Sarah Vaughan read English at Oxford and went on to become a journalist. After eleven years at the *Guardian* working as a news reporter, health correspondent and political correspondent, she started freelancing. *The Art of Baking Blind* is Sarah's first novel. She lives near Cambridge with her husband and two small children.

THE ART OF BAKING BLIND

Take five strangers with nothing in common except a passion for baking. Add a hotly contested competition and beat to stiff peaks. Bake to just the right degree of tension . . . The search is on for the new 'Mrs Eaden', an amateur baker so talented they are fit to emulate the author of the classic cookbook *The Art of Baking*. Each contestant has a reason to bake. Jenny faces an empty nest; Claire has sacrificed her dreams for her daughter; Vicki struggles with motherhood; and Karen is determined not to let her façade slip. As alliances form and secrets emerge, making the choicest choux bun seems the least of their concerns. For they will learn — as Mrs Eaden did — that while perfection is possible in the kitchen, it's very much harder in life.

SARAH VAUGHAN

THE ART OF BAKING BLIND

Complete and Unabridged

CHARNWOOD
Leicester

First published in Great Britain in 2014 by
Hodder & Stoughton
An Hachette UK company
London

First Charnwood Edition
published 2015
by arrangement with
Hachette UK
London

A catalogue record for this book is available
from the British Library.

ISBN 978–1–4448–2460–5

Published by
F. A. Thorpe (Publishing)
Anstey, Leicestershire

Set by Words & Graphics Ltd.
Anstey, Leicestershire
Printed and bound in Great Britain by
T. J. International Ltd., Padstow, Cornwall

This book is printed on acid-free paper

For Ella, Jack and Phil.
With love

Things fall apart; the centre cannot hold;
Mere anarchy is loosed upon the world

W.B. Yeats: 'The Second Coming'

I truly believe that life is improved by cake.

Dan Lepard: *Short & Sweet*

Prologue

April 1964

'Imagine your perfect home: a gamekeeper's lodge or rambling farmhouse, the walls wreathed in wisteria, brick warmed by the sun. Picture the garden: bees drunk on the nectar of hollyhocks, the air shimmering with summer. An apple tree rustles and drops early fruit.

'Now imagine this house made of gingerbread, its sides gently golden; royal icing piped along the rooftop and studded with sweets. Plant sugar canes in the flower beds; drench with jelly tots; pave with smarties. Pause and admire this culinary doll's house. Your ideal home and all-too-brief treat.'

Kathleen Eaden puts down her pen and chews her bottom lip in dissatisfaction. That wasn't what she wanted to write.

She places her creation on the floor and stretches out in front of it, tweed skirt rucking up and long legs splayed like a child's behind her. The Axminster carpet feels comforting and she wriggles deeper, slim waist pulled upwards, the thick pile snug against her pubic bone.

Propped up on her elbows, she peers at the house and breathes in the scent of Christmas: ginger; cinnamon; golden syrup; muscovado. Orange zest. A touch of cloves. The roof tiles are dusted with sugar and if she reaches, ever so carefully, she can adjust that heart-shaped knocker that's slipped on its still-wet icing.

There, that's better. With one gentle tweak, the sweet shifts on its iced glue.

It's still not perfect, though, this kitsch delight she has spent the past four hours constructing. The tiles are wonky and the cut-away windows should be better aligned. She bends closer. Light slants through them and disappears into gingery darkness. Oh, schoolgirl error. She reaches for her pen: 'Use a ruler to position your windows.' Or perhaps they should be mullioned? Her lips move silently as she lays out instructions for the readers of *Home Magazine*. Her hand speeds so fast she ruffles the cream Basildon Bond but her writing remains immaculate: gracious loops that chase across the page in Quink of royal blue.

She re-reads what she has written. She's still not got it. Not captured the reason she loves making gingerbread houses even though doing so makes no earthly sense at all. She tries to clear her mind to stave off the anxiety of a deadline. The jangling chords of the Beatles' latest hit crowd her head, the melody upbeat and addictive. 'I don't care too much for money,' sing the Fab Four and though, at twenty-seven, she is too old to be swayed by mop-haired boys, she finds herself momentarily distracted by the jauntiness of the tune.

She must get on. Lowering herself, she squints through the gingerbread windows. Perhaps she is approaching this from the wrong angle? Why would Susan, her six-year-old niece, love this — and what appeals to the six-year-old in her?

A gingerbread house is more than the sum of its parts: more than sweeties and gingerbread soldered with royal icing, glossy with egg white and thick with sugar. There is something fantastical about this fairytale house . . .

And, suddenly, she has the answer.

Tears burn. She blinks hard. Not now. She hasn't the time for this. She must finish her column. Breathe deeply, she tells herself: in for two, out for five; in for two, out for five.

She sits back on her haunches then lifts the house to her desk and busies herself with her papers. A cup of cooling Earl Grey rests on the top and she almost spills it as she reaches to take a sip. The self-pity is still there — a knot so hard she imagines it visible through her slight ribcage — and she tries to swallow it down with a bigger gulp. Still there? Yes, of course. Only ever a breath away: so close it can readily overwhelm her. But it can't do. She needs to get on top of this.

She picks at a spare dolly mixture and squishes it against the roof of her mouth. The sweetness seeps through her tongue and slips down her throat, insubstantial yet distracting. She takes another sip of tea. There, that's better.

'The doyenne of baking with the enviable figure' wouldn't behave like this, would she? The description — concocted by Harper's — usually provokes a sardonic smile. Now, though, she tries to accept the compliment at face value. Her hands flutter to her waist as she smooths down her skirt and tries to right herself; her thumbs rest in the shallows of her hip bones. Perhaps there are some benefits, after all.

She leans back and straightens the paper.

Now, if she can just ignore the sadness that corrodes her stomach, she might be able to finish this column. She sniffs brightly and tries to re-read her last paragraph. The script wobbles and blurs.

Oh for goodness sake, Kathleen. She uncaps her fountain pen in a flurry and, determined to ignore the tears that prick, yet again, despite her best efforts, Kathleen Eaden begins to write.

Cakes

People often ask me the secret of my baking. Shall I tell you? There is none. Anyone can bake provided they master a few basic principles and, at least until accomplished, follow the recipe to the letter. Nowhere is this more important than in making cakes. A variation in the temperature of the oven or in the measurement of ingredients; a failure to sift or to fold in sufficient air can lead to the most dismal sponge. But get it right and the most ethereal of cakes is entirely possible.

So the rules: always use eggs at room temperature and fat, either butter or a margarine like Stork, that has softened. Use flour containing a raising agent, sieve it to introduce extra air, and fold in lightly to encompass more. Always prepare your tins before cooking and preheat your oven. Place the tins in the oven gently, and shut the door softly as though leaving a sleeping baby. And never check your sponges until at least two-thirds of the cooking time has elapsed.

Once your golden creations have been removed from the oven, leave them for a couple of minutes before you ease them from the tin. Then place on a wire rack so that air can circulate. When cooled, sandwich with the finest jam and dust with icing sugar. Serve with a pot of afternoon tea.

The perfect Victoria sandwich must be light, moist and scented with fresh eggs and vanilla. It should feel decadent but not excessively so. A slice of Victoria sponge, filled with raspberry jam or, in summer, whipped cream and freshly hulled strawberries, is a daily treat you can feel justified in indulging. Just take three eggs and six ounces each of sugar, fat and self-raising flour, and heaven in a cake tin can be yours.

Kathleen Eaden: *The Art of Baking* (1966)

1

January 2012

Vicki Marchant breathes on her chill French windows and carefully traces a heart. A fat tear of condensation slithers down and she stops it with her finger and writes an A for Alfie. The letter weeps and she wipes the pane gently, chasing moisture with crisp squares of kitchen roll.

I must be going mad, thinks Vicki. Either that or I'm just plain miserable. Outside, ball bearings of hail pound the frozen blades of grass.

Well, it's hard to feel cheerful in January. The joy of Christmas — a joy felt so wonderfully through three-year-old Alfie — has rudely ended; packed away along with the decorations: this year, golden pears and partridges; rococo cherubs; icicles and stars.

January — or bloody January as she tends to think of it — is all about abstinence, penitence and being sanctimonious, as friends embark on an alcohol-free, dairy-free, wheat-free month. No one wants to come to dinner in January — and if she can persuade a fellow mum to lunch it's a frugal affair: broccoli soup without the Stilton languishing from Christmas; all offers of home-made stollen, Florentines and mince pies laughed aside quite firmly. 'No, really, I couldn't,' her neighbour, Sophie, had insisted yesterday as Vicki pressed a full cake tin on her, and had sounded quite panicky as if she were going to force-feed her.

Yet it's not the general abstinence that most frustrates her but the sense of limbo. The sub-zero temperatures mean Alfie can't race around the garden and there are only so many times a week she can go to a soft play barn. Without the gift of snow or sunshine 'the big freeze', as the media has dubbed it, has become one long grind of de-icing cars and salting paths, of finding sufficient layers and contending with Alfie's whingeing if, as invariably happens, she forgets his welly socks.

She gives a sigh, thick and laboured. Outside, the hail has stopped abruptly, the only evidence the icy marbles nestling in the grass. The grey sky is as unyielding as ever; the bare trees still; the ground quite barren. No sign of the snowdrops and tête-à-têtes she and little Alf planted in October. Her garden seems devoid of hope.

She turns on her coffee machine and measures out enough grains for a double espresso, hoping a burst of caffeine will reinvigorate her and improve her morning. For, if she is honest, and she always tries to be, her frustration has nothing to do with the weather at all.

My name is Vicki Marchant, she imagines announcing at yet another interminable play-group, and I am a fraudulent stay-at-home mother. A mum-of-one with none of the demands of numerous offspring or any of the pressure of having to work. I have a beautiful, healthy boy who loves me. And I do adore him. But I'm still not sure I'm very good at or — whisper it — always *enjoy* motherhood. Oh, and here's the joke. I'm an 'outstanding' primary school teacher, according to Ofsted. Someone who's supposed to know what they're doing. So why do I find it so hard looking after my own small child?

It wasn't meant to be this way, she thinks, as the machine groans then belches hot coffee grains at her. When Alfie was born, the plan had always been to give up work to immerse herself in her baby and subsequent children. Her Shaker kitchen would be covered in poster-paint masterpieces; her lengthy garden would boast hens, herbs and flowers; and each day would bring new adventures for her Petit Bateau-clad child. She hadn't counted on the drudgery of early parenthood with a child who refused to sleep and a husband who refused to get up; or on her rage when her boy decorated her Farrow & Ball walls with his handprints; or her impotence when a fox massacred the hens.

You would have thought a primary school teacher would have known that toddlers prefer church playgroups, with their interminable rich tea biscuits and weak instant coffee, to babyccinos in Starbucks; and that a trip into town would *always* lead to dramatic meltdowns, Alfie's body as taut as a board as he struggled against being put in a buggy, as powerful as a coiled spring as he wriggled free of her grasp.

She should have known that glitter would always be sprinkled all over the kitchen and that, at three, he could not hope to produce anything other than a sodden clump of papier mâché. Yet, somehow, she had forgotten, or been naively optimistic. She had thought she could conquer any problem with a calm voice and an endless supply of smiley stickers. No, motherhood isn't turning out quite as she'd envisaged, at all.

There's just one thing she feels she can do with Alfie, she reflects, as she wipes the coffee grains from the surface and refills the machine, and that is baking. And so this is an activity in which they have started to excel. They began with cupcakes, over which she maintained overall artistic control. But they soon progressed from gingerbread men to tuiles; from pizza bases to sourdough; from jam tarts to tarte tatin.

Alfie, who quickly learned that he got a strong reaction if he slopped water on to the floor or glue on to the table when painting, has discovered he gets a better one if he cracks an egg correctly, the slippery white slopping into the mixing bowl 'without bits of shell'. Mummy sings when she bakes, and if her brow creases when he becomes over-exuberant with the sieving — and flour and cocoa sprinkle the floorboards — any irritation is momentary, dissipated by the heartening smell of sponge cooking and the sensual experience of licking the bowl.

For Vicki, baking with her boy is tangible evidence that she is a good mother.

'Did you make these yourself — and with Alfie?' her friend, Ali, had quizzed her only on Monday as she had handed her a vintage cake tin with a smile of dismissal.

She had felt a distinct glow of satisfaction at her friend praising not only the creations but the fact that she had made them with her child.

'God, how do you stand the mess?' Ali had continued. 'Must be the teacher in you! I never bake with Sam.'

As always, she had felt mild pity.

'He loves it.' She had shrugged, with typical self-deprecation. And, on cue, her tousle-haired boy had looked up and given her a quick grin, his hand slipping into hers as he offered Ali's three-year-old a home-made biscuit. 'And so do I.'

Today, however, that sense of satisfaction evades her. Irritation niggles as she takes in the sea of Lego, the washing wilting on the maiden, the socks wrenched off on a whim and discarded, one dangling from Alfie's ergonomically ideal chair, the other kicked under a toy box and curled like a stale croissant, waiting to be swooped up.

She sighs then forces herself to breathe more calmly, taking in the aroma of lemon, sugar and butter now flooding her kitchen, bathing her in a delicious citrus fug. A timer pings and she opens the oven, and brings out an exquisitely cooked tarte au citron. The viscous yellow glows against the crisp golden pastry, blind-baked to perfection. And Vicki smiles.

2

When baking, it is important not to scrimp on ingredients or to cut corners. You must not believe you can get away with the minimum. Your family deserves the best.
I am all for moderation and economy, but no one wants a mean sponge or a poorly risen loaf of bread; a scrag-filled pie or a pitiful pudding. Remember: when you bake, you cherish.

Jennifer Briggs, pummelling focaccia on the granite worktop of her farmhouse kitchen in Suffolk, pauses for a moment and looks out at her walled garden and beyond. Her arms are beginning to ache from punishing the mixture: stretching it then kneading it then stretching it once more to release the gluten. Her nose itches and she scratches it with the back of fingers that are lightly floured.

A cat — one of two that check up on her as she bakes — stalks across the kitchen and miaows, insistent; then sits and glares at the oversized fridge.

'No, you're not getting any food yet,' Jennifer tells her. Then, amused, 'Oh, you're wondering about that too, are you? Well, Tabby, I don't think that's going to happen somehow.'

The cat blinks, impenetrable, and begins to wash herself but Jennifer continues to look at the advert, neatly clipped from *Eaden's Monthly*, and attached with a heart-shaped magnet to the fridge.

'Calling Britain's Best Bakers' it declaims, in a mock-up of the iconic First World War Kitchener poster. 'Your country needs you to produce the nation's best bakes.'

In excitable italicised font, it explains that Eaden and Son are searching for the New Mrs Eaden, an amateur baker so talented they are fit to emulate the wife of the store's founder, who published her classic cookbook *The Art of Baking* in 1966 and died only last year. The winner will receive a £50,000 contract to advise the supermarket on its finest baked products, will contribute a monthly magazine column, and will front their advertising campaign. The New Mrs Eaden will then be able to launch her, or his, own baking career.

Jennifer, an avid baker, has been intrigued by the competition — and, much to her surprise, has entered. Well, she was brought up on *The Art of Baking*, her mother deferring to Kathleen Eaden and her odes to the most decadent of cakes.

Jennifer shops at Eaden's and believes this will be a proper baking competition — despite the rather silly YouTube clips each task's top two bakers must make. The judges are certainly credible: Dan Keller, that attractive artisan baker, and Harriet Strong, author of over thirty cookbooks and star of a long-running cookery series. This isn't a reality TV show but a contest run by the country's most upmarket supermarket: a business that champions high-quality, free-range and freshly produced food and assumes its shoppers love nothing better than to bake.

Well, Jennifer is one such customer and submitted an application form just before Christmas. She is still chafing with disappointment at not having been contacted. And yet she is not surprised. In small print, the competition website explained that the supermarket reserved the right to choose applicants who accurately reflect the nation's different demographic groups. There had also been excessive emphasis placed on the importance of candidates submitting photos, and she suspects that, at fifty-two, she is too old and too fat to be a contender.

She sighs and imagines how she must have been viewed by those sifting through the applications, young adults, she assumes, not much older than her three newly grown-up girls. Hair cropped in a sensible short bob: unflattering, boring, but eminently fitting for the wife of the local dentist and member of the W.I. A broad, open face, flushed with rosacea, testament to her wholesome living and her apparent lack of vanity. And a weightiness that allows her to be seen as a caricature: the fat, jolly, asexual cook.

She resumes her kneading.

Fat, she accepts as she pounds more vigorously in a sudden flush of anger, is something she has grown used to as her burgeoning love of baking has coincided with her expansion into middle age.

'Never trust a thin cook,' she sometimes twinkles as she folds her still neat arms beneath a bosom — it is definitely a bosom now, rather than distinct breasts — that continues to swell as she moves up each dress size. Now a size twenty, she can no longer be described as voluptuous, curvy, or even cuddly. Her thighs, which rub together when she walks, are silvered with stretch marks like the tears appearing in her stretched focaccia. Her stomach flops with the moist consistency of softly whipped cream.

Her daughters, if they ever bothered to consider it, would assume that their mother is nonchalant about this. Jennifer looks what she is: a rosy-cheeked mother earth figure; an excellent home cook who will rustle up a dozen scones or a Victoria sponge with eggs from her own Sussex Whites if friends give her twenty minutes' notice; the ever capable linchpin of their family.

Only Lizzie, her youngest, who has just started at Bristol, wonders if her mother is truly as happy as she claims.

'Are you OK, Mum?' she had asked her, tentatively, at Christmas. 'Do you mind rattling around here, just cooking for Dad, now we're all at uni?'

Jennifer had smiled. 'Do you mean: what do I do all day?'

The elder girls had been less concerned. 'Oh, it's what she loves doing, looking after all of us, taking care of the old grump, isn't it?' Kate, now twenty-three, had chipped in.

'Course it is. She's our mother hen, aren't you?' Emma, twenty-two, and more typically acerbic, had slipped a slim arm round her waist and squeezed her. She had felt discomfited by the sentiment, but relaxed into the hug.

'Well, I do have plenty to do: there's still loads of cooking and gardening . . . and the hens, of course.' She had sought to make herself sound busy. The girls, wanting to believe the best, had laughed.

'Stop fussing, Lizzie,' Emma had bossed her younger sister. 'You heard what she said. She's just doing what she's always done.'

It did not seem to occur to them that, once, she had had a career, though, admittedly, she had stopped nursing when she had her first baby. By the time the girls were at school, nobody wanted her to work out of the home — and so she stayed there.

Now, when she worries about her, Lizzie fires off a loving text and is reassured by a swift and cheery response. 'Lovely to hear from you, darling. Had a glorious day in the garden and now making sticky toffee puddings. Xxx'

Jennifer, who has agonised over getting the tone of the text just right, watches the phone, willing it to ring. It remains silent. And so, alone in her kitchen, she bakes and bakes.

3

When serving cake, always provide a cake fork and a napkin. And never press your guests to eat. Cake should be something chosen once you've weighed up the potential effect on your waistline — and decided that it is so delicious it is worth succumbing. Either give in to the seduction wholeheartedly — or savour the satisfaction of knowing you can resist.

Karen Hammond is perched at the island in the centre of her chaste kitchen, the line between her eyebrows deepening as she examines its marble surface with disdain.

Watery sunshine slants through the substantial roof light, picking out her copper lowlights. The cleaner is due later and a few specks of dust dance in the sunlight, bestowing a dirty halo that shifts as she grimaces.

A smear of grease, a tell-tale thumbprint at its head, mars the island's glassy smoothness. How could she have missed that? She reaches for the anti-bacterial spray and polishes. Her face ripples in its surface and she pauses for a moment, struck by her reflection: a study in concentration; unforgiving; tense.

The imperfection erased, she puts the cleaning products away and surveys the room. Her fingernails, coated in Chanel Rouge Noir, click against the worktop in a minor drum roll. A call to action; a call to perfect.

A carrot cake sits on the opposite counter, its frosting sparkling. Fat sultanas wink at her from the orange crumb: she breathes in the sugar, the spice, the egg. It teases her, this cake, like a cocksure teenager leaning against a street corner. 'Come on. You know you want me. Just a little nibble? A taste of my icing? Tell me, darling, where's the harm in that?'

But Karen resists. The kitchen implements have been put in the dishwasher; the mixing bowl, with its cloying icing, long since washed, dried and stowed away in its cupboard. For one moment, she had imagined sweeping her index finger around it and sucking the heavenly combination of mascarpone, sugar and just a squeeze of lime. Yet, even as she thought it, she knew she would never do it. Control and self-discipline are the key to everything. She has long known that the brief elation of surrender just cannot compare with the thrill of denial.

Jake, her seventeen-year-old, half man, half boy now, saunters into the room.

'All right, Ma?'

She tenses at the public school affectation.

He thrusts his hands into his jeans pockets, pushing them lower as he opens the fridge and surveys its contents. His T-shirt rides up and she can see the cleft between his slight buttocks. She wants to yank his jeans up. Tell him to dress properly. Instead, she looks away.

'Got anything to eat?'

The question is rhetorical. He begins to pile up cheese and ham, butter and bagels, a seemingly limitless number of calories which his

22

six-foot-two frame can more than tolerate. She tenses as he plonks them on the surface, instantly destroying her order.

His eyes sweep across the sterile kitchen to her latest creation.

'Ah . . . cake. Don't mind if I do, do you, Ma?' he continues as he thrusts a bread knife into it and cuts himself a sizeable chunk. He eats as if ravenous. Moist crumbs sprinkle the floor and a dollop of frosting, still not set, drops from the knife.

She cannot bear it.

'For God's sake, Jake. If you're going to devour it, do it nicely.'

She reaches for a porcelain side plate and a silver cake fork.

'What's that for?'

'You know what that's for. It's a cake fork. Eat it properly.'

He looks at her with mock incredulity. 'God, Ma. Anyone would forget you were born in Sarf-end.' He elongates the word in a mock Essex accent. 'Since when did you get so up yourself?'

His tone cuts her like a scalpel. Since my son started mocking me, she wants to reply. Since he and his sister entered a different social sphere with their rugby matches and cello lessons, their skiing trips and Latin gerunds. Since they entered a different world to me.

But she doesn't. Instead she contemplates her beautiful boy, his patrician features, mercifully untouched by acne, now marred with derision.

'If you want to eat my cake, you follow my

rules,' is the best she can manage. It comes out fiercer than she intended. Less of a command; more of a hiss.

He brays a laugh. 'Chill, Ma. Calm down.'

He looks at her as if she were from another planet then continues to demolish the cake, jaws moving efficiently.

'This is good, by the way. Here, try a bit.'

He holds it out to her, pushing it towards her lips. She recoils, suddenly fearful.

'I'm fine, thank you.' Her voice is tight. 'I'm not hungry.'

He gives a shrug. Goes back to finishing the cake.

'What about the icing?' he persists as he cuts himself a second, smaller, slice. 'Here, just taste it on the knife. Go on.' His upper lip curls as he holds it in front of her, a reward for good behaviour. It is dangerously close to her mouth but she refuses to flinch.

'I said: 'No.' '

It comes out almost as a shout. He raises an eyebrow. She forces herself to soften her voice and breathes deeply.

'I'm fine, thank you, darling. I just wish you'd listen to me.'

She busies herself to deflect attention from her outburst: begins to put his food back; takes a can of Diet Coke from the fridge. The caramel liquid fizzes in a crystal tumbler then burns as the bubbles run down her throat. It is her poison of choice now she has ditched the nicotine: a wonder drink that has zero calories but appears to fill her up.

24

Her son is still watching her, his hands now raised in supplication. 'I don't get you. You make these gorgeous cakes and you won't even taste them. What's that about? It's not like you're fat or something.'

He takes in her size eight frame: the flat abdomen and pronounced sternum; her skin taut against her cheekbones; her upper ribs radiating across her chest. He shakes his head, as if he were the parent bemused by the offspring, and ambles away.

She is about to remonstrate — to tell him to help clear up — when he lobs his parting shot: an insult tossed so casually that, at first, she wonders if she has misheard him.

'You're fooling no one, Ma,' he drawls as he slopes away, hands thrust deep in his pockets. And, again, under his breath, almost as a whisper: 'You're fooling no one.'

★   ★   ★

What the fuck did he mean by that? Fear powers her as she runs from her substantial Victorian house in Winchester towards the edge of the city on a forty-five-minute run that will burn a good 565 calories, she calculates, and, she hopes, extinguish her sense of shame.

She keeps up a brisk pace: feet striking rhythmically heel-to-toe, torso erect but at ease, breath regular and even. The houses blur, their price tags diminishing as she leaves the centre of the city: Georgian town houses blurring into cutesy terraces; merging into more modern

25

detached properties; the majority nondescript, the rare one a suburban gem.

She has come a long way, she tells herself as she powers past the law courts, the railway and the hospital towards open countryside. She has come a long way and she is not going to let it all crumble because her son, this beautiful boy-man she often cannot believe she produced, thinks he knows something that will put her back in her place.

Her stomach corrodes. *You're fooling no one, Ma.* A general reference to the working-class roots she refuses to discuss or something more specific? What does he know? Which of her two dirty secrets has he picked up on? Or is he chancing it?

Has he told Oliver? Still her husband, though with him spending the week at their London flat, their lives are increasingly separate. She sometimes wonders if he even cares for her, so immersed is he in his work, so completely is he drifting away. What about Livy? She thinks of her serious girl — so different from her at fifteen — and finds her fists are clenched, as if she were trying to cling on to her daughter's innocence.

She thinks back ten years: Jake, aged seven, scoring his first try in tag rugby, knees grazed, shins mud-splattered, pride stretched across his face. And the person he had run to for a victor's hug wasn't Oliver, or his coach: it was her, freezing on the touchline. 'I love you, Mum,' he had whispered into her neck, his arms tight around her, his voice fierce with passion. She

26

was his world. 'The best mum in the world — in the universe.' The passion had continued for quite some time. So why, now, was there this contempt?

The question niggles as the run becomes harder: a steeper incline to the crest of one of the high hills in the area. A chance to push her body. There is no pavement here and she runs on the tarmac, segueing on to a grass verge hedged with brambles when a car thunders past, spewing water at her legs.

She glances at the running watch strapped to her upper arm. Nearly halfway. Three point one miles; twenty-two minutes; 257 calories. She surges forward. She needs to burn more, run faster; she should be able to run faster.

Her breath is ragged and uneven now. She tries to hum, as if to block out her anxiety. Keep going, she tells herself. He knows nothing. Just keep going.

Blood floods her head in solid waves out of sync with her iPod. Just keep going. Keep going. He knows nothing. She repeats the mantra — and wishes she could believe it.

And then, suddenly, she is at the top of the hill and her voice comes out in a burst: a yelp of relief and a cry of achievement. Behind her, Winchester spreads: all affluence, heritage and privilege. You have come a long way, she reassures herself. You have come a long way.

The flooded water meadows shimmer and, as she catches her breath, a ray of sunshine illuminates the cathedral and the prestigious

27

school. She resumes her jogging, breath steadying as she runs for a while on the flat. Her pace picks up; fast and rhythmic. You've come a long way; you've come a long way; and you are going to hold tight to this.

4

If holding a coffee morning, always ensure that your coffee is Eaden's finest and your biscuits, it should not need saying, are home-made. Do not allow your standards to slip even if you only offer a hot beverage. You do not want to be the sort of hostess who offers merely a cup of instant coffee.

Three weeks later. A wet and windy February morning and Vicki is scuttling through the raindrops on the King's Road, Chelsea, on her way to the Search for the New Mrs Eaden audition.

Her watch says she has plenty of time — that she's fifteen minutes early — but Vicki hates being late for anything, just as she hates being unprepared. She pulls a wicker basket tight towards her, and peeks under the gingham tea towel cover in case her home-made blueberry muffins and Emmenthal croissants should have somehow escaped. Of course they haven't. Fat raindrops splash on her cake tin and she walks faster, readjusting her umbrella.

Just stop being so nervous, she tells herself as she spies Eaden and Son's flagship store, with its elegant lettering and all-glass frontage. Look, you're here now. Just enjoy this. This is what you wanted: a chance to bake; to excel; to do something outside the home.

Oh, but will Alfie be all right? She feels her

habitual twinge of guilt at the thought of his tear-streaked face as she left him at Ali's. He was just putting on a show for your benefit, her rational, teacher-voice reassures her. But was he? Perhaps he was coming down with something and she hadn't noticed? Why else would she have to pull away from his grasp?

For a moment she considers ringing Ali again, just to check, but she has already texted her since leaving Sloane Square station and she fears looking neurotic. Her phone pings in her pocket. A text from Ali: 'Of course he's fine. Now go and enjoy yourself!'

She grins — given permission by another mother — and, with a lighter heart, almost runs the last few steps to the store. There. She is not a bad mummy. Not really. She is just seizing a rare opportunity to shine.

Walking into the store, it actually feels incredible that she is here, summoned to the audition. She only applied right at the last minute, on 31 January, the entry deadline. It wasn't that she didn't want to do it. The advert, cut from *Eaden's Monthly*, had been pinned to her fridge since early December, fighting for space among Alfie's potato cut prints and stick drawings. But she had dithered: reluctant to commit to something that meant time away from her boy. And then there had been one particularly lonely morning and she had realised, somewhere between tidying up the train track and the Lego, the play-doh and the farm set, that, if she didn't get out more, she would combust with bad temper, or go quite quite mad.

And so she is here. Hardly the most intrepid destination and yet this feels thrillingly exciting. Trepidation replaces anxiety as she takes in the table by the entrance, arranged with bottles of Prosecco and elaborately beribboned boxes of truffles, and breathes in the scent of freshly baked pain aux raisins.

Everything in Eaden's flagship store looks perfect: the apples, piled in pyramids on reproduction market barrows, are without blemish; the cavolo nero dark and prolific; the bread — sourdough flutes wrapped in artfully ripped brown paper — looks as if it has been crafted in the early hours by an artisan baker. The butcher's counter boasts vast hunks of topside, generous fillets of sirloin: rich, succulent, vermilion. The sea bass and langoustine shimmer on a mound of crushed ice.

Even before 10 a.m., the shop hums with contented shoppers as they select their fresh produce and deliberate over their espresso coffee, their fair trade tea bags, their 85 per cent cocoa chocolate, their organic oatcakes, their cantuccini.

The wide aisles can easily accommodate two trolleys and Vicki watches three middle-aged women negotiate the space. As one squeezes past, there is no tension, no rancour, just an apologetic smile and a gracious nod of acceptance. This isn't the sort of supermarket where customers swear at one another, ram trolleys into heels or try to beat fellow shoppers to the checkout. Eaden's embodies old-fashioned values such as good taste, quality, refinement.

Above all, it stands for courteousness.

There's no one here to greet her now, though, and so Vicki makes for customer services, glancing at the baking aisle as she does so.

An elderly gentleman is peering at the flavourings. Mustard cords; cravat; a tweed jacket that has lasted forty years and will see him out; a face that is markedly florid. He looks distinctly lost.

'May I help you, sir?' A slim young assistant smiles in concern.

'Looking for fresh vanilla pods. My wife insists she needs them. Damned if I can find them.'

'If you just come this way, sir, I can show you.' She holds out an expansive arm behind him but does not touch him. 'There you are: three choices but, if I was baking, I'd choose this one.'

'Really?'

'Less expensive but grown on the same plantation so the same quality.'

'How extraordinary . . . '

'May I help you with anything else?'

'No . . . No, that's fine. Thank you.'

Leaving him to scrutinise the withered black sticks in their minute test tube, the girl melts away.

'Vicki . . . Vicki Marchant?'

A young woman with a neat blonde bob and pearl earrings is smiling at her.

'Oh, yes. Sorry.' She immediately feels wrong-footed.

'Welcome to the Search for the New Mrs Eaden competition!'

Vicki smiles, suddenly filled with excitement.

'I'm Cora Young. Eaden's marketing assistant.'

She holds out a neat hand with a signet ring on her little finger. Vicki wipes her own sweaty palm before taking it.

'The interviews are in our conference room upstairs, in the head office. If you'd like to come this way?'

★   ★   ★

Someone is already waiting in the conference room above the store. A middle-aged woman who looks like the epitome of a baker, with her gentle smile, her broad face, and a bosom so ample that Vicki's eyes are instantly drawn there.

She looks nervous — and lovely. A proper mum, or a proper, young, granny. Alfie would love her. He'd nestle against that chest and gaze up adoringly in his own version of small boy heaven.

'Hello. I'm Jennifer.' The older woman moves towards her and holds out a hand, slightly self-conscious.

'Vicki.' She grasps it. Jennifer's fingers are cool and her handshake surprisingly firm for someone who looks so diffident.

They smile, both searching for the start of a conversation.

'Did you . . . ?'

'Are you . . . ?'

Their voices collide.

'No, after you,' Vicki defers to the older woman.

'I was just going to ask if you were nervous. I

33

know I am. They only rang me two days ago, and I can't quite believe it. I keep expecting them to say they've made a mistake.'

'Oh, I'm sure they haven't. You look like you know how to bake — oh, I don't mean that rudely. I mean, you just look experienced . . . ' Vicki's voice tails away in embarrassment. 'Oh, I'm digging a bigger hole, aren't I?'

Jennifer laughs. 'Not at all. It's just nerves. Good to know we're both feeling the same.'

She glances at a framed black and white photo of Kathleen Eaden, standing outside the building they are now in, which takes pride of place on the wall opposite.

'She, on the other hand, doesn't look as if she was ever nervous, does she?'

Vicki looks at the shot. The woman is dressed in the style of that 1960s icon, Jackie Kennedy: a dark bouffant bob, the ends curling up at her shoulders; pale lipstick; lightly kohled eyes. Her face is striking rather than pretty with an intelligent gaze and high cheekbones. Her smile is alluring. She wears a dress coat with oversized buttons and a shift dress ending just above her knee. Slim calves taper down to kitten heels.

'It's the same picture used in here, isn't it?'

Vicki draws out a copy of *The Art of Baking* from her capacious handbag: a glossy duck-egg-blue hardback, with lavish photographs, published to coincide with Kathleen Eaden's death the previous year.

'Oh! A real Kathleen enthusiast.' Jennifer waves her own paperback copy: dog-eared, besplattered, and at least forty years older than Vicki's edition.

'Is that an original?' Vicki feels as if she has been trumped though she doubts that was Jennifer's intention.

'My mother's. I was brought up on Mrs Eaden. So I thought this should come along.'

She passes it over and Vicki spends a few moments flicking through the pages. Recipes for Chelsea buns, Bakewell tart and apple Charlotte catch her attention; Battenburg and lemon meringue pie; salmon and watercress quiche. The black and white photos in this original book are sparse but most show Kathleen Eaden smiling as she holds up a finished product. Her smile mesmerises so that the reader's eyes are drawn only to her, and not the tart or pudding.

'I just love this book,' Vicki enthuses. 'I only discovered her a couple of years ago. Of course I'd heard of her but it wasn't until they reissued this that I tried out all these recipes.'

'In my childhood, she was what every baker aspired to,' says Jennifer. 'I can remember my mother saying, 'I'll just consult Kathleen,' just as we might turn to Delia. Amazing, really, that this one book had such an effect.'

'And she sounds like such a wonderful woman. Did you read that interview in *Eaden's Monthly*, after she died, with her daughter, Laura?'

'Oh, I know. What a glorious childhood. It sounded completely idyllic: bonfires on the beach; surfing; flying kites — and all that wonderful baking.'

'I'd love it if my son ever remembered me that way.'

The words fly out of Vicki's mouth before she can stop them, and she wants to curl up in embarrassment. Jennifer looks away tactfully.

'Oh, I mean, I'm sure he will. Well, I hope so. But I can't quite imagine it,' Vicki hears herself over-explaining. 'It's pathetic really. I absolutely adore him but it doesn't seem to come as easily to me as it did to Kathleen. I find it quite hard at times.

'Do you have children?' she hurries on. 'You look as if you might have — ' She blushes as if the older woman could somehow detect her thought process: that Jennifer's stomach, voluminous under a tunic, is one that has surely expanded to cope with more than one child.

The older woman seems impervious. 'Three girls. Nineteen to twenty-three so all grown up now — or so they like to think.'

'I've just the one. A three-year-old,' Vicki repeats herself as if she needs to apologise. As if to confirm it, her womb gives a dull ache.

'The first one's always the hardest. The biggest shock to the system. I found my first a real thunderbolt. It gets easier with the second, and eases over time.'

Jennifer smiles. And while Vicki would usually find this patronising: a platitude uttered by someone who had effortlessly had multiple children, from this woman it merely sounds kind.

Far from being diminished, she feels instantly reassured, immediately acknowledged. As if she might have just met a possible friend.

* * *

Three minutes to ten and Vicki feels increasingly nervous. The door swings open and Cora ushers in a man who is apologising profusely: dark hair flecked with grey; a neat physique; early forties; somewhat anguished deep brown eyes.

'Thank God I made it.' His face, anxious, pleasant, largely unexceptional, relaxes, as he sees that only two people have arrived so far. The line between his eyebrows eases into more of a furrow, less of a crevasse.

'So sorry I'm late,' he continues. He shrugs off a large rucksack, containing what must be his baked products and rearranges his damp trench coat. The blue shirt underneath has been badly ironed.

'Coffee?' Cora chirrups as she gestures to the table, covered in coffee cups.

'An espresso would be lovely,' he answers. Then, as he catches sight of the catering flask containing filter coffee made an hour ago, 'Ah, just an Americano then.'

He takes the standard white cup and saucer with a smile and hovers over the plates of goodies. Chewy oat and raisin cookies, baby blueberry muffins and mini pains aux raisins.

'The cookies are good,' Vicki says with a gesture, skirting the table. 'Not home-made, but still.' She bites her lip, aware that Cora may take this as an insult. 'I'm sure they're freshly baked downstairs.'

He selects a muffin then touches his rucksack as if in reassurance. I wonder what he's got in there? thinks Vicki. Panettone? A spelt and honey loaf? Or something less interesting. Then: I

37

wonder how good he is; and what made him apply to be here?

'Hello.' Jennifer is more welcoming.

'Sorry . . . Hello. Mike. Mike Wilkinson.' He offers his hand and a firm handshake.

'Jennifer.'

'Vicki.'

They smile broadly and chorus their delight.

Mike nods encouragingly but they lapse into silence. The sound of cups chinked on saucers fills the void.

'Oops.' Vicki slops weak coffee over her hand. She grimaces in embarrassment, then grabs a paper napkin and dabs ineffectually at the few splashes christening her vintage-style tea dress. Jennifer smiles, eyes brimming with sympathy. Mike, keen to avoid witnessing her mortification, turns aside.

'I'm suddenly really nervous. Stupid really,' Vicki burbles in explanation. Her stomach fizzes with fear.

'We all are,' reassures Jennifer. 'It's only natural. There's no guarantee we're going to be selected for the competition, even though we've got this far. And, if you're anything like me, it just feels like such a big thing!'

They segue into conversation: their interest in the competition; their apprehension; their expectations for these interviews; and what each of them has brought to woo the judges: croissants aux amandes and a chocolate torte from Jennifer; a devil's food cake and brioche from Mike.

'There have to be more of us than this,

though?' Vicki queries. 'Cora said they were looking for five contestants. Any fewer and they won't have enough variety for the YouTube clips.'

On cue, the door swings open. Another competitor? Their chatter peters away.

The woman who enters looks dressed for battle: knee-high boots; a crisp white shirt; dark indigo jeans; a mane of expensively low-lighted brunette hair. Her face glows with the lightest dusting of bronzing powder and a glimmer of excitement. She carries a grey wicker basket and the air of someone holding a delicious secret they can barely suppress.

Mike blushes and looks a decade younger. Jennifer's smile is characteristically welcoming, if a little guarded. Vicki feels instantly apprehensive.

'The Search for the New Mrs Eaden audition?' says Karen superfluously and somewhat self-consciously. Then, with a touch of irony, 'Well, let's bake.'

Kathleen

She wishes she were baking, she thinks, as she stands at the entrance of the one hundredth Eaden's, ready to cut the ribbon and open the store.

Around her, staff smile in expectation while the gentlemen of the press just restrain themselves from jostling like a crowd of children promised cream cakes and slabs of chocolate; sweet ginger beer; warm custard tarts.

Yes, she wishes she were baking — or writing. Creating something, at any rate. A blowsy choux bun to be wolfed down in a moment or a description that lasts just a little while more.

Instead of which she is here, on the King's Road, Chelsea, being buffeted by a brisk April breeze and wishing she were wearing something more substantial than a light dress coat and the sheerest of stockings. Her new heels pinch and she feels distracted by the nagging pain and insistent cold.

'A smile for us, Mrs Eaden?' It is one of the reporters. Flashbulbs fire as she shoots them a beam.

What if she'd refused? The thought occurs as a gust of wind flares against her and she reaches to check her bob: impressively backcombed, stiff with Elnett. Well, of course she wouldn't. Being

Mrs Eaden — George's wife; culinary authority; and Eaden's asset — is who she is; is what she does, even if, at times, she would rather be spinning words or sugar. Pose, smile, nod, that's her job: and, latterly, to her relief and unexpected delight, write and bake.

Just another five minutes, she estimates, trying to warm herself by rubbing her arms; then twenty meeting the staff inside the store and exchanging pleasantries. It is not much to ask, and she knows it is central to the success of their company — and good for her career, if she is going to write her *Art of Baking*.

The voice of an older woman, straining to see what is going on, proves the point.

'Who is she? Is she in the movies?' The question blows towards her.

'No. She's Kathleen Eaden. Owns this shop and writes that fancy column. You know? That one in *Home Magazine*.'

'Pretty, isn't she?' Her friend is reverential. 'And much younger than I thought.'

'Bit skinny for my liking but that's the look now, isn't it?'

'She's beautiful.' A third voice joins in.

'Who? Kathleen Eaden? Oooh. I didn't realise.'

'It's Kathleen Eaden!'

'Who?'

'Kathleen Eaden. You know, Mrs Eaden.'

'Ooh.' The voice sounds hushed. 'I like her.'

The fact filters along the pavement, towards the newly opened Habitat with its whitewashed brick walls and wooden-slatted ceiling, its waif-like assistants and glamorous young customers.

41

'Mrs Eaden,' the five-deep crowd pulses, and she wonders how long she can cope with this pressure. Like champagne bubbles thrusting against a cork.

'If you're ready, my dear?' It is George, coming to the rescue.

'Of course, my darling.'

'Here are the scissors. Do be careful.'

He hands them to her, blades down, thick fingers wrapped around them, as if she were a small child in need of protection. For one awful moment, she imagines the havoc if she grabbed them and snipped wildly at the air.

'Darling?' The look George gives her is one of concern clouded by love: as if he still cannot believe his luck, three years into marriage.

'Just a moment,' she reassures him as she opens the scissors and places the blades either side of the satin, stretched taut. Let me make a wish. Let me wish for the thing I always wish for. She closes her eyes for perhaps three seconds then forces them open. The ribbon slices in two and the satin slithers to the floor amid cheers and applause.

Perhaps it's a good omen, she thinks. If Eaden's can burgeon like this — from a handful of grocer's shops to one hundred branches in ten years — then, perhaps, I too can burgeon? Women do it all the time.

'Kathleen?' George places his hand in the small of her back and ushers her into the supermarket of the future: all fluorescent lighting and self-service freezer cabinets.

And Mrs Eaden switches on her smile.

42

5

Never assume that to be a good baker you need to have attended cookery classes, whether at your local Women's Institute or at the Cordon Bleu. Anyone can learn to bake, and while a good teacher will undoubtedly help you, you can educate yourself. Some of the most exquisite baking I have ever tasted has come from the humblest of homes.

The rain that has splattered Vicki and drenched Mike is drowning the cathedral city of Exeter, fat raindrops running down the hills and sloshing the pavements, impervious to the brimming drains.

Claire Trelawney is spending a lacklustre morning at the checkout of the local Eaden's reaping the benefits of the downpour: the store is less crowded than usual, though time drags just as slowly.

She gives a mother with a small baby a quick beam as she begins to load up the conveyor belt but most of the smiles she bestows are wan; a common courtesy expected by her bosses and normally delivered with some enthusiasm. But not this morning. The rain lashes the windows in a sudden squall that leaves shoppers stunned — and blasts others inside, escaping the dripping canopy. I am going to get soaked, thinks Claire, taking in her regulation black trousers, which chill her thighs when drenched, and her cheap slip-on shoes, already sodden. She tries to rally herself but is half-hearted. What is there to smile about in a provincial superstore on an overcast mid-February morning?

She begins to scan the items, the scanner beeping with monotonous regularity. Nappies, beep; wipes, beep; milk, beep; butter, beep; Dairy Milk chocolate, beep; beep; beep.

'On special offer.' The mother gives a guilty grin.

She must have displayed some emotion. You can tell a lot about people from their shopping. You don't just root out the bulimics or the alcoholics, but the obsessives, the ones who stick rigidly to their lists; the ones who never cook; and the ones who cook perpetually.

Take this mother. Now her haul is getting more interesting. Perhaps she was wrong to judge her over her kilo plus of Dairy Milk for here are organic eggs, icing sugar, caster sugar, mascarpone, cream cheese, vanilla essence — the expensive stuff in its tasteful brown bottle, not the extract — digestive biscuits.

'Making a New York cheesecake?'

The question is involuntary.

Claire lowers her head in embarrassment and goes back to the scanning. Self-raising flour, beep; raisins, beep; carrots, beep; courgettes, beep — both organic.

'Yes.' The mother smiles, and her voice is educated but friendly. 'However did you guess?'

I could recite the recipe, thinks Claire. Not that I can afford the ingredients to make it — or not unless they're up to their best-before date and I can scrounge them from the staff room. Is she doing Nigella's version, she wonders, Rachel Allen's or Mary Berry's?

The question flies out before she can stop it.

'Nigella's,' the woman replies quizzically, and the unspoken question hangs in the air: Why would someone like Claire be so knowledgeable about such sumptuous puddings?

'Do you like to cook?' the woman continues.

But Claire has spotted Margaret, the checkout supervisor, watching her. She is meant to scan eighteen items a minute, and, while she is supposed to be friendly, excessive chatting slows her down. 'Erm . . . I just read recipe books; food porn, mainly,' Claire replies with a quick beam.

The customer blushes. Food porn. Did I say that? Claire cringes. The woman stabs her pin number into the chip and pin and they wait in silence for the transaction to go through.

'Well, bye then,' the customer manages. She sweeps her jute bags into her trolley and rushes her baby away from the skinny girl who has unsettled her by showing some character; surprised her with her unexpected quip.

It's true, though, I do read recipe books, thinks Claire defensively. And watch re-runs of *Saturday Kitchen*; and *The Great British Bake Off*; and *MasterChef*. What else is a single mum to do with no money, a nine-year-old girl and little social life?

Much of the time she is too exhausted to put these recipes into practice, or too skint to buy the ingredients for the more complex ones. But she and Chloe regularly make sponges and pastry; gingerbread men, cupcakes, saffron bread, even Cornish pasties. Recipes that don't require expensive ingredients or excessive skill but that fill their tiny flat with the scent of a buttery hug and the promise of good times.

At twenty-seven, she knows she is unusual in taking the time to bake but she is only doing what her mother Angela has taught her to do. 'Just carrying on the Trelawney tradition,' she tells Chloe and her tangled-haired daughter crimps the edges of the pasties or fashions gingerbread stars before launching into a dance routine, her skinny legs taking her out of the cramped kitchen in one leap.

'You're a natural.' Claire's mum nods approvingly, though she can't quite resist tweaking the leaves on her pie crust.

'Oi!' Claire feels a familiar stab of irritation. It looks better, though, and she leaves it in its place.

'I wish you'd go back to baking,' Angela tends to continue; meaning, I wish you'd stop sitting on a checkout and go back to working in a bakery. But the hours are better in the supermarket, she always answers; how could she start work at five or six with Chloe?

'Well, what about going back to college?' her mother suggests, and the catering course curtailed by an unplanned pregnancy. But they both know that's a pipe dream. The days of being a student; of dreaming about working in a revered — perhaps even a Michelin-starred — restaurant disappeared nine years ago when

46

she was handed a screaming, mucous-and-blood-coated baby. She in no way regrets Chloe — how can she when she offers the purest, most unconditional love she has ever experienced? But getting pregnant at seventeen soon put paid to such fantasies. Claire Trelawney doesn't have the luxury of dreams.

★ ★ ★

In the marketing department of Eaden and Son's, Cora Young is staring at a photo. A slight young woman cuddles a long-legged girl who could almost be her sister were it not for the premature lines of anxiety above the woman's brows and the passionate ferocity of that hug. Lank hair is scraped off a pale face from which blue eyes shine with an unexpected intensity; and there is a look of tension and energy about her limbs; as if constantly vigilant, poised to spring into action.

Cora, faced with an almost exclusively middle-class array of candidates, decides the fact this one works for Eaden's can be brushed over; she won't be seen as having snuck through the back door, but rather as having fought her way there, she will be an asset.

She takes another look at the photo.

I like her, she thinks. I'll make the call.

★ ★ ★

When the call comes for Jennifer confirming that she sailed through the audition, she is in the middle of making short-crust pastry. Her squat fingers are coated in butter and flour and she has just bound the crumb together with iced water and a fat orange egg yolk, the wet ingredients marrying the dry in an act of culinary alchemy.

She is making a chicken and tarragon pie with buttered new potatoes and green beans for Nigel, her husband — though whether he will want it is a different matter. Perhaps the potatoes if he can catch her while they're still steaming and before she can slather them with butter. Then he'll toss them with the beans and some little gems into an undressed and unsatisfying salad. On second thoughts, he may allow himself a splash of balsamic vinegar.

Once upon a time Nigel was as much of a foodie as she is. But at fifty, his younger brother, Tom, suffered a massive heart attack and it was — as Nigel repeatedly, and somewhat sanctimoniously, puts it — 'a wake-up call'.

Out went the evening whiskies, the chocolate after dinner, the slab of cake when he got in from work, the generous helpings of red meat. And in came running. Not a gentle jog round the block. But the obsessive, relentless running of a fifty-two-year-old man who has felt mortality snapping at his heels and is desperate to outrun it. A man who, in middle age, has decided to become a marathon runner.

'Well, it's better than having an affair, Mum,' Lizzie, their youngest, chastises her when she ventured to comment on how their father had altered.

And of course it is, though in its way it feels like a betrayal.

It is not just the hours he puts in: the thrice-weekly runs with a twelve-mile one each weekend; the weekly running club meets, where he runs alongside fearsomely toned women triathletes; the marathons themselves — and, in just over a year, he has already clocked up four. It is his rejection of their former way of life at a time when, in a cruel twist of fate, all three of their girls have also fled: Lizzie, immersed in her first year at uni; Emma in Montpellier in the third year of her French degree; Kate, post-finals, who has just set off for a year's travelling in Australia.

She knows, of course, that she should try to be the good wife she has always been and accommodate his new needs; bend to his will; adapt her cooking. But her whole identity is tied up with providing rich food for him and every time she serves a steamed sea bass with a Thai salad or, pre-race, a bowl of pasta with a tomato-based sauce, not an unctuous carbonara, she feels a pang of resentment. She is also hungry. She eats the steamed sea bass and, of course, appreciates its delicate sweetness but she is left hankering for carbohydrates. As she clears up, she reaches for the ever replenished cake tin, or opens the fridge. With Nigel safely dispatched from the kitchen — 'No, I'll tidy up, darling, don't you worry' — she undoes the good she has done and gorges on chocolate torte or egg custard tarts.

Of course, she knows this behaviour is

unsustainable. She realised it at Christmas when Emma, always the one with the sharpest tongue, had quipped to Lizzie that Nigel had become a 'Jack Sprat'.

'And what does that make me?' Jennifer had retorted — challenging them to finish the nursery rhyme.

Em had had the decency to blush. 'But we like you cuddly,' she had tried to reassure her, putting her arms around her mother's waist and trying to nuzzle into her neck as she had as a child. But the damage was done. For once, Jennifer had pushed her away, rejecting the child who was typically the most frugal with her affection. 'Try to think before you speak,' she had hissed. 'I do have feelings.'

Nigel, wandering into the room as she stalked out, had rolled his eyes at his grown-up daughters and offered his opinion. 'Menopausal.' She had heard the girls' laughter, and though she knew they were just trying to hide their embarrassment and placate their father, it had struck her as the cruellest betrayal. She had looked down at her stomach, bulging against the waistband of her velvet trousers after a particularly lavish Christmas lunch, and had been filled with self-loathing. More than that, standing beneath the mistletoe, her broad feet planted firmly on the seventeenth-century flagstones of her hallway, she had felt hollowed out with despair.

Of course, Nigel was right. She is menopausal but her relentless baking has nothing to do with this and everything to do with trying to fill the growing emptiness in her life.

She feels bereft. She has lost the role she has played for twenty-five years but, like a hamster racing neurotically on a wheel, she cannot stop and adapt to changing circumstances. She has always cooked for her family and the fact that no one wants her food — or, seemingly, her attention — does not deflect her. The pies and cakes keep coming; for village fêtes, charity coffee mornings, elderly neighbours. When friends comment on her generosity, her response suggests it is natural; that it is a reflex. 'Well,' she says. 'Food is love.'

'Jennifer Briggs.' The voice on the end of the telephone breaks into her reverie.

'Jenny, yes.'

'We're calling from the Search for the New Mrs Eaden. You auditioned on Tuesday? We'd like you to take part.'

Standing in her kitchen, gripping the phone with still damp hands on which tendrils of wet pastry cling, Jennifer's heart swells.

Kathleen

She bakes, as she prefers to do, in her Chelsea town-house kitchen. Sun streaming through the sash windows, bathing her in light.

Her scales are neatly aligned; her ingredients arranged in size order. A reporter's notepad and a pencil sit on a side table — ready to jot down any tweaks to her recipes or thoughts for *The Art of Baking*, the book she has confirmed she will publish next year.

Today, though, the page is empty. Inspiration unnecessary, or, perhaps, refusing to strike. She has already written the next column: an ode to the joys of cake baking in which she somewhat rashly promises 'heaven in a cake tin' by mixing fat, flour, sugar and eggs. And so there is no demand that she bake. She can just potter; creating sponges or biscuits, meringues or patisserie for the sheer thrill of doing something she enjoys.

She is systematic, though, and prolific. Intently focused, she bakes from memory, making batch after batch of the most familiar sponges: Madeira cake; coffee and walnut cake, and a Battenburg, coloured with almond essence and sieved raspberries. A chocolate cake comes next, to be topped with a rich fudge icing; then madeleines — chaste in contrast to such decadence. By lunchtime, the table heaves with sponges in various states of readiness; cooling; complete; or freshly anointed with the most exquisitely judged icing.

Despite herself, she finds she is reaching for her notebook, conjuring up the cakes' deliciousness with a few choice words: the fudge icing is 'muddy'; the Battenburg 'scented'; the coffee cake 'just the right side of bitter'. No, that's not right. The coffee cake 'marries sweetness with sophistication: the butter cream lifting the sponge; the walnuts adding a certain creaminess'. Is that correct? Are walnuts more creamy than bitter? She nibbles one, then crosses out the description and provides an unsatisfying alternative. 'Creamy bitterness?' she writes and underscores the question mark.

Perched at the table, she takes a sip of Earl Grey and allows herself to sample one small madeleine: the blandest of cakes, perhaps, but comforting, nevertheless. She wraps a couple for George to enjoy later and places the coffee and walnut cake in a tin to give to her cook, Mrs Jennings. But most of these beauties are destined for a different home.

By mid-afternoon, the cakes have been boxed and sent two and a half miles away to the Westminster Children's Hospital, situated on the corner of Vincent Square.

The consultants are bemused that a hospital treating severely malnourished children should receive such unsolicited goodies. But the nurses enjoy them for their tea break.

6

Try to involve your children as much as possible in your baking. They will love the chance to work alongside their mother and it is never too early to teach both little girls and boys to bake. Remember to show patience and good humour, to smile at their endeavours, and you will be assured of a willing helper ever eager for your praise.

'Quickly, Alfie. No, not that way.' Vicki is struggling to pinion her resistant child into his car seat as a chill wind whips her body and threatens to slam her with the car door.

It is seven forty-five on the day of the first round of the competition, and Vicki has to get Alfie to her friend, Ali, in Putney, before driving to Eaden's country estate in Buckinghamshire for ten o'clock and the start of the competition. She should have masses of time but that is without contending with the vagaries of London traffic — and of her son.

She is already braced for the inevitable meltdown — 'But Mummeeee, I need you' — and has factored in twenty minutes to deal with it. She could write the script: twenty minutes of initial reassurance, followed by firm parenting, followed by blatant bribery. She will only extricate herself from his clutches, as they both know, with the desperate promise of Lego. And then his tears will miraculously evaporate.

She will race to her car and then inch her way up an exhaust-choked Fulham Palace Road at the peak of rush hour. She will feel guilty, stressed, angry. Just anticipating it makes the band of tension around her forehead tighten.

'I said: 'No'.'

A friend once told her the way to deal with car seat resistance was to punch your child in the stomach. At the time she assumed it was a joke, the kind of black humour the more witty of her mummy friends trade in; the sort of comment you see on Mumsnet where bored mothers vie to churn out the best one-liners. Now she is not so sure. She contemplates her offspring grimly. He is grinning cherubically, trying to swipe the felt hairclip holding her fringe while she uses both hands to try to force the central seat-belt buckle together. His torso, fast becoming that of a strong little boy not a cuddly toddler, strains against her, his back arching. She jerks her head away from his clutches and simultaneously forces him back in his seat. The seat belt is buckled. He holds her gaze, the smirk melting into a bottom lip wobble. She repeats, with a somewhat steely satisfaction: 'I said: 'No'.'

Since when did she become this hectoring figure? she wonders, as she slams his door unnecessarily aggressively, opens the driver's door, and buckles her own seat belt. She does not want to be a shouty mummy. It is, as one health visitor once told her, somewhat euphemistically, 'not helpful'. And it is certainly not what outstanding teachers do.

It is also not what mummies with only one

child do. If she had a car full of children, and a job to get to, it would be more understandable. But she has just one child, as the dull ache of her monthly period reminds her; one child on which to lavish all her time and attention. As things stand, her behaviour is just not acceptable.

All the same, she excuses herself somewhat petulantly, as her Freelander slips its way into the stream of traffic, she does not have it completely easy. This morning, for instance, she could have done with some help from Greg, but where is he? Just like every morning, he was out of the house by a quarter past six. True, as a commercial lawyer he likes to be at his desk by seven fifteen at the latest, and it's his willingness to do this that allows her the luxury of being at home with Alfie. But, even so, she would love it if he could sometimes be around.

He is barely aware of what she is doing today. Of course, he knows she is in the first round of a cookery competition run by the supermarket where they shop, but she is sure he wasn't listening properly when she reminded him of the details last night; nor when she paraded various outfits in front of him, his eyelids sinking before he excused himself and, with an apologetic smile, fell into bed. She suspects that he thinks she will be knocked out at this stage — an idea she has gently nurtured despite there being no elimination element to the competition. At least she hopes this is the reason he shows so little interest. His only concern is that Alfie, and the apparently effortless efficiency with which she runs their home life, will not be disrupted.

'But what happens if you get past this cake round?' he had queried when she had heard back from Eaden's last week. 'Who's going to look after little Alf?' Panic had suffused his even features. 'I can't help with childcare.'

'Oh, I'm certain it won't come to that,' she had reassured him. 'And if it does, I'm sure Mum or Ali will step in. You won't be affected at all.'

Oh, yeah, she thinks, as she nips across the traffic and into the side street that leads to Ali's. If I get through this round there'll be competition rounds every other weekend, and her mother, with various weekends away, her volunteering commitments and an Easter holiday booked, might not be up for looking after her feisty grandson after all.

You might just have to do some parenting, she thinks, as she spies a tight parking space and parallel parks with the cool efficiency of a Londoner. The tank eases its way in expertly. She is somewhat surprised. Perhaps it's a good omen.

'Come on then, boyo,' she says, catching her son's eye in the mirror. His face is pale, his large eyes tremulous. His bottom lip quivers as he steels himself to cry.

A ripple of weariness rolls over her. Perhaps she should cut straight to the bribery. She twists to face him. 'If you let Mummy go off and do her baking, and if you play nicely with Sam, I'll buy you a Lego helicopter.'

Kathleen

Well, it isn't a gingerbread house.

When George said he had bought her a house
in the country her first, irrational thought had
been that it would be a gatekeeper's cottage:
something turn-of-the-century, with gables, and
scalloped cornicing and rich red bricks looking
like gingerbread and softened with age.

It hadn't occurred to her that he would buy
something so huge and — though she would not
dream of saying this — so pretentious. And yet, if
she'd thought about it, it was precisely the sort
of monstrosity a grocer's son would buy if he
were trying to flaunt his recently acquired wealth
and impress a judge's daughter. She had sighed.
She loves him because of his background — not
despite it. So why does he feel this continual
need to prove himself?

'You do like it, don't you, my dear?' George,
ever anxious to please, had put his arm around
her as they stood in the grounds of Bradley Hall,
the Gothic mansion he was showing her for the
first time, and which he had bought for her
birthday. A bead of perspiration pricked his
brow.

'Of course, my darling.' She had kissed him on
the cheek, and reminded herself that he hadn't
meant to be vulgar. He had only done this

58

because he adored her. 'What a clever surprise!'

'I thought you would love it, you see,' he had continued, as they had walked up the gravel drive towards some horrifying griffins. He paused, newly nervous. 'There's so much space. I could imagine you having the most fantastic study. Look.' He gestured to a bay-windowed room on the first floor. 'It has wonderful views. A room with a view. That's what you said you needed, didn't you? Or was it a room of your own?'

He had flushed; and she had felt a rush of love for a man who had actually listened as she'd talked about Virginia Woolf, and who had read a novel by E.M. Forster, not so much for his own benefit — though he was frank about wanting to better himself — but because he knew it would please her.

'A room with a view would be just perfect.' She smiled.

'If we want to publish *The Art of Baking* early next summer, you need to crack on with it rather.' George the businessman suddenly surfaced: more earnest than her and — though he would never put it like this — more aware of her growing value as part of his brand.

'I've finished cakes.'

'You can't write a book just about cakes.'

'No . . . But I've made a start on biscuits . . . Then it's bread; pies and pastries; puddings and, perhaps — though I've not decided — a final section on high teas.'

'Sounds like we need to install you in that room.'

'Yes . . . or the kitchen.'

'Yes,' he had said with a smile. 'That sounds more logical. We need to get you beavering away in that kitchen.'

They had walked on in companionable silence, Kathleen suddenly excited at the thought of a country-house kitchen with its vast ovens and yards-long tables on which she could roll out complex pastries and lay out tray after tray of biscuits. *The Art of Baking* could be written here — not in some grandiose study or secret garret, squirrelled away under the eaves, but in the heart of her home. The words would flow as the pastry puffed up and dough rose; sections forming in the time it took for a batter to transform into a sponge in the oven. Sentences sometimes stall in her drawing room, as if she needs the scent of melted butter, eggs and sugar to work.

'I also thought' — George's voice had cut through her thoughts and he had flushed more deeply — 'that this was just the sort of place to bring up children. I could imagine it filled with our little ones.'

The magenta had tinged his hairline and burnished his ears.

Her throat tightened, and she had smiled and patted his arm; given a laugh that — surely, even to him — must have tinkled with insincerity? How to tell him what he must suspect? That the heir he craved — the Son in his Eaden and Son — seemed to have no intention of materialising any time soon.

'Oh, we've plenty of time for that, darling.' She had leaned up towards him and planted a kiss on his lips, her own slightly open. I want it too, George, she had wanted to tell him. You know how important family is to me; you must know I so want it. But I can't seem to find the words.

Instead, she had sought to placate him, uttering a line that wasn't an untruth, she reasoned. It just didn't come close to the truth.

'I don't think we're in any rush, are we? There's plenty of time for babies. Let's just spend a little longer enjoying being the two of us.'

7

When presenting your cake or tart, do take care. A mismanaged flip of the wrist, a moment of distraction, can cause your sponge to crumble or, worse, tumble to the floor. You have taken time to create your cake or pudding so take time over its presentation. Substance and style are required.

'Oh. My. God.' Claire Trelawney cannot help her reaction as she sweeps up the gravel drive to Bradley Hall, the former home of George and Kathleen Eaden, and the setting for the Search for the New Mrs Eaden competition.

'Not bad, is it?' The cab driver glances at her in his rearview mirror, taking in her wide eyes, the neat mouth hanging open. She looks gobsmacked.

'Bloody hell. Did they really live here — and am I going to stay here?' She laughs with incredulity, a bubble of excitement bursting as it wriggles through the nerves knotting her stomach. She cranes forward, peering up at the sandstone Gothic revivalist mansion, taking in its turrets and ornate arcading, its excessively high windows glinting in the rare February sun.

'You part of the competition then?' The cabbie, who has picked her up from Reading station, slows his pace to let her take in its full splendour. The cab crawls along the gravel so that she can see the croquet lawn on which a stray pheasant struts.

'Yes. Yes, I am.' Claire — who has been silent through nerves since getting into the cab — laughs at the sheer unlikeliness of the situation. The idea still seems ridiculous.

'Not used to this sort of luxury, then?' he jokes.

She gives a rueful smile. 'No, I'm not.'

She takes in gargoyles leering from the roof, and, as the cab growls to a halt, the stone lions flanking the entrance.

'Nor me, love.' He laughs. 'Well — enjoy it! A mate of mine's working on the restoration and it's meant to be like a boutique hotel.'

'Right . . . '

Claire does not even try to imply she knows what the interior of a boutique hotel is like, nor does she mean to give him much attention. She is too busy gazing at the arched windows — like the windows of castles in Chloe's old fairytale books.

'Mind you, it was in a complete state when they started: roof falling in; dry rot; terrible electrics. Just goes to show things aren't always as good on the inside as they look on the outside.'

'Uh-huh.'

She is barely listening.

'As so often in these cases, it can be a question of all style and no substance.'

He kills the engine, takes the keys from the ignition and turns to face her properly.

'I shouldn't really say this but their plumbing

was up the creek. Shit everywhere, if you'll pardon my French.'

He gives her a wink, like some sort of all-knowing local.

'Just you remember that.'

★ ★ ★

Am I really in the right place? thinks Claire as she pushes open a solid oak door and is confronted with Bradley Hall's faded beauty. Entering the impressive hall, she finds no one to greet her and little to suggest this is anything other than an ornately furnished country-house hotel. She pads over the parquet flooring, her trainers making no noise, and peers up the mahogany staircase into a forest of William Morris rose briars.

'Hel-lo?' Her call is tentative.

She repeats it, feeling increasingly self-conscious. Her voice, soft with its Devonian burr, barely resonates.

Still no answer.

She drops her overnight bag and fumbles in the pocket of her jeans for her mobile and a print-out on which there is a number. Her stomach grips even tighter as the phone rings.

'Hello?' The voice on the other end is efficient, confident, well-spoken.

'Ummm. It's Claire Trelawney . . . I've arrived for the baking competition but I'm not sure I'm in the right place?'

She hates herself for squirming. She looks down at her legs, one crossed over the other. No

64

wonder she feels off balance as well as out of place.

'Claaaire.' Warmth floods down the phone and into her ear. 'Fantastic. We've been waiting for you. I'm Cora. Where are you? In the entrance hall? *So* sorry. We're in the kitchen. There should be a sign? Can you see it?'

A piece of A4 paper with 'The Search for the New Mrs Eaden competition THIS WAY' and a large black arrow is taped to a light switch.

'Oh, sorry. Yes.'

'Fantastic. Well, you just follow that and you should be with us in a minute.'

'OK.' Her relief is so extreme she sounds joyful. But Cora has already gone.

Glancing at the sign, she feels a tiny rush of reassurance, the blackness of the pen, and the confident hand in which it is written, making the situation seem more real. The notice may be temporary but it is Sellotaped firmly. Someone has taken no chances that it will flutter from the entrance, be trodden on and crumpled. It is tangible: the stuff of everyday not of dreams.

Claire has found it hard to keep her usual firm grip on reality for the past four days. Everything has happened so quickly. On Thursday, her mum had rung her at work, itself a rare occurrence, and asked, in a voice tight with nervousness, if she could meet her to pick up Chloe.

'Everything OK?' Claire's throat had constricted though she kept her tone light.

'Fine, my lover. Wonderful.' The reassurance had rushed from her. Then: 'I've got some great news.'

She had lied to her manager; said school had rung asking her to pick up Chloe immediately; fled the fluorescent oppressiveness of the store and hared to her parents' former council flat, her battered Ford nudging forty in her desire to be there fast.

When she arrived, Angela's face glowed with excitement, a beam breaking out across her broad features.

'But what's the matter?'

Fear had tumbled from her.

'Nothing. I told you. I've some fantastic news for you. But I'm worried you're not going to like it.' Her mother had paused. 'I've been meddling — but it's for your own good.'

Bill, her dad, had been grinning too. 'Spit it out, love,' he'd told his wife, rocking back on his heels in anticipation and then, uncharacteristically, coming forward to hug his youngest daughter.

Their behaviour was making her increasingly nervous.

'For God's sake, Mum. You haven't tried to contact Jay, have you?'

Incomprehension flooded her mother's face at the reference to Chloe's absent father, who she had repeatedly tried to get to show an interest in his daughter.

'That waste of space?' her mother had virtually spat. 'Don't be ridiculous.'

Putting her arm round Claire's tense shoulders, she had at last managed to spill her delicious secret.

'You see, my lovely. You know how good you

66

are at baking . . . Well, I entered a competition on your behalf . . . that Search for the New Mrs Eaden thing run by Eaden's? And, well, they want you to take part . . . '

'I don't understand.'

'I filled out an application form, telling them what you could make: cream horns, jam puffs, saffron bread and buns, pasty, stargazy pie, Chloe's birthday cakes. And, um, I sent them a photo of you. They want the area manager to audition you tomorrow — just to check you can string a sentence together and that you really can bake — and then they want you to go up to the competition, in Buckinghamshire, on Saturday. They want you to take part.'

She hadn't known whether to feel intense irritation or just sheer incredulity. Standing in their cramped kitchen, her fingers clutching the chipped Formica surface of the units, as if to steady herself, her stomach hollowed then fizzed with adrenalin.

'But what about Chloe? What about work? I can't just swan off to some competition. I haven't the clothes, I haven't the money . . . '

'We'll sort it.' Her dad, ever dependable, could barely contain his pride.

'Of course we'll sort it,' echoed Angela. Eaden and Son would pay expenses, including train and cab fares; her parents would look after Chloe for each of the six rounds.

'But what about work? I can't lose my job.'

'You can swap your Saturday shifts, and Cora, the lady who contacted me, said she would talk to them; it's in their interests to have an employee who's going to be a celebrity cook and a 'culinary consultant'.' Angela, getting somewhat carried away, had clearly worked it all out.

'Let's face it, what's the worst that can happen?' Bill had asked, his face creasing with laughter.

'I can lose my job. I can lose my income. I can get even poorer.' She had been engulfed by rising panic.

'Love.' Her mum had smiled, and she shook her head as she marvelled at how sensible her youngest child was; how sensible she had had to become. 'If you win this, the world's your oyster. You'll be their star employee. You'll probably be running the whole baking department! They won't be able to get enough of you.'

That was four days ago. Now, on a freezing Saturday morning after catching the 6.52 Paddington train, it is difficult to mimic her parents' bravado. And yet she knows she has to show some chutzpah; to be the feisty seventeen-year-old who believed she could take on the culinary world.

This is her chance. Her chance to do something more interesting with her life; to break away from the torpor of the checkout; to offer Chloe a better future. This is her chance not to be scared; to glimpse a future where she does more than survive on little more than the minimum wage and to enjoy a present in which she is not constantly financially sensible. This is her chance to be audacious; her chance to dream — but she is no longer sure if she knows how to.

She pushes open the swing door and follows the A4 signs proclaiming 'Competition Kitchen'. Peeping through the window in the door she sees a massive hangar of a room, with five work stations and, at the far end, what looks like the judging table.

Despite the vast space, the kitchen is trying to be homely. Pastel bunting garlands the walls; vintage cake stands festoon the oak surfaces; four cream fridges stand guard. The limpid March light filters through windows fringed with potted-out herbs: flat-leaf parsley, rosemary, sweet basil and thyme. Halogen spots direct more reliable beams.

A door at the far corner of the room opens and, to her horror, a line of people enters. She watches as the competition weaves its way into the room: a plump matronly woman; a rich one; a yummy mummy; a middle-aged bloke, trying not to look stressed.

She hadn't realised she was so late; that, by taking an early morning train rather than leaving Chloe last night, she would automatically feel on the back foot. She takes a deep breath. I can do this, she tells herself, though she barely believes it. I'm as good as them. And then with a bravado that feels hollow: this can be mine.

'Claire,' a strong, confident voice greets her from the front of the room, where an elegant, middle-aged woman is standing. 'Good of you to join us.'

The room turns to look at her.

'I'm Harriet Strong, one of the judges, and this is my fellow judge, Dan Keller.'

The woman strides towards her and thrusts out a hand, sparkling with an antique cocktail ring. It crushes against Claire's fingers.

'Pleased to meet you,' she manages.

Harriet gives a businesslike nod and returns to the front of the kitchen. She smiles, removes a microscopic piece of fluff from her blouse, then waits for their full attention.

'Welcome to the first Search for the New Mrs Eaden!' she declares. The room swells with nervous laughter.

'This is the baker we want you to emulate: Kathleen Eaden.' She gestures to a large black and white photo.

Claire recognises her immediately. The same face smiles down in each Eaden's bakery department, and on the boxes of teal polka-dot crockery sold as part of the Kathleen Eaden range. Still, she is struck by how proper she looks. Hardly rock and roll. She wears a pencil skirt and a tweed jacket. Didn't she live in the Swinging Sixties? Perhaps it passed her by.

'This photo was taken in 1963, two years after Kathleen married George,' Harriet explains. 'She turned out to be a huge asset. As I'm sure you know, by the time they sold Eaden's to the Marshall Group in 1967, George's father's grocers had expanded to 208 supermarkets. Kathleen was key to that exponential growth and success.

'She was everything an Eaden's customer aspired to: beautiful, elegant, refined. And women loved her. She introduced them to new ingredients but she did it gently: persuading them that they could bake beautifully and providing recipes that proved they could do it.

'Her writing style was firm but could be playful. Like her contemporary, Robert Carrier, writing in the *Sunday Times*, she delighted in writing about cooking. And, crucially, she wasn't just style and no substance. She baked not only simply but exquisitely too.'

She smiles. 'So, we have set a high standard — and the winner of the title, and the contract, needs to meet this. Needs to cook as perfectly as Kathleen Eaden.'

There is a pause. Bloody hell, thinks Claire. I can't do that. What was Mum thinking? Everyone here's older, more experienced, more like Kathleen Eaden than me.

She takes a deep breath and through eyes that are beginning to well reads the first recipe, on a laminated card: Victoria sponge. She wipes her eyes. The words are still there. She isn't imagining it. Victoria sponge. The easiest cake in the world. Something Chloe makes on her own and has been doing since she was seven. Child's play.

'We thought we'd ease you in gently.' Harriet appears to be smiling at her directly.

And, like a child, like Chloe, she begins to bake.

★ ★ ★

Half past ten and the room vibrates with the gentle hum of collective concentration. Five people all focused on one task; all industrious; all

71

showing a meticulous, unwarranted level of attention.

Jenny, to her surprise, is working with painful deliberation. She can make a Victoria sponge with her eyes shut — and must have made over a hundred — and yet she is weighing everything with exaggerated precision. Golden caster sugar, self-raising flour — held aloft and sieved into a bowl twice — baking powder, and pale unsalted butter: each is treated as if they were a class A drug or potentially fatal medicine. A gram over? She is taking no chances. She removes a smidgeon of flour.

Of course, she knows baking is about precision: too little raising agent, too little air, too much mixing, too cold ingredients, too hot an oven, too long a cooking time — each of these variables can reduce the perfect sponge to a flat, dry or greasy parody of the garden fête ideal. But, even so, her care is excessive. Holding the instructions, her hand shakes with nerves and she knows she is measuring so carefully to try to dispel these. But she is also being assiduous to try to block out all other thoughts.

Her stomach grumbles with anxiety, not just because this competition has become suffused with importance but because she cannot shut out Nigel's brutal words last night. She cannot reconcile her knowledge of him as a gentle man, the father of her children and her husband of twenty-five years, with someone capable of such derision. Or perhaps that's not true. She has always been aware of his sharp side, but it has never before been directed at her. Barbs and put-downs have been reserved for malingering patients and been tempered with a laugh. Now she is in the firing line, and laughter is absent.

It had happened, of course, in the kitchen. She had just brought a fresh batch of blueberry muffins out of the oven and had torn one apart: ostensibly to work out if the buttermilk and bicarb made it more aerated; in reality, to gorge on the jammy blueberries and warm, moist sponge.

Nigel had burst in after a ten-mile run, sleek in his running Lycras. Freezing-cold air blasted into the fug of the kitchen as the stable door flew open.

Despite the sub-zero temperatures, he'd looked exhilarated rather than chilled. His still-handsome face was red and glowing; his top was darkened with sweat patches, and his breathing was shallow and quick. Yet he didn't cut a ridiculous figure, the archetypal middle-aged man desperate to recapture his youth. If anything, Jenny had thought, his physique was better than thirty years ago: hardened and lean, where before it had had the softness of a studious youth.

Breathing out noisily in the kitchen, he was like a wild animal: not a cheetah — that would be to flatter him — but a fox, or a wolf. Yes, she had thought with amusement, with his dark locks, flecked with grey and slick with sweat, and his hairy legs there was definitely something vulpine about her husband.

And then, like a wild animal, he had turned.

'Not baking again?' And where once there

would have been affectionate amusement, now there was a snarl. 'Don't you think you should lay off it a bit, Jen? It's nearly ten o'clock at night. I'm sure that even you don't need to be baking now.'

The attack was like a blow to her stomach. She had been tempted to retort that he too was pursuing his hobby at an unsociable time but remained silent, focusing instead on the way he gulped down some water, his Adam's apple rising as the liquid ran noisily down his throat. A spurt gushed from the bottle and splashed on the flagstone floor.

'I'm just practising for tomorrow's competition,' she had excused herself, as she reached for a cloth. She bent down to wipe the small puddle, biting back a bubble of anger. 'I just wanted to get these perfect.'

'It's becoming a bit obsessive, though, isn't it?' he had needled her. 'No one in their right mind needs to cook to the extent you do. And,' he continued, 'I'm not sure it's good for your health.'

'It's fine for my health.' Her voice was sharp, keen to prevent the unspoken criticism. But this time it was spoken.

'It's not, Jen. Your BMI must be in the obese bracket. You're becoming, no, you've become, fat, my love.'

The word had ricocheted round the room. He had never called her that before. Cuddly, voluptuous, curvy — these have been the chosen euphemisms, uttered only when she has sought reassurance. Recently both have avoided any

74

reference to her widening girth.

Now some unspoken contract had been breached.

She had turned to face him, tears welling in her pale blue eyes, and searched for reassurance. But his look was cold and cynical.

'I mean it, Jen.' He was matter-of-fact, his tone frank. 'You need to get a grip. This cookery competition is sheer indulgence. No one needs to gorge themselves on pies, cream cakes and biscuits. Least of all you.'

He had turned the knife casually as he reached into the fridge for a bottle of apple juice: 'A bit of exercise wouldn't go amiss either. If I were your GP, I'd be advocating a strict exercise routine as well as a diet.'

'Then it's a good job you're not,' she had hissed.

'Well, yes. I'd see you as a drain on NHS resources,' he had retorted.

She had searched for a glimmer of humour, but there was no attempt at a quip.

He had raised an eyebrow, the look of censure unwavering. 'I'm going to bed.' And she had been left alone, as ever, in her kitchen.

On autopilot, she had wiped the surface, taken the cooled muffins from the rack and placed them in a tin, and then, very deliberately, taken the half-eaten one and crammed it into her mouth.

Even that had offered no succour. The soft crumb was dry against her throat and she had spat it into her Belfast sink, rasping as she coughed up a sob. Clutching the cold enamel, she had let the tears come, crying out of self-pity for a lost marriage and a lost self.

Today, that excess of emotion has left her feeling hollowed out. The puffiness around her eyes has died down, and been disguised with foundation and a touch of blue eyeliner but the sense remains of a bridge crossed. She cannot dislodge a line remembered from some long-forgotten A-level text: 'Things fall apart; the centre cannot hold.' Now, who wrote that? The poet — of little use after that English exam; and of none when she started nursing — remains elusive but the words take on a mantra as she creams her fat and sugar. She imagines the mixture curdling when beaten with eggs that are too cold. The sponge can still be enjoyed, but it won't rise as well; it won't be up to scratch. It's a prosaic analogy but seems apt: with a knot in her stomach, she wonders if the same will be true of her marriage?

It seemed clear on the way down on the train, this morning, that she has a choice. Either she can do as Nigel wishes: give up the competition before even starting, give up baking, seek to starve herself; become the slim, healthy-looking wife she is now in no doubt he would like, perhaps even take up a sport — though the thought of running is laughable; maybe something suitably pedestrian, like golf. Or, she can run with this: bake like fury, bake with passion, find an outlet for her creativity that is recognised and applauded. And then, at the end of this three-month process, she can take off the blinkers, step on the scales, and step back into the role of a wife — albeit one with a marriage in tatters.

Put like this, the decision is clear and so this competition — this simple sponge — has taken on a disproportionate importance. After nearly three decades of tending to others, she has the chance to do something for herself. She can shine at what she does but, equally, she realises with a glimmer of excitement, she can redefine herself. She does not need to be a corpulent cook, the jolly fat lady of the competition — though she is aware Eaden and Son have pigeon-holed her as this. Perhaps she could even ask that they use Jenny, her name as a girl, not the more matronly Jennifer. Perhaps she could be Jenny once more.

She focuses on the cake. Eggs, their fat yolks orange and spherical, plop into a mixing bowl and are quickly beaten before being whisked into the mixture. Self-raising flour and extra baking powder are sieved from thirty centimetres above the bowl, and folded in lightly. A splash of milk makes the mixture moister still. She eases the batter out of the bowl with a gentle push of a spatula, guiding it into the greased and lined cake tins, taking excessive care to check they are evenly distributed. She weighs the tins just to check. The tops are caressed with a palette knife and then the tins are placed side by side in the centre of the oven as she waits for the alchemy to begin.

★   ★   ★

Eleven o'clock and Karen, her sponge in the oven, is watching her fellow bakers. Vicki folds and spoons, creams and beats as if enjoying an elegant courtly dance. Claire works precisely: movements swift and economical; no time for indulgence here. Jennifer seems excessively nervous. And Mike bakes with a cavalier disregard for instructions. As if there has been enough in his life to be anxious about without him fretting over a cake.

While Harriet darts between the contestants, her fellow judge, Dan, is ambling down the side of the work stations, moving with the cool confidence of a handsome man in his early thirties with the world at his feet.

Karen drinks him in. Thick dark curls wreath his shapely head; his eyes, behind hipster glasses, are frank and bright; and his jaw line and cheekbones strong and exquisitely defined. He is, she thinks, an Adonis, plucked from some Mediterranean glade and placed in the most prosaic of settings: a kitchen. His skin, the silkiest olive, gleams with health; his full mouth curls as if contemplating a kiss.

But it is his body that most invites comparisons with the Greek gods: firm pecs hinted at through a cotton shirt unbuttoned just one button too much; a torso tapering to a slim waist; and the height — he is six feet four inches — glutes and legs of an Olympic rower.

In late middle age, he could run to fat were he to immerse himself in the bread, pasta and kuchen that he claims he was brought up on. But she suspects he is too narcissistic — and canny

— for that. His cookery book may have reached number three in the non-fiction charts in the run-up to Christmas, but he must know the public's appetite is less for his recipes than for himself. He is one of those rare creatures with true charisma. He is delectable, dangerous — and unattainable.

Or maybe not. Karen's assessment of individuals is automatic. A throwback to a childhood when the need to check out the opposition was instinctive: the first thing done as she entered a room. And her instincts, honed over forty years, are largely right.

But now she senses danger: the danger of flirtation — and potential seduction. She watches him walk towards her station, his movements fluid but purposeful, and waits to meet his gaze. His eyes are warm; that upper lip curls.

'Hello.' He smiles and there is a palpable frisson.

Oh, fuck, fuck, fuck, fuck, fuck.

'Hello.' Her tone is polite, rather than inviting, but her chin is tilted up as if in challenge.

'And how are you doing?'

The question is ludicrous. A non-sequitur. What does he mean, how is she doing? She is taken aback by his physical beauty; she is wrong-footed.

'I mean the sponge?' His smile is encouraging.

'Oh, the sponge.' As if she could have been thinking of anything else. 'Oh, perfect — well, I hope so, we shall have to wait and see,' she hears herself burble. She never burbles. He thinks I'm stupid, she fears. *I need to get a grip.*

'You should be thinking about getting your cakes out of the oven.' Harriet's voice rescues her, and cuts through the hum of activity. The sponges are soon perched on wire racks, eased out of their greased and lined tins and set to cool.

'And five minutes.'

The bakers caress their cakes with warmed palette knives, smoothing raspberry jam over the sponge. Jennifer would like to add butter cream, or replace the jam with whipped cream and sugared raspberries but she appreciates the need for simplicity. Claire, dowsing her sponge with caster sugar, grimaces at her cake's relative lack of height.

'And — tools down.'

A shriek rips the air. Vicki, hands clutched to her head, is paralysed in horror. Her cake is splayed upside down, icing sugar dusting the floor, jam oozing out from between the dislodged sponges.

'It's OK, it's OK, it's OK.' Red-faced and frantic, she looks close to tears as she gesticulates that others should leave her. 'I was just trying to move it on to a better plate.'

She bends to scoop up the ruined concoction, breaking a sponge as she does so. Then noisily, messily, unbelievably, she begins to weep.

'Oh, poor love,' Jennifer murmurs.

At the back of the room, Claire exhales.

Kathleen

The first time it had happened, she had barely allowed herself to believe she was pregnant. Of course she had known. She had held the secret tight inside her, incapable of telling anyone, least of all George, in case she gave him false hope. For four whole weeks, as she baked and wrote and opened supermarkets, she had walked around knowing she had exciting news and just longing to share it. Her breasts tingled and, if she looked very closely, she imagined she could see a slight swell.

Afterwards, it had helped that she hadn't shouted her joy from the rooftops; hadn't even uttered a whimper. It had helped her to half convince herself it was just a late period, delayed by the stress of writing her column. A period four weeks late.

There had been little pain. And that had made it all the more confusing.

For there had been a surprising amount of blood.

8

A Battenburg may seem a little complicated to make but, I assure you, it is worth the effort. Few cakes are as guaranteed to raise a smile. There is something celebratory about a Battenburg and something frivolous. And no one can doubt the care and effort required to bake it. This is a cake to make for someone you love.

When Harriet approaches her to discuss how to make a Battenburg, the advice is unnecessary. Well, it would be a Battenburg, thinks Vicki. Battenburg is the cake that started her whole baking-for-validation obsession.

It began, of course, with her mother. She was going to bake a Battenburg for Frances's fortieth birthday. Vicki was thirteen. A ludicrously ambitious cake for a thirteen-year-old to bake. But then Vicki was nothing if not her mother's daughter. Weaned on ambition, Frances used to joke — and Vicki remembers the laughs of her mother's friends: uncomfortable and insincere.

As a small girl, Vicki had loved shop-bought Battenburg. She would ease apart the coloured squares of cake, the synthetic pink and lemon yellow, her fingers sticky with jam and the sugary marzipan she would unfurl like a delicate ribbon. She would nibble each square daintily, imagining herself to be a fairy princess. And then she would savour the peeled-away ribbon, rolling it tight then unrolling it, tearing off strips to melt on her tongue.

Eating Battenburg was a rarity. The most exquisite treat. Frances refused to buy her daughter cake, though flapjacks, made with black treacle not golden syrup, and carob brownies from the local health food shop — heavy with wholemeal flour, dry with walnuts, disappointingly un-chocolately — were allowed.

Battenburg was something she only got to sample at her best friend Nicola's — Nicky's — house. In the warmth of her kitchen, or at the bottom of her garden, they would dissect the tessellated squares into quarters and put them on her toy tea set to make fairy sandwiches for their Tiny Tears.

Of course, at thirteen, she was long past playing with dolls but the thrill of Battenburg — its status as a joyful, celebratory, somewhat illicit cake — remained with her. And so, buoyed by Nicky, she decided to make one for her mother's forticth birthday.

She did have one moment of hesitation.

'You don't think she'd prefer a carrot cake, do you?' she had asked Nicky. 'I've never seen her eat a Battenburg — or anything so pink.'

'Don't be stupid,' Nicky had scoffed. 'You don't make someone a carrot cake for their fortieth birthday! What is she, a rabbit?' And so she had ignored her reservations and blocked them out in a flurry of giggles.

With Nicky's mother's help, they had found a recipe and spent an industrious afternoon concocting the sponge. The pink squares were a livid pink, the lemon, an aggressive yellow; the cake tapered slightly at one end where the tessellation was imprecise and bulged, barely perceptibly, in the middle.

But the thirteen-year-old Vicki had tried to remain optimistic.

'Do you think she'll like it?' she had asked Nicky and her mother, as she gnawed on a fingernail, biting the cuticle so that it tore and sprang salty blood.

'Like it? She'll love it,' Nicky's mum had reassured her, watching, concerned. 'She'll love it because it's fantastic and she'll love it because you made it for her.'

She had presented it to Frances the next morning — the day of her birthday — with her usual breakfast of half a grapefruit and a cup of Earl Grey tea, black with a slice of lemon. She had meant to keep it until teatime but the anticipation was too intense.

Frances, uncomfortable at being expected to remain in bed — she normally rose at six thirty — had laughed, incredulous.

'Oh darling. Did you make it?'

'Yes.' Vicki's cheeks flushed pink with pleasure. Suddenly she was no longer thirteen but eight, seven, six. Coming home from school with birthday cards, love letters, Mother's Day cards for Frances: the spelling somewhat erratic, the sentiment — a cry for love, for attention — always the same.

'I don't know quite what to say!' Frances had assessed it from either end, her left eyebrow raised in mock horror.

Say it's lovely, Vicki had willed her, hotly aware her mother wasn't supposed to react in this way.

'Well, it's certainly interesting. What strong colours! Did you mean it to be quite so psychedelic?' Her laugh had tinkled.

Vicki had flushed.

'They're not meant to be psyche . . . so bright,' she had tried to excuse herself, her voice small and tight. 'It's supposed to be delicious.'

'And I'm sure it will be,' Frances had cut in, just in time.

Twenty years on, Vicki can still recall the relief when she heard this — and the shame when her mother then undermined this reassurance.

She had brightened, momentarily. 'Do you want to try a bit?'

'Oh not now, darling.' Her mother had sounded instantly anxious. 'Maybe later — at teatime. And just a little bit. I'm not sure that much food colouring is good for anyone.'

Now, in the Eaden's competition kitchen, Vicki realises she has a chance to right that wrong. To bake a Battenburg that will scare no one with its colouring and that will win the validation she has sought for twenty years. And so she bakes with a determination that eluded her earlier. She is going to bake the most exquisite Battenburg and surprise not just the judges but, more importantly, her mother.

★   ★   ★

Twenty minutes in and Claire, recalling her truncated catering diploma, is still trying to persuade herself she can do this: that she can pour different-coloured batters into separate compartments and structure them so expertly they form a checkered square. She is naturally neat and precise: her milky-tea hair tied back in a high ponytail; her apron strings double knotted; her trainers new for the occasion; her tiny jeans ironed. Her fingers shake as she folds the parchment-lined foil neatly in half and then forms a four-centimetre pleat to separate the different-coloured mixtures, but she is sharp with herself: 'Pull yourself together; you can do this; you know you can.'

Her fingers still shake. She imagines her daughter — soft brown hair framing great big eyes that trust her as emphatically as when she was a baby. The image calms her. 'You have to do this — for Chloe. You don't have a choice.'

* * *

Karen, too, is trying to focus, concentrating on a recipe that allows her to achieve order, if not perfection. She is still acutely aware of Dan's presence; his height as he saunters down the aisles, those broad shoulders, those startling blue eyes. She tries to zone him out, imagining instead her daughter, Livy, at fifteen already a beauty, or, indeed, Jake.

No, better not think of Jake. She barely understands him now, this boy-man she produced whose truculence perturbs her. Or perhaps she understands him too well. She bites down a flicker of fear. Is his shift in attitude

86

towards her just down to teenage hormones, or is there a basis for his derision? *You're fooling no one, Ma.* Did he see them? And, if he knows, has he exposed her? Has he told Oliver?

Baking — and, more specifically, setting herself up as a baker in a cookery competition — is supposed to be a means of avoiding such anxieties. Of reinventing herself: acquiring a more appropriate, more *maternal* hobby than starving herself, exercising fanatically, or obsessing about her ageing, increasingly unattractive body. In her most lonely moments — and she has plenty of these — she imagines she is becoming the wicked queen to her daughter's Snow White. Or a Mrs Robinson to Jake's friends. Either way, she fears she is an embarrassment to her kids.

And so she bakes: beating and whipping, scraping and caressing, measuring, timing, assessing. Digital scales and a sugar thermometer make her precise, though nothing compensates for her refusal to taste. Nevertheless, she is competent and assured; determined and, potentially, ruthless. She is channelling her energy into this Battenburg as if its creation is the most important thing in her world. And, for the moment, on this bleak day in early March, it is.

★ ★ ★

An hour later and the bake has become supremely technical. Butter icing is smeared between strips of pink and golden sponge and the pieces tessellated to create a checkerboard effect. White marzipan is rolled in an oblong and the icing-covered sponge then wrapped in this like a choice present. Five Battenburgs sit squatly, some more even than others; a couple clearly lumpy; one with irregular cuboids of sponge. Queen Victoria — for whose granddaughter the cake was invented — may not have been amused. Mrs Eaden may have been appalled. But in the competition kitchen, there is a sense of accomplishment — and relief that the job is done.

'And — tools down.' Dan's voice — deep, mellifluous — fills the air and the contestants stop what they are doing. Five golden cakes, set on white cake stands, are carried to the display bench at the front to be cut. Vicki allows herself a small smile and tucks her hair behind her ears. Even from this distance, hers looks the clear front-runner: neat, plump, majestic. A knife plunges in and reveals perfect gold and pink squares. The epitome of kitsch, it tantalises and looks particularly good to eat.

The judges agree.

'The crumb is perfect,' declares Harriet, a moist fragment clinging to her lipstick before her tongue swipes it away. 'Our two winning bakers this week then — the two who must appear on YouTube — are Jennifer, for the Victoria sponge, and Vicki.'

Vicki, receiving a verdict she has waited two decades for, cannot suppress a massive, heartfelt grin. Perfect. They think my cake is perfect. Her grin widens until she fears she looks ridiculous. But she cannot stop herself. Finally, she has the validation she needs.

Biscuits

A home-made biscuit is a thing of beauty. Light and ephemeral, sweet and buttery, it should melt on the tongue and leave guests pining for more.

Our American friends may eat cookies, soft plates of dough studded with chocolate, and our young children may find these appealing. But the best of biscuits are more delicate. With an exquisitely curled brandy snap, a piped coffee kiss, a raspberry macaroon or a melting moment, the ordinary housewife can conjure up indulgence, refinement and elegance. She will delight those at her coffee mornings — and astound them with her skill.

The rules are simple. Handle the bound dough as little as possible and be sparing with extra flour: it may stop it sticking but will make the biscuit less tender. With rolled or shaped biscuits, rest the dough in the refrigerator for a good half-hour before shaping. Chill the dough for refrigerator cookies for considerably longer. Simple flavourings work best: a little grated orange or lemon rind: ground cinnamon or ginger; ground almonds or instant coffee; vanilla essence or cocoa powder.

Biscuits do not need to be expensive. But they do need to tantalise: stoking your appetite so that you will need to be restrained in eating just the one. Like the petits fours served in the most sophisticated French restaurants, they are entirely frivolous. And, perhaps because of this, they are all the more irresistible.

Kathleen Eaden: *The Art of Baking* (1966)

Kathleen

She is baking, now, in her Bradley Hall kitchen: a vast, high-ceilinged room in which her cook is also working, preparing an evening meal for sixteen while she, Kathleen, bakes solely for her delight.

Her book is going well: the biscuit section halfway complete, the words flowing freely, covering page after page of cream paper, as her delicacies crisp or turn toffeeish.

Today, though, her notepad is in the drawer and she is making biscuits just for the hell of it. And not just any dull cookies but the most childish and evocative of biscuits — baked not to impress but to provoke a smile of utter joy. Plump, chewy and brown. Glinting with sugar. Studded with dark raisin buttons and eyes.

She works the dough for the gingerbread men, rolling it lightly. The scent of the ginger, the mixed spice, the touch of cinnamon are perhaps unseasonal. But Susan and James, her niece and nephew, will hardly mind.

She presses the cutters down: a mummy, a daddy, and two babies — a girl and a boy. The block of marble is soon covered with two families: her older sisters, Esme and Mary, their husbands and offspring; a single man, her roguish younger brother Charlie; her mother,

Celia; and a childless couple, George and herself.

She cuts out another man: her father, Alexander. Mr Justice Pollington. Strong, authoritative, indefatigable, dependable, who nevertheless keeled over with a massive heart attack on her seventeenth birthday leaving a hole that cannot be filled by any gingerbread shape.

She scrunches up the dough and surveys his remaining family: extensive and ever extending; warm; inclusive; yet never quite making up for his absence, though Charlie — fifteen when Daddy died — does try. They are bossy, frequently judgemental, tolerant of George and his wealth — but never entirely accepting. By no means malleable yet soon to be transformed into pieces of gingerbread.

And then, slowly and ever so tenderly, she presses the boy cutter into the dough once again. Another baby. She has told no one yet: not George, not her mother. But her period is late and her breasts feel different. They tingle. She has made an appointment to see her doctor. She is almost sure.

She dithers over whether to bake the baby or to roll it back into the dough: is she tempting fate if she creates it, or if she expunges it? She has waited so long for this and she doesn't want what happened before to happen once more.

Don't be ridiculous, she tells herself sharply. Stop being fanciful. You are baking; nothing else.

But just to make sure, she creates a string of small boys and girls: sturdy, compact, and when baked, harder and stronger than their parents.

9

I have rarely met a man — whether a husband or a son — who is not partial to a sweet little something. A chewy macaroon, a chocolate-coated biscuit, a buttery Viennese whirl sandwiched with butter cream.
They may proclaim to love all things savoury but that does not preclude their hankering after a titbit that is tempting and wickedly sugary.

Vicki is in her default position: standing at her kitchen island, the surface strewn with ingredients, gazing out at her frozen world.

Inside her Edwardian semi she is toasty. Warmth seeps through the oak floor of her retro kitchen while the red Aga expels heat with the blithe confidence of a global-warming denier. Yet the cold is insidious. Condensation clings to the French windows, numbing her fingers. A reminder of how closeted she is; how vicious the elements are.

The big freeze continues to be unrelenting: encasing the earth with frost, punishing the few brave crocuses. People speak of it in hyperboles: 'The most intense cold for thirty years'; 'The most sustained cold snap for half a century.' To the weather forecasters, thrilled at having something sensational to broadcast, there is ill-disguised glee in such extremity. To the nation as a whole, there is a peculiarly British pride in showing fortitude in the face of adversity. To

Vicki, it is just bloody annoying.

She turns to her kitchen table and the fruit of her morning's labours: eight wire racks laden with melting moments, oatcakes, chocolate chip and hazelnut cookies, shortbread, macaroons. Crisp round the edges, chewy in the centre, the biscuits gleam, plump with sugar and butter. She breaks a cookie in half and nibbles the sweet buttery crust oozing rich dark chocolate. Perhaps she has achieved biscuit perfection.

She turns to smile at a photo of Kathleen Eaden, white-tacked in a prominent position on the door of a cupboard. Her head on one side, Kathleen holds a mixing bowl aloft and is stirring with a wooden spoon. You make it all look so effortless, thinks Vicki. But you clearly had drive and ambition: you weren't just some model who took a good picture. The woman seems to smile at her, down the decades. Help me, Vicki wills her. Help me do my best. Help me to bake well enough to appear again in one of those mini films on YouTube. And help me to win the competition.

Her eyes flit to the clock and she realises that she has been baking for over four hours. In this time Alfie has helped her, played with his train track — and been slumped in front of CBeebies for the past hour and a half.

She knows this is bad parenting but, in her desire to work her way through five recipes, finds it easy to excuse. Greg would not be impressed. But then, as always, Greg is not around.

She goes into the playroom and switches off the television, to instant screams from Alfie. She should have given him a five-minute warning or counted down while shaking a shaker, as she did as a teacher, but, really, he has watched too much.

'I'm sorry, my boy.' She tries to bundle him into her arms. 'But you've had it on for ages. How about some lunch? You could have a warm chocolate chip cookie after your cheese on toast?'

'Noooooooooooo!'

The bellow fills the room as hunger, boredom and frustration at being ignored combust in his small body. He tosses his head in anger, writhes with surprising ferocity, and lashes out at her. She holds his legs, strokes his hair from his reddening forehead and tries to kiss away his tears of rage.

'I'm sorry, my lovely,' she soothes him. 'I'm so sorry.' The screams continue but are more half-hearted; the fight gone as he nestles into her breasts and inhales her unique scent of Eternity and melted butter. He begins to whimper, appeased by her touch. She loves him so much like this. When he allows himself to be pacified by her and, momentarily, is less a little boy than a baby or small toddler. When he buries himself into her as if he wants to curl up, safe inside her. Soft with exhaustion; and briefly compliant.

Hand in hand they traipse to the kitchen where Vicki puts bread under the grill and begins to slice cheddar, cube avocado, halve cherry tomatoes. How many middle-class children are being fed this at lunchtime? she wonders. Tomatoes, cucumber, raisins, carrot sticks, bread sticks: the staple healthy snacks offered at children's parties — and the offerings habitually swept up into black bin bags at the end, untouched.

She would like to pretend her boy chose these over mini rolls, party rings and chocolate fingers, but, like most children, he'd prefer a bit of cake. As if to illustrate this, he is swiping a warm chocolate chip cookie from the bounty on the table and cramming chewy morsels into his mouth. Dark chocolate from a large chip oozes on to his chin and the crumb is smeared on his cheeks. He giggles and she turns.

'Oh, Alfie. Not before you have something healthy. I said *afterwards*.' Her tone is beseeching. But then she looks at those mischievous hazel eyes, that dimple, the look of utter delight in doing something unsanctioned but within the safe confines of his kitchen, and she relents.

'My gorgeous boy. I can't really expect you to obey me if I leave them out for you, can I?' And she too takes a cookie, bites into its yielding centre, and shares a moment of rare complicity.

★　★　★

In her Suffolk kitchen Jenny — she has decided she is Jenny now — is also grappling with biscuits, though, really, she finds it the simplest type of baking of all. Buoyed by winning the first task of the competition, she too is optimistic. With no elimination element, she knows she cannot be knocked out but she wants to do more: she wants to excel, even if it means having to appear on those silly clips put up on the Eaden's website and on YouTube. But if she is to do this, she requires perfection.

And so she is practising with a ferocity that patently irritates her husband, abandoning her usual high standards of housework, as she works in the kitchen from breakfast until late afternoon. It is the more delicate, elegant creations she is focusing on: brandy snaps, almond tuiles, Florentines, melting moments. These are biscuits that require precision: the delicate placing of the exact amount of mixture on a baking tray, or the piping of same-sized shells. These are no homely cookies, created by dropping slapdash spoonfuls of dough, but exquisite mouthfuls which exist to tantalise. This is baking designed to showcase her substantial skill.

She has run out of ground almonds though, and, while the internet order containing these will come tonight, she cannot wait and so pops to her local Eaden's, keen to track down the ingredient. It is lunchtime and the store is more packed than usual with office workers queuing with sandwiches and drinks or fitting in a quick shop. As she crosses the car park, she notes a Volvo estate with a familiar registration plate. Nigel's car. She feels a jolt of surprise at seeing it out of context. Her bearings have shifted. His domain is the surgery, so what is he doing here?

This morning, she dispatched him with a Thai salad served with marinated — skinless — chicken breast. But maybe he does crave pasta?

Perhaps he is not really abstemious and has sneaked out for a secret stash of carbs? To her surprise, she finds this endearing, not merely irritating. Maybe he craves her cooking and she can surprise him. Mentally, she prepares a meal of seduction: steak with brandy sauce, dauphinoise potatoes and a token side salad of rocket and watercress.

She moves between the parked cars, intent on finding him poised over a Belgian bun or snaffling a pork pie — though both choices seem unlikely. And then she stops. He too is making his way through the cars, and he is not alone.

His head is thrown back in laughter, and there is a joyfulness about him that makes him look younger than his fifty-four years. His stride is purposeful, suggesting he is a man of energy and vigour. But it is the subtle closeness of his body to that of Gabby Arkwright — wife of the local GP, keen triathlete, and a family friend — that draws the eye. The way he leans towards her as she turns to him to share her joke, her pretty, neat features lit up, her dark eyes intent on his. The way his arm moves behind her back, not touching but guiding her with a gentle solicitousness as they wend their way through the moving vehicles. He is just being Nigel, she tells herself; ever courteous, ever charming — particularly to the more attractive of her friends. And then his hand comes to rest in the small of Gabby's back, snug against her gym Lycra, and it rests there; no longer just guiding but proprietorial. And she knows, without needing to look — though she is transfixed; she cannot look away — that his strong fingers will stroke the small of her back before brushing over her bottom. And with that small gesture — so fleeting that any acquaintance, or patient, could dismiss it — her world, as she knows it, turns upside down.

Shielded by a silver Land Rover Discovery, her bowels slacken. Then, acrid bile spurts into her mouth. Her body is betraying her: her heart pounds and her vision blackens. Things fall apart; the centre cannot hold. She leans against the solid metal of the car and bends forward, hands squarely on knees. Her breasts encase her as she puts her head down, waits for the faintness to subside.

She does not know how she gets home; driving her Renault Espace on autopilot through country lanes she has known for the past thirty years. She would like to think she drives safely — she always drives safely — and yet there is an uncharacteristic recklessness to her as she careers round corners. Things fall apart. And middle-aged women drive with abandon.

She feels numb. And yet her head spins; thoughts kaleidoscoping as she pieces together a shared lift here, a dinner-party joke there. When did it start? Where is it going? And how could he — how could *she* — do it? Twenty-five years of marriage and twenty-odd years of friendship have proved as fragile as the cobwebs jewelled with dew drops clinging to the hedgerows. That small gesture has blown the one apparent certainty in her life apart.

In moments of crisis, Jenny does what she

always does: she cooks. She needs to preoccupy herself. To excise the hatred, the sorrow and the shame. This is a day to pound, to knead, to bash. This is not a day for millefeuille but for tenderising steak with a rolling pin; for pummelling dough; for downing glasses of robust Merlot as she concocts a beef pie that smells of iron and fortitude, that will offer the ultimate comfort, and that she cannot bear to eat.

She rips the brown skin off an onion, discarding its paper-thin coating; cuts swiftly, the knife slipping through the onion's core and prompting extra tears. Olive oil and butter are hurled into the Le Creuset and fizz, the heat on too high. She tumbles diced steak with mustard and pepper, and starts as she watches her fingers: painted with crimson red; transformed by the brightness of the blood.

It is only once she smells the sweetness of the onions softening in butter that she realises this is the same meal she cooked as a seventeen-year-old, for her father and sister on the night her mother died.

And it is then that the tears fall; tears for a relationship that has spanned three decades and for a bereaved teenager, taught to cook by her mother, for whom food has always been love.

10

If you are lucky enough to have a daughter, do pass on your love of baking. You will teach her a desirable skill — and grow even closer as you work together.

'So, is this how you spend your mornings?' There is a whisper of scorn in Frances's voice as she sweeps into her kitchen, taking in the array of biscuits still resting on the wire racks.

A chill air has entered the room and it is not — Vicki thinks — purely down to the blast of sub-zero wind that whisked through the hall as she let in her mother. The faintest hint of disapproval tinges the atmosphere, imperceptible to anyone other than her daughter who has had a lifetime to become attuned to its every nuance.

'I've been productive, haven't I?' Vicki is brisk. She smiles as she takes her mother's coat, pulls out a chair and moves trays of biscuits.

'Coffee?'

'I'll have a hot water and lemon, darling. Don't worry. I've brought my own lemon. I expect you've used all yours making another tarte au citron.' Her voice tinkles: as delicate and painful as a shard of glass.

Vicki smiles sweetly. She has been in the house two minutes, she thinks, and already she is trying to make me feel inadequate. Well, not this time. She reaches for her own unwaxed organic lemon and shakes it triumphantly. Then washes it with soap, and dries it, for good measure.

Her mother assessing her every move, she places a neat slice in a fine bone china mug, adds boiling water then supplies a silver teaspoon and small saucer for the fruit.

'You didn't pour *boiling* water on it?' Frances looks pained.

'Oh . . . I'm sorry! I'll do you a fresh one . . . '

Vicki cuts a second slice, chooses an untainted mug, pours the acceptable, just-boiled water.

'Here you are . . . I hope this is better.'

Frances, svelte, neat, exacting, glances at her daughter, green eyes narrowed like a newt's.

Does she think that was a dig? Vicki's stomach twists with its habitual tightness. She smiles, and in that gesture tries to convey what she always feels: I only want to please you; I only want your approval. Frances, stirring her hot water, fails to notice the appeal in her eyes.

Vicki waits and identifies, for the thousandth time, with the rebellious pupil summoned to her mother's office. Stop being ridiculous, she tells herself. You are not in trouble. She is only your mother.

Frances lifts the slice of lemon with a teaspoon; presses it against the side of the mug; drops it in the saucer. Then at last, she switches on a smile.

'So are these for this cookery competition?'

'Yes.' Vicki is surprised but delighted that her mother is showing an interest. Frances has made a point of downplaying her achievement in getting into the competition, failing to congratulate her — or even acknowledge it.

104

That failure had hurt. A recently retired head teacher, Frances understands auditions, exams, achievements. Her whole career has been predicated on them. But she only values *academic* success, thinks Vicki. She seems to view her daughter's love of baking as worthless — or, rather, as an embarrassment. It is as if she believes I have chosen to shine at this just to spite her, she thinks. As if it wasn't enough merely to scrape through my A-levels, or abandon my career to look after Alfie. As if I really wanted to annoy her by choosing to excel in the domestic sphere.

'So, you wanted to ask me a favour?' As ever, Frances comes straight to the point. Vicki imagines her chairing a staff meeting. Efficient, authoritative, intimidating.

Her bowels melt. 'I wanted to ask if you could help Greg to look after Alfie over the coming weekends of the competition.'

There is a pause during which her mother takes a sip of the almost-scorching water.

'I think I could do quite well, you see, but it will mean overnight stays for five weekends — and it's a lot to ask Greg to do it all on top of the hours he's putting in at the moment.'

Frances allows her lip to curl while she contemplates an answer.

'Isn't that what fatherhood's about? Not that your father stayed around long enough to find out.' She cannot resist a dig at both men in Vicki's life.

'Well, yes, and of course he should do all the childcare each weekend without complaining

— but that's not reality, is it?' Vicki feels a frisson of irritation. Her mother really isn't making this easy for her.

'Besides' — she decides to appeal to her better nature — 'I thought you might want to support me, and to spend some time with Alfie. He's so glorious at this age and, at this rate, he's the only grandchild you're likely to get so it would be wonderful for you to see him a bit more . . . '

She feels herself welling up, and busies herself tidying away some biscuits, placing them carefully on baking parchment, filling three tins. Surely you can see how lovely he is, she thinks; surely you can hear what I'm saying? I'm telling you that I don't think I'm able to have another baby. That I'm infertile. Barren. I'm asking for your help.

The memory of another old hurt emerges and she wonders if she dare allude to it. She backs away, the possibility disappearing even as it forms. It's the nuclear option. One day I'll be brave enough, she thinks. But not today. She slams on the tin lid. Let's get this skirmish over first.

Frances, meanwhile, is watching Alfie push a Playmobil ambulance around her chair and flinching as he rams it against the table legs. He's being particularly cute today but Frances looks unconvinced that looking after him would be a bonding experience.

She has frequently commented that children only become interesting when they reach secondary school — when they 'become intelligent' as she once memorably put it — or, if

106

she is honest, when they become young adults. She has never seen the appeal of infants however endearing she knows, objectively, they are.

Vicki knows all this but still hopes she will make an exception. Did she make one for me? she wonders. In the privacy of her own home, did she kiss the creases of my fat toddler thighs? Did she watch me as I slept, marvelling at my childish peacefulness, just as I watch little Alf? Did she bury her face in the nape of my neck and breathe in my warm, milky smell? Did she stroke my plump cheek and wonder how she had managed to produce someone so unblemished? So utterly perfect.

She has no memory of Frances playing with her: of her entering her imaginary world and absorbing herself in her games. Nor can she remember her responding to her endless questions without irritation; her tolerating the repetition, the inanity. The teacher in her winces now at her mother's sharpness and questions why there was little joint imaginary play; little interaction beyond drawing and reading. If she wouldn't play with me, she thinks, why would she do it for another child?

Of course, she knows her mother is busy. She has been retired for less than a year but shows no intention of slacking. Each week she works as a volunteer at the Bodleian Library. She swims every morning; helps run the local Oxfam; has resumed piano lessons; and is taking evening classes in Italian. She has begun an advanced IT skills course and, in September, will start a part-time MA in child development. And then there's her travel: unconstrained by a partner, and with a carefully accrued private pension, she is planning a trip to Laos and Cambodia this summer, and to Sicily at Easter.

And all of this is great. Of course it is. Her mother has no intention of becoming one of those grandparents conscripted to provide free childcare, their sciatica worsening as they push incarcerated toddlers around in buggies, their features clouded with exhaustion.

And nor would Vicki want this. She accepts and applauds her mother's full life. Frances has worked hard and it can't have been easy bringing up a daughter on her own while scaling the career ladder. So now it's her time to be selfish — not that Vicki would ever describe her as such. But sometimes, just sometimes, it would be nice if she were a bit more engaged with her grandchild. She doesn't expect her to *dote*. She is realistic. But it would be nice if she showed some interest, any interest at all.

Her mother takes her time to answer.

'Oh, darling, I'd love to. But I just don't think I'd have the time. I can't really commit to that with everything else I've got on at the moment.'

The lie is automatic. And, though Vicki expected this response, she still cannot hide her disappointment.

'Of course. Stupid of me. Forget I asked. So sorry.' She keeps her head down, continues to put the biscuits in their tin.

But Frances must have heard the catch in her throat.

'Well, of course, if it's impossible for Greg to

do it all, then of course you could call on me. But I can't sign up to five weekends. And I'm sure that's not what you're asking me to do, is it?'

'Of course not.' Vicki, glimpsing the chance of some support, hurries to placate her. 'Perhaps just one of the days each weekend, or perhaps just every other . . . '

'Every other weekend?' Her mother's anxiety is palpable. 'Oh no, I don't think I could do a full weekend. Perhaps the Saturday, if Greg could drop him off and pick him up?'

'Or I could do that. Or you could stay at ours?' Why, thinks Vicki, is she making this so hard for me?

'Well, I'd rather be in my own space.' Frances gives a sniff, taking in the clutter of toys; making it clear that, if she is going to do her daughter this favour, it will be on her turf — and on her conditions. And so it is agreed. Vicki will drop Alfie off in Oxford before hurtling back to Buckinghamshire. Frances will provide childcare on three Saturdays with Greg, who won't relish the drive but will be relieved he's not shouldering all the childcare, collecting him at 6 p.m.

'Thank you, Mum.' Vicki's gratitude comes out in a rush. She bends forward to put her arms round her mother, brushes her powdery cheek with her lips, gives her a tight hug.

Frances seems wrong-footed, her body inert, unable to relax into the embrace.

'Be careful of my drink.' She makes a show of moving the porcelain mug aside, discomfited by this sudden display of affection.

'Of course.' Vicki moves back, head down, embarrassed by the rebuff.

But her mother isn't finished. 'So are you going to offer me one of these delicacies?'

Kathleen

The baby seems to be growing. Much to her surprise, it has been nine weeks since her last period and, warm inside her, her baby — she does not think of it as an embryo — is bedding down, relying on her for life.

There is no sign of it. Every morning she looks at herself sideways in the mirror but her stomach is still flat, or possibly convex. The 'doyenne of baking with the enviable figure' still exists, much to her frustration. For, without a gently curving belly, she fears she is imagining it all.

Dr Sharp has reassured her, however, as has James Caruthers, an eminent obstetrician whom the good doctor has referred her to in Harley Street. And, of course, she has that other tell-tale sign of pregnancy: morning sickness. Or, rather, constant sickness. Waves of nausea pick her up then spew her forth like a sailor battling the high seas in a small vessel.

She is taking quite a battering.

The only thing that curbs the sickness is sweet carbohydrates. Soft and undemanding. Scones and tea cakes; brioche and buns. And so she is baking. Ignoring the bile that rises as she binds the dough, imagining the relief that comes, all too briefly, when she crams the sweet bread into her mouth.

She writes about this as well: racing through descriptions of tea breads and Shrewsbury buns as fast as she can bake them, her manuscript thickening even though her waistline remains svelte. Despite the nausea and the tiredness, she enjoys the restless creativity: she bakes, she writes — and she nourishes a baby. She exists in a productive whirl.

'My bread section's coming along well,' she tells George at the end of another fruitful day. 'The book's almost half finished.'

'Well, you won't have time to write once you've had the baby.' He smiles, indulgent.

'Oh, I will.' She is emphatic. 'I can write when it's sleeping. I can do many things — write, bake, grow children — all at once.'

'Perhaps we could have a child a book?'

He slips his arms around her waist and her smile wavers.

'Let me have this one first,' she tells him, fear crowding in, then tries to sound more optimistic. 'But, in theory, yes. Let's fill this great big house.'

It is around this time that she perfects her Chelsea bun recipe. Chelsea buns for my Chelsea girl, says George, as she brings out a further batch from the oven. It is a short-lived obsession.

She is photographed proffering them for publicity shots, she writes about them for *Home Magazine* — and then, quite abruptly, she goes off making them.

She finds her appetite for them has completely stopped.

11

In baking, organisation and preparation are of the utmost importance. Mastering both will ensure you bake calmly and efficiently. The same may be said of life. Take the time to prepare yourself, whether for an appointment or for your husband, and you will reap the benefits.

Saturday morning, mid-March, the day of the biscuit stage of the competition and Karen Hammond is trapped inside her Porsche Cayenne outside Bradley Hall waiting for the weather to clear.

It is still raining; relentless driving rain that hammers down on her windscreen, impervious to the sluice of her wipers. She turns off the ignition. Better wait for it to subside. Her blow-dry will be ruined if she makes a dash for it.

Forced to rest, Karen leans back against the warmed leather seats and takes in the mansion in front of her. She can see why it might appeal to a self-made man like George Eaden — a man keen to demonstrate his wealth with a fairytale palace with lots of phallic turrets — but she imagines Kathleen Eaden would have preferred something more intimate; a little less grandiose.

Bored, she reaches into her glove compartment for a leaflet given to each competitor. George bought the property in 1964, some months after the Profumo affair occurred at nearby Cliveden, she reads. Perhaps he got it cheap because of that — or perhaps he was hoping for his own naked moonlit swims? She glances at his black and white photo: a broad, stolid figure, with sandy hair, a cheery smile and the look of a market trader. Yes, you'd have an eye for a bargain. Too conventional, though, for skinny dipping.

She stretches and carries on reading about the hall's extensive renovation. 'When finished, it will boast a visitors' centre detailing Eaden's growth from humble grocer to FTSE 100 Corporation; become an elegant retreat for star employees; and house the entire Kathleen Eaden recipe archive,' she reads.

A photo shows the hall flanked by herbaceous borders and bathed in summer sunshine. The archetypal eccentric English stately home.

Today, the skies are leaden; the borders barren. It is a setting fit for a Gothic novel.

★　★　★

After twenty minutes, the rain peters out and a watery sun peers through the mass of grey. Karen grabs her leather overnight holdall and decides to risk it, neat ballet pumps crunching across the gravel and dancing up the puddled stone steps to an elaborate entrance hall. From now on, the contestants will bake all weekend — and so, today, she will get to stay overnight and explore the hall. Her heart flutters, not from the exercise but from excitement. She feels refreshingly energised.

Inside, she picks up the keys to her assigned room and climbs the stairs, pushing past the rose briars reaching for the ceiling like the thicket encasing Sleeping Beauty's castle. On either side, black eyes — captured in oil; surrounded by gilt — watch as she dares to venture further. They really need to crack on with the refurbishment.

Yet Karen's room, when she flings open the heavy oak door, feels airy and contemporary: freshly painted pale grey walls; white eggshell picture rails and cornicing; a new iron bed — king-sized, she notes — a slate mohair throw; crisp white bed linen from an upmarket company.

It is as if she has stepped into a boutique hotel — though the clean white en suite boasts no complimentary toiletries. She places her bags on the floor and sits on the mattress — firm; just the way she likes it — then allows herself to lie along the length of the bed and — insofar as she ever does this — tries to relax.

The preparation for this moment has, she realises, been immense. Like Vicki and Jenny, she too has been seeking biscuit perfection and has been moulding warm tuiles over oranges and warm brandy snaps around wooden spoons just as *The Art of Baking* dictates.

But she has also been perfecting herself. The list of beauty treatments she would usually spread over a three-week cycle has been condensed into three days. And so she has been pruned and honed, pummelled and irrigated;

115

stripped back and defoliated as if she were a particularly lush garden that has grown rampant and needs to be wrestled under control.

Many of these processes are supposed to be enjoyable — pro-lift firming facials, luxury manicures, body wraps and full-body massages — and they have cost her over £600. And yet undergoing them has seemed onerous as she has counted the vacant hours away from her kitchen. There is no doubt these hours perfecting herself were necessary, just as it was necessary to have her lowlights retouched and to put in five spin classes as well as her daily gym sessions. Her children have barely seen her — though as day boarders they are not home until nine. The house has felt as calm, as empty, as whitely sterile as ever. Oliver has stayed in London all week, apparently working on some commercial take-over. God knows what she has to do to attract him these days. She doubts he even notices.

She sighs and looks at herself in the reproduction Venetian glass mirror, taking in the fine smile lines now traced on her cheeks, the deeper crease above her eyes. So much for that anti-ageing facial. She smooths her forehead as if to erase the tell-tale signs of ageing. How much longer can she stave off the Botox? Just a matter of months.

Perhaps that's what Jake meant with his casual, 'You're fooling no one.' You're no longer an attractive young woman. You're mutton dressed as lamb. Her stomach twists. She knows at heart it's not that, or not just that, for then his

116

contempt would be general; not so cutting; so scalpel-sharp.

She thinks back to the conversation she had last night with her daughter, slim, studious Olivia. At fifteen, her world view is far safer than her mother's was. She may flirt with boys on Facebook but she wouldn't dream of touching them. Passion is something found in books and, very sensibly, she is waiting for her Heathcliff, Mr Darcy, or Edward Cullen.

Despite this naivety, Livy is wise, so much so that she often appears older than her brother. Those grey eyes appraise her, and Karen has an unnerving sense that this beautiful, innocent girl — so different from herself as a teenager — can see right through to her core.

Her children are close: the nineteen months between them meaning that Jake confides in his sister and is protective of her in a way that confounds Karen — recalling her own experience with Steven, the older brother she hasn't seen for twenty years. If Jake has a specific reason to hate his mother, then Livy is likely to know. And, even though she is unlikely to trick her into betraying that confidence, Karen needs to try.

She had interrupted her as she sat reading some English set text, long legs curled beneath her on the sofa.

'Livy . . . Do you know if there's something bugging Jake?'

'Male adolescence?' her daughter had drawled without looking up at her.

'Something more specific.'

117

She had forced the words out as if they choked her.

'Something he's particularly angry about . . . Something, perhaps, to do with me?'

Olivia had looked up then, and had gazed at her through those heavy-rimmed spectacles Karen wished she would swap for contacts. She always felt they distanced her: making her more implacable; her expression harder to gauge.

'If there is, Mum, then that's not a conversation you need to have with me.'

Her daughter had swung her legs off the sofa and got up to leave the room.

'It's a conversation you need to have with him.'

Of course, she hadn't dared to. It had been much easier just to provide food, clear away their plates, remind him of the time he needed to get to rugby and that she wouldn't be there the next evening but that Oliver should be back to check on them. Easier just to slink away that morning without popping her head round his door and saying goodbye; to pretend that she was just thinking of him and his need for sleep.

You're fooling no one, Ma. The words cloud her head. No, she hasn't fooled him, nor — seemingly, now — her daughter. The fear that she has slipped in both their opinions — that, perhaps, they deplore her — cuts like a Sabatier knife.

But the rest of the world? Well, she has to try. She has to keep on trying.

She focuses on the familiar face staring at her in the mirror. With the eye of a connoisseur, she

118

reaches for the metallic leather make-up bag in her handbag, takes a pair of tweezers and prises a stray hair free from her eyebrow. She reassesses herself, then brushes her mane with firm, even strokes, forcing any softness away. Finally, she reapplies lip pencil and a neutral lipstick, her hand shaking ever so slightly, and kisses a white tissue, leaving a jammy print. She smooths down her shift dress; rolls back her shoulders, and, before leaving the room, takes a very deep breath.

★ ★ ★

Downstairs, the contestants are taking coffee in the drawing room, their excitement palpable as they adapt to the grandiose surroundings. Claire is the most nervous; unable to relax on the chintz floral sofa; fearful of spilling her tea. She tries to steady her cup and succeeds in slopping liquid into the saucer. Has anyone noticed? Her stomach tightens like string pulled into an impenetrable tangle as she counts down the minutes to the next ordeal.

Incapable of sitting still, she gets up and walks over to the huge, arched windows, overlooking the impressive sweep of gravel. A battered Ford Focus estate has just drawn up and she smiles, feeling an unexpected flicker of relief. Mike Wilkinson, buffeted by the rain, wrestles an overnight holdall from the boot and trudges across the drive, head down. Who's he left behind this weekend? She barely spoke to him last week but had spotted his wedding ring and overheard a reference to children. And yet there was an air of sadness about him.

Watching him dodge the rain, she realises she has instantly warmed to the lone man in the competition. She senses a conspirator: someone who isn't sure how he got here but will try to enjoy the ride. For some reason — perhaps his dogged trudge or the hint of a sense of humour — she suspects that Mike is like her: someone who may feel a little lost in life but who has more to them than meets the eye.

As for Vicki, she seems very self-assured. Well, she won at the Battenburg. But Jenny also seems on edge. Last week, she had gone out of her way to be friendly; now she doesn't start conversations — or seem to welcome them. Looking closer, Claire sees that she is not just preoccupied or distant but that her eyes seem almost dead. It is as if something has occurred while they have all been practising their chocolate macaroons and almond and cherry biscuits. Life has happened, away from a preheated oven and a greased baking tray.

★   ★   ★

'Hello, everyone. Are we all ready for the Search for the New Mrs Eaden to continue?' Cora, dressed in tapered navy trousers and a Breton top, smiles at them in expectation, eyes sparkling, head to one side.

The contestants have two hours in which to prepare melting moments, shortbread, macaroons and almond and chilli biscuits in a test of

120

time-management as much as baking skill. Poring over her recipes at the back of the room, Jenny is relieved to be offered something more complex than a Victoria sponge: something that requires her to make calculations and to act swiftly, the adrenalin flowing as she works out a timetable.

Jotting down the timings, she has a sudden flashback to her mother baking, churning out butter biscuits, shortbread fingers, jam tarts for the church summer fête. A batter-splattered *Good Housekeeping* book is open on the table, but a couple of years later it could equally have been *The Art of Baking*. Lucy, her neat figure hidden by a cotton overall, would flit from one to another, comparing recipes and scribbling notes.

Standing on a chair in the kitchen, the only room that was ever warm in that draughty rectory, Jenny dips a fat finger into the mixture, sucks at a curl of buttery dough.

'Now, Jenny. You should ask before you do that,' her mother remonstrates but with a smile. At her feet her sixteen-month-old sister sits, squat, banging a wooden spoon on a saucepan lid. Eleanor looks up at her four-year-old sister for titbits. Jenny obliges, her mother's back turned. The two girls smile a gooey, buttery smile as they share their secret: a secret more delicious for being so cloyingly sweet.

If only life could have remained that simple, she thinks, gathering together caster sugar, unsalted butter and plain flour, required for the shortbread. Cheddar, chilli and garlic are lined up for the savoury biscuits — her second job.

Cocooned in warmth, the scent of melting butter coming from an Aga, her baby sister at her feet and her mother at her side. The squidgy sensation of sweet biscuit dough seeping into her mouth. Outside, sunshine and a vast country garden. Life could not get any better. For a moment, she wants to regress.

Back in the present, the hum of steady work fills the stable block, interspersed by Harriet's questioning as she makes her way between the work stations like an exacting science teacher.

Jenny rubs her unsalted butter into the flour, sugar and salt, watching the crumb sprinkle back into the bowl as she lifts her squat fingers. Lightness of touch, she reminds herself automatically. In baking as in life.

She combines the crumb into a dough, wraps it in clingfilm and places it in the fridge then repeats a similar process for the cheese biscuits, beating butter with Cheddar and dried chilli; then adding flour and water. Plump blanched almonds are caressed with the mixture before she rolls it into firm golden cylinders and puts it in the fridge to chill.

Now it's time for the fripperies and she allows herself a small smile as she contemplates the moreish mouthfuls. She whisks egg whites into airy peaks then gradually adds caster sugar to form a glossy meringue. Ground almonds mixed with icing sugar are gently folded in and the gleaming concoction piped on to non-stick baking paper in neat circles, three centimetres in diameter. She taps the baking sheet gently to pop any air bubbles, flattens peaks with the tip of a knife then leaves them for an hour for a skin to form.

And then, finally, it's the melting moments. After forty minutes of quiet industry she contemplates the final recipe. Her freshly washed whisks whizz yet another block of softened butter with icing sugar. Vanilla extract, flour and cornflour are added and mixed until smooth. Then comes the fun bit. With characteristic dexterity, she paints a straight line of pink food colouring inside a piping bag, spoons biscuit mixture inside, and pipes twenty-four perfect swirls. Glossy with butter, they sit: precise and symmetrical. There is nothing healthy about a melting moment. And yet there is a primness to them. They are not decadent like a chocolate torte or mascarpone cheesecake. She thinks Mrs Eaden would have approved of these.

With this final tray of biscuits chilling, and the oven warming up, she moves outside, craving a moment of quiet away from her fellow competitors.

The rain is lacklustre now, splashing the cobbled courtyard as if apologising for its earlier bravado. She draws her puffa jacket around her as she shelters in the stable block and pulls out her iPhone. Nothing from Nigel. She switches it off and on to check again. Still nothing. Disappointment throbs like a gobbled lump of pizza dough.

She does not know why she had hoped, against all experience, that there would be some conciliatory gesture from him. Some text, if not of love, then of good luck. Of course, she hasn't brought up the chance sighting of him with Gabby Arkwright. To hear an admission would be more than she could bear; but, then, so would a lie. Besides, she does not know how to begin that conversation with a man she no longer seems to know. She fears he would brazen it out. Twist it so that she would be left feeling guilty for having the audacity to suspect him of such a betrayal.

Rather than confronting him, she has tried a typically conciliatory approach to the impasse that has widened since the night he broke their unspoken verbal agreement and accused her of being fat.

Tears burn her eyes as she recalls that row and teeter as she dwells on the humiliation of the previous night.

They had been in bed, a super-king-sized expanse they had bought years earlier to accommodate early morning cuddles with their three small daughters but which has latterly allowed them to sleep all night without touching one another. These days, bed invariably involves wearing a long nightie; a demure affair that smacks of Victorian prudishness and drapes her in virginal white. It acts as a signal; as clear as Nigel's donning pyjama bottoms or, in happier times, a Tampax box left out in the bathroom. Not tonight, darling.

Last night, she had slipped on a shorter version: still a sensible cotton jersey; still pristine white; but distinctly un-Victorian. She had tugged at the fabric clinging to her saddlebags and hoped her ample cleavage, framed with soft

124

white lace, would provide sufficient distraction. Twenty-five years ago, and six stone lighter, she had flaunted her breasts for him, occasionally flashing them in private. She cannot remember the last time that happened. She had also delighted in energetic sex, approaching it as she might a sport, and making up in enthusiasm what she lacked in finesse. Recently, any lovemaking has been diligent and curiously joyless, Jenny willing her weight to melt into the mattress as she endured the missionary position; loath to initiate anything more exciting for fear of exposing herself.

Nigel, his back turned to her as she entered the room, had ignored her. She had slipped under the goose-down duvet, enjoying the softness of the fresh sheets, and steeled herself for action. Tentatively, she had stroked the front of his thigh, surprised at the tautness of the muscle, its contrast to her own dimpled softness. Her hand had crept to the softest skin between his legs, velvet where leg met groin.

'Don't.'

The voice was tight. His hand had reached for hers and shoved it away, crushing her knuckles.

'I'm not interested.'

Chill had separated every word.

She had rolled to her side, hot tears seeping into her pillow, fist pressed to her mouth to stifle her sobs.

The evidence of her distress seemed to thaw him and he had turned towards her, propped himself on one elbow, placed his firm fingers on her arm.

'I'm sorry . . . I'm just not in the mood; and, if you're honest, neither are you.'

He had waited for her conciliatory nod, her confirmation he was right.

'I've just got a lot on at work and I'm tired. This marathon training's taking it out of me.'

Not to mention Gabby, she had wanted to mutter.

'Of course,' she had said, suppressing the image of them having wild sex in her mind.

She had bestowed an understanding smile; received a benedictory kiss on her forehead. Satisfied, he had hunched up on his side of the bed, turned his back, and was rewarded by sleep.

She, however, had spent the next three hours consumed with anxiety, wrenching the duvet around her, then kicking it off, her mind crowded with images she still cannot force away: Nigel biting Gabby's pert breasts, squeezing her buttocks, moving inside her; Nigel, shuddering with the impact of an orgasm; Nigel, his face tender in a way she remembers — but now never sees.

When sleep finally came, it was disjointed. She dreamed of a lithe triathlete riding her husband and screaming hysterically.

It had been a relief when the fluorescent numbers on her alarm showed 5.30 a.m., and she could abandon the pretence of sleep.

The image fills her mind, once again, in that sodden courtyard as she brushes the face of the iPhone. She needs to get a grip, she tells herself, as she swipes away her tears, smudging mascara across her cheek.

Sending a message to her girls will cheer her up. She is strict in rationing her contact to them. When she first got the phone she adopted their behaviour, texting liberally, straining to keep the umbilical cord taut. An exorbitant phone bill and some gentle joshing from Lizzie — and a less than gentle barb from Emma — had put her in her place. Incontinent texting was for teens; occasional cheery messages for mums. She allows herself one text conversation every other day with her youngest; a twice-weekly text — sometimes, to her anguish, not responded to for a day — to Kate and Em. She had gone cold turkey yesterday so feels justified in reaching out to her baby today.

'Just at the Mrs Eaden biscuit auditions. Bit harder than last time! Wish me luck!' Her fingers tap lightly as she conveys false chirpiness. Is she allowed some sentiment? 'P.S. I love you, Mum.'

The satisfying swoosh sounds, and then, more gratifyingly, a ping.

'Go, Mum, go! Talk later? Luv u 2.'

Warmth floods Jenny's heart and she re-enters the kitchen lit by the flicker of a smile.

* * *

Back in the kitchen, there is a heady scent of warming butter and sugar. The macaroons come out of the oven, and sugary meringue and subtle nuttiness fill the air. Vicki looks up and spots Jenny's tear-streaked face.

'Are you OK?' she asks, touching the older woman's arm.

127

Jenny nods, and smiles reassurance. 'Fine now. Nothing to do with my biscuits.'

'No . . . I didn't think it was . . . ' Vicki's eyes are pools of concern.

'Just . . . preoccupied by something.' Jenny feels she has to explain, or perhaps she wants to open up to this attractive young woman. 'Oh, I don't know . . . I was just trying to make contact with my husband. I don't know about yours, but mine is absolutely useless when it comes to answering the phone. Doesn't understand the concept of a mobile. But I guess that's just men!

'But it's all absolutely fine now. And I've had a lovely text message from my youngest daughter. Yes, everything's absolutely fine.'

★ ★ ★

There is to be an hour's break and the contestants leave, eager for a drink and an escape from the tension of competition. Like divers signalling to one another underwater, Mike and Claire head for one another with the bashful smiles of those keen to make each other's acquaintance but unsure of how to start.

He holds the door open for her and then falls in line as they splash their way through the kitchen courtyard to the rear door of the property. The silence is initially companionable; then strained as each waits for the other to initiate conversation.

'Good baking?'

The words tumble out as Mike makes the first approach. He glances at her, taking in the gentle

128

flush that now colours her pale features.

'Not really, no.' She gives a rueful smile that turns into a grimace. 'Oh, I think I've cocked up — sorry.' She checks to see if he's offended.

He shakes his head in reassurance.

'My macaroons aren't crisp enough and I had trouble getting them off the baking parchment. But there isn't time to remake them before filling them.' She bites her lip.

He nods, wary of offering trite reassurance but keen that she should not stop talking. He seems to have forgotten how to make simple conversation.

'What about you?' She helps him out.

'Oh, OK.' He does not tell her that he has found today's session surprisingly easy.

'Bit fancy, really, aren't they?' he manages. 'Not the sort of thing I'm used to baking.'

'Oh, what's that?' She smiles encouragement, liking his self-deprecation, his hesitancy.

'Oh, you know, kids' stuff. Endless cupcakes and birthday cakes; gingerbread men; baked puddings — custards, junkets, rice puddings. Bit of bread when I can get organised.'

'Your wife must love you.'

'Oh, I don't have a wife.'

Colour suffuses Claire's cheeks. 'I'm so sorry. Your ring. I presumed . . . '

'She died two years ago.' He smiles to make it easier for her; stops; places a firm hand on her forearm. 'Please,' and his eyes beseech her. 'Don't worry. You weren't to know.'

They continue walking.

'It was cancer. She — Rachel — was forty. I

sometimes think people should be warned before they meet me, given a handout, a potted biography; perhaps we should all have that.' He gives a laugh that manages to sound both nervous and bitter.

'She had a mastectomy but it was a particularly aggressive strain and it spread to her bones. She died just before Sam, my boy's fourth birthday. Pippa was six.'

He is silent; reluctant to add to the brutal facts; aware he has already shocked a stranger. She too is silent, running possible responses through her head; dismissing each as trite. The silence stretches between them like a piece of elastic pulled to its most taut, waiting to ping.

'The kids are fantastic, though.' He provides happier, common ground, and she rushes to it with relief.

'Eight and six now? I've a nine-year-old girl, Chloe. First time I've spent a night away from her, and I'm missing her like mad.'

'Bet she's having a whale of a time with her dad?' It is his turn to probe.

'I doubt it. We don't bother with one of those.' It is Claire's turn to shock, and she laughs — feeling that his gaffe has somehow cancelled hers. 'Well, I mean, I did bother once — didn't use a sperm donor or anything. But not for a long time. Not since she was a baby. And we're just fine.'

He doesn't pursue it. Already in the distance from the kitchen to the rear door of the hall they have covered more emotional ground than anyone else in the competition, exposed their

130

souls, for a few fractured seconds, shared an intimacy lacking in their lives.

Their smiles are fulsome, this time. He has lovely eyes, thinks Claire with a shock. Deep brown and frank. When you look at him closely he's not that old, either. Wonder what he looks like when he laughs?

She has a lovely smile, thinks Mike. And a real vibrancy. She doubts herself, but she shouldn't. Bet he hurt her like hell. But she's a survivor.

12

If baking with friends — for a W.I. show, perhaps, or a church fête — try not to become overly competitive. Baking can be the most inclusive of activities.

Karen rests her head against the back of a Windsor chair in the bar of Bradley Hall, which has been opened for the contestants, and allows herself a gentle sigh.

It is the end of a long day and the bakers have gathered here to ruminate on their baking; muse on the judges; assess their chances. The atmosphere has mellowed, for no one — not even Karen — can sustain high levels of competitive tension. We are beginning to know each other, she thinks; perhaps we will even like each other.

Why else would we be here? she wonders, as she looks around the bar — yet another room ripe for refurbishment. Mike and Claire are perched on a burgundy leather banquette thrust against mahogany panelling; Jenny and Vicki on nineteenth-century rush-seated chairs. Beer mats are scattered over the heavily varnished wooden table which looks — no, is — distinctly sticky.

She gets up.

'Excuse me.' She smiles at Jerry, the barman. 'Could you wipe our table? It feels a bit dirty.'

He looks at her sharply but if he imagines an innuendo, he seems to think better of it. She smiles sweetly. Her voice is honey; her eyes flint.

The table wiped to her satisfaction — or not really her satisfaction for she is not convinced that the cloth is sufficiently clean — she tries to settle for a second time. Her cheeks glow with the warmth of the well-built fire, which spits and flares in the inglenook fireplace before Mike coaxes consistent flames. Karen takes a sip of her Diet Coke and notes what the others are drinking: Claire, a vodka and tonic; Mike, a bottle of Beck's; Jenny and Vicki, a bottle of Eaden's First Reserve Merlot though she doubts they will finish it. Despite the more mellow atmosphere, no one will risk a hangover.

She has, she reminds herself for the third time today, come a long way from the spit and sawdust establishments she slunk into as a fifteen-year-old: or the end of the pier where she nursed a bottle of cider and traded kisses, and more, for single cigarettes. She shivers, as if remembering the chill wind whipping her thighs as it swept up the Thames, the smell of vinegar and chips and sulphuric mud flats, the taste of smoke and sour saliva. Her mother, Pamela, would be collapsed on the sofa in that mean, pebble-dashed house, scoffing Fry's peppermint creams and Wagon Wheels in front of *Blind Date*. She never questioned what her fifteen-year-old daughter or seventeen-year-old son were up to; for her, ignorance was bliss.

Karen shivers again. Well, she got the hell out of there and that's all that matters. And now she needs to stop thinking about it. Perhaps it's time to liven things up a bit? She is suddenly bored of her saccharine drink: her security blanket in the torturous world of food and alcohol. She pushes it aside and announces she is in search of some sparkling water.

'Can I get anyone anything else?' The invitation is directed to the group but her eyes linger on Mike, the sole male and so the obvious focus of her attention.

He looks surprised at the intensity of her gaze.

'Another Beck's, was it? And Claire, another V&T?'

'No, I'm fine thanks,' the younger woman demurs.

'Oh, come on. Live a little.'

She sashays to the bar, ignoring Claire's protests.

'I might even join you,' she says.

'Two vodka tonics, a big bottle of sparkling water, and a bottle of Becks.' She smiles at the barman as she takes a crisp £20 note from her oversized wallet, her nails clicking against its patent leather.

'Here, I'll help you.' Mike's natural chivalry emerges and he joins her. She is surprised to note how much taller he is than her. There is suddenly something very male about him as he stands beside her. Not touching but indisputably with her.

She wonders if she should risk a little flirtation. Well, where's the harm in that? Mike is the sole man among four females and even though he's not her ideal — too old; insufficiently muscular; insufficiently beautiful — determining that she would be his choice among them is instinctive. A reflex that comes as naturally as breathing. Besides, there is something alluring about those sad eyes; about his status as a widower, for Claire has relayed this gossip. She wonders if he's had sex since his wife died. She glances sidelong, behind long lashes. He fails to notice. She doubts it very much.

They make their way back to the table and Mike, his diffidence eroding with this second bottle of beer, asks each of them why they have entered the competition.

'What about you, Jenny?' His smile is encouraging.

'Why did I want to become the New Mrs Eaden?' She prevaricates as she tries to form some sort of honest answer.

'Well, I'm fifty-two — so I grew up with my mother using Kathleen Eaden. I've been cooking since childhood and I thought I might as well show what I've learned over the years.

'I'm a housewife — but now my girls have left home and my husband, well . . . he doesn't need me to bake for him the whole time. He's often busy doing marathons and things or he isn't around; so, for the first time in a long while, no, for the first time ever, I've the time to do something for myself.'

She smiles. 'When I saw the competition advert I thought: I can do that. I'm not saying I'm wonderful, or anything, but I know all the basics. And this felt like a proper baking competition. I mean, I know there are those silly YouTube clips we have to do, and we're on the Eaden's website and we'll have to be in *Eaden's*

Monthly, but I wouldn't have to go on television. It didn't feel exploitative.'

She takes a sip of her wine.

'I suppose, overall, I just felt that this would be something I would enjoy. A bit of a challenge. And I felt that I might — just might — do well at it.'

'I feel a bit the same way.' It is Vicki who is chipping in, offering Jenny a smile and a means of deflecting attention. 'Not that I've got grown-up girls, or anything like your experience, but I do have a little boy, who's just started at nursery, and I'm on a 'career gap'. If I'm honest, I'm not quite sure what I want out of life.

'I used to teach. Primary. Key stage one. And I loved it and was good at it, so I thought I'd love channelling all my energy into my little one. But it's harder than I expected. I don't seem to have such control over him, and I don't have the same satisfaction: he's too young to be interested in phonics or even mark making; and you can't have the sort of conversation you can have even with a five- or six-year-old. I suppose this competition lets me be in control, then; lets me do my preparation and see the results — just as I did when teaching. And it lets me do something for me.'

'What about you, Mike?' Karen turns the question on to him. She leans forward so that the hint of a breast is exposed, and looks at him intently.

'Oh, I expect it's an early midlife crisis — I'm forty-two.' His tone is light, as if he's wary of revealing anything too intimate.

136

'Like all of you, I love baking and, I suspect like all of you — you too, Jenny — I like the idea of competition. Survival of the fittest and all that.'

He twists his wedding ring then continues, as if determined to be honest. 'After Rachel became ill, I re-trained and became a teacher. And though that brings its own challenges' — he smiles at Vicki — 'I miss the adrenalin of my old job in the Treasury. I miss the edge. Yes, I know you need to be on top of your game all the time in teaching — aware of being caught out; anticipating each tricky question — but I'm dealing with secondary school kids not government ministers. I miss that need to perform at the highest level every minute of the day.'

He laughs, as if in apology. 'It sounds a bit pathetic, but this competition provides a bit of that. Plus — and this sounds even worse — it gives me some validation, doesn't it? I think I'm doing an OK job as a dad but there's no one to tell me that, to tell me I'm OK. At least this way, I've got some proof that I'm doing something right. That I'm feeding them well — or, at least, making them good cakes and bread.'

There is a pause, each taking in his confession and with it his breaking down of barriers.

'It's not pathetic at all.' Claire puts a hand on his forearm and gives it a quick squeeze.

A bit tactile for this early in the evening? notes Karen, and shifts the attention to her pretty swiftly.

'So, Claire. What's your motive?'

Claire withdraws her hand immediately.

'Why did I do it?' Claire looks uncomfortable, hunching her slight shoulders as she cradles a glass tumbler.

'Um, well, I didn't have much choice — my mum put me up for it and it wouldn't do to disobey her.' She laughs as if in recollection.

'Seriously, it was a surprise: this isn't the sort of thing I'd ever put myself up for. I'd never have applied on my own. I've my mum to thank — or to blame.'

'So why go ahead with it?' Karen persists. Her gaze is intense: not unfriendly but challenging.

Claire meets it. 'Well, apart from the fifty grand, I guess I'm doing it for my little girl, Chloe. She's never known that her mum could do something as exciting as this; that she's capable of achieving something. And, perhaps for the same reason, I'm now doing it for me.'

A bubble of irritation wells up inside her as the vodka hits home. 'I'm not like you, you see, or Vicki, or Jenny. This isn't a game for me. It offers me the chance of a better future for my kid.

'Working in Eaden's, I watch women like you decide whether to pick sirloin or rump steak, double cream or mascarpone, while I sit and think about which variation on a pasta sauce I'm going to have to make. I didn't apply. So what? That doesn't mean I don't want to do well at this. I've got to do my very best.'

It is the longest speech she has ever given and it feels like an inappropriate, somewhat aggressive outburst. There is a pause as the contestants take it in, give it the emotional weight it needs.

The silence draws on, becoming uncomfortable. Jenny racks her brain for a platitude that won't cause offence; Vicki gives a smile of contrition. Tension wells, as taut as the surface of a pond before being cut by a skimming stone.

'And what about you, Karen?' Mike, having initiated this soul-searching, is keen that the person who provoked Claire's outburst shouldn't evade the question.

'Oh, you know, bored middle-class housewife who makes a mean tarte seeks excitement with Dan Keller.'

'Karen!' Vicki is delighted. The self-parody, and pun, has had its desired effect.

'Well, what other reason is there? I'm very interested in his strudel,' she deadpans.

Vicki, two glasses of wine into the bottle, gives a delighted snort.

'His strudel . . . Whose strudel are you interested in, Claire?'

'Oh, no one's.' She blushes, but is keen to lighten the atmosphere she has clouded. 'Strudel — proper strudel — over sex for me, any time.'

'What a waste,' says Karen, and checks if Mike agrees.

'Not really.' Claire is defiant again, angered by Karen and her judgements. 'It's just easier that way, isn't it? No one interfering, mucking me around, telling me what to do. Just me and Chloe.'

'But don't you miss it?' The vodka, not something Karen would usually touch, burns her throat and makes her direct.

'Wa-hay. I'll need to drink a lot more before I

start answering questions like that and I'm not drinking any more tonight. Talking of which, I'm going to head off now to try to call Chloe; nice to get to know you all a bit more.'

She gathers her bag and cardigan together and makes a rapid exit, a slight figure flitting through the bar and out the other side before anyone can persuade her to stay.

'Did I scare her off?' Karen downs her vodka, as Mike watches Claire leave in dismay.

'Well, probably.' The Merlot is making Vicki more forthright than usual. 'But I wouldn't worry about it. I think she's the dark horse; the one who's more focused than you'd think in this competition. I think she's going to slay us with her gingerbread house tomorrow, and she's just off to check how to make the ultimate caramel.'

'Talking of leaving, I'm going to make a move too.'

It is Jenny, uncomfortable at the turn of conversation, and, suddenly, feeling old. 'I didn't sleep well last night — too apprehensive — and I'm not sure about my caramel recipe, either. Perhaps I need to check it too. Just talking about it is making me nervous,' she burbles away.

'Are we the more foolhardy ones?' Karen wonders, raising her glass to the two remaining.

'Actually, I should check on Alfie — or rather, Greg, make sure he's done everything right.' With a sigh, Vicki makes her excuses. She wends her way through the bar, banging her hip, squeezed into skinny jeans, against a bar stool in her hurry.

Karen regards her with amusement as she pours a glass of sparkling water. One to watch, or just another insecure middle-class mummy who likes making cupcakes?

She glances at Mike. 'She can't hold her drink, can she?'

The bar falls rapidly quieter. There are only the two of them now, and a table of staff drinking quietly in the corner. The fire glows; white embers falling into ash. In other circumstances, the setting could be romantic. But she doesn't need romance; she needs distraction. Anything to ward off the demons, unaccountably crowding in from the past.

Mike rubs his eyes, as if bemused at finding himself alone with her. Karen softens her smile. He is very vulnerable, she reminds herself. She is going to have to take this gently.

'So' — she raises her glass to him — 'then there were two.'

He looks startled. Damn. Wrong tack. She tries again.

'That was very moving. What you said about entering the competition to gain validation . . . '

'Oh.' He rubs his forehead as if exhausted with parenthood and his status as a widower.

'I can't believe I came out with all that. Utterly ludicrous, really, inasmuch as we're all seeking it, aren't we?' He looks pensive. 'Though perhaps not you.'

'Oh, I wouldn't be so sure.' She laughs, and thinks, How little you know me. *You're fooling no one.*

'Well, you do a good impression of being less

141

needy than many of us.' He smiles. 'Here I am desperate for a bit of praise for being a parent: someone to tell me I'm doing as good a job as any mother because I can make my kids panettone. But you seem far more confident.'

'Oh, I think we all need it, Mike,' she demurs, keen to steer the conversation away from herself and his unwelcome foray into psychoanalysis. 'But, understandably, you may need it more than most.'

He is silent. Perhaps she has gone too far. She sips her vodka while contemplating her next move.

Then: 'Tell me, do you get much emotional support at home?'

'Well, the kids are great — always telling me they love me.' He smiles in recollection. He is being surprisingly obtuse.

'But . . . no support from another adult? No partner?' The intrusion feels crass, but there is no subtle way to ask.

'Oh, no. No, not at all.' He shakes his head as if to dislodge the very idea.

There is a pause.

'That must be very lonely?' Her eyes are suffused with understanding — and the hint of invitation if only he would see it.

'Well, yes, I suppose it is. But you can be lonely in a relationship as well, can't you?' He takes a swig of Beck's and looks preoccupied for a moment.

'Anyway. Back to you. This is all getting a bit deep.' He gives her a friendly smile, the smile he would give to the parent of a pupil.

She is knocked sideways. She wasn't anticipating this. Inasmuch as she had thought about it, she had envisaged a little gentle flirtation with the hint of a further something: something discreet, understated and understood between two consenting adults.

She hadn't realised she was dealing with someone so emotionally raw and so out of practice at reading sexual signals. She sips her vodka. Well, he would be a challenge but she is not sure she has the energy. She feels apathetic all of a sudden.

'So . . . Dan Keller . . . He was a lure for you, was he?' He is smiling as if straining for conversation.

She sits back — and decides to give it one last try.

'Well, he is rather lovely, though perhaps too narcissistic. He's far too aware of his beauty — and that's never attractive in a man.'

She looks at him frankly, dark eyes assessing him, lips curling into a smile.

'I find it much more attractive if someone is totally unconscious of their good looks. That's far more alluring.'

The penny still hasn't dropped. She feels exhausted. What am I doing? she feels like crying. I am teasing the poor man like a cat toying with a shrew. No, that's wrong. A shrew would be all too aware it was being teased; he doesn't even seem to have noticed. The thought hits her with the clarity of the vodka shot burning the back of her throat.

'I need to go.'

She groups the glasses with crisp efficiency, removes the empty bottles to the bar, swings her capacious bag over her shoulder in the time he realises he may have missed a compliment.

'Oh . . . night then.' Mike looks befuddled. Perhaps he has noted the shift in mood; the tension shimmering through her sudden brisk movements.

'Night, Mike. Sleep well.'

For a moment, she considers running a hand through his thick hair or kissing his cheek and then pausing by his lips, but the moment has passed. Or, rather, it never happened.

She congratulates herself on managing an impersonal smile and maintaining a saunter as she leaves the bar.

13

A gingerbread house is a culinary doll's house; a world created by a baker's imagination — and modest quantities of sugar, spices, eggs, butter and flour. Anyone can live in a gingerbread house: not just a wicked witch intent on luring children, but a kindly grandmother or a loving mother with a string of children. It is — or can be — the ideal home.

Eight in the morning and watery early-morning sunshine filters into Karen's bedroom, illuminating her like a biblical Old Master. Inside her mouth, a mouse appears to have died. An unfamiliar bitterness, morning breath mixed with something more noxious, coats her tongue. Her teeth, tentatively licked, feel furred. Someone is tightening a thin band of metal around her forehead.

The shower is punishingly hot. Molten streams of water cascade down her back and between her breasts, scalding her torso, blanching her face. She swipes the dial to cold. The shock is immediate. She gasps, skin tingling into goose bumps, whitening. Then comes the glow of extreme cold. The water caresses her body, as invigorating as plunging into the Channel on a dank December day.

The cold galvanises her. She lathers shower gel over her body, sweeping her limbs, washing her deepest crevices, working shampoo, then conditioner, into her locks. By the time she steps from the shower the metal band has been loosened. The dead mouse has been rinsed away with icy water, but its residue remains. She picks up her electric toothbrush and scrubs at the fur. Then flosses, and spits blood.

Walking into the bedroom, she stands in front of the full-length mirror, drops the fluffy white towel to the floor, appraises herself coldly. The body she sees is lean and strong. The legs of a woman half her age; an enviably flat abdomen that fails to betray two pregnancies; breasts with nipples pointing upwards, asking to be teased. She turns. Her buttocks are toned and smooth, glutes as hard as rocks when she squats. Her back is still youthful: no tell-tale signs of wrinkling, and no excessive fat. Her feet are neat, the claret pedicure immaculate. Her hands, carefully moisturised, always French manicured, score less well: with a shudder, she notes a sprinkling of brown age spots.

She moves on to her face, forehead strained by a towelled turban. A neat nose, alluring mouth, quizzical dark eyes, but around them, the tell-tale etched lines of ageing. Stripped of make-up, reddened by a shower, naked of artifice, she sees a face that has lived through four decades — and a little more. What must he have thought of me, she recoils, recalling Mike's confusion? Perhaps he failed to recognise her automatic, half-hearted flirtation, though Jerry, the barman, dark eyes appraising her, saw it for what it was. *You're fooling no one.*

She tears the turban from her head and

146

roughly dries her hair. Then she pulls the towel around her body and scrubs and scrubs.

★ ★ ★

'We're giving you a harder task today. One of Kathleen Eaden's favourites.' Harriet, neat in pearls and a twinset, appraises the quintet as they stand behind their work stations.

'We want you to build us a gingerbread house, your own ideally. Let us see a little bit into your lives.

'We do want solid constructions, though, and interesting ones: so do bear that in mind if you live in a suburban semi. You have four hours in which to build your ideal home out of gingerbread.'

Vicki gives a smile. This is the sort of challenge she loves: ordered and pretty. Never wildly inventive, she thinks of the ultimate Hansel and Gretel house made more kitsch. Bedecked with scalloped white glacé icing, it will have lollipop trees and chocolate button tiles; jelly tot flowers and sugar paste — not gingerbread — children: a boy wearing a cap and Little Lord Fauntleroy britches, and his blonde, pigtailed little sister.

Jenny, working alongside her, is following the brief more strictly and will attempt a Queen Anne farmhouse, the symmetry being easy to replicate though she thinks she will ice the window panes. Melting butter with dark muscovado sugar and golden syrup, and mixing this with flour and ground ginger and cinnamon, she ponders over who should inhabit this home.

147

Should she model a middle-aged jogger, white sugar-paste limbs protruding from red running shorts? Should she add three beautiful, grown-up daughters? Perhaps it should be just herself, holding a mixing bowl, working away in the kitchen of the house.

Claire is also preoccupied. Harriet said not to build a suburban semi so what would she make of a two-bedroomed, 1960s council flat? Should she fashion a leaking flat roof, or a concrete staircase perfumed with piss?

She thinks laterally. Harriet said create your ideal home so where would that be? By the sea. She will build a gingerbread beach hut complete with her parents brewing a cuppa on a Calor gas stove. The time she would have spent building a bigger construction will be used to fashion sugar paste shells and pebbles. A sugar paste Chloe will play outside the hut, performing handstands.

Karen will be more ambitious. Paracetamol, caffeine and, unusually for her, carbs — half a slice of granary toast spread with thick honey — have sent her hangover packing. She considers replicating her Victorian home: the gingerbread will mimic its red bricks and she is sufficiently competent with a piping tube to cope with its elegant curves. But this is a chance to create an ideal, the sort of home she would have had in another life. She will build a minimalist penthouse in the heart of the City: all unforgiving glass and sharp architectural lines. Sheets of hardened caramel will form two glass walls and she will use a protractor to ensure precision. There will be no infantilising dolly mixtures; no chocolate buttons; no kitsch. And there will be no sugar paste children. Hers is an entirely adult world.

Mike is dispensing with children as well. True, his first thought had been to build a tree house with a boy and girl at the centre of his design but he is unsure of how to fashion a sufficiently strong tree and unconvinced he is creative enough. Instead, he is going to be ambitious. In a playful reference to his old life, he is going to build 10 Downing Street. His gingerbread will be dark: made with black treacle instead of golden syrup; flavoured with cloves to replicate the blackened brick.

For four hours they work, the mid-March morning taking on the scent of Christmas: cinnamon, ginger, treacle and cloves. From early on, the front-runners are Mike and Karen, the most intelligent in their construction, producing the neatest edges, cut at an angle, to ensure the strongest gingerbread house.

Yet anyone watching, more interested in the personalities of the contestants than their skill at baking, would be drawn by Vicki, using a lip brush to paint pink flowers on the tiny girl's dress. Her gingerbread cottage is perfectly acceptable — a textbook version of what it should be — but her interest is in the miniature figures. She scrutinises them, then bends the arm of the sugar paste boy child and puts it around his little sister. The girl's sugar paste hair has been plaited.

Next to her, Claire is positioning her girl child with care: holding her upside down, legs splayed in a cartwheel, before icing her to a beach.

In Jenny's home, there are no children and no husband. But there is no Jenny, either. To position herself alone in her kitchen, as she had originally intended, would be to divulge too much. There is a curiously sterile look to her creation.

'And . . . tools down.'

The four hours of intense concentration are up. Karen is surprised by how nervous she is as she places her penthouse in front of the judges. It has nothing to do with Dan's presence, though the jolt of lust is automatic. It has everything to do with her pride in conceiving and realising this idea. If gingerbread and caramel can look architecturally edgy, she has managed it.

'Well, I'd like to live here.' Dan is looking at her creation — and herself — with frank admiration. 'I think it's fantastic. Something I'd never have thought of. A really original take on a traditional idea.'

The glow starts in her stomach, spreads through her chest, suffuses her face.

'Thank you,' Karen says, and, for the first time in the contest, she gives an honest smile.

Bread

Tell me your favourite scent. The smell of a baby's neck? The aroma of fresh violets?

To my mind, there is none so delicious as that of freshly baked bread.

The French may have their baguette, the Italians their ciabatta, the people of the Middle East their flat breads. But the good honest loaf is still the staple for most British families. And there is nothing to beat the taste, or the smell, of your own bread as it emerges piping hot from the oven.

First, a little science. The raising agent that bread uses is yeast, a living organism that requires gentle warmth. It also needs food, which it gets from flour, and moisture, from water. A culinary miracle then takes place. Bubbles of carbon dioxide form, which produce the bread's light and airy texture. It is most important not to hurry this stage — the proving — and, once complete, to remember to knead lightly. You want a crumb that's light and the loaf, topped with a golden crust, to be bouncy and soft.

Many people tell me they do not have time to make bread. And why, they argue, should they bother when commercially baked loaves, such as those made by Eaden's, are so good and so widely available?

I agree that bread takes time and may not be the bake of choice for the busy housewife, still less the career woman. But, with good time-management, a home-made loaf is within the capability of all who pride themselves on producing good cooking. And when you see the look of rapture on your husband's face, or the delight of your small children as they smell the fresh warm bread and slather it with butter, you will know it was all worth while.

Kathleen Eaden: *The Art of Baking* (1966)

Kathleen

The cramps start as she writes: a nagging clutch that grabs at her womb and squeezes it tight so that she has to bend over, head thrust towards her knees. She knows at once what it is. No period pain but something far more brutal. Something destructive. A vicious wrench that leaves her grasping the side of the desk, fingers whitening against the oak, pen weeping where it lies discarded. She begins to straighten before being felled by another gasp of pain.

She tries to breathe deeply, fighting now against pure panic. This can't be happening. This can't happen. It can't be like the last time.

Her womb clutches even more tight.

Then, she had barely allowed herself to believe she was pregnant. Just a late period, she continued to tell herself. Delayed for four weeks by the stress of writing her first column. But the amount of blood had told a different story.

And here it is again. There is a whoosh — and she has soaked knickers. Has she had an accident? She touches the top of her thighs above her stockings and feels the stickiness, warm and wet.

Her fingers are painted crimson and she stinks of brine. Frantic, she wrenches down the nylons. The blood runs down her inner thighs; thick, vibrant, unstoppable. Where does it keep coming from? she wonders, though the answer is obvious.

Somehow, she gets to the bathroom. Every ten or so minutes there is another gush: the blood turning deep crimson and clotted; dense with guinea-sized clumps. She dreads something larger coming. I can't let him come out like this — into the toilet. I can't let him get dirty, and she hauls herself up, padding herself with a towel.

The bathroom floor is cold but she shakes more from shock than the chill of the tiles. Her teeth chatter like a cartoon character's. Pull yourself together. Pull yourself together. Her words come out as a sob.

Try to breathe. In for two, out for five; in for two, out for five. Oh, how can that help? She stops trying to be rational and dabs at the floor, desperate to banish all evidence. It's a losing battle. Every time she wipes the checkerboard tiles, there's another smear, or gush, or trickle. She moves, and sprinkles blood.

Cocooned in towels, she curls into a ball and waits for what she now knows is inevitable. She thinks she is — she was — twelve weeks pregnant. Yesterday, she had still felt nauseous. Today the sickness had gone and she had felt such intense relief. She had spent the day baking, watching the dough rise and imagining her stomach growing, stretch marks forming like the tears on its surface. And she had kneaded the dough without dreading the rising bile.

Now, she would do anything for such sickness.

For such proof that a baby was growing inside her; lengthening by the day; preparing for life.

George will be so disappointed — and as for herself? Children are what her family does; what they expect and what they — what her father — would have wanted.

Her womb contracts and, in a rush of blood, she expels what would have become her child.

14

Baking is much like having a husband: there will be times when you must pay attention to your dough and show it some sensitivity.

It is the thump that wakes Greg. A muffled thudding. Far more gentle than a bang, and rhythmic, as if someone were counting out bars of music in a softly shuffled 4/4. He glances at the clock radio: 5.13. That frustrating no-man's-land time, too close to his 5.45 a.m. alarm call to allow him any sleep, yet — in the chill of late-March — too early for a dawn chorus to justify the end of night and herald a new day's start.

There's the thump again. Half awake, he rolls towards Vicki, hoping to luxuriate in her warmth, to snuggle up and siphon sleep from her soft body. His arm stretches over tepid sheets. Her side of the bed is empty with only the faintest residue of warmth.

He looks back at the clock, properly awake now: 5.14 a.m. It is, he realises with increasing frustration, Saturday, the one day he can get some sort of lie-in, Sunday morning being taken up with Alfie's ridiculously early swimming lesson in which the small child just screams and clings to the side of the pool. Saturday is the morning when he can curl up to Vicki and fantasise about the possibility of early morning

158

sex — though it's rarely achieved thanks to the clockwork wake-up call provided by Alfie at around six thirty. At 5.14 a.m., it's a possibility though, if only Vicki were around.

Lying back against the pillows, it occurs to him that the rhythmic thudding probably has something to do with her absence. Disgruntled, he swings his legs out of bed, grabs a hoodie, and stumbles for the door. The faint sound becomes more persistent as he reaches the bottom of the stairs and follows the light filtering from the kitchen across the stripped oak floorboards. Thump, shuffle, shuffle, shuffle; thump, shuffle, shuffle, shuffle; thump, shuffle, shuffle, shuffle. Thump.

Vicki, wearing an oversized jumper, bare legs and an apron, is flinging dough on to a granite worktop. Entirely absorbed in her work, there is something ritualistic about what she is doing: throwing the glutinous mass, then kneading it, then folding it in a repetitive dance. A smile plays on her lips. For someone so controlled in her daily life, so concerned with the pursuit of perfection, she seems to be relishing such casual brutality. Pushing her dirty blonde hair back from her eyes with the back of a floured hand, she flings the dough down with a particularly solid thud.

'Vicks . . . What are you *doing?*'

Greg does not share her enjoyment.

'It's five in the morning. On a Saturday. You've woken me up.'

Concern floods her intelligent eyes.

'Oh, my love, I'm so sorry.' She approaches to

159

hug him but her hands sprinkle flour.

'I'm making bagels. I thought you could have them fresh for breakfast. Don't worry: I'm coming back to bed now because I need them to prove for an hour and a half before I shape them and then boil them. I'll do that at seven. You'd be having them for lunch if I hadn't started now.'

Characteristically perky, it all appears to make perfect sense to her. But Greg is incredulous.

'You got up before five so I'd have them fresh for breakfast? Why would I want you to do that? I'm not married to a baker.'

She grins. 'Ah, but you see you are.'

'No, I'm not. I'm married to someone who's become obsessed with a cooking competition. Well, that's great. I'm pleased for you. And I know you want to practise. But you're taking authenticity too far.

'You don't need to bake in the middle of the night. You need to sleep like normal people. Or perhaps you need to think about making a baby. I thought that was what you wanted?' Exasperation clouds his even features then begins to dissipate as he takes in the bizarre image of his wife standing bare-legged and dusted with flour in the middle of the kitchen in what still counts as night.

Despite himself, he begins to stir. There is something surprisingly sexy about her doing all this baking. She rubs her nose, depositing flour, and he notices smudges of tiredness below her eyes. She is pushing herself and he realises for the first time just how much she wants to win

160

this competition. A wave of tenderness subsumes him. Seeing her, blinking under the harsh halogen spotlights, love mingles with desire.

'Well, let's go back to bed then.'

She places the dough in a bowl, covers it with clingfilm, rinses her fingers and moves towards him to placate him. It strikes him that she is using the same reasonable tone and distraction technique she would use on their three-year-old. But it's unnecessary. When she looks at him like that, he is putty in her hands.

'I can't sleep now. I'm too wide awake.' He grins at her, all innocence.

She smiles up at him, reaches cool fingers up his inner thigh inside his striped cotton boxer shorts. 'Who said anything about sleeping?'

She knows him too well. Much as he would like to resist — to make some statement about being irritated at being woken up — there really is no point. He is incapable. They kiss: a chaste kiss of contrition that morphs into invitation, her tongue probing his mouth, her hands caressing his neck. He reaches for her buttocks, naked, he discovers with a thrill under the hastily thrown-on sweater. The discovery excites him more than he would have thought possible and, with something of a stumble, for she is nearing ten stone now thanks to the extra baking, he lifts her on to the counter. Her bottom pushes through the soft sprinkling of flour. She pulls away; then gives a giggle as her thighs are coated with the white powder.

'Don't.' He wants to freeze this moment. To preserve it, untainted by humour.

She looks at him, taking in his expectant face, softened by desire.

'There are far better things to be doing at five in the morning than baking,' he mutters, embarrassed to admit to his need for her.

And she reaches down and begins another rhythmic dance.

15

Most of the time you will need to be firm with your dough. You will need to control this changeable, organic substance: working it; determining how much it should expand; knocking it down at the correct time; and knocking it into shape. You will need to behave, in other words, like a clever wife who knows the secret to marital happiness lies in educating her husband to appreciate her needs.

Nigel Briggs is naked in his en suite bathroom — a former dressing room — performing his morning routine. Eyes heavy with sleep, he stands in front of the toilet taking a boyish satisfaction in the hot hiss of his pee as it strikes the cold toilet bowl and his ability to aim it in different directions. Urine drips from the end of his penis as he gives it an affectionate flick and lands on the granite floor in a neat, sticky circle. It does not occur to him to wipe it up. Jenny will follow with the Dettol spray.

He turns to the basin and begins the process on which he lectures his patients. Floss; brush with an electric toothbrush, spit splayed in concentric circles; swill with mouthwash, rinsing the plaque away. A shower — brief; cold; invigorating — comes next. And only then, once he is alert and can concentrate properly, is he ready for the main event.

Naked again, he stands on his wife's

raspberry-coloured digital scales experiencing a frisson of excitement as the display fluctuates, raising then dashing his hopes, determining his weight. Eleven stone, 8.9 pounds. Better than yesterday's eleven stone, 9.2 but still not good enough. He gives a moue of dissatisfaction and wonders, for the umpteenth time, how much difference it would make if he'd had a shit.

A towel around him now, he wanders back into the bedroom and jots down his weight in the small notepad. Once dressed, he will add it to a spreadsheet on his laptop to be translated into a graph detailing his consistent weight loss over the weeks. Yet there is no need for the memory jog. Eleven, 8.9 will be branded at the front of his mind throughout the day, governing his food choices, determining how far he should run that evening. He does not need a graph to tell him that, at six foot, he is still nine pounds off his target weight.

'I'm still a long way off my target.' The information is barked at Jenny, who, fully dressed, has entered the room with a cup of breakfast tea for him. It does not occur to him that she might not find this information interesting.

'Hmm?' She shows a modicum of interest, fine-tuned over twenty-five years of marriage. Sufficient not to rankle yet some way short of the level of enthusiasm he would like.

'My target weight? I'm a long way off it. For a six-foot man, running a marathon, I should be under eleven stone — 15 to 20 per cent less than your average six-footer. I'm eleven, 8.9; that's

164

only about 10 per cent less than the average. I'll have to check my spreadsheet for the exact figure. Seb Coe was more than 20 per cent.'

Bombarded with this flurry of statistics, Jenny tries to work out a response that will sound informed but reassuring.

'Are you sure you should be comparing yourself with a double Olympic gold medallist?' is the best she can manage. It does not have the desired effect.

'Of course I'm not comparing myself with an Olympian.' He splutters as if the idea is preposterous. 'Nor am I comparing myself with a middle-distance runner. I was using him as an example of an elite athlete. And yes, actually, Jenny, that's what I'm aspiring to be.'

He looks incandescent, and faintly ridiculous, as he stands in his socks and boxer shorts, rifling through his wardrobe. Despite his lean physique and dark good looks, he remains a middle-aged man — one who should have been working on his fat ratio three decades earlier if he wanted to join the athletic elite.

He continues chuntering as he searches for a favourite shirt, spurning the three she had ironed the previous evening, and she sidles out of the door, keen to escape the disdain that accompanies much of his comments these days. Head in the wardrobe, he seems to sense her departure, and calls her back, like an owner bringing a dog to heel.

'Jennifer.'

'Yes?'

'I asked you a question. Did you confirm the

165

Paris hotel booking for the marathon weekend?'

'I haven't but I will.'

'April 14–15. Don't forget.'

'April 14–15.'

As she repeats it, she realises there is a problem. Now three weeks away, April 14–15 is the weekend when they will be making pies and pastry. Feather-light home-made puff pastry is her baking signature. Making pies is her forte. Missing this — missing out on the chance to shine in the competition; effectively to drop out — is not a possibility.

It is not the ideal time to bring it up but she forces herself to do so.

'Nigel. I won't be able to join you, darling.'

His face forms a question mark.

'It clashes with the pastry stage of my competition. I can't miss that. I'm so sorry.'

The look on his face changes from incomprehension to derision. If eyebrows can sneer that is what his are doing.

'April in Paris versus pies in Buckinghamshire?' His voice drips with sarcasm. 'Your choice, my love, your choice. I would have thought you would have welcomed a romantic break away — quite aside from the opportunity to support your husband. But no, you go back to making pastry.'

A hard ball of fury forms in her chest. She wants to scream at him; to puncture his self-righteousness, and point out that he could support her for a change. It is on the tip of her tongue to suggest that Gabby Arkwright might be partial to April in Paris but she cannot bring herself to go there. Instead, she takes a deep breath and wills herself to be calm. When her voice emerges, she is surprised by its steeliness.

'I do support you, Nigel, of course I do. But I need to do this.'

Her tone remains firm; no hint of beseeching here.

'I am not going to give this up even though I won't be able to cheer you over the finishing line. I'm very sorry but I do need to do this.'

The silence goes on far longer than she would have expected. Derision has drained from his face and his expression is one of incomprehension once more.

Jenny walks from the bedroom feeling visibly taller; her head raised high, her footsteps brisker than usual. It is only once she is in the sanctity of the kitchen that she notices her hands are shaking.

★　★　★

'I can't believe you're not going to be there to support him.' Emma Briggs, ever opinionated and forceful, is summoning as much indignation as she can muster when Jenny phones her to tell her she won't be going to Paris to cheer on her father.

'It's not like it's a local 10K run, Mum. This is the Paris marathon. A big event. And we were all going to meet there, weren't we?' Her voice, on a mobile phone line from Montpellier, is as insistent as if they were standing in the same room.

Jenny feels exhausted. With the self-righteousness that comes with being twenty-two, her middle daughter is managing to convey extreme disappointment in her mother while being oblivious to her petulance. Her voice goes on and on; hectoring, questioning, challenging in her self-appointed role as Nigel's advocate. Jenny lets the barrage wash over her, keeping half an ear open for when her daughter mentions Mrs Eaden. It is a long time coming.

'And what is this baking competition, anyway?'

Jenny has to remind herself that her daughter is living a far more interesting life than hers in a different country. While the competition is of huge interest to bakers who shop at Eaden's, it has not reached the radar of the average student: certainly not a third-year enjoying an academically light year in the south of France. Of course, Jenny has mentioned it but Emma persists in feigning ignorance as if to suggest she has better things to do with her time than look at YouTube clips of middle-aged women making shortbread biscuits. As indeed she has. Jenny refuses to be riled.

She takes a deep breath. 'You know what it is, darling. It's the Search for the New Mrs Eaden — you know, the competition that I told you was being judged by that rather attractive baker, Dan Keller. It's going on for three months and, at each stage, the winner and runner up are filmed demonstrating their baking on YouTube. We appear on the Eaden's website and we'll be in their magazine, too.

'The winner's just chosen by the judges though. If I win, I'll get a big enough cheque to help write off uni debts for the three of you — and I'll get the chance to write about, and advise on, baking.'

'So, it's quite a big deal then?' Her daughter still sounds bolshie.

'Yes. Look, I know I'm letting Dad down, and that he's disappointed, but I can't give this up to watch him from the sidelines. I want to be doing something for me.'

There is a pause, so lengthy that Jenny wonders if Emma has lost her mobile signal.

'Emma? Em, are you there? Say something.'

She hears her middle daughter give a sigh plump with disappointment, and she knows she's in for an emotional ride.

'I just think it's a shame. Put like that, of course I understand. But Daddy' — Emma resorts to the name she used as a child to convey her loyalty — 'has put so much into this and it's just a bit sad you won't be there to support him.

'It's no one's fault', she continues, adding a dose of martyred magnanimity. 'But I can see why he's so disappointed about it — especially as we were all going to meet up, and make it a family celebration.'

The idea of a cancelled family reunion — already mythologised — obviously rankles. Jenny is just wondering how to atone for this when Emma mines a different emotional vein.

'You've put me in a bit of a quandary now. I don't know who I should support.'

Her mother, familiar with her daughter's skill

at manipulation, recognises her cue. 'Oh my darling, it's not a competition but you must support Daddy if that's what you feel you'd like to do.'

'You don't mind, do you?' Emma can afford to be conciliatory now that her Paris weekend is no longer in jeopardy. 'You won't feel that I'm not supporting you, or that I'm taking your place?'

'Of course not, darling.' She too can be magnanimous now that the aggression has been defused. 'In fact you'd be doing me a favour, and making me feel much less guilty. You go and have fun.'

16

To make two basic white loaves, take strong white flour; yeast; warm water and a smidgeon of butter, sugar and salt. Time, a little skill, and the wonder of nature are then all that are required.

Sunday morning, late-March, and Mike Wilkinson is as close to happiness — or what constitutes happiness, post-Rachel — as he is likely to be.

Pippa and Sam are sprawled on the floor next door, watching a slapstick TV game show, and chortling with the infectious laughter unique to very young children. Not for the first time, he wishes he could remember how to laugh like that and wonders at what age they will lose their capacity for sheer glee.

He pokes his head round the door. Heads close together, all bickering is forgotten as they delight in the misfortune of the competitors, slipping down slides, splashing into water, wading through mud.

'What's so funny?' Like the permanent outsider, he is keen to be in on the joke.

Sam, for whom the forbidden words bum and poo can still provoke manic giggling, can barely contain himself. 'The man . . . the man . . . got hit by a . . . ' His red face creases with the effort of getting a sentence out, and convulses as a fresh wave of giggles rises up from his belly.

171

'Idiot,' his sister joshes him. At eight, Pippa likes to think she is above such unrestrained hilarity. A second later, her behaviour undermines her.

'Look . . . Daddy, did you see that one?' She gives a squeal, her exquisite face flushed with excitement as she turns towards him. 'He fell all the way down!!!!'

Mike reckons he has forty minutes of peace, tops, and, for once, feels justified in sticking them in front of the telly, their remote parent. He has just taken them on a four-mile bike ride and their mud-splattered legs will be aching — though he knows that, after lunch, he will have to run them round the rec.

Forty minutes gives him time to whack his casserole in the oven, put on the mashed potatoes and crack on with his bread-making. The bread stage is next but Mike, a realist who knows he is not going to win the competition, is not intent on practising. He is going to make bread for the sheer joy of doing it.

Late last year, he had been baking one Sunday lunchtime while indulging in one of his unashamed middle-class fetishes: listening to Radio 4's *The Food Programme*. As he'd begun his gentle kneading, folding the dough towards him then pressing down with the heel of his hand; turning the dough around and repeating the process, the programme — in one of those rare moments of coincidence — had described what he was doing. More to the point, it had talked about making bread as therapy. Veterans of Afghanistan who had set up a bakery were interviewed, as were victims of torture who met for a bread-making session every week. The rhythmic kneading of dough was a means of soothing and calming when intrusive thoughts and memories threatened to overwhelm them, explained the charity organiser. And the smell, taste and texture of bread transported them back to happier times — baking bread with their mothers, perhaps — before their trauma.

Listening to the programme, Mike found he had tears running down his cheeks, not just for the torture victims — refugees from Iran, for the most part — but for himself as he tried to achieve some sort of equanimity after Rachel's death. He hadn't seen his bread-making as therapeutic, but he suddenly realised he could date its start from the week after her funeral, when grief, initially staved off by adrenalin, engulfed him. Pounding the dough — rather than lightly folding and gently punching it as the books advised — was cathartic; a means of distracting himself when he had felt over-whelmed with anger, just as more active men might go for a run or pound a punch bag in a gym.

Now, making bread is a regular weekly fixture and has become not just therapeutic but creative. Where he once used it as an acceptable means of releasing his anger, he now views it as something more positive: a means of creating something unique, of providing for his children in the most basic way. He also loves the sense of continuity it gives him: even the Anglo-Saxons made bread, he is fond of telling his pupils, and, as hunters

173

rather than farmers, had been so terrified of wheat growing and dough swelling that they cast spells at every stage of their bread-making. Bread is intrinsic to British culture and language, he tells them. Think of the phrases taken from milling: grist to the mill; nose to the grindstone; and the colloquialisms: make some dough; earn a crust; upper crust. Even Jesus — and here he is on shakier ground, having been agnostic even before Rachel's death — recognised its centrality to human existence, describing himself as 'the bread of life'.

His enthusiasm for bread-making and its place in British culture has led him to experiment in a way he avoids with cakes or puddings. He bakes with spelt or rye flour; sprinkles poppy and sunflower seeds; adds olives and rosemary, pancetta and caramelised onions, blue cheese and walnuts. And yet his trademark loaf remains a standard bloomer, slashed three times across the top to allow for satisfying gashes in the crust, and a basic wholemeal. He knows he will have to shine in the competition; to demonstrate that he can make naan, or bagels, or challah loaf. But, for today, in his warm kitchen, for his hungry children, it'll be his bog-standard farmhouse white.

* * *

Claire Trelawney is also baking — in her case hot cross buns, saffron bread and tea loaf — as she works alongside her mother and daughter.

Her hands move lightly but her jaw is set as

174

she flings the dough down on to the worktop and stretches and rotates it. Chloe's father, Jay, has been in contact and she always makes bread rather than more delicate cakes and pastries when this happens, reaching for the strong white flour, just as other women might launch into a flurry of obscenities; open the vodka; light a cigarette.

'Easy, love.'

Claire looks up to see Angela raising an eyebrow.

'Sorry.' She smiles and takes in grandmother and granddaughter: two generations united in the simple pleasure of mixing a handful of ingredients — flour, yeast, water, salt and sugar — and witnessing culinary magic take place.

'Am I doing this right, Mum?' Chloe, ever keen for parental approval, is struggling with the sticky bun dough, which clings to her fingers.

'You want a little more flour — not too much.' Claire's voice rises to a squeak as Chloe tips a mound of strong flour on to the surface.

'You don't want tough, dried-out dough.'

'Leave it to me, my lover.' Angela, the matriarch and the acknowledged premier baker in the family, despite what Claire might think, takes over, scooping up the flour and putting it in the packet, pulling the dough from Chloe's fingers and kneading it on the worktop for her.

'Let her do it for herself, Mum. She needs to learn.' Claire is irritated by her mother's involvement.

Angela is implacable. 'No point letting her struggle. I was just helping.'

'It's great now, Nanny. Look, it's gone more stretchy.' Chloe looks from one to another as she points at the smoother dough her grandmother is creating. Her enthusiasm dampens the spark of tension.

'That's fantastic, lovely. Really well done.'

'Now just work it for about ten minutes like that: we want it silky smooth and elastic,' advises Angela, handing over to her granddaughter. 'These are going to be really bouncy hot cross buns.'

The three work on in companionable silence, Claire creating the saffron dough by pouring lukewarm milk, liquid gold, on to dried fruit, sugar, yeast and buttery crumbs. The soft, rich dough reminds her of the play-doh she made for Chloe when tiny: sensual; tactual; elastic. The smell is better though: the scent of dried fruit and earthy warm yeast gentler than the saltiness of the child's dough; and the texture is softer: not scratchy but smooth.

'Smells good, don't he?' Angela looks on approvingly, her own mixture now rounded to a smooth sphere and placed in a bowl, a damp tea towel stretched over it.

'You're getting to be a fine baker.' She says this with a verbal wink; a tacit admission that her daughter has every right not to take her advice now that she is doing well in the competition.

Claire smiles at the compliment, rarely bestowed and all the more precious for it. 'Thank you! Yes, I'm getting better. Not there yet, though. Not by a long shot.'

'Well no, but you can get there — can't she, Chloe?'

Chloe's delicate face breaks into a grin, nose wrinkling between her freckles, wide eyes sparkling with pride and excitement.

'Course she can. She's the best baker and the best mum in the world.'

'Oh well. I'm getting better. They liked my gingerbread house.' Claire cannot help smiling, but her kneading becomes heavier as she recalls the result of it being good enough for her to appear on YouTube: Jay bombarding her with emails and texts.

'Not worrying about it, are you?' Angela, ever attuned to her youngest child's anxiety, notes the crease deepening between her eyes.

'Well, a bit. Well, a lot really. I know I won't win, I'm not stupid, but I want to do all of us proud.'

She smiles, trying to mask her continual sense of responsibility for Chloe's sake but failing as her voice trembles. She is back to being seventeen and telling her mother she is pregnant. 'I don't want to let you down.'

Angela is all arms, all bosom, as she gathers her daughter, and a concerned Chloe, into her apron. She smells of Pears soap and baking. 'Oh, my lover, you'd never do that.'

They stand there for a couple of seconds before Claire extricates herself, embarrassed by her mum's soppiness and wary of scaring Chloe.

'That's wonderful, my lovely.' She gestures at her daughter's dough, now placed in a bowl with a plastic bag over it. 'Will you just go and put that by the radiator? Then wash your hands and you can put a CD on?'

Her daughter nods and carries her dough; solemn with responsibility. Then she flies to the bathroom, freed from the responsibility of worrying about her mother, fired by the thought of a dance.

'So . . . what's bothering you?'

There is no point, Claire has long realised, in hiding anything from her mother. She delays her answer as she finishes wiping up the flour.

'Jay's been back in touch.'

Angela wrinkles her nose as if someone had farted.

'He saw my gingerbread house on YouTube.'

'I wouldn't have thought baking was his thing,' Angela notes drily, as she rinses her fingers of flour.

'I think his sister put a link to it on her Facebook page. Or anyone I know could have done. It's had quite a lot of hits now. Fifteen thousand. Can't quite believe it.' She cannot hide her surprise at the number — or her pride.

'Oh.' There is a pause while Angela digests the news and the unfamiliar power of the internet. She dries her hands thoroughly with the towel.

'Well. You're not going to see him, are you?'

'Course not.' Claire flushes. 'Why would I do something as stupid as that?'

'OK.'

'You don't believe me.'

'I didn't say that.'

'You don't have to.'

Her mother gives her a look.

'Oh, I'm sorry, Mum. I'm sorry. No. I haven't said I will. No.'

Her answer fails to convince her mother.

'I just know you, my lover. And I know how he gets under your skin.'

'I know . . . I know. But it's so difficult. I'd love Chloe to see him. I'd love him to play more of a role in her life. I'd love him to be a dad to her.'

'You think he wants to do that?' Angela looks sceptical.

'He says that . . . He says the YouTube clip — the fact it was me making a beach hut for Chloe — made him realise what he's missed out on.' She tries to convince herself. 'If I see him, it's for Chloe's sake.'

Angela gives a snort.

'Mum.'

'You know what he's like, Claire. You know how he treated you before. You don't need that. Especially now you're doing so well for yourself.'

'I know.' Claire smiles, intending to convey reassurance. 'I know.'

Her mother gives a harrumph and Claire buries her head in a cupboard, suddenly anxious to find some vanilla essence.

17

I know it is fashionable to limit the amount of bread one eats, and perhaps to substitute it with crackers or Ryvita. But never deny yourself everything. Food is there to be enjoyed. And substitutes are rarely quite as satisfying.

Vicki is humming as she potters up and down the aisles of her local Eaden's: a gentle, insistent hum, half a semitone out of tune. It is early afternoon and the store is as quiet as it ever gets, emptied of the workers who raid the shelves of pastrami on rye or goat's cheese and roasted vegetable wraps during their lunchtime foray from the office; not yet invaded by the hassled mothers towing disgruntled children as they drop in for an emergency bag of brioche after school.

Vicki is humming in part because she has had an unexpected phone call. The sort of call that has got her mind racing, and opened up the possibility of a different sort of world. Amy Springer, the year three teacher at her old school, St Matthew's, has rung to say she is just pregnant and due to go on maternity leave in September. The job would be hers for the taking. Of course, she won't apply for it. It's Alfie's pre-school year and the deal had always been that she would give him her undivided attention until he started reception a year later — and that she'd have another baby. But that doesn't seem to be happening. And perhaps this would distract her: stop her feeling life is standing still while she fails to get pregnant. Yes . . . it *is* tempting. And it's lovely that Amy immediately thought to give her the heads-up. That she thought she was perfect for it. She wonders if she should give Colin Johnson, her old head, a call.

No, of course not. It's just a flattering fantasy. But she wonders what her mother would say if she announced she was to return to work? She has no doubt she would love it. Frances has always taken it personally that she abandoned her career, after the sacrifices she made in the seventies and eighties to ensure it was a given. Recently, she has stopped asking when she will return but the issue of her not working throbs in the background, as oppressive as an imminent thunderstorm.

Well, she wants no such tension this weekend. She turns her attention to her immediate job: concocting something delicious for her mother. A thank you for looking after Alfie; another bid to win her admiration; her approval.

She meanders down the store. It is lovely to be here and to be childless, she realises with a spasm of guilt: to have time to stop and assess the products; to smell the mangoes and press the avocados without Alfie — who refuses to sit in the trolley — pulling at her belt, at her waist, at her handbag and then racing out of sight.

It is an entirely different experience, shopping without a child. A pleasurable experience in which she can allow her mind to wander — to consider what she might bake at the next round, and how she can ensure she wins a YouTube slot as she did for her Battenburg cake (18,928 hits when she last checked, an hour ago). That recipe was more emotionally charged for her than any other and she wonders if her bakes have to be associated with bad memories for her to do herself justice.

Come on, Mrs Eaden, she thinks, as she pushes her trolley to her favourite aisle, the baking aisle, help me out here. What do I have to do to shine: to set myself above the star of the gingerbread house, Karen, or the clear front-runner, Jenny? Jenny's lovely — though there's clearly something going on with her husband — but I do so want to win. If I'm not going back to teaching then I need to show my mother I can excel in this field. To win her over, it's not enough to come second. I need to be the best.

She turns into the baking aisle. It's bread next. Never her forte. Should she focus on different grains, or different flavourings? What would Mrs Eaden do? What would the judges like?

She appraises the bags of strong flour: organic; rye, granary and a spelt mix, and spends an inordinate amount of time looking at them before selecting a bag of strong white and a bag of organic, stoneground wholemeal. She pauses then adds a third bag: gluten-free, organic bread flour.

I bet you didn't have a mother like mine, she thinks, as she picks up the organic undyed apricots, giant golden sultanas, flame-red raisins and candied peel required for her hot cross buns.

If she uses gluten-free flour, she can bake a cake for Frances. I'm doing it again, she thinks. Baking a cake to make her happy — though this one will have no colouring, no artificial flavouring, no gluten, and, if I can avoid it, no fat or sugar. What sort of cake can I bake to please her? Or could I try bread? A bread made with gluten-free bread flour? No, I'm being stupid. It will still contain yeast — and that gives her terrible bloating.

Her tranquil state of mind is disappearing fast and so she hares back to the fruit aisle to pick up vegetables that will, surely, please her mother. She could abandon the cake idea and make her a Thai salad, high in flavour with soy, red chillies, coriander and ginger; minimal in calories. She picks up peppers, baby corn, beansprouts, sugar snaps, then pauses. The peas say product of Zimbabwe; the baby sweetcorn, Kenya. She puts them back, emphatic. Her mother will only lecture her about the air miles.

What about an apple crumble? English apples; gluten-free flour; oats; minimal brown sugar, fat ... No, that won't work. Will she eat extra-low-fat sunflower spread?

Perhaps it would be best just to make her an apple compote and serve it with some low-fat organic natural yoghurt? Then choose some sustainably farmed fish and serve it with organic, locally produced broccoli? She deliberates, stymied by indecision; wanting to do everything right, to achieve some sort of perfection. Eventually, she selects the choicest vegetables, knowing, as she does so, that, in some way, they will be found wanting. They won't be as fresh, as flavoursome, as vegetables grown on a friend's allotment, but they will have to do this time.

The products chosen — and the choices still niggling — she needs some light relief and flits over to the magazine section. She picks up a CBeebies magazine for Alfie, imagining his smile as he discovers the Rastamouse stickers inside. Last night, she had read him a tale of the rapping mouse's exploits and he had listened intently as she'd stumbled through a rap in a cod Jamaican accent.

'Sorry it doesn't sound right,' she had apologised.

He had shaken his head and produced a new word: 'It's awesome.'

And he had snuggled up to her, warm, docile and seriously impressed.

Sometimes I get it right, she thinks as she turns to the baking magazines: *Baking World, Baker's World, Cakes and Decoration, Cupcakes and Pop Cakes*. The titles spring out at her in a haze of pastel yellow and pink.

She spends a few guilty minutes rifling through them: trying to assess where her £3.95 would be best spent. None will help her with bread: all are preoccupied with sugar and confection. And, really, though the decorations are technically difficult, the ideas are run-of-the-mill. Staid.

A woman is peering at her quizzically, head cocked to one side, a smile on her lips. 'It is you, isn't it?'

Vicki's face is blank.

The woman elaborates. 'Vicki? Are you here to promote the competition — not that you need to?' She gestures at the copy of *Eaden's Monthly* she is holding.

Vicki takes the magazine. She had not realised the April issue would be out yet. And there she is, on the front cover, perfecting her gingerbread house alongside Claire and Karen. She looks confident; accomplished. She looks happy.

'Don't you look beautiful?' The woman seems star-struck. 'Well, you're my favourite. You remind me of my daughter. I'm going straight home to view your film on YouTube again and to put another comment on the website. I just loved your Battenburg cake.'

'Thank you ... Thank you so much.' Bemused, Vicki suddenly remembers her manners.

'I know it's not very 'cool' of me,' the woman continues, 'but ... I don't suppose you would ... would you mind?' She draws a Parker ballpoint from her handbag and gestures at the magazine.

'You'd like me to sign it?'

'If you don't mind. I know it's not very sophisticated. But my daughter will never believe me otherwise.'

'I'd be delighted.' Vicki's ability to speak appropriately seems to have returned. She giggles, self-conscious, excited. 'I've never done this before. My first taste of celebrity!'

'Your first — but not your last, my dear.' The woman smiles. 'I doubt it will be your last.'

Kathleen

His comments had struck her as hugely inappropriate, even though she knew, rationally, he was just trying to be kind.

Minutes earlier she had lain on his couch, in his consulting room in Harley Street, her legs in stirrups, as he examined her to assess why — two weeks after the event she refused to put a name to — she was still bleeding so heavily.

'I'm afraid we're going to have to do a D and C to check you haven't anything nasty still inside you,' James Caruthers, Fellow of the Royal College of Obstetricians and Gynaecologists, had informed her, stripping off his gloves and washing his hands vigorously. She had reddened, reluctant to meet his eye after his clinical probing inside.

'Anything nasty . . . you mean, my baby?'

'No — retained tissue; the remains of the placenta.' He turned to her briefly, then continued scrubbing between his fingers, his manner not unfriendly but matter-of-fact.

Her sorrow had swirled around the room as the gynaecologist had detailed the nature of the procedure and the risks and benefits. The words washed over her: general anaesthetic; risk of infection; bed rest; prevention of sexual intercourse; required to facilitate a second conception

186

in time. He might as well have been speaking ancient Greek or some other equally esoteric language, so alien were the words.

She had stared hard at a silver-framed photograph on his desk: James Caruthers, his elegant wife and their three small boys in prep school uniform. Blond-haired, highly privileged, impervious to life's difficulties. The youngest had a dimple and an irrepressible smile.

And then she had felt the tears prick, hot and fast. Julie, his nurse, had handed her an ironed cotton handkerchief with a cluck of reassurance. Mr Caruthers had been forced to abandon his lecture and his pacing around his wood-panelled study. He had stood, briefly confounded, then perched on the edge of his partner's desk, freckled hands placed firmly on his thighs.

'Look,' he began, and his tone was calm and rational. 'I think the best thing you can do is to build up your strength in preparation for another pregnancy. Eat some of the food you write so well about: not so much the cakes but the pies and the wholemeal bread. The recipes that are particularly nutritious. Lots of red meat and green vegetables — that sort of thing.

'I must say,' he went on, warming to his theme. 'I think it's marvellous you have this interest. Mrs Caruthers is really quite a fan. Reads your column every month and says you're writing a book — is that correct?'

'Um . . . Yes. *The Art of Baking*.' She was bemused and tried to remember what she was supposed to say about this project that had stalled in the last fortnight, as if her ability to

187

write had also seeped away. She had managed to cobble together a column for *Home Magazine* — a rehashed ode to the joys of the crumble — but had written nothing good enough for the book. How can she spin sentences about nurturing one's family with baking when she doesn't have one? Or rather, one that just comprises George and her?

She looks at the obstetrician afresh, and sees that he is a stranger. Someone who thinks she might want to talk about writing and baking when all she wants is an answer to why she lost her child.

But James Caruthers looks pleased with himself, as if he has found a solution that will make up for the failings of medical science.

'Well, then.' He leans back and gives a wide smile. 'We're going to tidy you up and have a good look at you. And I'm sure there's no reason why you won't be able to have a bonny baby. We might just have to try a little longer; give you some time.

'But you're lucky. If things don't work out quite as you'd like . . . well, there's a Plan B, isn't there? You'll always have your baking and your writing to fall back on.'

18

Lardy cake — my husband's favourite — may seem somewhat old-fashioned: a sweet tea bread layered with lard that oozes stickiness, each bite yielding sultanas, sweetness and spice.
Historically they were seen as celebration cakes since sugar, dried fruit and spice were dear. These days, we need have no such qualms, and the only limitation will be how strongly we value our waistlines.

'Morning!' Karen Hammond tosses a smile over her shoulder as Dan Keller walks past her in the competition kitchen, assessing her technique as she makes her signature leaven bread.

She thinks she is on to a winner: a spelt loaf topped with rye flakes. Wheat-free, unusual and contemporary. Claire's saffron bread, Mike's cardamom and fennel loaf, and Vicki's hazelnut and honey wholemeal will have nothing on this.

'Do you always knead like that?'

Dan's question, delivered with wry amusement, takes Karen by surprise.

'I . . . uh.' She stops what she is doing, thrown by his physical presence; the proximity of his arm to hers; fine hairs almost touching as he reaches over and takes the dough.

'You're using spelt, aren't you? So you're going to have to knead for longer than with a usual dough. Do you mind if I demonstrate?'

'Is that allowed? Isn't it cheating?'

The thought of breaking the rules in this open environment thrills her.

'I'm not going to do it all for you — but a quick knead is permitted.' His words seem suffused with sexual innuendo and she glances around. Her competitors, ensconced in their kneading, seem oblivious and continue with their work, heads down.

She moves along the bench, giving him excessive space so aware is she of the need not to be physically close. He glances at her and then begins to stretch and rotate the dough, his hands moving quickly and lightly though she can see the strength of his biceps, straining against his shirt.

'Now you try.'

He moves aside as she takes his place and puts her hands on the dough, warmed and softened by his touch. Push, turn, fold; push, turn, fold; push, turn, fold. She mimics his movements, concentrating fiercely as she tries to ignore his presence beside her, the thought of her fingers being where his have been, the heat in her groin.

'Much better.'

He gives another smile and ambles off, leaving her watching his pert glutes enhanced by his slim-fitting jeans, the triangular tapering of his waist, his broad shoulders. She feels played — like a teenage girl pining for the school pin-up, who throws her a casual smile, then flings an arm around her classmate, oblivious to her desire.

She returns to her kneading. What is it that makes him so attractive besides the obvious good looks? she wonders. Perhaps, on a basic level, there is something very manly about the fact that he can provide. He can bake pies, make bread, could feed a family with some flour, yeast and water and the skill of his hands. She has little doubt that, if returned to the wild, he is the sort of man who would instinctively know how to build a shelter, hunt and skin small mammals, spear fish, construct a fire that blazed — not fizzled. He is physically capable as well as physically desirable.

He reminds her of Dave, the builder who constructed their £200,000 double-storey extension five years ago, and who spent three months, on and off, camped in her kitchen. Initially she had dismissed him as boorish: a labourer who read the *Sun* on his numerous tea-breaks; who seemed to be forever retiring to his van to eat rounds of sliced white sandwiches; who insisted on turning up for work before 8 a.m. but would knock off as soon as it became dusk.

But he soon grew on her. There was humour and intelligence in his dealings with her and his crew of brickies, chippies and plumbers; genuine embarrassment on the day he turned up just after seven before she had dressed; a gentle courtesy as he tried to tiptoe over her kitchen floor, giant hobnailed boots trampling detailed footprints of mud.

Above all, he was capable — in a refreshingly physical, practical way. When the council planning department decided that another wall should be knocked down, he dealt with it within the day and organised a skip for its immediate removal. When a nail pierced a pipe and water cascaded through the ceiling, he found the source of the problem, summoned his plumber from another job and stood over him, swearing gently, until he put it right. When snow fell and temperatures plummeted to minus twelve, meaning the tilers were unwilling to scale the scaffolding, he began their job for them, putting them to shame. At one point — the one occasion when she lost her cool over the build and nearly cried when a £40,000 roof light arrived broken — she half expected him to put his arm round her, and somehow fuse the fractured pieces of glass. Instead, for a couple of seconds, he had looked nonplussed. Then he reached for his mobile and demanded a replacement from the suppliers.

The employer/employee relationship was maintained — scrupulously on his part; more shakily on hers — and it was a relief for Karen when the build was finished and she no longer had to contend with the extra testosterone swilling around her home. But her experience of Dave made her realise the attraction of men who did physical work. Compared to Oliver, who worked in an alternative universe — playing with numbers, accruing and sometimes losing vast sums of money that he would never touch and she could never visualise by responding to a computer — Dave could build her a home. She had no desire to be married to someone like him; Oliver's job might seem risible in contrast but she appreciated his salary and bonuses. But she wouldn't have minded shagging Dave. And think how much she could have fed him. She could definitely see the allure.

★ ★ ★

Well, of course she wins the bread challenge and comes second — to Jenny — when they later make lardy cake: plump, glossy, sticky; saturated in fat. The thought of eating it makes Karen gag, and she flits round the kitchen, trying to offload her caramelised rectangles, inwardly shuddering at the trickles of lard that seep between currants and sultanas.

'Can I interest you in my wares?' She is in front of Dan, whose eyes wrinkle in amusement.

'I feel like a seventeenth-century serving wench,' she finds herself explaining, and to her horror fears she is about to blush.

'I'd be very interested in your wares,' he replies, taking in her slightly heightened colour and the glow of success that somehow softens her; making her mannerisms less calculated; her features less angular. He holds her gaze for a fraction too long.

'As for your lardy cake . . . delicious though it was, I have had to try five samples in the last half-hour, and a couple of those' — he glances at Vicki and Claire, the least successful contenders in this challenge — 'were dripping in fat.'

He laughs. 'I guess that's where the expression 'getting lardy' comes from. I'm now desperately in need of a stiff drink . . . or some exercise?'

There is something about his manner that

193

invites flirtation, or at least that is how Karen manages to explain her behaviour, later.

'Well, I'm sure I could oblige,' she hears herself reply. 'The exercise, I mean,' and then, as he raises an eyebrow, she elaborates, slowly yet with a distinct gurgle in her voice. 'I've got my running kit with me. I was going to go for a five-mile run, if you're interested?'

'I'm not sure I'm meant to fraternise with the competitors.' He smiles.

'Why? Scared we'll beat you?' The challenge is automatic, and works.

He draws himself up to his full six foot four. 'Oh, I think I could put you through your paces, Karen Hammond. Meet you at the back of the hall in twenty minutes.'

'I'll look forward to it.'

★ ★ ★

It is dark when they meet; a clear late March night in which a full moon has risen and the stars gleam preternaturally in an indigo sky. Karen's breath forms clouds of mist as she runs on the spot, in an attempt to keep warm. She wears no hat or headband — her hair being her best asset — just a hot-pink fleece and black Lycras that sculpt her legs.

Lit initially by the floodlights leading up to the hall, and then by the moon, they take the path from the mansion, then make a circuit of the perimeter of its grounds, running along paths where possible but making forays over grass and leaves. Dan takes the lead, running at an even

194

pace that allows him to talk without breaking into a sweat or showing the least sign of breathlessness. Karen keeps up, powered not just by her aerobic ability but by a determination he should be cowed by her. She wants to turn the tables: to have him in her thrall, not the other way around.

For a while they are largely silent, both focused on achieving a consistent brisk pace — an eight-minute mile — as their feet pound the musty leaves and damp grass. Karen realises they are breathing in time with one another, and concentrates on the synchronicity, delighting in the power of their bodies, and how well matched they are in terms of fitness, as they storm up a hill and begin to run on higher ground.

The more even ground allows for some conversation but it is minimal, as if both want to focus on the physicality of what they are doing. Words — the usual currency of flirtation — are superfluous.

'Faster?' Dan asks the question; refrains from a challenge.

'But of course.' She ups her speed, pushing her legs faster, feeling the blood pound in her head. Her heart feels as if it will burst.

'Easy . . . ' He gives a laugh, between breaths. His breathing has become more laboured, as if his heartbeat were audible. 'I didn't mean a sprint.'

They slow down, taking a dimly lit path into a copse shielded from the moonlight.

'Glad I'm not alone,' she pants.

'Glad I'm not either,' he says.

To either side, thickets rustle. A rabbit streaks across the path, the flash of its white tail catching in the minimal moonlight. The ground is more uneven, causing them to slow down further.

'Fancy a rest?'

'Are you slacking?' She laughs over her shoulder, powering through the trees, exhilarated by her strength, by the flirtation, by her sense of being pursued. It would be so easy to pause in the privacy of the copse, unzip her fleece — 'God, I'm hot,' — and see what would happen. But Karen rarely takes the easy option. Besides, she wants the thrill of the chase.

They leave the clump of trees, and the grounds open up in front of them to reveal Bradley Hall in all its Gothic splendour.

'Not much further.' Dan has caught up and overtakes her, shooting a grin over his shoulder as he pounds past. She raises her pace once more and is swiftly alongside him. He slows down to a more companionable speed.

Her breathing is ragged now. Pearls of sweat bead her cheeks but the freezing air wicks them away. She hopes her flush is attractive.

'We're a good match,' he says, as their feet crunch over gravel.

'We are.' She slows down, running more gently in a cool-down then beginning to stretch.

'We'll have to do this again,' he persists, looking into her face as she glances up after stretching a hamstring.

'Are you sure that's allowed?'

'I'd have thought it was a necessity, given all the fat I'm going to be consuming in the next few weeks. What is it: pastries and then puddings? I think you'll need to put me through my paces.'

The smile he bestows hints at a complicity between them; an understanding — or at least that is how Karen reads it as she takes in the frank invitation in his eyes. He likes me, she thinks with a jolt; he likes me and he desires me. She feels a flicker of joy.

* * *

Watching from the window of her bedroom, where she has gone to draw the curtains, Claire cannot see the couple's faces. But she can read their body language: the way he bends towards her, puts his hand on her shoulder, and then fleetingly — there's no doubting it now — caresses her cheek. How long has it been since a man touched me like that? she wonders; as if he couldn't help showing some tenderness? As if, at that moment, I was the only thing that mattered to him in the world?

There has only been one person who has ever made her feel like that: the man who has caused her the greatest pain, and the greatest excitement. Sexy, charming, unreliable, unconsciously cruel Jay. She picks up her phone; re-reads his message; and wonders, for what must be the hundredth time, what would happen if she replied.

Kathleen

Two days after the D and C, Kathleen Eaden is back on form and by George's side for another opening. Then it's time for a photo shoot in which she is pictured cradling a home-made bloomer: heavy as a newborn and still warm.

'Kathleen? Are you sure you're all right?' George, his arm placed protectively around her, was solicitous as if questioning if he had pushed her too hard by suggesting she still go ahead with the photographs.

'Of course!' Her tone was bright and she heard a sharpness, not usually there. 'I mean' — and here she gestured at the callow photographer — 'he's hardly David Bailey.'

'He comes very well regarded.'

'Oh, I know, my darling.' She regretted her tone in an instant. 'I just meant: it's not very cutting edge. This poster campaign. It's not as if I have to be a Jean Shrimpton.'

He pulled her close, and dropped a kiss on her forehead.

'I don't want the Shrimp. I want Kathleen Eaden — and so do our customers.'

'Oh, I know.' She tried to laugh off her silliness. That's not what I meant, she thought as she extricated herself from his hug. For a moment, she had a flash of a different life: one in

198

which she swanned around London with lovely young men and behaved like a girl in her early twenties. Someone required to look beautiful without the burden of having to behave like the ideal, domestic woman. A girl, not a woman, permitted — no, expected — to have fun.

She smoothed down her dress — no miniskirt but a demure shift.

'Come on. We'd better get on with the rest of the photos.' Her voice was brisk.

'If you're absolutely certain?'

'Of course. The show must go on!'

He had looked at her and some kindness in his face made her pause and admit to her vulnerability.

'No one here knows, do they, that there was a baby?'

'Oh, my darling. Of course not.'

'I'm just being stupid. So silly.' She smiled and swallowed a sip of water, trying to dislodge the hard lump stuck at the back of her throat.

19

To make a succulent Chelsea bun, you need a sumptuous filling: sugar, cinnamon, sultanas, raisins and chopped dried apricots, all enveloped in melted butter, and rolled up tight. Tack down one end of the dough; scatter with the filling, and then roll, tightening as you go. Imagine you are swaddling a newborn baby and then holding her close.

'We've got a real treat for your final bread challenge.' Harriet is beaming, and making Claire nervous as her definition of a treat, she suspects, will vary wildly from hers.

'Chelsea buns: something Kathleen Eaden provides a glorious recipe for in *The Art of Baking* and which seemed to have a particular significance for her. She and George had a Georgian town house just off the King's Road, where she spent a lot of time, and he would often joke that she was his 'Chelsea girl'. They appealed aesthetically and emotionally. You cannot hope to be the New Mrs Eaden without getting these little beauties right.'

Oh, bloody hell. Claire glances at Vicki, who she cannot help liking, and mouths: 'So, no pressure!' But Vicki, like an extra-keen pupil, is hanging on Harriet's every word. Jenny and Mike appear equally interested and only Karen, inspecting her nails, seems the slightest bit preoccupied. She looks particularly smug this morning, in her skinny jeans, silk shirt and high leather ankle boots that look completely impractical. Claire glances down at her jeans and imitation Converse. She must feel pretty confident she's not going to coat herself in eggs or flour.

Claire is feeling distinctly bad-tempered this morning. Not a feeling she often experiences, and not one she feels good about. Her whole body aches: her back is stiff and her mind fuzzy from lack of sleep. She has had a bad night, thinking of Karen and Dan, and of her and Jay and their hopeless relationship. Obsessing about what she could have done, if anything, to keep him: to stop him running off when Chloe was three months old and then flitting in and out of their lives ever since. Agonising — yet again — about where it all went wrong.

To counteract this, she has drunk too much sweet black coffee and now feels distinctly shaky. Her heart pounds and she is restless; she can't stand still and keeps jiggling her feet. She is also nervous. Can she create a perfect Chelsea bun — soft, light, with toffeeish fruit and an exquisitely judged filling? Her lardy cake was rubbish; her saffron bread unsophisticated. Her chances of winning the next YouTube slot — let alone the competition — are evaporating as fast as a sugar syrup furiously boiled.

Harriet is continuing to drone on. Something about the buns needing to be regular. She had better concentrate. 'They require precision. We want neat circles with the filling — a perfect combination of spices and vine fruits — evenly distributed,' the established baker explains.

'We also want them uniformly baked: we don't want charred fruit; we don't want undercooked dough; but nor do we want corner buns that are dried out even if the central ones are deliciously moist. There must be regularity.'

Well, they don't want much. With a sigh, Claire mixes salt, yeast and flour then forms a well in the middle; pours in liquid; and binds into a dough. She works it hard, turning it on a floured surface, making it smooth and elastic. She keeps her head down, hiding her reddening face, afraid that she might cry.

What really annoys her, what really *upsets* her, she realises, as she works the mixture, is that Jay might not have gone if she had been more of a Karen: a woman who knows how to play men, how to use them, how to get on in the world.

Good old Claire had bumbled along, believing his promise that he would stand by her when she got pregnant; trusting he would be loyal; that he would love her even if, for such a short time, her hair was greasy and her trackies milk-stained; her bras stretched and grey not brightly coloured and taut.

Stupid, naive Claire had thought Jay was her mate. Someone who would stick by her through those first tough months and not go out on the lash with the lads at every opportunity; who would understand she was too tired for sex and not go sniffing around for it elsewhere.

She had assumed he would grow up, just as she had had to do. That having a baby daughter would turn him into a parent, and that, because he said he loved her and Chloe, he would want to be by their sides.

She turns the dough viciously. Of course, she hadn't counted on Jade Russell and the joy of a carefree shag, or the promise of a bar job in Ibiza. The two combined proved far easier, and more appealing, than life in Exeter with Chloe and her.

When he'd told her, he'd given her the old 'it's not you it's me,' explanation — one he'd repeat when he returned at the end of the summer and then disappeared the following April.

Angela had told him where he could go then. And Claire, crushed and confused, had let her. He had flitted in and out of their lives ever since, seeing Chloe whenever he visited his mum in Devon. It had seemed selfish not to let him; though, when he stood their daughter up the last time, she had vowed never again.

The pathetic thing, she thinks as the dough takes the brunt of her anguish, is that, really, there has been no one to match him. A couple of flings but no one she liked enough to introduce to Chloe. No one she has trusted enough to let into their world. She is like a goose. Something that mates for life. A stupid goose who tried to mate with a peacock. She grimaces at the thought. Well, that was always going to be messy.

The dough is smooth now. She places it in a bowl and, as she does, her emotions shift. Self-pity sharpens to anger — at herself, initially, and then at Karen. She looks up and watches as she smiles at Dan sauntering past. He smiles back and, to Claire, the look seems plump with promise. Karen lowers her head, bashful as a teenager. And Claire has to look away.

It's just not fair, she thinks, as she covers the bowl with clingfilm. That she's flirting with a competition judge. She would never point this out; never betray her. But still. The injustice cuts as deep as a butcher's knife.

There are two types of women in the world, she realises. Those like her, and, she guesses, Jenny and Vicki. Kind women, who put others first; and sometimes struggle in the world. And there are those like Karen. Who are ruthless. Who grasp life and take what they can for it; and who shine in a more forgiving, more obliging world.

*　*　*

Two and a half hours later, and the Chelsea buns have been taken out of the oven. The exhausted bakers appraise their creations, assessing their relative merits: the extent to which the vine fruit have caught; the neatness of the cinnamon swirl; the uniformity of the buns; their softness; the merits of simple caster sugar versus an apricot glaze and drizzled icing top.

'This one's superb.' Harriet has taken a bite from Claire's offering. Her mouth works as she ruminates. 'Light and sticky, soft dough . . . just the right blend of toffeeish raisins and sultanas. Punchy spices but not overpowering . . . and dusted with the most moreish sprinkle of caster sugar.'

'Oh dear, this one's less good.' She prods at

Vicki's, which is undercooked, the dough too pale, the bun flabby. 'Oh dear, oh dear.' She prods it again. 'Someone wasn't sufficiently precise about their baking time.'

The analysis continues. This bun is too charred; that too leaden. Vicki has turned red: shame at her undercooked offering spreads across her face. Claire's despondency vanishes. Slowly she realises that none of the judges' comments on the others' buns has come close to their enthusiasm for hers. Harriet is comparing hers and what she assumes to be Jenny's and appears to have come down in her favour. She glances at Mike, who gives her a wink.

Harriet delivers her verdict. 'The clear winner of this bake is Claire. Well done. I'm delighted.'

Applauded by her competitors, she looks at each of them, incredulous. Vicki and Jenny beam back; Mike seems genuinely thrilled for her. By the time she meets Karen's eyes, Claire is laughing. A great big laugh that sings of surprise, relief and pure delight. Holding the older woman's gaze, she smiles even more broadly as if to include her in her excitement. And, tentatively, as though the emotion triggering this is unfamiliar, as though she cannot quite trust it, Karen smiles back.

Kathleen

Like the good girl that she is, she has taken James Caruthers' advice and is baking to enrich her increasingly thin body: making seed-encrusted breads and iron-rich meat pies.

Steak and kidney feature strongly in her kitchen; lamb, chicken and rabbit. Green vegetables, particularly broccoli; eggs and salmon. She bakes and eats compulsively, visualising her blood being enriched, her womb lining strengthening with each mouthful she forces down.

George, ever loving, ever ineffectual, does not know how to help. He sits, watching, as she ladles out another lamb casserole, her face a mask of concentration as she tastes it; her manner devoid of joy.

'You seem very . . . diligent,' he ventures.

'And how should I be?' she snaps, and is shocked by the look of surprise that crosses his face. The utter incomprehension. She has never spoken to him like this before.

Mrs Jennings, her long-standing cook and chief recipe taster, understands her better.

'Mr Eaden mentioned his favourite, lardy cake, the other day. He wondered if you could make one for him. I'm more than happy to do it — but I haven't got your lightness of touch.'

And so she had obliged, reluctantly at first for

it seemed wrong to be baking anything with questionable nutritional value, but, as the dough squished through her fingers, with an increasing sense of delight. The sun had streamed through the window and as she worked, she remembered what a joy it was to bake just for the fun of it. To create something that oozed fat and sweetness and decadence — and that made her poor husband smile.

She was on a roll then. Cakes and pastries; buns and biscuits; tarts and croissants: she revisited old favourites and tweaked the classics. The kitchen was suffused with the scent of spice, sugar and butter as the two women worked, side by side.

Mary came to stay and Susan and James 'plumped up', as they put it, on a diet of sausage rolls, cream horns and mini Bakewells.

'It's a good job you don't have children. They'd be roly-poly,' her sister commented, more than a touch disparagingly, as she watched her offspring race around the grounds.

But her niece and nephew looked good on it: their legs sturdier, their cheeks ruddy as they played tag before picnicking on doll's-sized pork pies and crisp Coxes from the orchard.

'Can we stay with you longer? You cook nicer food,' James had whispered and she had felt an unsisterly pang of delight.

The words began to flow, too. Her section of bread and baked goods almost wrote itself and she was soon testing out pie fillings and thinking of synonyms for flaky and butteriness.

'This will be written on time,' she told George,

and for the first time since her loss, she actually believed it: she would create *The Art of Baking* even if she could not create a child. Her writing became better, each sentence revealing how she loved to bake — both the end product and the process. She crossed out little, and surprised herself with her taut, evocative prose.

At times, when her pen sped across the page, or a new tart proved particularly successful, she wondered if there was a limit to her creativity. Could she really write well, invent new recipes and hope to conceive a baby? Wasn't that sheer greediness?

And, then, as autumn turned to winter, something miraculous happened that disproved that theory.

She became pregnant for the third time.

20

If friends and acquaintances delight in your baking then accept the compliment. To do otherwise is ungracious.

Easter and, alone in her small flat, Claire is experiencing an uncharacteristic bubble of excitement as she flicks open her battered laptop and waits for the connection to YouTube.

There she is, demonstrating how to make Chelsea buns: slightly earnest but almost pretty for once as she tries to explain the process. She wished her hair looked shinier but at least she doesn't sound stupid. And there's the evidence of her success: 15,407 hits. Two hundred and three more than two hours ago. Over fifteen thousand people have seen her winning bake — and, judging from the comments, they have liked it.

Her phone pings. One of them is texting her now. Jay.

Well, of course she rang him. Her mum would be furious if she knew the real reason she was babysitting Chloe tonight but it seemed petty not to meet up, not now that he'd moved home with the intention, he said, of being a real dad.

He seems to have settled down a bit, becoming, of all things, an estate agent. She can see him doing well at it: wearing a sharp suit; driving a company car; selling some sort of dream. Penthouses on the New English Riviera are his speciality, he had told her when he had called last week to suggest they meet up, by which she assumes he means the expensive flats overlooking the beach at Exmouth. If anyone could convince buyers this beach — with its sudden squalls and strong currents — was Britain's answer to the south of France, then she guesses it would be him.

And so she is meeting him to discuss more regular contact with Chloe, she tells herself, though that doesn't explain why she is putting on make-up. Not just the cursory lick of mascara but a silvery eye shadow that throws glitter over her cheekbones, a smear of lip gloss that makes her lips look fuller, a flick of eyeliner that defines her eyes.

She up-ends her hair and ties her ponytail higher; hangs hoops from her ears; tugs her top beneath her trademark hoodie a little lower, puts on boots with a slight heel — polished but in desperate need of re-heeling. I'm not doing this for him, she tries to convince herself; I'm doing this for me. To feel good about myself. Oh yeah, comes a whisper deep inside her. Who are you kidding?

She is still telling herself this as she walks towards the bar on the seafront at Exmouth and spots him coming towards her. Hands in pockets, green eyes smiling from a face bronzed through windsurfing; a lean, well-toned physique. It is less of a saunter, more of a strut: the peacock parading his plumage in front of an interested female. He still fancies himself, thinks

Claire, but the galling thing is: he *is* still fanciable. Despite the hurt he has inflicted through his hands-off approach to parenting; despite the fact he loves himself and is immature and selfish, she still finds herself responding to that lazy smile.

'All right?'

She is back to being seventeen, charmed by the cool boy at college.

He holds out his arms. 'Can I get a hug, Miss YouTube queen?'

Despite herself, she smiles, and accepts the embrace. Her body remains stiff, cocooned against his muscles.

'Still angry?' He looks down into her face, strokes her cheek. The tips of his fingers are warm and she can feel the heat of his chest.

She shakes her head, turning her cheek from his fingers, and moves away.

'Come on. Let's get us a drink. I've got a whole crowd, desperate to meet you.' He slings an arm around her shoulders, friendly but proprietorial.

'Oh . . . I thought it was just going to be us.' She falters then blushes. 'I wondered if you wanted a walk on the beach?'

'Thinking of the old times? You dirty girl!' He whispers his delight in her ear. 'You'll have to wait till later.'

'No, I didn't mean that.' She blushes, furious at herself and at him. 'I meant I thought we were going to talk about you seeing Chloe.'

'Of course we are. Of course we are.' He is all sincerity. 'But first I want to introduce you to the lads. Show them how fantastic you are!'

His hand drops to the small of her back as if to guide her to them.

They have reached the bar: nondescript, modern and heaving with a young clientele propped against the bar or clustered around long, wooden tables. He opens the door and they push through a fug of lager and sweet white wine.

'Here she is!' he calls to a table at the window, where five young men — three of whom she recognises from their teenage years — are clustered. 'The New Mrs Eaden!'

'I am not,' she hisses in embarrassment.

'Well, all right, not yet. But she will be. And the next celebrity cook. That fit Chinese one had better watch out.'

'Can you *stop it!*' She is furious.

'Sorry, sorry. Everyone — remember Claire? Mother of my child, light of my life, the new star of YouTube?'

'I am NOT.'

'You are!'

Sean, Ethan and Jason — the lads she remembers from college — grin into their lagers.

One of the others, Rob she thinks — tanned, laid-back, good-looking — hands over his smartphone. 'I'd say you were. Here, take a look for yourself.'

The clip of her making Chelsea buns shows 16,760 hits — over a thousand more than an hour earlier.

'And look at that gingerbread beach hut.' Fingers stroke the screen: 31,462 hits. They flick back to the Chelsea bun film: 16,781.

Someone hands her a vodka and tonic, and she finds herself relaxing into the seat as she scrolls through the phone, checking the hits for her film against those of Jenny and Karen.

'Look at the comments on the Eaden's website.' Jay puts an arm around her lower back, draws her to him.

'Yeah — not Jay's usual sort of site — but now his favourite,' Jason teases.

'Yes, well. I didn't know a culinary goddess before now.' He drops a kiss on her head and she tells herself he is just being friendly; just proud of her; almost like a big brother.

'Hey, enough of that. Look at this.' Ethan hands over another phone showing the Eaden's website.

She squirms as a photo of herself holding a dish of Chelsea buns comes up then begins to smile at the stream of comments from Eaden's customers: 'The most likeable of the contestants: we want you to win'; 'Fantastic baking. Those look delicious'; and, predictably — though she doubts he is a regular Eaden's shopper: 'Claire, love. You can handle my buns any time!'

'Do you believe what a sensation you are now?' Jay is looking at her intently.

'Hardly a sensation,' she says, though her cheeks are flushed with pleasure.

'Well, I don't know what else you'd call it? None of the others are getting the hits you are — apart from that Karen woman. And I don't think they're interested in her cooking. Bet they love you at work?'

213

'Well, yes — I guess I'm good publicity.' She is still getting used to the idea. She can feel herself blushing with the attention. Just enjoy it, you deserve it, she tells herself.

Jay smiles; runs his hand up her back; gives her a quick squeeze that makes her insides flutter.

'You, Claire Trelawney, are a complete star.'

★   ★   ★

'So, obviously, when she's brought out her book in time for Christmas and started her second series, we may want to speak to you — but, frankly, we'll probably be holidaying in some foodie mecca like Rome, Paris — or maybe Dubai . . .

'As her manager, I will, of course, have to accompany her on all her filming commitments — particularly those in hot countries. And Chloe and I will get first choice on the tastings. Forget this six pack' — and here Jay raises his T-shirt slowly to wolf whistles. He blows Claire a kiss. 'I am going to get well FAAAT!'

There is a drum roll of hands on the table and he downs his bottle in one, then leans over and gives her a jokey smack on the lips. She wipes away the lager, stung by the sensation and a flood of memories.

He is on a roll, and she has to admit he is funny. Fuelled by his friends and numerous bottles of lager, he has launched into a comic fantasy about how she will win and he, as her self-appointed manager, will lead a life of luxury.

At least she hopes he knows it is a fantasy.

He is being Jay at his best: gregarious, charming, attentive. And she has missed this: this camaraderie and good-humoured banter; this sense of feeling protected, for once, and flattered. And the suggestion, that, if she decides she wants to, she could have him — for one night, at least.

So why can't she relax entirely and lap up the attention? Perhaps because he hasn't focused on their daughter, or asked her even once about her day-to-day life as a mum.

In fact, she realises as she takes another sip of her vodka and tonic, for most of the evening they have talked exclusively about her success in the competition. And much of the conversation has been about Jay and his comic fantasies — and not about her at all.

★ ★ ★

'That was a laugh, wasn't it?' he had said later, when they finally escaped the bar and she got to walk along the seafront. The sea was a millpond, the tide stroking the shore.

The air was chill though, no duvets of cloud cushioning the air, and she had thrust her hands deep into her pockets. Her shoulders hunched around her ears as she shivered in her thin jacket.

'Here.' He had put his arm around her, and, self-consciously, she had slung one around him, resting it on the taut skin beneath his jacket. Force of habit, she told herself. And a good way to keep warm.

'You were fantastic in there. You are fantastic.' He had smiled down at her, his eyes, green flecked with gold, full of amusement. And he had squeezed her close.

But something had bugged her. 'I'm not just about this competition, you know. There's a lot more to me than that.'

She had dropped her arm; scuffed her feet like a truculent toddler.

'Hey. Easy . . . I know that. I know everything you've done for Chloe. How hard everything's been for you with me being so hands-off.'

'You mean absent.'

'OK. Absent.' He had shrugged off the criticism as if the word were unimportant. 'But you should enjoy how excited everyone is for you. You should be thrilled you're doing so well.'

'I am. But . . . ' She had wanted to articulate her fear — that he was only interested in her because of her new-found fame; that he had reappeared after her clip on YouTube — but he had stopped her.

'No more buts.' He had smiled and planted the gentlest of kisses on her mouth. His lips felt warm and familiar; his mouth forbidden. She had tasted lager — and leaned in to enjoy the kiss.

The image of Angela, face masked in disappointment, came between them: *I know how he gets to you.*

'I can't do this.' She had broken away, almost tearful.

He recoiled. 'Don't be a tease.'

'I'm not . . . I just . . . I can't. Not yet. Not at the moment.'

She had turned away, face pinched, shoulders hunched, head down. Hating herself for being overwhelmed with doubt; for not giving in to the moment; for being the sort of woman who would be used by him — not the sort who would use him without giving it a moment's thought.

21

Simnel cake is the traditional Easter cake: decorated with balls to symbolise the eleven loyal disciples and packed with fruit, spice and marzipan — all forbidden during Lent.
I prefer to serve a large custard tart — the colour of daffodils; crammed with fresh golden eggs — to celebrate the idea of birth and renewal.

Jenny, at home in her kitchen, is in her element, the preparations for an Easter weekend of foodie decadence well under way. Her brood has returned. Not Kate, who will remain in Sydney, but Lizzie, back from Bristol, and Emma, home from Montpellier, laden with traditional chocolate fish and exquisite eggs from a local chocolatier.

'Aren't these gorgeous, Mum? Do you want to save a few to decorate your torte for the competition — can you do that?'

Jenny had been delighted to see her daughter's almost childlike excitement — and her sudden, unexpected support.

Nigel, sweeping through the kitchen on his way out for a run, was less enthusiastic. 'Very nice, but none of us needs to be gorging on those — least of all your mother.'

She had stood there, so stunned she was unable to think of a response.

But Nigel hadn't finished. 'And if you're going

to eat them, you need to remember to clean your teeth thoroughly half an hour afterwards.'

The girls had been incredulous.

'Do you think we'd get an 'I've been to the dentist' sticker for doing that?' Emma had asked, as he slammed the kitchen door and sped off in a display of bad temper and sprayed gravel.

'Bet he confiscates my mini eggs,' said Lizzie. And then: 'Has he always been that bad-tempered?'

'He's just worrying about his weight for this marathon,' Jenny had excused her husband. 'It's making him grouchy. But I've got a feast planned for tomorrow that, for once, might make even him break his diet.'

*   *   *

The Georgian mahogany table in Jenny's dining room — laid for special occasions — would suit a Dickensian Christmas, or a lavish photo shoot for a glossy magazine. The leg of lamb, cooked to perfection, its pink flesh encased in succulent fat and studded with garlic and rosemary, takes centre stage. A jug of red wine gravy sits alongside it and redcurrant jelly, made with redcurrants from the garden, together with pungent mint sauce — also home-grown and home-made.

The roast potatoes, cooked in goose fat, are a master-class in how to cook them: crisply golden on the outside, light and fluffy within. There are toffeeish roast parsnips; chantenay carrots sautéed in butter and honey; green beans cooked

219

al dente; and, since Nigel prefers them, unadorned home-grown spring greens and a bowl of unseasonal new potatoes. She has steamed them with mint, sprinkled them with ground black pepper, and, with some difficulty, refrained from adding butter. They sit chastely: the abstemious exception in a glutton's feast.

Jenny has been working for the best part of four hours on this meal and she is glowing: not just from the heat of the kitchen — and it is a relief to come into the cooler dining room — but from excitement at having two of her three girls home. For just over a fortnight, she can pretend she can turn the clocks back: back to a time when the house was noisy, filled with chattering, bickering, sometimes squabbling daughters who would always require help with homework, advice with friendships, and — for all three were sporty and required a vast amount of calories — her always nutritious, sometimes indulgent, food.

Despite Nigel's barbs, and his increasing obsession with his pre-marathon weight loss — or lack of it — she also hopes that this meal will remind him of the importance of family — and, by extension, the importance, to him, of herself. Of course, an imaginary Gabby Arkwright is constantly in her peripheral vision; mocking her when she smooths down then discards a wrap dress she had hoped might be forgiving; tutting when she slices cold butter into mashed potato; flitting around Nigel, laughing unnecessarily loudly at his every utterance; gazing at him in adoration.

Recently, when they have met socially — at a mutual friend's drinks party — Gabby had barely spoken to them. But Jenny was constantly aware of her presence and had feared their friends and acquaintances could discern the skeins of attraction that bound her to Nigel.

They had left the party early. Later that night, she had heard him making a furtive call on his mobile. He had killed the call when she entered, and she then had to endure the repeated ping of a barrage of text messages.

'Someone wants to get hold of you,' she had cracked.

He had feigned nonchalance. 'I expect one of the girls has sat on their phone by mistake.' And then, with a lie so brazen she wondered if she was imagining things: 'No, it's a wrong number.'

Today, however, she is putting aside her fears about her relationship. Nigel has already completed a ten-mile run so that he can be at home for the festivities and this acceptance of the need to attend a lavish family meal fills her with hope. Despite his reference to her weight, she has overheard her daughters speculate about her having become lighter. Quite unintentionally, her waistbands have grown looser. The stress of her deteriorating relationship and her participation in the competition have meant she has become obsessed with baking — but not with eating. Excessive familiarity with sugar and butter means she no longer craves it. Sometimes, she is too exhausted, or preoccupied, to want to eat much of the food.

But not today.

'This looks gorgeous, Mum.' Lizzie is all smiles as they sit down. 'I haven't eaten like this since Christmas.'

'Me neither. Not sure what the French would make of this: they'd definitely approve of the meat, but perhaps just served with the green beans,' pronounces Emma, dissecting the meal.

'Well, you can always just eat them.' Jenny refuses to be ruffled. 'But I made the parsnips especially for you.'

'Oh no, I'm going to devour it all.' Emma gives the laugh of a slender girl whose metabolism allows her to consume vast amounts of food without losing her litheness.

'What about you, Dad?' she chivvies her father. 'Can you drop the diet for one day? Let yourself be just a little bit bad?'

There is a moment of tense silence. Oh, just let him help himself to whatever passes muster and don't draw attention to the decadence of the food.

Nigel looks up from the lamb he is carving and smiles graciously. 'The Paris marathon's only a week away, Em. So, no, I'm not going to undo everything I've been working on with, what would you call it, a 'blow-out'. Your mother's gone to a huge effort, and I'm sure we're all very grateful, but that doesn't mean I have to be pressurised into eating all this food.'

His words discolour the atmosphere like a dirty paintbrush dipped in a jar of clean water. For once, Emma is momentarily silenced and contents herself with piling carrots on to her plate. Lizzie looks to her mother for reassurance.

Jenny passes her the red wine gravy, her face a study in calmness.

'No one's pressurising you to eat anything, darling. We all understand about the marathon. I just wanted to cook a celebratory meal and people can pick and choose as they like.'

As if to demonstrate, she begins to place beans and carrots on her plate alongside the lamb and its claret-red gravy. But she feels constrained from reaching for her favourite part of the feast, the roast potatoes and parsnips, so aware is she of the need not to antagonise her husband, to pass judgement on his choices, or invite comment on hers.

The girls, meanwhile, cannot help observing what their father has chosen: two slices of lamb, the fat meticulously removed and discarded at the side of the plate, like the innards of a mouse the cat has tortured; a single new potato, naked in its creamy purity; and a pile of green beans and spring greens, proclaiming their health-giving benefits with their aggressive darkness.

'Is that all you're having, Dad?' Emma cannot refrain from passing comment.

'For the moment, yes. Some of us don't feel the need to gorge ourselves.'

The colour rises in Emma's cheeks and Jenny knows she should spring to her defence, to point out that no one is over-indulging — or, if they are, well, isn't that part of the point of a feast.

But Emma is more than capable of sticking up for herself.

'I'm not gorging myself, Dad; I'm just enjoying Mum's cooking. And I'm interested in your diet. Really. I'm amazed that you can put in your distances on such a limited intake of food.'

Nigel continues to chew, his jaw working meticulously on what must be the only tough piece of meat in the joint or a particularly stringy spring green. The delay increases the tension but when he speaks he remains good-humoured; the *pater familias* indulging his youngsters.

'Well, Emma, I'm trying to reduce my body weight so that I can run faster. Elite runners are on average 10 to 15 per cent lighter than non-runners — so, for me, that means being under eleven stone: something I'm still half a stone off which, with the marathon a week away, I won't achieve now.

'For every pound I lose, I will gain two seconds a mile. So, if I lose ten pounds, I'll gain twenty seconds. Over the length of a marathon that means shaving nine minutes off my time.'

Emma ponders this information, finishing her mouthful.

'Well, you've clearly lost a lot, Dad, and that's very commendable. But surely starving yourself, or significantly reducing your calorific intake, this close to the race is dangerous?'

Nigel leans back in his chair, and feigns amusement.

'Surprisingly, I've found no evidence for that.' He smiles and his tone becomes more patronising as he explains his theory. 'Every pound I lose is going to help my race time and give me a new personal best. So I'm going to carry on trying to reduce my weight as much as I can.'

'I just wondered if this was the most effective way.' Emma doesn't know when to stop. 'Aren't you meant to carb load in the week running up to a race? You know you need those complex carbs to give you a slow release of energy. If you dramatically reduce the amount of carbs you eat, you risk lower glycogen stores — and hitting the wall.'

A vein throbs on Nigel's temple. His voice becomes tight.

'With all due respect, I think I know a little more about this subject than you. Yes, I know I need carbohydrates but I will carb load just before the race — not, as you're suggesting, a week before. When I do eat carbs, they will be slow-release complex ones: porridge, for instance. Not roast potatoes and parsnips saturated in fat or the rest of the stodge your mother insists on putting on the table.'

He pushes back his chair and glowers at the assembled women. Jenny, seething at the criticism of her food but wary of antagonising him, looks at her plate, concentrating on chewing a mouthful of food she cannot swallow. Lizzie blinks like a startled rabbit. Only Emma returns his gaze unperturbed. Implacable.

Eventually, he breaks the silence.

'Well, well done for ruining the meal, Emma. There's nothing quite like destroying someone's appetite by analysing what they're eating and criticising their food choices. You need to bear that in mind, my girl.'

He waits for an apology.

'OK, Dad.' Emma assumes a sunniness that

suggests she is innocent of any involvement in the argument. 'Don't let's have a ruined meal, though. Mum's made her Mrs Eaden's trifle, or there's Sachertorte and simnel cake?'

The look on her face could be interpreted as a taunt, though Jenny cannot believe Emma is quite so reckless as to do this. Her father turns puce; the vein on his forehead pronounced as the blood rushes to his face.

'Are you intent on mocking me?' He rises from the table, thrusting back the chair, all pretence at even-handedness abandoned. 'Why the hell would I want cream or chocolate if I can't even eat a roast potato?'

For a moment, his face is that of a petulant child forbidden chocolate at a party and Jenny feels a rush of sympathy. Then he dispels it.

'I'm going out.'

He turns on his heel, banging the dining room door behind him. They wait then hear the front door slam and his feet pound over the gravel. A moment later, his Volvo drives off, wheels screeching in his hurry to depart.

His wife and daughters look at one another.

'Another parsnip, Lizzie?' Emma tries to lighten the mood.

'Oh, Emma, how could you?' Jenny exudes frustration.

Immediately, Lizzie rushes to her side. 'Don't cry, Mum. This is all delicious. It's not your fault Daddy's become obsessive — and so bad-tempered.' She glances at the door as if fearing he can hear her. 'Really, it's not.'

Jenny gives a furious smile and wipes her

watering eyes with an ironed linen napkin. 'It's all right, darling.' She rubs at the mascara smear.

Emma sits mute, pain etched across her face. Slowly she rises, joins her mother and sister and puts her arms around them.

'I'm sorry, Mum.' The apology is heartfelt. 'I didn't mean to antagonise — but really, he's talking bollocks.'

'Emma.'

'I'm sorry, Mum, but he is. He's like some male anorexic. And he's not going to have the power to complete that marathon. Serves him bloody right, too.'

Lizzie gives a guilty snigger. 'Perhaps that will do him good. Make him realise he's being excessive — and bumptious. And make him realise he's bloody lucky to have Mum, and her food.'

Jenny sits there, held by her daughters, taking in the sweet smell of their hair, a smell she found intoxicating when they were children but in which she can now rarely indulge. She wants to hold this moment for ever: the feeling of being cosseted that she experienced in the arms of her own mother, but which has been absent as an adult.

She holds the tableau a moment longer then, self-conscious, forces herself to break it.

'Talking of food, I don't really feel like any more main course — but would either of you like some pudding?'

'You bet!' Emma whirls away from her, clearing plates with an expertise gained from Saturday work as a waitress. Lizzie continues to hold her, but looks up into her face and smiles. Together they stack plates, wipe mats, and clear away cruets with a quiet efficiency born of familiarity with each other and their home.

Only later, when the dishwasher has been stacked and the cakes placed back in their tins — Lizzie cutting a last sliver; Em stealing a last mouthful — do they refer to their errant father.

'Does he often storm off like that, Mum?' Emma broaches the subject.

'Oh, only very rarely,' is Jenny's less than truthful reply.

'Where does he go to?'

'Oh — for a run, I should think.'

'With Gabby Arkwright?'

She stops washing the roasting pan.

'Well, sometimes, yes.'

'He's seeing rather a lot of her, isn't he, Mum?'

'Yes.' And in that syllable there is admission, and a warning to go no further.

'I don't want to talk about it. I don't want a hug.' She flaps the girls away with her wet hands, then turns her back and plunges her reddened fingers back into the washing-up bowl.

Lizzie and Emma stand nonplussed; a childhood certainty dismantled with the most casual of questions. On the kitchen table, the trifle disintegrates, thick whipped cream slumping into a pool of custard, kirsch-soaked cherries and sodden sponge.

Kathleen

The third time it happened, she had half expected it. And yet it had still come as a surprise.

What made it even harder was that she had done everything she could to prevent it. As soon as she had known, at six weeks, that she was pregnant she had taken to her bed, as instructed, and for eight lonely weeks she had lain there, straining to listen, through her open window, to the chatter of shoppers, the click of heels on the King's Road nearby.

'UTTAM!' Mr Caruthers, with his love of acronyms, had been insistent. 'That's the treatment for habitual abortions.'

'UTTAM?' she had queried, not daring to question his other terminology — with its associations of illegality, back streets and murder.

'Up to toilet and meals. Apart from that, you must rest. And rest properly. Let's give this little fellow' — he did not seem to consider that the baby could be a girl — 'the best chance we can, shall we?'

She did not like to say that she had tried to do that all along.

There had been progesterone injections, as well. Administered by Julie, who came weekly to plunge a needle into her buttocks. And an instruction that George should refrain from his husbandly duties.

'No marital relations, I'm afraid. No sexual intercourse.' James Caruthers had been explicit.

'No, no. Of course not.' George, attending the consultation, had flushed puce.

'I know all this is rather a pain' — the doctor had sounded languid — 'but it's imperative for Mrs Eaden — and for baby.'

'What about my book — and my baking?' she had ventured as he had doled out instructions. 'I'm supposed to finish it by May: that's less than four months away.'

He had looked at her sternly.

'I'm afraid building up your baby is your work now.'

She must have looked crestfallen for he softened.

'You can write from your bed but no baking. No getting up and going down to the kitchen, or even sitting at a desk. You must remain propped up in your bed or largely supine. Your baby's health comes first.'

She had smiled at that. She had long since stopped viewing herself as an individual, as someone whose needs should be considered while she got on with the vital work of carrying a baby. She was a vessel whose sole role was to nurture a new life. And she was happy with that. What could be more important than keeping a child safe, especially an unborn one? Nothing was more important, or, for her, it seemed, more difficult.

Still, she was going to write. Propped against four pillows, her notepad perched on her knees, she honed her descriptions of succulent pies and the lightest of pastries. Mrs Jennings helped: baking to her instructions and bringing the results straight up to the bedroom to discuss pitfalls.

'You should be my co-author,' she had half joked as they sampled quiche.

Mrs Jennings had been flattered but dismissive. 'Oh, my dear' — she had finally stopped calling her Mrs Eaden, at Kathleen's insistence — 'I don't have your way with words.'

So the time passed. And, of course, she had visitors. Charlie popped by, incongruous and embarrassed in his sister's bedroom; and Mary came with the children, who brought home-made butter biscuits, painstakingly written cards, and — in Susan's case — her favourite cuddly toy.

During their visits, staying in bed was bearable — even, occasionally, enjoyable when Susan curled alongside her, badgering her for a story; or James perched on the end of the bed and, legs swinging, lined up his latest Matchbox treasures. They improvised an assault course in which the cars raced up and over her legs, in and out of the slippery folds of the eiderdown. Briefly, her bedroom pulsed with childish laughter.

Still, perhaps she had done too much.

Eight weeks later, she had woken to find her thighs drenched in blood, the white cotton sheets bowed under the weight of a crimson puddle. Her womb tightened then throbbed.

For long, slow seconds shock muted her cry. When she finally wept, the sound was alien. Primeval.

She had not known that was the true sound of grief.

Pies & Pastries

It is often said that pastry is the test of a good cook. For, while the ingredients — flour, fat, air, an egg yolk or water to bind — could not be simpler, the baker must practise to acquire the desired lightness of touch.

As in all areas of baking, there are rules to follow; and, here, I may seem more exacting than most. For the basic principles — handling as little as possible; resting between rollings and before baking — are absolutely crucial if you are to attain perfection.

Nowhere is this more evident than when baking blind: a technique that ensures you may pull off the seemingly impossible: a delicately cooked filling surrounded by a crisp pastry case. A leap of faith is required — for you will not know if the pastry is soggy before you release it from the tin — and careful attention to detail. But, get it right, and you will have achieved a culinary Holy Grail.

Having mastered this trick, the clever housewife can produce such treats as crème pâtissière-filled French tartlets and tarte au citron, or reinvent British classics. Try creating a crisp-bottomed treacle tart or using home-made egg custard in a feather-light custard pie.

Of course, you may prefer to bake savoury pies: the ultimate comfort food for a hard-working husband or a gaggle of hungry children. Steak and kidney; chicken and mushroom; rabbit with bacon, cider and cream. There can be no more loving way to greet your family on a cold winter's night; no better meal after a vigorous walk in the country. Just the smell of the buttery shortcrust and succulent meat as they come back home will remind your loved ones of just how much they are adored.

For a lighter meal, a spring luncheon perhaps, try a French savoury tart. Or save your pastry for the pudding and delight your family with a Bramley apple pie, the fruit fluffy and coated with cinnamon, or the ultimate in sophistication — a lemon meringue pie.

Pastry is unforgiving: no other area of baking is as good a test of your skill. But persevere and you are guaranteed to thrill.

Kathleen Eaden: *The Art of Baking* (1966)

22

When making quiche, try to marry flavours and colours that will create an exquisite picture. This is food for women: almost too beautiful to devour. Though quiche can be hearty, my favourite are savoury tartlets: rich with eggs and double cream but sufficiently small to be delicate. You may wish to guzzle large quantities of pastry but moderation is sometimes called for.

Mid-April, and spring has sprung with vigour, determined to spurn the threat of frost that lingers, jubilant at having survived the 'big freeze'. Primroses carpet the ground: gold and white crocuses thrust up, their buds bursting open. Bluebells burst through a soft palette of white, yellow and green.

In the competition kitchen, Karen gathers together ingredients for a quiche and watches as Dan ambles towards her.

'Not for real men,' he quips, gesturing at the recipe.

She had forgotten his wit could be so pedestrian. Not like Oliver's, she thinks.

'So, how's your pastry been going?' He seems gratifyingly reluctant to leave.

'Fine. Though I'm in need of running it off.'

'I'm looking forward to it. Ten K tonight, after a two-pie challenge?'

'If you're sure you're up to it?'

'Oh, I'm up for it.' He grins, and his eyes flicker over her body.

She rewards him with the rare brilliance of a true smile.

★ ★ ★

'The quiche, or savoury tart, was something that Kathleen Eaden championed,' explains Harriet. 'She had eaten it in Paris in the fifties and had loved its simplicity. Served with a well-dressed green salad it was far lighter than the standard diet of meat and two veg she had grown up on in Britain. It took a while for Eaden's to stock them but Mrs Eaden introduces a recipe in her *The Art of Baking*. Not the smoked salmon and watercress she loved — that would have been a step too far for customers — but a hearty bacon and onion one that was her take on a quiche Lorraine and that she hoped would be palatable for husbands. And she served exquisite savoury tartlets at her lunches for her girlfriends or as starters at the more relaxed of her dinner parties.'

'We want you to take Kathleen Eaden's basic recipe as your inspiration and show us what you're capable of,' Dan takes over. 'Salmon and watercress; quiche Lorraine; or perhaps a purely vegetarian option?

'We want to assess your skill at blind baking. Can you give us a crisp case that's perfectly coloured before adding your filling? We don't want pale, insipid pastry — but neither should it be browned beyond golden. We want a sumptuous filling that doesn't leak and we'd like you to aspire to prettiness. Kathleen Eaden was famed for her exquisite use of colour: tiny broccoli florets with flaked salmon; beetroot with white goat's cheese; sliced tomatoes with courgettes; even butternut squash with Stilton. We'd like you to be equally artistic and innovative.'

At the front of the kitchen, Jenny works swiftly: poaching salmon and sautéing shallots for her filling, then beating together eggs and cream. Blind baking should be the means of acquiring a perfect pastry case, she muses. A technique for ensuring the pastry remains crisp and lightly golden; as delicate as the food it holds inside. Yet so much can go wrong. The pastry can bubble up or shrink away from the sides; the filling can seep through the fork pricks; one baker's light golden is another's undercooked. Despite the best of intentions, it doesn't always lead to perfection. If she fails to concentrate, it can be as unpredictable as the rest of life.

Which leads her to Nigel. The Paris marathon is tomorrow and the past week has seen them live increasingly separate lives: Jenny more than matching his running hours with hours labouring over pastry and pies.

A phoney war has been played out in their family home: both fortifying their trenches; neither prepared to throw the first grenade to blow apart their marital limbo. Neither has mentioned Gabby or where he disappeared for ten hours on Easter Sunday. It had been a relief when he set off for Paris four days later.

Like the good wife that she is, though, she is conditioned to be supportive. And so she had sent a text message this morning: a cheery greeting for the day before the race; a good luck message. There has been no reply.

She still feels guilt at not being there to cheer him over the finishing line, and doubt: would Paris in the springtime have been the setting for some sort of reconciliation? She doesn't think so but hates to feel she has not seized every opportunity. They have not made love since December. Did the affair with Gabby start after this, or beforehand? Was it at the Gibsons' Christmas Eve party? Or was he briefly screwing — she winces at the word — them both?

She beats her cream and egg savagely, air bubbles forming then bursting. Was that last, unsatisfactory, coupling spawned of duty or pity? Did it just confirm their incompatibility — both sexual and non-sexual — and send him hurtling back into Gabby's arms?

She has a sudden memory of a hazy afternoon in a cornfield, the wheat crushed by their bodies, stalks scratching her bare skin. Her body was firm and peachy, not yet irrevocably altered by childbirth, and she had a confidence, born of pride at working on a children's ward in a large hospital and knowing she was making a difference. Nigel, young and eager, was clearly smitten. Bathed in stultifying July sunshine, she had watched him trace the curve of her breast with his lips then bite her nipple. She shivers as if savouring such pleasure. Such memories belong to a different time.

The timer pings: high-pitched and insistent, and she brings her tart case out of the oven. It's too pale; it needs a minute longer. She brushes it with egg wash before putting it back in again. She focuses; readjusts the timer; reassembles her ingredients to make more pastry. Just in case her blind baking fails.

To the side of her, Vicki has no such worries. Her quiche Lorraine is to be a masterpiece for she has practised this recipe three times and is fired by the certainty that she is too well-prepared to fail.

'There's quite a lot of your mum in you, you know,' Greg had commented as he had consumed the third quiche the previous evening.

'What do you mean?' she had snapped, though she guessed the answer.

'Well, your perfectionism; your determination; your clear-sightedness. Your teacherly love of preparation. When you want something, you really go for it.'

'Is that supposed to be a compliment?'

'Well, you went for me, didn't you?' He had grinned through a mouthful of crumbling pastry.

Then, more seriously: 'They can be good qualities, yes. They can make you bloody annoying — but they could also make you win this competition. They'll make you go far.'

Claire, however, shares none of her focus. Indeed, she is distracted by the figure of Karen, standing straight in front of her. Dan appears to have been taking an excessive interest in her technique, questioning if the pastry case is sufficiently golden, suggesting she brush it with egg white.

She tells herself to concentrate but his behaviour smarts like a thorn from a bramble, jabbing into soft flesh, marring blackberry's fun. I am envious of *her*, she realises. Of her confidence. She would have known how to behave with Jay. She would have used him — not broken away, confused and embarrassingly tearful. And she would have had him begging for more.

★ ★ ★

At the coffee break, after Karen has presented her winning smoked mackerel and horseradish quiche, garnished with pea shoots and a side salad of baby spinach and watercress, Claire's sense of inadequacy threatens to overwhelm her.

Seeking distraction, she finds Vicki and Mike.

'Didn't you see them?'

Mike is nonplussed; Vicki intrigued.

'Who? What are you talking about?'

'Dan and Karen. He's helping her. I'm sure he is. Advising her on how long she should cook the pastry; suggesting she uses egg white not yolk; hinting she should check the oven.'

'How do you know all this? Weren't you busy with your own quiche?' Mike is bemused. 'I didn't notice anything. Too busy keeping my head down.'

'I thought he was chatting to her quite a lot — but he always does.' Vicki is pensive. 'He always seems quite drawn to her but he can't help her cheat, can he? What's in it for him?'

Claire raises an eyebrow.

'Oh . . . no . . . ' Vicki gives a nervous giggle, excited by the prospect of salacious gossip.

Mike moves off to read a paper, raising his eyes in disbelief.

'There's something going on,' Claire continues. She needs to open up to someone and Vicki, the closest to her in age and the most approachable despite being a bit of a posh girl, seems the most likely confidante.

'How do you know?' Vicki is intrigued.

'They went for a run together on our last weekend here, and there was some pretty heavy flirting going on.'

Vicki snorts with laughter.

'I know it's none of our business but I can't help being a bit jealous. Not at the thought of flirting with Dan Keller, just of having the confidence to do that. I could never do it.'

'Me neither.'

'Really?' Claire is surprised. She had assumed Vicki, resolutely middle-class, determined, focused, beautiful, the clear star of the *Eaden's Monthly* feature as she sees it, could do anything she put her mind to.

'God, no. I'm hopeless. I'm all right standing in front of a class of little kids — though sometimes I have to psyche myself up for that — but I've been terrified in this competition. And I certainly wouldn't dream of joking — let alone flirting — with a judge. I just don't have the self-confidence. The mere thought of doing anything spontaneous, anything risky like that, freaks me out completely. When it comes to them, I really have to steel myself to speak.'

Claire feels stunned.

'I just assumed — you just seem — so *together*. I mean, apart from the Victoria sponge . . . '

'What a disaster!' Vicki laughs. 'I suppose I'm quite good at putting on an act. Teaching forces you to do that. But you try being at home with a small child who doesn't do anything you say all day. That soon saps the confidence out of you. Oh . . . I'm sorry. Perhaps you experienced that with Chloe?'

'Not really. She was always a really good little girl — still is.'

'Lucky you! Well, that's a testament to your good parenting. Perhaps that's why you always seem strong.'

'Who, me?'

'Yes, you. Just look at what you've achieved.'

Claire gives a laugh, embarrassed and incredulous.

'Like what?'

'Bringing up a child on your own. From what — eighteen? Such a young age.'

'I just had to get on with it. That's life, isn't it? And I had my mum's support.'

'But not your partner's, from what you said?'

'Well, no. He was worse than useless.' She wonders whether she should open up to Vicki. 'Still sniffing around a bit, to be honest. Don't know if I should give it another go.'

'Oh, Claire, you mustn't.' Vicki looks horrified. 'I know it's none of my business but I really wouldn't. I always think you have to leave bad mistakes behind and not be held back by them. Just try to move on. Onwards and upwards. Not that I'm very good at it, myself.'

For a moment, she looks sad as if remembering a particular incident. Then she gives herself a little shake and looks kindly at Claire.

'Going back to what I said about you achieving so much, I don't think I could have coped with being a teenage mum. Well, no, I know I couldn't. I was still a child myself: far too emotionally needy, far too angry with my own mum, far too immature to have been responsible for anyone but me.'

Claire looks at her in surprise. The conversation has taken a shift, and Vicki sounds as if she might be speaking from experience.

For a moment, she looks as if she is about to launch into a confession. Then she smiles.

'We'd better get back. They'll be starting without us.'

And the moment is gone.

Kathleen

She is back in James Caruthers' consulting rooms, George beside her, as the gynaecologist details his treatment plan.

The day before she had undergone yet another internal examination under general anaesthetic and this time the doctor had inserted metal dilators inside her to assess what he persists in calling the competence of her cervix. She suspects she is incompetent.

Thankfully, he comes straight to the point.

'As we suspected, there was no resistance before insertion of a Hagar 8 dilator and that leads me to diagnose incompetence of the cervix.'

'And that means, doctor?' George, a man who fought as a teenager in the war and commands silence in the boardroom, looks petrified at the diagnosis.

'It means Mrs Eaden's cervix is abnormally weak. It dilates — opens up — before the baby reaches full term which accounts for the habitual abortion.'

She wishes he would not keep using that term.

'Is there anything I can do?' Her voice is controlled though her insides plummet.

'Well, yes. A fairly modern, and, because of its novelty, somewhat controversial technique: the McDonald suture.'

The doctor looks more animated than she has ever seen. 'We can insert a stitch at the neck of the cervix, seven or eight weeks into the next pregnancy and then remove it once baby has reached an age at which it can be born — at around thirty-six weeks.'

'And will it work?' She surprises herself with her scepticism but this third loss has made her harder, as if the kernel of hope she had managed to nurture throughout this last pregnancy has shrivelled and turned into dust.

He raises his hands, palms up.

'Mrs Eaden, obstetrics and gynaecology is a tricky business and this procedure is fairly new. But I am confident that with this, enforced bed rest and the other measures we have discussed — weekly progesterone injections and, ahem, the ban on sexual intercourse — we will give any future baby the very best chance of life.'

23

If you bake as assiduously as me, you may need to exercise. A slab of cake can be offset by a leisurely walk or a swim at a gentle pace.

It is a less picturesque night than their earlier meeting. Cloud half obscures the moon and snuffs out the weaker stars though Venus shines bright. The two figures, sleek in running garb, have no idea they are being observed as they set out from the front entrance of Bradley Hall for their ten-K run, just before six thirty. Bouncing lightly on the forecourt before they sprint off, both runners are studies in self-absorption. It would not occur to them that they are being spied on from separate rooms in the house.

They begin by heading off as before, down the stately drive sweeping away from the mansion, and then around the perimeter of the grounds, running clockwise this time, towards a more substantial wood. The terrain becomes harder, the twigs and bark of a forest floor mingling with rotten leaves, obscuring the odd tree root.

'It's too uneven to run through this,' Dan decides, leading them back out again. 'Let's head back to the grass.'

Running over softer ground, there is an automatic spring to their step, though the grass is uneven and tufty, kept down by a flock of sheep and periodically smeared with dried cow pats.

'This feels like proper cross-country.'

'Bet you excelled at that, as a girl.'

Karen shakes her head, recalling the concrete of her urban school playground, the shards of glass glinting on the tarmac, the fetid litter bins, the graffiti on the walls. A playground where she learned to trade herself for cigarettes, and use the cigarettes to stave off hunger.

'Not that kind of school.'

Her breathing remains measured. The hour-long runs she has put in at the gym, each day for the last fortnight, are paying off. Her cheeks glow but with exhilaration rather than exertion. To his surprise, Dan begins to trail behind.

She takes the lead and wonders yet again if she should make a move, or whether she should rely on him to do so. She decides on the latter. Despite her determination to take the upper hand, she feels uncharacteristically vulnerable. She is not used to rejection but she senses that, were he to spurn her, she wouldn't take it well.

Karen glances over her shoulder. He is chasing her now. She feels nervous, like a teenage girl flooded with desire yet fearful of what she is about to get into. A sickening, delicious feeling; this feeling of being scared — of being alive.

I felt like this once with Oliver, she thinks. In that sweaty West End club as I snared my prize, my banker. And later, once I got to know him. Before marriage; before children; before I realised that work was his real passion — the thing that always had to come first.

Or was that fair? Was he alone to blame for the distance between us? Didn't I push him away, certainly once we'd had the kids and I wanted to do everything my way, but, in truth, much earlier: almost from the very start?

A memory crowds her head: the bathroom of their honeymoon suite in Rome, moonlight streaming through the window, and the look of incomprehension on her husband's face. He had found her again eight months later, while skiing in Val d'Isère, and this time had begged her to see a psychotherapist. He'd even made the appointment. Of course, she hadn't kept it but had made sure he never again caught her. She became more and more controlled, more distant, more private. Life — children, exercise, meals — were run with rigorous organisation. And passion, warmth, love, humour: all of these ebbed slowly away.

Dan is closing in now. She maintains her pace, letting her sorrow ease away from her, steadying her breathing.

'Have you been practising?' he asks as he catches her up.

'My tarte au citron? But of course. Just wait till you taste my tarte tatin.'

'I meant the running.' He is exasperated. 'You seem to be getting faster.'

'Whatever gave you that idea?' Karen ups her speed and runs off. Blood gallops in her head; she is sure her heartbeat is audible. She begins to sprint; pushing her body to its extreme, exhilarated by her power — physical and sexual.

He is in pursuit now, chasing her down a

gentle incline that swiftly becomes far steeper than she anticipated. Her foot catches in a hidden rabbit hole and jolts her. She falls, arms raised to her head as she tumbles, twisting three times before she rolls to a stop.

In a second, he is by her.

'Are you OK? Are you all right? You haven't twisted it, have you?'

Her heart judders but she feels shock at the fall, not pain. How could she have been so stupid? Jake's jibe rings in her head: *You're fooling no one.*

Dan's face is masked with panic: does he fear their meeting being exposed or is he just concerned for her? Compassion and shock jostle.

I look old, she thinks. I'm older than he thought.

'I'm OK. Really. It's not twisted. I'm just a bit shaken.'

She tries to put some weight on the ankle, and avoids wincing.

Her voice becomes more abrasive.

'Help me up, won't you? I said I was fine.'

He places firm arms around her back. With some effort, she resists softening into them; she keeps her body ramrod straight; her manner formal.

'Thank you. Now, let's get back.'

'If you're sure . . . ' But she is off, tentative at first but increasing her pace as they hit even ground and she becomes more sure-footed. A mantra pounds through her head: I'm fooling no one; I'm fooling no one; I'm fooling no one; I'm fooling no one.

251

I'm fooling no one at all.

He trails behind as if chastened by her curt tone and fearful of offending her. As they sweep on to the gravel, he calls out: 'Can I check on you later? I'd like to check you're OK . . . I mean, I'd like to see you.'

She glances at him, unsure of what to make of this admission: is he expressing concern for a woman who has injured herself, or something more ambiguous? She cannot read words shorn of innuendo; freed from the artifice of flirtation.

Karen feels suddenly weary. She craves a hot bath and then the comfort of being held. The thought shocks her. She is not a cuddly person. She craves sex — not affection.

She takes in his open face: unexpectedly gentle.

'All right . . . I'd like that,' she says.

24

A tarte au citron is the most disarming of desserts: in small quantities, sharp and refreshing and yet, at heart, hugely rich. The citrus cuts through a heavy meal but then, suddenly, you are sated. Unable to manage another mouthful. The clever hostess serves only a sliver of it.

'Dan?'

Harriet's voice, as she spies him watching Karen jog up the central staircase, is that of a disappointed headmistress.

'Could I have a word if you have a moment?'

She moves aside from the doorway of the lounge where she has been waiting, gesturing that he should enter, and closes the oak door.

He stands before her; the Platonic ideal of a desirable man, made concrete. She takes in the dark curls softened by beads of sweat; the glow of his face; his broad chest. He is twenty years younger than her and has a lot to learn about celebrity. She is not sure, though, if he will listen to her.

'It's a little delicate.' She pauses to check if he knows what she's talking about and pats her hair, somewhat nervously. 'You know me. I'm hardly censorious . . . but do you think it appropriate to go running with a contestant — someone whose work you judge?'

He sighs.

'It looks bad, Dan. And as we both know in this game, appearances are everything. Your jaunt may have been entirely innocent but you need to make absolutely sure it looks it — and that it remains that way.'

'We only went for a run,' he begins.

'Oh, Dan. You must think I was born yesterday.' She looks at him as if he were a pupil risking expulsion about whom she cannot help caring.

'If this got out, the *Daily Mail* would have a field day. The brand, and your image, would be tarnished. Eaden's would drop you like a shot and that would be such a loss. You've such a promising career.'

She smiles and pats her hair again. 'I'm not being entirely altruistic. We're a good team; we work well together. You've refreshed me. Given this old boot a bit more career longevity.'

She grimaces at the admission. 'Please, Dan, just stop whatever it is you've started.'

★   ★   ★

It is not until nearly midnight that Karen accepts he has taken the coward's way out and will not come to her. In the intervening four hours she has cosseted herself: taking a languorous bath, silky with essential oils; slathering herself with body lotion; tending to her ankle, whose purple bloom is beginning to appear. She has pulled on sleek black underwear under a delicate cashmere hoodie and Pilates bottoms, tweezed her eyebrows and reapplied her make-up. Her feet, she has checked, are exquisite: the nails professionally painted in Chanel's appropriately named Vamp, and a silver toe ring hinting at a rebellious streak.

Easy-listening ballads play on her iPod. Tracks she knows are hardly hip but which she cannot help but relax to. David Gray, Katie Melua, Dido, James Blunt. A few soul classics are incongruously interspersed: Marvin Gaye begins to croon about getting it on. She jabs the iPod, pressing the forward arrow, seeking to silence him.

For the first hour she is busy with preparation; for the next, giddy with anticipation. She flicks through her copy of *Vogue*, then turns to *OK!* seeking distraction in inanity but the identikit smiles of the D-list celebrities grate. She wonders how many of the relationships celebrated here in exclusive, eight-page glossy photo shoots will last a year. For a moment, she thinks of Oliver. Balding, cerebral, prosperous but still a man whose good opinion — she no longer expects affection — she craves. Did they ever look at one another with the adoration that perky little actress is feigning? She is pretty sure he once did. Before Rome, before Val d'Isère and, perhaps, for a little while after. As for her, she has never done adoration.

Infatuation she can do though. An antidote to an absence of love. A heady drug that gives her a rush; confirms her vitality and vibrancy. All-consuming and immediate, it is the reason she books the same Eaden's delivery slot each week: Ryan, tall, tattooed and barely twenty and hers from 11 a.m. to noon on Wednesdays; the reason she swam when Jamie, a mere twenty-two and still boyishly beautiful, was on his lifeguard shift.

She had thought she had had it bad then, but with Dan her infatuation has reached a new level: a groin-juddering, heart-thumping obsession that dictates her actions — what she wears; what she bakes; what she says — and dominates her thoughts. It is not just his beauty, not just his charisma. It is the fact that the attraction seems mutual. Apparently reciprocated, her infatuation fuels her. She believes herself to be as beautiful and charismatic as him; she believes herself to be worthy of his desire.

So where is he? In the third hour, anticipation turns to trepidation. Perhaps he is waiting until the coast is clear; until he is less likely to stumble upon the other contestants; until it is so late that his intentions — turning up at her bedroom in the night — are sufficiently unambiguous. Perhaps he got caught up in a discussion with Harriet and was unable to sneak away. Or perhaps he has had second thoughts.

In the fourth hour, trepidation turns to despair — and then self-flagellation. How could she have been so stupid as to have thought she was being anything other than played? She looks at her face in the mirror: the exhaustion of a hard day's work and the shock of her fall perceptible under her eyes despite a generous application of Touche Éclat. *You're fooling no one, Ma.* She sees her forty-seven years. How could she have believed he wouldn't notice them?

256

As the fourth hour passes, she knows what she must do. She pulls on ballet pumps and a long cashmere cardigan and leaves the room, walking lightly but purposefully towards the competition kitchen. To her surprise, it is open. A shaft of light filters from the corridor, illuminating her way as she slips into the room and finds her work station. She turns to the nearest fridge and opens the door, bathing her face in the unearthly glow. Quickly, she reaches in and grabs what she was looking for.

Her tarte au citron has been tested by the judges but is still more than half complete. She plunges a knife in and cuts a sliver; then immediately a second, larger, slice and a third. The triangles sit quivering in the gloaming. The fluorescent yellow filling wobbling; tantalising her. 'Eat me, eat me.' She takes a breath, then obliges.

Crouched on the floor, shielded by work stations, she crams the first slice into her mouth, barely tasting the tart citrus fruit, the buttery pastry. Then comes the second, more substantial piece, closely followed by the third. Her mouth fills with cloying softness cut through with sharpness. Her stomach — empty since a small chicken salad at lunchtime — feels immediately bloated.

She is tempted to continue cutting, chipping away at the semicircle until there is only a third then a quarter then an eighth left but her self-loathing is already overwhelming. She thrusts the plate back in the fridge; rinses and dries the knife; buries it in the drawer. Then she

257

slips from the room, almost running now in her desire to be rid of her taut belly. She needs to purge herself of the gelatinous mass lining her stomach, or making its way to it, just as she needs to purge herself of her self-disgust.

Later, this is the only explanation she can give for using the toilets off the kitchen rather than running the two flights up to her room. Immediacy — the fear that she will not be able to rid herself of the food before it hits her stomach — appears more important than privacy. The stalls are empty. She enters one, locks the door, ties back her hair and, toilet paper in hand, lifts the seat.

With her clean, right hand, she puts her fingers to the back of her throat, finds her gagging reflex and pushes. A spurt of vomit spews into her mouth. She makes herself press again, and unleashes a torrent. She rocks back on her heels then forces herself to push a third time, lurching to the toilet bowl to release the bile. Her throat burns and she is spent. Briefly, she rests her head against the cool of the toilet wall before the dangling toilet roll and sweet stench of urine fill her with repulsion. She wipes her mouth with a piece of paper, flushes, checks the vomit has cleared, and then unlocks the door.

Claire is waiting by the sinks, her eyes wide as she sees that it is Karen who emerges.

It is a shock for them both.

'How long have you been here?' Karen is peremptory.

'Uh . . . I've just come in. Bit of a late night in

the bar. Stupid really. I just got chatting to Mike for too long. Then I felt hungry so thought I'd sneak to the kitchen.' She is rambling.

The question remains unsaid.

'Are you OK?' Claire ventures.

'Why wouldn't I be?' Karen turns away from her, presses the soap dispenser with the back of her hand, lathers suds under running water.

'You just . . . you just sounded as if you might be feeling a bit poorly.' She meets Karen's gaze in the mirror but there is concern not rancour in the look she gives.

'Nothing gets past you, does it, Claire?' Karen gives a sharp laugh as she dries her hands then turns to face her. 'To be honest, I think I've got a touch of food poisoning. I've a really gyppy tummy.'

She pauses, pained to make a request but realising she needs to. 'Please don't mention it to the others, will you? I'm sure I wouldn't be able to compete, for health and safety reasons, if they knew about this.'

'No, of course not . . . But are you sure you're OK to carry on?'

'Of course I am. It's a bit of food poisoning. Nothing contagious. I'm not going to die of it.' She is brisk. 'Nothing I can't get over by drinking plenty of water and having a good sleep.'

She brushes past the younger woman but holds open the door, gesturing that they should both leave.

Claire takes it but watches as Karen walks along the corridor, her head held high though her colour is pale.

Food poisoning? She must think I'm stupid. Yet the alternative is more incredible. She has a sharp recollection of the toilets at her comprehensive; the stench of disinfectant; the shine of toilet paper; and Hazel Adams, the class fatty, making herself sick.

Is that what was going on there? She makes her own way to bed, a knot of sorrow pressing in her chest like a granite pebble: her mind trying to process what she has just seen.

Kathleen

Still no baby, there is still no baby. As spring bursts into summer and summer melts into autumn, she no longer wants to play this exhausting game.

At first she had blamed the writing. The day after her loss, she had ripped up the entire section on pies and pastries and stuffed it in the drawing room hearth. The flames had licked the cream sheets of paper then gobbled them up in one greedy whoosh and she had felt nothing but relief.

George had been somewhat dismayed.

'But all that work ... You were two-thirds done.'

'And I'm not going to finish it,' she had insisted, not minding that she sounded melodramatic. 'Is that all that matters, George, that I write this book? I couldn't include those recipes. They feel tainted.'

'That's ridiculous.'

'No it isn't. Not to me.'

The deadline is pushed back indefinitely and George refrains from commenting. Nor does he complain when, three months after her loss, she is still pulling out of store openings. She fears she is not doing her bit for their business. For Eaden's. And yet, selfishly, she does not care.

261

The columns keep coming, delighting the readers of *Home Magazine* who have no idea of her anguish. She finds she is writing about the most frivolous of puddings: meringues, baked Alaskas, croquembouche, vacherin. Nothing sustaining, as recommended by Mr Caruthers, and nothing to do with pastry.

Her prose sparkles, as bright as beads of caster sugar, as brittle as spun caramel. And yet she feels it is soulless. She knows she is writing entirely from the head.

If she can dazzle in print, in life she is increasingly sombre; retreating into herself and away from George.

She flinches from his touch now. There can be no habitual abortion, as James Caruthers insists on referring to it, if there is no sexual intercourse. And yet intercourse is required if she is to chance another pregnancy. Intercourse and a massive leap of faith.

In September she decamps to Bradley Hall, and the move to the countryside, and her once vulgar house, seems to free her. The estate is fecund. Trees drip fruit; the kitchen garden provides limitless squash, plums and pears.

Even the grass yields treasures: wild mushrooms, dark-gilled and dewy, and conkers, fat and burnished; shiny like chestnut leather. She caresses them like prayer beads as she picks up apples and roots out acorns; feet scuffing through leaves as she circles the grounds.

With Mrs Jennings struggling to cope with this autumn bounty, it seems almost immoral not to return to the kitchen. The cook smiles and

George breathes a deep sigh of relief.

One Saturday, he slaps a brace of rabbits on the scullery table.

'And what am I supposed to do with these?' She strokes the short brown fur and the softer white belly, and thinks of Peter Rabbit.

'Make a pie,' George, flushed at playing the country landowner, challenges her.

And so she does, creating the most flavoursome concoction of bacon, shallots, carrots, thyme and rabbit, simmered in stock and cider and finished with cream.

She serves it with purple sprouting broccoli from the garden, and finds, at the end of the meal, that not only has she cleared her plate for the first time since March, when she lost her baby, but that she is smiling.

'Kathleen?' George looks as if he is wondering if he can smile too.

'George?' And for the first time in months there is a hint of humour in her voice, the suggestion, however tentative, of a tease.

For a moment, she is the Kathleen who spied him at the Carltons' dinner dance and went after him: this older man, who offered both the chance of rebellion — with his humble roots initially scandalising her mother — and the ultimate stability.

She looks at him — this man who has been unable to ease or even understand the full extent of her sorrow but who is nevertheless her rock: the person she relies on — and burrows herself deep into his arms.

25

I am a firm believer in the importance of breakfast. Not a fry-up or even going to work on an egg, but a slice of home-made toast spread with blackcurrant jam and a cup of Earl Grey. This is my minimum requirement, without which I am liable to be crotchety. However modest, a breakfast balances your blood sugars and sets you up for the day.

Eight hours later, the morning of the Paris marathon and Jenny is perched on the edge of her bed, brow furrowed in concentration, as she struggles to construct the right text. Her fingers fumble on the screen as she tries to get the balance right: to send a message to Nigel that is supportive but in no way imposes expectations. She ends up being girlish. 'The very best of luck! Thinking of you, my darling!' She cringes the moment she sends it. Why be so effusive? Why call him darling? She no longer thinks of him as her darling.

When no reply is forthcoming — she hadn't expected one, but still she hoped for it — she sends one to Emma, pulling the umbilical cord tight: 'Thinking of Dad and wishing him all the best. Please give him a hug from me — and one to you of course!'

Emma responds quickly. 'Huge excitement here. He's very pepped up and hoping for a good personal best. Hope the baking competition's going well. Thinking of you too! Xxx'

All is well in the world. Jenny allows herself a small smile, gratified that her daughter is acknowledging the importance of this competition to her. Then a second message pings, and her happiness dissolves like sugar gently heated with water.

'Just seen Gabby Arkwright. Very over-friendly. Going to watch with me as Peter's running too.'

A chill runs through her as she tries to decode the message and Emma's reason for sending it. Is she being naive? Is Gabby's husband really in Paris? Why hadn't Nigel mentioned this? She does not need to ask.

'How nice. Please call me if you have a minute,' she texts, then tries Emma's number, as frenzied as a jilted lover. It rings out: an unfamiliar, nasal French beep. She leaves a message: her voice shaking with false cheeriness; the words — 'Em, when you have a minute, please could you call?' — conveying nothing, and everything.

She is too jittery to eat much breakfast. A pot of Earl Grey is swapped for a black coffee; a sliver of cold toast smeared with butter and blackcurrant jam is discarded. Food, for so long a great comfort, provides no succour today.

'Jenny? Do you mind if I join you?' Smiling from the next table, Vicki looks as if she wants to intervene. She picks up her cup of white coffee and hovers, as if reluctant to pull out a chair until she is sure it is OK.

'Oh, of course.' Jenny tells herself to pull herself together; to welcome the intrusion. She forces a smile. 'How are you this morning?'

'Oh, I'm good, thank you — and you?'

'Me?' She gives the automatic answer: 'Oh, I'm fine.'

'Really?'

'No, not really.' She grimaces at trying to fool her. Vicki's kindness makes her falter. 'Not really at all.'

'Can I get you something nicer to eat?'

Jenny demurs, and Vicki bustles about, selecting the choicest morsels from the buffet: a couple of warm pains aux raisins, some fresh granary bread and a cold pat of butter, christened with a pearl of water; a bowl of Greek yoghurt; a bunch of red grapes.

'I'm not really hungry.'

'I can see that,' says Vicki. She butters the thick bread and spreads jam; cuts it into four triangles; gestures that she should take one, treating her, Jenny can't help thinking, much as she might her little one — what was he called: Alfie? 'But I always think that, if you're feeling a bit down, you need to eat.'

Jenny forces herself to take a mouthful, then a second. The bread, coating the roof of her mouth, tastes of nothing. The jam is good, though: fat apricot halves coated in a thick golden syrup that gleams.

'Better than the blackcurrant,' Vicki says, nodding at the discarded dry toast. 'Oh, wait just a minute and I'll tidy that away.'

She bobs up again, removing all evidence of the rejected breakfast, and returns with a bowl of berries.

'Have you tried this compote? Here, have a bit with some Greek yoghurt . . . You're sure? Oh, well, I might have to sample it.' Vicki winks as she plunges her spoon into the blackberries, deep juice spilling over the mounds of whiteness. For a moment, they eat.

Is she going to question me, wonders Jenny, and, if so, can I be honest? For a moment, she considers confiding in her about Gabby and Nigel — and just as quickly dismisses the idea. This lovely young woman has probably only been married for what, five years? Long enough to know that it's not all hearts and flowers but not long enough, she hopes, to understand that a husband might stray.

'So . . . Is there anything I can help with? Anything you'd like to talk about?'

Vicki looks embarrassed to be asking and Jenny suspects she is rarely this direct.

The younger woman shrugs. 'It's all right. You can tell me to mind my own business. I just thought you looked as if you could do with offloading a bit.'

'Am I really that transparent?' Despite herself, Jenny smiles.

Vicki nods.

'Gosh . . . How embarrassing. My girls always say they can read me.'

Vicki smiles once more, sips her coffee, and quietly waits.

Unable to articulate the real cause of her anxiety, Jenny reaches for a more general sense of unease. 'Well, I suppose that — as usual — I'm just feeling guilty. My husband's in Paris, running the marathon this weekend, and I feel I should be there to support him. It feels hugely self-indulgent to be here, making *pastry*, when he's got that going on.'

'What about him? Why isn't he here to support you?'

'Oh, well, it doesn't really work like that . . . ' Her voice trails away, incapable of explaining the balance of power wrought over a quarter of a century of marriage and now firmly tipped in Nigel's favour. She takes another bite of bread to avoid having to talk.

'If you don't mind me saying' — Vicki watches her carefully — 'I don't think you've anything to feel guilty about. I know it's something we're good at: I feel guilty every minute I'm not with Alfie, every time I dump him on my friend Ali, or my mum, or Greg, and yet I know it's a complete waste of time.

'You're fantastic at baking. Head and shoulders above the rest of us, though I hate to admit that! And you deserve to be here, showing off what you can do every bit as much as your husband deserves to be running a marathon. Perhaps you've even more reason. He's not going to win it, is he?' She looks at Jenny for confirmation.

Jenny shakes her head, emphatic.

'Well, then. Unless Karen or I improve immensely, you could — you *should* — win this. And, then, he should be cheering you on — supporting you in that way.'

'Oh — I'm not sure that's going to happen.' Jenny's face clouds over and, for one dreadful

268

moment, she thinks she is going to start crying.

'Well, he should be,' Vicki says staunchly. 'Please don't cry. What I'm trying to say is that you could win this hands down. You have real talent and you deserve to shine every bit as much as Claire, or Karen or me.'

'Thank you,' Jenny manages to utter. 'But I'm not sure that's true.'

'It is!' Vicki's voice rises in frustration. 'Of course it is. But you won't win this if you don't recognise that and if you persist in this . . . it's more than self-deprecation . . . this self-doubt. You have to believe in yourself. Believe you can do this.'

She pauses. 'Pep talk over. I'm sorry. I don't mean to be sharp. I just think you're fantastic — we all do — and it's about time you realised it.'

She gulps her coffee and puts the cup back on the saucer with a decisive chink. For a moment, Jenny thinks she has offended her.

'I wish I shared your confidence.'

To her shock, she sounds almost bolshie. She looks at Vicki, alarmed: she has just complimented her and she has dismissed it.

'Well, you should. You're the best,' Vicki says simply.

Her eyes are still on her face and Jenny thinks: I wouldn't want to be in her bad books as one of her pupils. For all her warmth, there is a steeliness about her: she is someone with resilience and strength.

Vicki seems to be reading her mind, for she reaches a hand out across the tablecloth.

269

Surprised, Jenny takes the warm fingers and squeezes them, grateful that the whole, uncomfortable conversation can be swept away.

But Vicki isn't finished.

'Jenny . . . I don't know if your husband appreciates how fantastic you are. But you look a little bit . . . cowed, if I can say that? And, here, among us, there's really no need.'

Jenny looks down at her plate and focuses on the floral pattern, willing the welling tears to disperse; embarrassed to admit that Nigel is less than supportive.

'Thank you,' she hears herself choke.

'Jenny . . . '

'Thank you,' she repeats, and manages a watery smile. 'You've been very kind.'

'It's not about being kind.' Vicki sounds frustrated again. 'Look, I don't want to intrude — or upset you. And I won't go on about this again but please hear what I'm saying.' Her voice softens and she sounds contrite. 'That you shine. That none of us can match you.'

Jenny looks at her and smiles with just a hint of conviction. 'Yes, I can see that . . . Thank you, yes.'

★　★　★

'Mike.'

Claire is skulking in the entrance hall waiting to buttonhole the only man in the competition as he walks back from breakfast.

'Claire?' His face lightens. 'What's with the cloak and dagger stuff?'

She pulls him into the lounge, checking as she does so that no one notices them.

'Come in a bit further. No, don't close the door! That will look suspicious.'

'Claire.' He takes hold of her shoulders. 'What's going on?'

She takes a breath, perches her bottom on the back of a sofa and lets the words flood out of her. Guilt, anxiety, shame: a jumble of emotions cascades so that he can make little sense of it all.

'Whoa. Slow down. Start from the beginning.' He puts a large hand to the side of each of her upper arms, pats her ineffectually then looks embarrassed by what he is doing.

'Sorry. I didn't mean to . . . You just need to start slowly, and calm down.'

And so the story comes out. How she popped into the toilet after their drink the previous night and heard someone retching when she entered.

'It was Karen. She said it was food poisoning.'

'And you don't think it was?'

She shakes her head. 'She was so defensive — like she was hiding something.' She spits out her fear. 'There was this girl at school. Used to stick her fingers down her throat the whole time . . . '

'Bulimia.'

'Yeah, that's what it's called. I think that's what Karen was doing.'

Her slight shoulders hunker around her and her head dips as if she wishes she could roll into the foetal position. When she looks up, her face is bleak with anxiety.

'I feel so guilty even telling you this. Like I'm

betraying her or something because she clearly didn't want me to know about it. But I needed to confide in someone because the stupid thing is, I was so jealous of her.'

Her shoulders hunch further.

'She seemed so glamorous and confident and everything. But I've just been a bitch, haven't I? All this time I've been . . . I don't know, in awe of her. And it turns out she was even more fucked up than the rest of us put together.'

He wants to put his arms around her, to give her a bear hug of reassurance as he would one of his children. But she is not his child and his feelings aren't purely protective, if he is honest. He contents himself with sitting alongside her, putting an arm around her slight shoulders. She is so attractive, he thinks with a jolt, as he takes in the curve of her cheekbone, the faint lines creasing from her eyes, her wide mouth, now pinched with anxiety. Her hair smells of citrus shampoo.

'First of all,' he begins, 'there's nothing for you to feel guilty about. If Karen has had a bulimic episode then it's probably occurred before. It'll be ingrained — a problem that's perhaps been going on for years. There's nothing you could have done to predict it — or to prevent it. I'm afraid you're not that powerful.'

She half laughs but the sound catches in her throat.

'Second, you being a bit envious of her — though God knows why you would be — bears no relevance to this. I bet she wasn't even aware you felt like that. And, even if she

272

was, it won't have offended her. She may even have been flattered.'

The half laugh comes again — and with it a look of tentative relief.

'Thank you.' She wipes away a tear with the back of her hand; sniffs to stop a bubble of snot.

'Here.'

He passes her a clean tissue.

'Thanks.' She blows her nose loudly then tries a joke. 'You're just as prepared as any mum.'

'I'm getting there. Done the poo on my arm bit; now I'm doing the girlie pep talks. Going to be completely unsexed at this rate.'

'Really?' She laughs despite herself, more at the reference to the poo than his neutering though, of course, he doesn't know this. He blushes and withdraws his arm from her shoulders, suddenly self-conscious.

They sit in awkward silence, his hip almost touching hers, the distance between them a centimetre. She must think I'm so straight, so sensible, he thinks.

'Well, thank you for making me feel a bit less of a bitch — though I still do, of course. Mostly, I just feel so terribly sad for her: that she feels like that. I won't be able to see her in the same way.'

'Perhaps that's a good thing.' Mike relaxes into the space next to her, the edge of his trousers touching her thigh now. 'Few of us are as straightforward as we first appear.'

26

The perfect French baguette should have a crisp crust and an airy crumb. It should give a satisfying crunch and then melt into nothingness. Serve warm, if possible, and fresh. This bread is deceptive: outwardly strong yet, inside, as soft as air.

Paris, Avenue Foch. A glorious spring morning, sun searing through skies of cerulean blue.

The marathon has been going for nearly four hours now and Emma is getting impatient as she is jostled on either side of her spot near the finishing line. Excitement at the thought of seeing her father streak past has long since been tempered by boredom at standing in the same position. The woman to her left — chic, French, impervious — steps on her foot: 'Pardon, désolée . . . ' Her eyes behind her shades are vacant. Someone behind her shoves, repeatedly. She has drunk so much water she is now bursting for the loo.

She knows she should be feeling heady on the atmosphere but there is only so much hysteria she can manufacture after being rammed in the same position for hours. Her sporadic cheers — for the first woman to cross the line; for an elderly albeit clearly fit competitor — feel self-conscious. Perhaps she is too British for this, too inhibited, or too lonely. She needs a group of friends — and, ideally, some alcohol — to get in a suitably celebratory mood.

Besides, her excitement is tempered by an unfamiliar sense of guilt: guilt at giving her mother a hard time for not attending, and guilt at standing here, nuzzled against Gabby Arkwright. For Emma, though lonely, is not alone. Gabby, who it transpired is staying in the same hotel as her and Nigel, has attached herself to Emma like a new, inappropriately old, best friend, drawing on fifteen-year-old memories of the days when Emma would play with her hideous son, Robert.

'You don't mind, do you, Em?' she had asked, and Emma had baulked at her using the name only applied by her sisters and parents. 'It makes sense our palling up. Peter's going to take hours to make the finish so it would be lovely to wait with you and catch up on old times, and I'd love to cheer on your dad.'

'Actually, no, Gabby. I don't want to wait with you because I can't bear the way in which you flirt with my father and the effect this is having on my mother,' is what she wants to tell her. Instead, good manners, the result of years of reminders from Jenny and an expensive education, take over. 'No, of course not,' she had lied, her courtesy to an old family friend automatic. 'That makes perfect sense. A great plan.'

Now, however, she is regretting not speaking her mind — just as she would to her family and friends, with whom familiarity has bred honesty. Every muscle in her body feels taut as she tries to keep her body away from Gabby, without appearing to do so.

Ever tactile, Gabby misinterprets her distance for concern at not invading her personal space. She gives Emma's arm a little squeeze of reassurance, and cosies up with a conspiratorial grin.

'Your dad's done so well in his training. He deserves a PB of around three hours forty.' She appears to be speaking a different language; one in which Emma, the linguist, has no hope of being proficient. 'His weight loss has been extraordinary and his stamina is amazing.'

Emma shoots her a sharp look, attuned to innuendo, but Gabby seems impervious.

'Peter, on the other hand, has been sluggish. I kept telling him: 'You're not going to get a PB below four hours unless you put in more miles — and, frankly, unless you get that, it's barely worth entering.' But, of course, he didn't listen. Quite honestly, I doubt whether his heart's really in it at all.'

'Why did he enter then?' Emma is aware some response is required, and hearing about Peter's failings is preferable to listening to Robert's successes.

'God knows. Force of habit, perhaps. He's been doing marathons for years. Residual competitiveness? He needs to compete against me at something! A desire to keep his paunch in check? Well, he's barely done that.' She gives a sardonic laugh. 'I can't fathom him out.'

There is a brief silence while Emma wonders whether she is meant to offer reassurance or comment on the state of their marriage, but Gabby sails on, oblivious. 'Your father, however, has shown steadfast determination. He's been a delight to train with. He knows what he wants, and he goes and gets it.' She gives Emma's arm another little squeeze.

Emma feels bleak. She wants to extricate her arm but knows that to do this would be pointed; and draw attention to Gabby's confidences. Yet not to do so feels increasingly disloyal to Jenny.

'You sound like you've been training quite a bit with Dad?'

'Three times a week. He's my protégé. I'm going to get him into triathlons next. He tells me he's a good swimmer.'

'Dad?' Emma laughs at a childhood recollection. 'He's a bit splashy. Empties half the swimming pool.' She gains some comfort from this exclusive knowledge.

'Really? That surprises me. Well, of course, he's more svelte than when you were a child, and impressively well-coordinated.'

Emma feels she has been put back in her place. She engineers removing her arm by pretending to search for a tissue, digging away in the pocket of her jeans until she unearths a particularly crusty one. Gabby glances at it with barely disguised disdain.

Blowing her nose, she takes out her phone and notices the missed call.

'Oh, look, Mum's phoned. I wonder what she wanted. Can I call her back now or will she be baking?' She looks at her watch; does the calculation. 'I think she'll be busy.' Thumb flicking, she checks her texts.

Gabby appears unruffled. 'They're chalk and

cheese, aren't they really, your parents? I mean, your mother's so creative but her hobbies are essentially sedentary — whereas your father's so active.'

Emma remonstrates. 'I don't think that's fair. Mum does lots of walking and she's hugely active in village life.'

'It wasn't a criticism!' Gabby looks amused rather than appalled. 'But you must admit, being active on the parish council and in local fundraising is hardly the same as running marathons. Your father operates on a different level.'

Before Emma can think of a pithy rejoinder, Nigel proves his lover's point, pounding past, red-faced and sweating profusely; oblivious to them; conscious only of the finishing line.

'Nigel, Nigel. Go for it, you can do it!' Gabby is ecstatic. She whoops, punching the air and turning to Emma, her face exuding pride.

Emma feels as if she has been punched in the belly. Stunned, she surrenders to her hug, joins in her squeals of excitement — then pushes to the finishing line determined to reach her father first, to claim the victor's embrace. Deep inside, fear and loathing combine. The affair, guessed at but not fully admitted to, is real. Her poor, poor mother. No wonder she has looked so closed, recently; so pinched.

It is only later, after Gabby has flung her arms around Nigel's neck and given him a massive kiss only to greet Peter with less enthusiasm; after they have had a celebratory sandwich on the Champs-Élysées: 'Nigel, you need to get protein in you within an hour of competing,' Gabby had admonished; after they have spurned Emma's idea of a celebratory beer — 'About the worst thing he could do; far too dehydrating,' Gabby had tutted. 'I'd better not then,' said Nigel — that Emma's phone belatedly pings with her mother's text.

She calls immediately but when it kicks in to Jenny's answerphone, she fears her voice will tremble. She kills the call and tries to formulate a text. What to say to convey her sympathy for what is happening; her unquestioning loyalty? 'Tried to call. Wish you were here with us, Mum. I miss you and love you. Xxx'

27

For a pie that sings of the countryside, simply sauté smoked bacon, shallots, carrots and rosemary. Add rabbit pieces, stock and cider, and simmer until the meat just slips off the bone. Stir in cream. Top with egg-washed shortcrust pastry. Serve with home-grown vegetables.

Jenny, of course, is oblivious to Emma's turmoil. Paris, the marathon, Gabby have all been relegated, for the moment, to the very back of her mind.

She has too much to think about. The bakers have been told to create a pie of their choosing, and, for Jenny, this is a chance to pay homage to her own mother. A rural child of the sixties and seventies, she can recall Lucy's rabbit pie, flavoured with rosemary, shallots and cider, far more vividly than the rare meals she has enjoyed at Michelin-starred restaurants. Just sautéing the bacon, takes her back to the rectory kitchen.

'What's that?' the six-year-old Jenny had asked, taking in the skinned rabbit being jointed by her mother on the stripped pine table.

'Just a chicken.' Lucy had smiled, looking up from her copy of *The Art of Baking*, from which she was adapting the recipe.

'This is the boring bit. You can help me with the pastry. Go and play.'

Even as an infant, Jenny had sensed her mother wasn't being entirely honest. She had hidden under the kitchen table, watching her deftly butcher the meat then add it to the frying bacon with the butter, flour, cider, aromatics and seasoning.

The heady aroma of alcohol simmering with braised meat and herbs had soon enveloped Lucy, bestowing a steamy halo. Later, Jenny had watched her strip hot rabbit from the bones, then transform it into something even more succulent by stirring through a dollop of cream.

Jenny had decorated the shortcrust lid — her usual job — and, as ever, had agonised over producing a fitting covering.

'That's lovely, darling,' Lucy, impatient to get it into the Aga, had reassured her.

'But I haven't got the chicken right.' Jenny's face had pinched in concentration. 'It looks like a rabbit.'

Lucy, her hands dusty with flour, had bent and dropped a kiss on the top of her head, breathing in the scent of clean hair and baking.

'Well, I prefer rabbits to chickens.'

Now, as Jenny tweaks the already imaginative recipe — adding a hint of garlic, a touch of tarragon — she hopes she is channelling her talent. More than that, she feels as if her mother were present: directing her moves, hovering by her side. Lucy's words mingle with Vicki's in a sweet polyphony of reassurance: 'That's lovely, darling'; 'You can win this: you're head and shoulders above the rest.'

281

Vicki, sifting her fat and flour into fine breadcrumbs, is thinking back to her childhood kitchen: a cold room, the cupboards half empty, the surfaces clear and sterile in which she ate supermarket quiche and watery iceberg while her mother marked homework upstairs.

In her early teens, Vicki tried to interest her in home-cooked food: attempting pasta with home-made tomato sauce or spaghetti carbonara; an overcooked kedgeree; an ill-conceived lentil curry. But Frances was too preoccupied, and too concerned with maintaining her svelte figure, to show much interest. The teenage Vicki found it soulless to try to cook properly and so subsisted on staples. Food became fodder. Jacket potatoes with cheese; fish finger sandwiches; pasta and tuna; boiled egg and soldiers; scrambled eggs.

Vicki has no memory of Frances ever attempting a pie. In fact, she is certain she has never made one. But she does remember Frances pulling a face as she nibbled a Cornish pasty on a rare holiday to St Ives.

'I'll eat it for you, Mummy,' the eight-year-old Vicki had offered, having demolished the egg and cress sandwich bought as the healthier option. The golden pastry heaving with steak had seemed exotic; its warmth reassuring against the wind whipping in from the Atlantic.

'Urgh, no. It's far too greasy. Quite disgusting,' said Frances. She had taken only two mouthfuls, then, when no one was looking, had tossed it into a bin.

Binding pastry, Vicki realises she has never known her mother to eat it. Every attempt to get her to try her treacle tart or her salmon and watercress flan has ended in a request for 'just a sliver', and the frustration of watching her dissect the filling only to push the pastry to the side of her plate, or hide it under her knife. She has never challenged her mother over this, just as she has never really challenged her over anything. Now, she realises, she wants to ask: Why can't you enjoy my food?

Increasingly, Vicki realises, baking is the means of creating a domestic idyll she has never experienced. Of cocooning Alfie and Greg in the homely fug of good cooking that she longed for as a child.

She has a clear flashback to sitting in her friend Nicola's kitchen after hockey practice, breathing in beef bourguignon, as Nicky's three brothers piled around the table. Nicky's mother, affluent, capable and apparently unruffled, had heaped plates high with buttery mashed potato and meat smothered in rich plum-coloured gravy. Nicky and her siblings had taken this for granted: joshing with one another through full mouthfuls; demanding seconds; barely thanking their mother. Vicki, unused to boys and continual teasing, had been cowed the first time she visited. But, as she lapped up the warm casserole, she had relaxed into her silence. Even now, beef bourguignon is her ultimate comfort food.

And so she is cooking a pie based on this: a

rich beef stew, seasoned with garlic, shallots, thyme and pancetta; simmered in red wine for as long as possible; topped with rich flaky pastry — egg-washed golden brown. As she sautés and simmers, binds and rolls, she drinks up the odour of an idealised childhood and imagines recreating it.

For a moment, she imagines having her own noisy brood: a trio of boys and a much doted-on baby girl, perhaps; or a more even pair of each — the teenage boys towering above her; the girls, exquisitely beautiful, long-limbed and long-haired.

A family with just one child seems so vulnerable. Three or four would be perfect. She sighs. Her period started this morning. She mustn't be over-ambitious. If she could manage just one more, she would be overjoyed.

But what about Amy's job? The question pops up at the most unlikely moments. No, she's ruled that out . . . unless she strikes herself a deal: if she is not pregnant by late June, the date of the application deadline, she could apply. It's only a maternity leave. She wouldn't be going back for ever. And it might be just what she needs.

★ ★ ★

For three hours the bakers work, binding and resting their dough; making their fillings; constructing the pies, and baking them until they are golden.

'You've all done very well,' Dan declares with

unfamiliar generosity.

Karen fixes a smile on her face and forces herself to look at him. He meets her gaze and gives a smile that is friendly but neutral. The sort of smile you would give an acquaintance whose name you cannot quite remember but who you feel obliged to acknowledge when you pass in the street.

'The pastry's a good colour on most of them, although this' — he gestures at Vicki's — 'is perhaps a little too golden. So it's going to come down to texture and taste.'

The judges probe and cut, taste and deliberate, cleansing their palates with chilled bottled water between each bite. Jenny's pie is clearly exemplary: the sweetness of the shallots complementing the gaminess of the rabbit, the cider cutting through the richness of the cream. Vicki scores well with a robust beef and red wine offering and Claire excels, surprising herself more than the judges, with a stargazy pie that is stunningly presented: heads and tails of pilchards bursting out of the crust as if streaking through a becalmed sea.

'I'm more surprised at this one.' Dan gestures at Mike's offering, a pie in which he has tried to conjure up memories of a fantastic Spanish holiday with Rachel by marrying beef with chorizo. 'A fantastic puff pastry and the steak is meltingly tender. But what's gone on with your seasoning? It's just too fiery. You've paprika and strong chorizo in here — and far too much sherry vinegar. Please don't take this the wrong way but it's as if this pie's trying to prove something.'

'Trying to be a bit macho, perhaps?' Mike helps him out.

'Well — yes. Not that you're not . . . '

Mike smiles. 'I think I've been rumbled.'

He glances at Claire, and she laughs.

Kathleen

New Year's Eve and she is lying in bed, listening to the chimes of Big Ben on her wireless. George is at a New Year's party. He had been reluctant to leave her, but she had been insistent.

'There's no need for both of us to be incarcerated, darling. You go and toast in 1966 for me.'

'Well . . . if you don't mind.'

'I insist. And enjoy it. Wish I was drinking champagne and dancing! Go on. Celebrate! This is going to be a good year.'

She smooths down her covers and ruminates on 1965. Not a good one by any definition. A year that has seen her experience three miscarriages in quick succession and almost throw her other baby — *The Art of Baking* — away.

This year, she is more hopeful. The book is almost finished. Reinvigorated by autumn, she has rewritten pies and pastries and romped through puddings. All that remains are a few choice words on afternoon tea.

She sips at a glass of elderflower cordial and allows herself a moment's self-congratulation. She is proud of the book now that she has tempered the brightness with a warmth that tells of her love of baking. Her belief it should be at the heart of the family.

She smiles and mouths the crucial word, tears springing to her eyes as she does so. Oh, she is being ridiculous — or perhaps just hormonal — but she still feels emotional whenever she reflects on this idea.

For, miraculously, she is pregnant. A baby is hiding inside her. Curled up safe for eight weeks, or perhaps a week more. Her Christmas present from George was a diamond bracelet from Boodles; from James Caruthers a stitch in her cervix. All she has to do now is lie very still.

The thought prompts her to take a deep breath and then to concentrate on breathing out slowly. In for two; out for five. In for two; out for five, she repeats, conscientious and self-conscious. She must do everything she can to stay relaxed. She smooths down her eiderdown again, holds up her wrist with its sparkling bracelet to the lamp and watches tiny rainbows dance on the wall beside her — then drops her arm. The problem with relaxing is that it is so tedious.

Voices float up from the street: New Year's revellers, no doubt first-footing. Their laughter and the clicking of the woman's heels drift away. Her life is quiet, now, but perhaps she should live somewhere more tranquil? Untouched and remote with the sea at the bottom of the garden and a golden beach stretching out of sight? They had spent their honeymoon in unsophisticated north Cornwall and the memory of being the first to step on to the sand, in the early morning, and mark it with fresh footprints, the exhilaration of plunging into water so icy it almost hurt before her skin tingled, remains vivid. Perhaps their baby could take its first steps there . . .

'And all that remains is for me to wish you a very Happy New Year.' She must have dozed off. The BBC Home Service announcer is signing off for the evening, his avuncular tone replaced by the clipped forecast for the coastal regions. 'Viking; North Utsire; South Utsire; south-westerly eight; moderate to good.' She switches off the wireless and tries to settle back down. A very Happy New Year. Yes, please. Her fingers cross automatically. Oh stop being superstitious. But anxiety gnaws away at her optimism.

What will 1966 bring? The war in Vietnam continues but Kathleen is untouched by world events. The news filters through her wireless or floats up from the pages of her *Times* and *Telegraph*, and yet all that matters occurs in this room. Inside her body. Inside her womb.

George had once wooed her by reading John Donne. She had been stunned when he'd stumbled through 'The Good-Morrow'. Who would have thought this grocer's son would have such a sensitive streak? On their wedding night, he'd blushingly recited 'The Sun Rising': 'Shine here to us, and thou art everywhere,' he'd told her after they'd made love for the first time and though the act itself was unspectacular — she had saved herself; and it had improved — the fact he had thought to quote metaphysical love poetry almost made up for it. Lying in his arms, being told she was 'all States', she had felt so loved. For the first time since her father died, she had felt totally secure.

Now, she picks up her copy of the *Collected Poems* and turns to that poem with its celebration of sexual love. The book opens easily on this page, as though it has been read more than any other.

'This bed, thy centre is,' she reads.

And it really is. It is the centre of her world.

Puddings

Who can resist a proper pudding? The sort of gooey, comforting pud that is as British as a rainy afternoon in February and is its perfect antidote.

We have a tradition, in this country, of steamed puddings: steamed apricot pudding, steamed gingerbread pudding, syrup pudding, Baroness pudding, or nègre en chemise, the French take on a chocolate and almond steamed pudding. We slather them with cream, for a treat, or a custard or raspberry sauce, and delight in their soft, warm stickiness.

Then there are the baked puddings. The milk- and egg-based desserts of our childhood: junkets, Old English rice pudding, egg custard, which soothe like a hug from a plump and pear-drop-scented granny. Next, the bread or suet-enhanced ones with which the economical cook can fill her family with her canny use of leftovers: bread and butter pudding, plump with egg custard and dried fruit, enhanced by a little orange zest; baked sultana roll with suet; apple Charlotte; rhubarb Charlotte; brown Betty; queen of puddings.

When the strawberry season is in full swing, or the apple trees are drooping with fruit, the careful cook can turn to fruit cobblers, apple hedgehogs or summer puddings. Gooseberry or rhubarb fools are a creamy treat. But, when summer dies, the family cook turns again to the comfort of a blackberry and apple crumble, nutty with butter, drenched in double cream.

Delicious though these puddings are, there will be occasions when more sophistication is called for. And then the clever baker can bring out the dinner party delights: lemon meringue pie or apple amber, decorated with angelica and glacé cherries; the French classic vacherin, a divine confection of meringue, cream and chestnut purée; a bavarois of raspberry, coffee or chocolate; crème caramel, crème brûlée or our own Cambridge cream.

It has become fashionable for women, worrying about our waistlines, to spurn such puddings, preferring a sliver of fruit or a Ski yoghurt, now available at any Eaden's store. But our husbands and children still hanker after a proper pudding — and feel cheated if we deny them. Make sure you serve one truly decadent pudding a week and watch them enjoy every last, creamy mouthful.

Kathleen Eaden: *The Art of Baking* (1966)

28

Very small children love to devour milky, creamy puddings. Reminiscent of their mother's milk, these are the easiest of nursery foods to guzzle and to bake. But do as the French do and try to develop their palates early. A three-year-old will demolish a white chocolate mousse or a chocolate soufflé.

'Alfie, I said no. Not now.' Vicki is feeling frazzled as she assesses her chocolate fondants, probing the sponge to see if the right amount of chocolate oozes out.

'Mummy, choc choc. Choc choc for Alfie.' Her three-year-old is tugging at her leg with surprising ferocity as she ignores his entreaties.

'No, Alfie. I said no. Mummy's concentrating.'

'Mummy, choc choc. Please, Mummy.' Alfie is insistent. His bottom lip begins to wobble and his eyes fill in preparation for tears.

'Can't you just go and play for a bit?' Vicki's voice feels close to a snarl as she turns to address her boy. She softens as she takes in the crestfallen toddler and feels immediate guilt at her harshness. She would never have spoken to a pupil that way.

'I'm sorry, lovely, but I'm busy. You can lick the bowl in a moment — or we can make something together — but just now I'm trying to work something out.'

The bottom lip juts and rage and frustration

coalesce in his small face. 'Alfie wants choc choc. Alfie help you.'

'Alfie, I've already told you. This is tricky. Mummy needs to do it on her own.'

He remains unconvinced, tugging at her jeans pocket then slipping a small hand under her top and trying to touch her puckered stomach. How would she deal with him if he were a difficult pupil?

As a last resort, she would suggest he see the only male teacher in the school, the year six teacher: older, taller, more experienced. More authoritative in every way. With a sigh, she removes his small hand and flounces to the bottom of the stairs.

'Greg?' She barks her husband's name, a single syllable packed with resentment.

'What?' His voice drifts from the bathroom.

'Are you finished yet? I need some help here.' Bloody hell, she thinks, kicking aside some Lego then wincing as she stands on a small piece. Where is he when I need him? Still having a shower after his Saturday morning lie-in.

Five minutes later, her husband emerges, as bouncy and refreshed as a Labrador puppy. His towel-dried hair is tousled, his eyes bright after sex followed by a decent night's sleep.

She, in contrast, feels weary. She has been up since six, trying to practise spinning caramel into baskets before Alfie woke up, and she has made chocolate fondants since giving him breakfast. Her hair, scrunched up in a hair band, is greasy and her body, clad in pyjamas that now need a wash, clammy with their juices and the scent of this morning's baking. She longs for a revitalising, cleansing shower to wash away her stickiness; and a triple espresso made by somebody else — ideally a barista in a city centre coffee shop devoid of toddlers — to kick her into shape.

She glances at the photo of Mrs Eaden, with her mixing bowl, and feels an unfamiliar twinge of resentment. Did you ever feel like this, Kathleen? She very much doubts it. How did you find the time to cook so expertly when you had a small child? I know you stopped writing before you had her but you still carried on baking — and playing on the beach, and surfing and flying kites. That interview, with your daughter Laura, was full of it: this idyllic childhood in which you managed to be both parent and ever enthusiastic playmate, painting with her, cooking, sewing. Creating homes in her tree house and doll's house. How did you manage it? She sighs. You were evidently much better at multi-tasking than me.

'You all right?'

Greg looks unnaturally, frustratingly healthy. A scrubbed face, pink from a hot shower and a good shave; a close-fitting jumper he can just get away with; a springiness to the way he moves around the kitchen, creating more clutter as he fills a glass with orange juice and fails to put the carton back in the fridge; pops a bagel into the Dualit toaster, leaving the packet out of the bread bin; switches on the coffee machine.

'Just a bit knackered. I'm finding it hard to get everything done with little Alf here.'

'Where is he?' Greg remembers he has a child.
'I put him in front of CBeebies.'
'Vicks . . . ' The syllable is suffused with disapproval.
'What? He hasn't watched any yet this morning and I needed to concentrate.' She folds her arms across her chest, aware she is being defensive and hating herself for it.
'It's only nine thirty. Of course he shouldn't have watched anything yet.'
'Well, lots of children are dumped in front of it as soon as they wake up to give both parents a lie-in.'
'Who?' He is incredulous. 'Well, that's immaterial. My son's not 'lots of children'. We don't need to bring him up by others' standards.'
'It's very educational.' She hears herself trotting out her excuses as he sweeps from the room to rescue his son from the imagined depravities of children's television. He doesn't hear and she swears out of earshot, out of frustration at feeling in the wrong.
She goes back to clearing up the detritus of cooking: putting packets of flour and pots of cocoa back in the cupboard, screwing up the 70 per cent cocoa chocolate wrappers, tossing eggshells in the compost bucket, putting butter back in the fridge. She wipes her index finger round the inside of the mixing bowl, sucks the sticky chocolate concoction from it then fills it with hot water. A sprinkling of flour is wiped from the surface; sugar and egg from the handle of the electric whisk.
Alfie runs into the kitchen beaming, his hand

snug in Greg's. Her husband looks self-satisfied.

'We're going on an adventure!'

'Are you now? Where are you off to?' She bends down to address her boy properly. 'The moon? To play with the pirates? I know, the jungle?'

'Nope.' Alfie cannot keep his secret any longer. 'Legoland!'

'Really?' Vicki straightens up, looks Greg in the eye.

'I'm doing some hands-on parenting for a change. You're always complaining I don't do enough of it. It'll give you plenty of time to do your baking.' He speaks without rancour but she feels he has scored a point over her. Mummy puts Alfie in front of the telly; Daddy whisks him off to small boy heaven with the promise of Lego goodies.

'I'm not sure he's old enough. I think we need to discuss it. I mean, it's a massive treat and maybe I'd like to join in . . . ' Her voice peters away and she realises she is sounding churlish.

'Well, you've just said you haven't enough time to get everything done so you definitely haven't got time to go to Legoland. Besides, it would be good for us to have a bit of boy time, wouldn't it, Alfie?'

'Yeah, boy time,' repeats his son, though he looks to his mother for confirmation. 'But Mummy come too?'

'Oh my lovely, I'd love to.' She is conflicted. On the one hand, she cannot bear to think of her beautiful boy experiencing a treat like this independently and she is incensed that Greg will receive much hero-worship for it; on the other, she craves some time alone — time to bake without someone vying for her attention; or to shave her legs without someone bursting into the bathroom and demanding that he float his Playmobil in the bath.

Greg senses her indecision.

'Mummy's going to stay here to get her baking sorted. Then she can relax with us and have a family day tomorrow.'

Vicki opens her mouth to protest.

'Good plan? I thought so.'

She bites down her anger at her enforced impotence. 'Well, he's going to need his rucksack and a spare set of clothes and his water bottle and some snacks.' She flits around the kitchen, gathering up a packet of raisins and another of oatcakes, grabbing his Thomas water bottle and going to fill it, her frenzied activity disguising the fact she feels redundant.

'No, he doesn't. I'm sure we can get drinks there. Come on, Alf.' He practically drags his son from the kitchen, bustling him into his anorak, and omitting to do up the zip, thrusting his feet into trainers.

'He'll need a pee.'

'Do you, Alf?'

Alfie shakes his head.

'Well, don't take his word for it.' Vicki's voice rises in exasperation. 'He's three. Of course, he's going to say that.'

Then: 'Come on, Alfie. No pee, no Lego.' She guides him briskly to the downstairs loo, lifts the seat, and stands guard as he manages to direct an impressive arc of urine.

She cannot, of course, resist commenting. 'You see, Alfie. You did need one.'

She is aware that Greg is glowering in the hall, irritated at her taking over and at her pointing out that she was right.

'You've got to let me be a parent,' he mutters as she brings Alfie back and pulls a woollen hat down over his curls.

Then: 'He's going in the car. He doesn't need that.'

'Bye, Alfie. Have lots of fun. Big snuggles when you get back.' She forces herself to hold a smile on her face, desperate to disguise the tension to ease the separation for her child.

Greg looks suitably uncomfortable, wrong-footed by his sharpness but inept at apologising. 'He'll have a great time. Sorry to snap — I just wish you'd stop mothering him all the time.'

She laughs; a yelp of incredulity. 'And how am I meant to do that? He's my baby. I'm his mum. It's in the job description.'

He pulls her close and places a kiss on the top of her head. Murmuring into her hair, he sounds suddenly weary.

'Well, perhaps you should do it less; or I should do it more.'

'Yeah, right.'

'Do you want a row about this? I am trying.'

'I know.' She gives up the fight and lets herself relax against his body. 'I know. Have a lovely day. I'll miss you.'

'Try to relax — and get those puddings sorted.' He grins at her. 'You can do this, you

301

know. Just write one of your lists and work your way through it. Be methodical.'

'I know, I know.'

'We'll expect to gorge ourselves when we get home.'

'Yes, all right.' She manages a half-smile.

'You're great at puddings. Seriously. Don't know what you're worrying about.'

She keeps the smile fixed on her face as she stands in the doorway, watching him strap Alfie into his car seat. The temptation to interfere; to take over with a brusque 'Not that way: I'll do it,' is so great she has to hug her arms around her. She just manages to resist.

Alfie presses his snub nose against the window, she imagines forlornly, and she breaks into frenzied waving.

'Bye, Alfie. I love you,' she calls as the car pulls off. Her waving feels almost frantic. She continues until the car has drawn out of sight.

Then she closes the heavy front door with its original stained-glass panels and rests her heavy limbs against it, pausing for a moment before confronting the chaos of the kitchen.

Stop all this mothering? She doesn't know how to. And even if she did, she wouldn't want to. Motherhood courses through her veins.

Which is not to say that she will not enjoy a day to herself. A flicker of excitement works its way through her body. She has a whole day in which to perfect her puddings, unencumbered by anyone else.

That's a thought. She pulls out her phone and fires off a quick text to Jenny and Claire.

'Practising puddings. Hope you're OK and managing to do the same? Xxx'

'Trying — with Chloe:/' Claire pings back immediately.

'Some done. Lots more to do,' Jenny's text reads.

Better get on with it then. But first, she needs to wash.

With a renewed spring in her step, she runs up the stairs to the bathroom and the oblivion of an uninterrupted shower.

Kathleen

March, and she is still in bed, still nurturing her baby. She counts the weeks: seventeen, eighteen, nineteen, twenty. Almost halfway through.

Her stomach has swollen into a neat hard-boiled egg, petite but emphatic. There is physical proof that, this time, something is living. She wishes she could flaunt it. But no one sees her bump besides those welcomed into the sanctum of her bedroom: George, Julie and Mr Caruthers.

Like a disgraced daughter, or a Carmelite nun, hers is a life of solitude. She does not mind. All her energy is focused on resting. On willing her womb to remain strong.

She flicks through the society pages of *Harpers* and *Tatler*, noting old acquaintances, and feels only mild interest. Much of the time, those dos were a bore. The Beatles claim to be 'more popular than Jesus', and the Moors murderers are due to stand trial. She will not read the reports in *The Times*. Her child feels newly vulnerable: at risk in the world as well as in her womb.

Propped up in bed, she rations herself to just half an hour's writing, wary of what happened the last time she spent her days with a book on her knees, her pen hurtling across the page until her hand cramped. The words spill out in her assigned half-hour: afternoon tea is distilled in neat slots and she spends the rest of her long weary day dreaming up more.

And then something happens that justifies such behaviour; that makes the caution, the isolation and the tedium worth while.

Stretching out in bed while re-reading *Lady Chatterley's Lover*, she feels a flutter so faint that, at first, she fears she has imagined it.

There it is again.

At twenty-one weeks, her baby moves.

29

It does not matter what you bake with your children though there is an argument for simplicity, and for tailoring the recipe to fit with their age. What matters is that you are spending time together: cosseting and nurturing them. Make the most of this when they are small for they may be more preoccupied with their education during the teenage years.

Karen, in her pristine white kitchen, is creating a baked alaska: the sort of dessert she often thinks she most resembles if she had to describe herself as a pudding. Glossy and crisp on the outside; ever chilly at the centre. Utterly desirable; always surprising. Only the sweetness and the initial warmth ruin the analogy.

Of course, it's not the kind of pudding she would ever taste but she takes great satisfaction from the various stages: the creation of the Swiss roll, the hulling of the fruit, the making of the meringue — whisked over a bowl of simmering water until it is stiffly peaked.

She has already made the fatless sponge: a tight roulade encircling home-made raspberry jam and then cut with mathematical precision into six two-centimetre-deep bases of light sponge. And now she places hulled and sugared fruit on top: blackberries, redcurrants and raspberries, which shine, ever jewel-like. She tastes just one: a raspberry she sucks on the tip of her tongue until the sugar dissolves away.

For a minute, she remembers her mother, cutting herself a slice of Bird's Eye Arctic Roll. A poor approximation of this most decadent pudding, with its piped strawberry jam and thin layer of sponge encasing a mass of yellow but, for Pamela, another Saturday night treat. More innocuous than the cigarettes and spliffs of her children. Almost infantalising. Wrapped in her small world of back-breaking work, telly and food, Pamela never asked any questions. Was she really so ignorant? Did she not know that Steven, charming but ever ruthless, was effectively pimping his sister? Or that Karen had initially gone along with it: desperate to please her brother, flattered to be in with his mates?

She begins the meringue, whisking egg whites and sugar with a cold, focused fury — yet still careful the gently simmering water doesn't touch the bowl and cook the eggs. The mixture gleams, glossily, like ice crystals sparkling on snow. She sets it aside and tops the fruit with ice cream then smothers each concoction with a sweet duvet of meringue. Three minutes in the oven, and she has six tiny Mont Blancs: dainty, golden and apparently symmetrical. She places them on duck-egg porcelain and, just for a moment, admires them: these works of art, too cute to eat.

Oh, but they're not though, are they? She takes a knife and thinks, as she grips it, of her brother. Her kids don't know they have an Uncle Steven. Well, she wants no connection. Imagine if he came across her beautiful, innocent Livy? She feels sick at the very idea.

And what about Jake? The same age as Steven when he started hawking her around, but a different class, a different generation. A different person — even if she no longer knows what sort of person that is. She must change that. She won't be a Pamela, choosing not to see what was in front of her. She will brave his hostility in a minute, and go and check up on him.

But first she will cut this baked alaska. The knife pushes to reveal a scoop of vanilla-flecked ice cream, the centre still resolutely cold. She probes further and a jumble of magenta fruits spill out, yielding their vibrant juices.

* * *

'Jake?'

'What?'

His tone, when she reaches his attic room, is less belligerent than weary — as if he cannot bring himself to speak to his mother: the habitual way in which he has communicated with her this year.

'Can I come in?' Karen is hesitant, poised at the door of his bedroom, wary of intruding into his space and of his mood if she enters.

There is a pause, then a sigh.

'If you have to.'

His rudeness riles her. Not for the first time, she considers the point of his expensive education — though she knows this contempt is reserved for her, and his friends' mothers reap the benefits of the extortionate school fees. She opens the door to his vast attic room, walls plastered with semi-naked female celebrities juxtaposed with motorbikes. Two blades — he is captain of his school's rowing eight — scull the ceiling. His duvet is rumpled on his bed; joggers strewn across an armchair. In one corner, a jumble of boxer shorts breed.

'That's hardly very welcoming.' Her tone is tart as she addresses her first-born, who is lolling in the chair by his desk, long limbs stretched out, watching her with ill-disguised antipathy.

'Sorry, Ma.' The apology is ironic. A lazy smile plays on his lips. She wants to smack him.

'I just came to say I'm going to the gym. Olivia's revising at Anna's for the day and it would be a good idea if you did some work too.' She looks pointedly at the unopened arch-lever files on his desk. 'Your mocks are what — two weeks away?'

He gives a snort.

'What's that supposed to mean?'

He shrugs.

'Jake?'

He remains silent but begins to kick at the corner of a rug, his size eleven foot, snug in rugby socks, ruffling it up then flattening it in an irritating tic.

She knows she should ignore such obviously adolescent behaviour but he has got under her skin.

'I asked what you were getting at, Jake?'

He looks at her full on, as if assessing how far he should go to hurt her. *You're fooling no one, Ma.* Perhaps now, finally, she will get to the bottom of what he meant?

'I just don't think you should lecture me when you never did A-levels — or even O-levels, was it?' he taunts her. 'And I don't think you should lecture me when you obviously don't give a shit.'

'Jake.' Her response is an automatic reaction to his swearing, to the charge — easily, lazily denied — that she doesn't care. She breathes a little more easily. This isn't the cause of his contempt. But still, it rankles. A knot of anger burns inside her and, inwardly, she counts to five.

'I do 'give a shit', Jake, which is why I've asked you to do some work. And if I'm lecturing you it's precisely because I don't want you to squander the chances I never had at your age.'

She hears herself metamorphose into the cliché of a haranguing parent, and, momentarily, gives in.

'You don't have a clue what my childhood was like, or why I didn't get any O-levels — or even CSEs — as you so kindly point out. You've never asked and I've never wanted to tell you. And that's the way it's going to remain. But don't you mock me for it and don't you mirror it. Don't take all this' — she gestures around the room — 'for granted. You have a far better life. And I am so bloody determined you are not going to repeat my mistakes.'

She goes to leave the room, furious at herself for losing control of her emotions and for her failure to get at the root of the problem.

'This isn't really about that, though, is it, Jake?' She gives a bark of a laugh and, with her challenge, opens the door to an honest

310

conversation. 'This isn't the reason you're so angry . . . or so contemptuous of me.'

He shakes his head in studied bemusement. 'Chill, Ma. I don't know what you're talking about.'

'About that dig. *You're fooling no one, Ma.* What did you mean by it?'

'Don't know what you're talking about,' he repeats. His face is blank, as if he has no recollection.

Did she imagine it? Perhaps she is crediting him with too much intuition? She is either being paranoid — or he is lying. His face remains a picture of innocence. He was never good at lying, even as a little boy, his mouth twitching in an instant give-away.

She feels in the wrong.

'OK, sorry. Sorry, Jake. Forget it. Forget it.'

She smiles at him, incapable of crossing the rift that is growing ever deeper between them. Standing in his doorway, poised in indecision, she wonders if she can attempt to breach it — or if she should fade away.

She takes the coward's route and makes her excuses — to his relief and her dissatisfaction. 'Just try to do some work, all right? I need to go. I've got to get to the gym.'

As she turns from the room, she could swear she hears him mutter: 'No shame . . . she's just no shame.'

★ ★ ★

In the changing room, she takes her time adjusting her hair in the floor-to-ceiling mirrors, eyes, apparently fixed on herself, busy spying. She is no voyeur but she charts the rise and fall in weight of her fellow gym bunnies just as assiduously as they do themselves. She may not know their names but she knows who has the baggiest stomach and who the breasts that flap like empty pockets. She can guess who starves herself and who overeats. She doubts that anyone else makes themselves sick.

In the spin class, she sits at the back, still assessing the other women and comparing herself to them. On a good day, she would perch at the front, vying for the attention of Ben, the muscular instructor. Today is not a good day. The class begins kindly: a light dance track with a strong beat that leads her to a light sprint. But within five minutes she is out of her seat for a ten-second sprint that sees her heart-rate soar to 85per cent of its maximum and her heart pound against her ribcage.

She sits back down, legs pedalling relentlessly; adds resistance and begins to climb to a rockier track, the beat slow and heavy. She ratchets up the levels until her glutes ache and her legs feel leaden. Next to her, a woman is pedalling faster; she glances over to double-check: her classmate's level of resistance is far weaker.

'You're at the top, now sprint down,' commands Ben, and she covers three kilometres in three minutes as a frenetic dance track takes over. Head down, legs powering, she imagines herself screeching down mountain roads, or climaxing.

For forty-five minutes, or twenty-one kilometres, she pushes herself in this way: rising and

312

falling, climbing and sprinting; grunting with effort and then with pleasure. Her face glows, droplets of sweat beading on a florid forehead. Damp blooms at her crotch and on the underarms of her Lycra sports top. Nobody said it was glamorous but it is the most efficient way she knows of burning calories.

Later, she pounds up the pool, pushing her body to her standard hundred lengths in groups of eight: backstroke; breaststroke; front crawl once again. She completes eight lengths of sprints, her body surging through the water like an underwater missile, arms rising and falling in a steady rhythm, head twisting to alternate sides. A textbook illustration of apparently effortless swimming; an example of fused elegance and power. Then it's four lengths with a float between her legs; four with a float at her arms; eight with paddles and flippers; a further eight sprints and back to sets of eight once again. Up and down the pool she goes; searing through the water, performing a tumble turn at each end. She thinks in terms of two hundred metres, and in terms of time. Always time. Time and, therefore, calories.

One hundred lengths in, she allows herself to stop. Checks the wall clock and her stopwatch. Thirty-four minutes thirty-two seconds. Two point five kilometres in thirty-four minutes thirty-two seconds. To her surprise, she has achieved a personal best. She allows herself to assess her fellow swimmers: the postnatal mothers desperate to lose their baby fat pushing themselves to try the crawl in the middle lane;

the octogenarian gentleman attempting a serene breaststroke at a walking pace; the women her age managing to swim lengths of breaststroke while chatting, and without getting their hair wet.

The ladies of the gym swimming club are vying with one another in their matching red swimsuits and silver swim hats. She gives one a nod of acknowledgement, taking in her increasingly honed arms and well-toned legs as she walks to the pool. She has lost a lot of weight recently. The speculation is automatic: how much has she lost and what does she weigh now? What is her BMI? What is her personal best?

As she leaves to plunge into the jacuzzi, her attention is caught not by another woman's physique but by an incongruous couple: the woman, perhaps in her late sixties, the man in his mid-forties — perhaps even her age. They are holding hands, but it is clear they are not lovers. Rather she is leading him, coaxing this soft-bodied bear of a man into the shallow end with an assiduousness born of years of attention. He gives a grunt of surprise, then a yelp which shocks as it reverberates around the pool, the sound amplified by the water. The breaststroke swimmers turn, their equanimity ruffled; even the octogenarian glances their way. The woman — small, bird-like — is unperturbed, easing her charge on to a giant float then towing him around the pool. 'It's OK,' she reassures him. 'It's OK.'

Karen takes in her face, worn with years of anxiety but still capable of experiencing the joy

314

of others. She is looking at the man carefully, assessing if the water is too cold for him, trying to elicit a smile.

The man gives another grunt. Less fearful, but still vulnerable. He clings to the float, shoulders tight with tension.

The woman smiles, and coos at him. 'It's OK. It's OK.'

He relaxes into the water, his white legs trailing behind him. He gives another yelp — of excitement this time.

The woman smiles, relief erasing her wrinkles; her burden briefly eased. She is, of course, the man's mother.

30

Your little ones will love to shape gingerbread or butter biscuits with you, creating plump teddy bears, stars or hearts. Should you feel inclined to rush their work, then stop. The closeness of that early baking will stand you in good stead in later years.

'Alfie?'

Vicki watches her little boy for a good two minutes before she disturbs him — so ensconced is he in his imaginary world.

Lying on his tummy, he lines all his vehicles up in size order and by colour. A rainbow of Matchbox cars snakes around the rug and disappears under the sofa. By his side are the chunkier dumper trucks: the cars his small hands would have curled around only a year ago but which are now deemed way too babyish for this more dexterous three-year-old.

'Now the people,' he chunters under his breath as he lines up the plastic Happy Land figures: children woefully out of proportion for his vehicles, though, this time, he doesn't seem to mind.

Is there something OCD about this behaviour? Should she worry he is somewhere on the autistic spectrum? Oh, don't be ridiculous. She thinks back to the reassurance provided by his nursery, where he now spends three hours each morning, freeing up her time for baking. He is bright, ordered, methodical. And he is just being a boy.

She kneels down next to him then lowers herself to his level. The world looks different from this angle: the fabric at the bottom of the sofa pilled; the odd tendril of fluff swirling like tumbleweed across the floor. She must hoover, she thinks automatically then stops herself. Today, she has promised, she is not going to worry about domestic things but will be guided by whatever Alfie wants to do.

'So — do you feel like doing some baking?' She watches as he straightens the line of red cars which stretches longer than all the others. Then comes the white and then the green.

'Why aren't there many yellow cars?' He looks perturbed as he neatens the lone yellow one.

'I don't know. I've never really thought about it. Perhaps people don't like their cars to be yellow?' The tiny vehicle is a particularly putrid shade.

'When I grow up, I'm going to have a yellow car.'

He continues to play and she watches his delicate features: that creamy complexion unmarred by a line, or even a freckle. How long can he remain in this state of perfection, without even the smallest of scars?

'Why you looking at me?'

He frowns, hazel eyes wide open, then presses his face close to hers so that she feels as if she is being subsumed by him. He blows a raspberry on her cheek.

'Don't do that!'

He bursts into giggles, delighted at the effect. 'Daddy taught me!'

'Yes, well . . . You can only do it if I can retaliate.'

'What's re . . . '

'Retaliate. Do it back. This.' And she grabs him around the waist, pulls up his Thomas the Tank Engine top and blows a loud, wet kiss on his belly.

'Mummy!'

He is delighted.

'Me do it back!' And he pushes her over and blows an even more enthusiastic one on her stomach. His breath is warm and the kiss wet with saliva.

'Enough. I give up.' She wraps her arms around him and laughs into his hair, slightly self-conscious yet relieved she can still provoke such delight merely by playing with her child. After a day 'sorting' puddings, as Greg put it, she feels calmer. More in control. And invigorated: as if she is more than capable of coping with — no, enjoying — her three-year-old. A day off has lent her perspective: made her miss him and realise how much she should cherish their time together.

'Do Lego now?' Alfie's eyes gleam as if he has realised that she is determined to make up for her irritability at the weekend and to give him enough attention. Or maybe not enough, for it can never really be enough.

Her heart sinks. She can pretend to match his enthusiasm for Lego for a few minutes but his capacity to play with it seems almost limitless.

318

'Lego then baking?' he bargains shrewdly, and she finds herself taken aback. Is he just mirroring what she often says or has he guessed that she lacks his relish for his favourite toy?

'That sounds like a good deal.' She smiles. 'Lego then baking. How about I help you make the fire engine and then you help me make gingerbread men — or would you prefer cupcakes?'

'Gingerbread men.' He is emphatic. It is the option he goes for, without fail.

'How did I guess?'

'Always gingerbread.'

'Always gingerbread,' she agrees.

'Gingerbread *after* Lego,' he reiterates.

'Yes, after Lego.' She rolls her eyes and is rewarded by him imitating her action, accompanied by a cascade of giggles.

* * *

Later, after she has made the Lego fire engine for him — a vehicle that requires him to be aged five to twelve according to the instructions, but which she still finds tricky — she finally manages to lure him into the kitchen. Rain splatters against the skylight and the French windows, making it feel even toastier than usual, and secure.

Though she knows the recipe by heart, she brings out *The Art of Baking*, and shows Alfie the photo of Kathleen proudly displaying a plate of cooked gingerbread men and women.

'They're too big,' he tells her.

'Too big?'

'Yes. They're grown-ups. I want to do babies.' And he runs to the drawer and rummages for the boy and girl biscuit cutters.

And so they make a wealth of biscuits, the smaller cutters doubling their numbers, and the remaining scraps re-rolled to make baby hearts and stars. Some of the dough seems to get eaten, Alfie squishing it into his mouth before she can stop him.

'No. No more — you might get tummy ache,' she remonstrates, worrying vaguely about the raw egg binding it.

He pops in another scrap and laughs, dough seeping between his teeth. 'Mummy. It's the best bit,' he tells her seriously, then beams, mouth wide open. 'It's deeeeelicious.'

Watching him like this, she wonders if it is possible to love him more. Certainly, today he has been at his most golden: ever loving, sparky, interesting but also, oddly, more compliant. Must be because she's given him her undivided attention, she thinks with a pang of guilt; or perhaps Kathleen Eaden was right and it's because they're baking? Doing something both of them love — she even more than him, if she's honest — which allows them to chat, and eat and investigate. To exist in their own happy bubble while the rest of life chugs on, oblivious.

'Why do you look sad?'

Alfie is staring at her, inquisitive.

'I'm not sad, my darling. I'm happy.'

'You look sad. Like when you saw Max's new baby sister.'

'Did I?' She gulps. Was she that transparent? 'I wasn't sad then, lovely, and I'm not now.'

She finds herself beginning to explain to him that sometimes people can be overwhelmed with good emotions, but she loses him quickly, his eyes flickering to the cooling gingerbread men before she has finished the sentence.

'Never mind,' she finishes. 'Now, how about we try one of those?'

Kathleen

The baby is staying tight inside her. Tight, tight, tight. Every hour she checks between her thighs but there is no blood. Then she makes herself wait two hours. Oh, thank goodness. Her inner thighs remain dry.

The baby kicks again. A flutter or a kick? A flutter kick. Perhaps she — for she feels as if she is having a girl — is learning how to swim. She imagines taking a little girl, her little girl, for swimming lessons and watching her streak underwater like mackerel spied from a fishing boat or a baby dolphin.

The flutter kick comes again. Perceptible. Definitely there. Perhaps you're a strong one, she addresses her belly. A strong one, and determined. Kick. There it is again.

She panics that the stitch will not hold, that her girl will break it with all this kicking, but Julie, now visiting her three times a week, reassures her. 'It's a good sign, all this action. It's when they're quiet for a long time that you start to worry.'

She can be quiet too, Kathleen wants to tell her. Sometimes I can wait hours without feeling a kick. And then, in the middle of the night, I lie, rigid with panic, fearing that she is no longer alive.

31

For the most indulgent of trifles, simply steep Madeira cake in kirsch, scatter with fresh cherries or raspberries, coat with a layer of melted chocolate, and then add home-made custard and velvet pillows of cream. Top with toasted flaked almonds or dark chocolate curls. Omit jelly and please do not think of including tinned mandarins or peach halves. This is a very adult, very sensuous, dessert.

'I am SO excited.' Vicki is practically trembling as she climbs the final flight of stairs, close on the heels of Cora.

The bakers, gathered for the pudding stage of the Search for the New Mrs Eaden, are being given unprecedented access to her recipe archive in the hope they might find inspiration there.

'I can't believe we're actually going to see Kathleen's writing. That we're going to get to touch her things,' she pants as they near the attic rooms at Bradley Hall, which currently house the recipe collection. 'It's going to be the closest we get to a master-class with her. Just incredible. Such a privilege.' She stops to catch her breath.

'She was only human.' Jenny is amused by her hero-worship; the self-conscious way in which she refers to her by her first name and then blushes.

'Oh, I know . . . ' Vicki is unconvinced. 'But she was something special — '

'She was lucky,' Claire cuts in, as they pause, slightly out of breath, half a flight from the former servants' quarters. 'I bet you could have been a Mrs Eaden, written books like her and got them published, if you'd managed to marry a millionaire who happened to develop a chain of supermarkets.'

'Oh no, I could never have been like her,' Vicki contradicts. 'She was way ahead of her age. Look at the way she writes: she makes you want to bake everything she describes and gobble it up at the same time.'

'Oh, all right. I'll give her that,' Claire says, mock-grumbling, as she rolls her eyes at Mike.

'I think she *was* special,' Cora, ever the loyal employee, chips in as she takes in the threatened mutiny gathering behind her.

'She was extraordinary,' Vicki agrees as they follow a meagre corridor to a larger attic room. 'Otherwise, why would any of us be bothering with this?'

They push through a green baize door and enter the warren of servants' bedrooms: low-ceilinged and poky compared to the grandeur of the rooms downstairs. A door at the end is labelled archive. Cora gestures to her and Vicki knocks, tentative.

Though the passages leading to it are dark, the attic room is bright. Sunshine floods through the casement windows and refracts off the white-washed floors, shocking them with an intense light. A line of glass-topped display cases streaks across one side, and an Ercol couch, elm frets splayed against the walls, provides a splash of burnt-orange tweed. What a beautiful room, thinks Vicki. Then: I wonder if Kathleen came up here.

A man, thin, stooped, dressed in a worn corduroy jacket and tweeds, emerges from a desk in one corner, exuding dust and diffidence. He wrings his hands, red-raw Vicki cannot help noticing, and massages his pronounced knuckles, but his smile, as he invites them to enter his world, is welcoming.

'Paul Usher. Delighted to meet you all — and to introduce you properly to Kathleen Eaden. These exhibits' — he gestures to the display cases — 'have all been catalogued. These' — he gestures to a pile of notebooks placed on the other side of the room — 'are still in the process of being assessed.

'You will find it easier — and I would prefer it — if you looked at the catalogued exhibits; but, if there's something specific you would like, we can plunder this pile.'

Vicki, Claire, Karen and Mike make straight for the catalogued items containing recipes for puddings, as they have been instructed. The notes are copious: pages upon pages of exercise pads detailing the best combination of ingredients, or the optimum heat, for an array of desserts.

Vicki cannot stop her fingers from trembling, as if the thought of touching the pages Kathleen had written on is overwhelming. Yet no one else seems the least bit tentative. Mike is rifling through an arch-lever file, and Karen flicking through a hardback notepad as casually as if it

325

were a well-thumbed magazine.

Only Claire seems to sense her trepidation, and gives her a smile. 'Come on. Don't look so worried. You need to get stuck in!'

And so she does, her nerves quietening as she becomes engrossed in the recipes. Every few minutes, she gives a squeal and calls Claire over.

'Look — her chocolate soufflé recipe. The one I've been practising. In her own handwriting! Isn't it beautiful? Looping and gracious — and such lovely ink. I wish I could write like that . . .'

'What's she written in the margin?'

' 'The ultimate pudding for a seduction.' ' They pause, then giggle.

'Well, lucky old George,' Vicki says.

'Or maybe not him?' Karen has overheard their conversation.

'Karen! She wouldn't. Not Mrs Eaden. Not Kathleen.'

The older woman gives a shrug and goes back to her reading.

'There's one for her trifle here.' Claire calls Vicki over.

'Oooh. Let's have a look: cherries, kirsch, home-made Madeira cake, whipped cream, custard, toasted flaked almonds — and a layer of dark chocolate . . .'

'I want to make it now!' Claire says.

'I'd never have thought of the chocolate.' Vicki bites her lip, cross with herself for being trumped by someone baking nearly half a century earlier. 'What a clever idea.'

'What about this one: a gâteau Paris — Brest?'

'They're such hard work. Have you made one?'

'No.'

'Oh.' Vicki feels the tiniest, guiltiest, bit smug. 'They're difficult . . . but impressive. Look — she gives directions for making the praline cream: you have to caramelise the almonds and then grind them down. That's interesting: she says you can use hazelnuts or a combination of both.'

'Don't think I'll be copying that.'

'No, but choux pastry always looks good.'

Having found a recipe for elegant choux pastry swans, Vicki takes the file to the sofa, a type she has always coveted but which Greg deems too retro.

It is, she has repeatedly told him, a design classic. Who cares if it is more suited to a Hoxton loft than an Edwardian semi bursting with toys?

'Rather stylish for the servants' quarters?' She smiles at Paul Usher, keen to display her style kudos.

'Kathleen Eaden chose it for her drawing room. It's from Ercol's 1965 collection and made just down the road in High Wycombe. But George felt it was too modern for the rest of the house, and Kathleen never got round to sending it to their house in Chelsea where she had similar furniture.'

On the other side of the room, Jenny is looking for something specific.

'I don't suppose you have her recipe for a rabbit pie — with cider, cream and bacon, do you?' she asks the archivist. 'I just remember my

327

mother making it. It was in *The Art of Baking* — and I'd love to see the original version.'

Paul Usher smiles. 'Believe it or not, I haven't catalogued her traditional pies yet — but they're in the notebooks I'm working on at the moment. If you'd be so kind as to put on these gloves, I'm sure we can find it together.'

Despite herself, she feels a thrill as she turns the pages of the notebooks, white silk gloves adding to the mystique. Kathleen's looping script swirls: firm, decisive, precise.

Jenny is surprised that the ink remains a bright cobalt blue, as if kept from the world for years.

'Have these not been looked at much?' she queries.

'Not those, no. Publishers have always been much more interested in her puddings and cakes.'

He gives a sniff. 'It's a shame, really. She's equally innovative when writing about savoury food but there isn't the appetite for it, if you'll pardon the pun. In my experience, people are always more interested in the sweet things of life.'

She continues with her search, passing the recipe for game pie mentioned by Kathleen Eaden that calls for pheasant, partridge, red wine and cognac. She finds the ingredients for chicken and grouse pie: one fat grouse, one chicken, six rashers of bacon, and six hard-boiled eggs. Yes, she checks, it really does stipulate eggs. There are recipes for raised game pies, raised veal and ham pies, pork pies; for quiches — lobster; asparagus; and sausage and leek. She is beginning to believe

328

that she imagined the recipe — or that it was entirely Lucy's creation — by the time she finds it. But here it is, neatly underscored in blue: rabbit pie, braised in cider and cream.

Seeing each step meticulously detailed takes her back, once again, to the rectory kitchen: Lucy enveloped in steam; Eleanor and Jenny playing as she sautés shallots, braises the meat. And yet there is something that halts her reverie, and distracts her. Tucked behind the page is an opened letter, folded in half, and addressed from . . . well, it looks like Cornwall. A couple of sheets of blue-grey Basildon Bond written in the same decisive script.

She glances at Paul, then at the others poring over their sweet recipes. Jenny has always held that it is bad form to read other people's letters; and yet, this is different, somehow. It is already opened and apparently discarded. And the date is 18 June 1972 — over forty years ago. Besides, there is surely something serendipitous about her finding it: as if it were waiting for her to stumble upon as she rifled for her recipe? Or perhaps that's a poor excuse. Perhaps she is just more inquisitive than she wants to believe.

She glances at the archivist. His head is in a file. Furtively, she lifts the recipe book to hide her opening out the letter, and begins to read. Her eyes flit as she drinks up the information then move more slowly as she seeks to process it.

Time seems to be suspended. Particles of dust dance around Jenny but life, as she knows it, doesn't appear to be continuing. She feels winded, just as she did when she spotted Nigel and Gabby on that wet lunchtime, back in March. There is no retching this time but a gnawing ache in her stomach. A profound sadness. Things fall apart, she thinks; the centre cannot hold.

Paul Usher is looking at her in expectation, taking in the flush to her cheeks; her disorientation.

'Thank you.' She blushes. 'I found it. Just as I'd hoped to.'

He smiles.

'Amazing,' she burbles, and feels she has to explain herself. 'To see it written out on the page.' She tries a joke. 'Well, at least I know my mother can't claim the credit for it.'

He returns to his books.

'There's just one question . . . ' She tries to sound casual. 'Who was Charlie? I saw the name written at the top of a recipe,' she lies — and blushes. She feels as if she has to keep the letter's existence hidden, and the fact she has read it. She needs to protect its author in all her vulnerability.

'Charlie?' His eyes narrow. 'Charlie Pollington was Kathleen's adored younger brother.'

'And Kitty?'

But she does not need to ask the question.

'Kitty?' The archivist leans back, assessing her properly now, and she wonders if the discovery of the letter wasn't really so fortuitous.

'Kitty was Kathleen Eaden.'

Kathleen

Twenty weeks. Twenty-one. Twenty-two. The kicks are getting stronger now. Less of a flutter; more of a poke.

'Hello, little one.' She smiles down at her stomach, trying to assess if she can spot a limb, if the surface has changed with the pressure. 'Don't try to come out yet. Just you stay in there, nice and warm.'

When George visits her, she takes his broad hand and places it against her cotton nightdress.

'Will I hurt it?' He looks alarmed.

'George. It's your baby. Look, touch my skin.' His fingers graze her pubic hair and he flushes. He has not touched her since James Caruthers sewed her up tight.

'Just hold your hand there — no, there.' She guides him until his palm warms the spot where the baby last kicked. He looks terrified, poor love, though she can understand it and only the regularity of the kicks and their increasing strength have reassured her that she can touch her stomach at all.

'Did you feel it?'

'Not sure . . . Not yet.'

'Just be patient. Here, try stroking it. She likes that.'

'She?'

She blushes. 'Didn't I tell you? I've just got this feeling . . . that we're having a girl.'

'No you didn't but I'll take your word for it.'

'You don't mind?'

He looks bemused. 'I'd be delighted. More than delighted.' And he smiles.

They wait: Kathleen fearful, as ever, that the kicks will stop; George noticeably nervous. He begins stroking her belly in clockwise circles, his flat, wide fingers surprising her, as ever, with their delicate touch.

'Wait a minute.' His eyes widen in surprise.

'Did you feel it that time?'

'Oh, yes! Definitely yes!'

'And again?'

'Yes. Goodness. That was strong.'

'She is, isn't she?' She laughs.

'Yes,' he replies in delight, and she sees that he has tears in his eyes. 'Yes, she most definitely is.'

32

To make the densely rich chocolate cake that is a Sachertorte you need only four ingredients. Oh, but what ingredients: dark chocolate, eggs, sugar, ground almonds — and for the ganache, more chocolate and double cream. It is just as well it keeps, for this is a cake to be eaten one sliver at a time. It is rich; it is decadent; and it is supremely grown-up.

Karen feels almost calm by the time she goes to bed after an invigorating run and a soothing bath — though no food. She is in the mood for abstention after being cajoled into tasting her concoctions today.

She is back on track. Her baked alaskas were superlative — Harriet's description — and it suddenly becomes more important to gain her approval than Dan's. Her Sachertorte also vied with Jenny's for the best bake: the ganache glassily smooth, her piped chocolate elegant — surprising given that her writing is usually so girlish with its carefully curved lines and fat 'a's.

She has not been able to resist purging herself this evening: emptying any remnants of her meringue and chocolate torte into the toilet of her en suite bathroom. Her throat burns in the aftermath but she has sought to soothe it, and her twisted stomach, with peppermint tea.

She feels virtuous. Slipping beneath the crisp, ironed sheets, she tries to relax. If there are no slip-ups tomorrow, and she sees no reason why there should be, she might be on course to win. She falls asleep contemplating tomorrow's challenge: a croquembouche, perhaps? Surely a tiramisu would be too easy? What about a form of patisserie involving a mousseline?

When her mobile rings, she is in a deep sleep and it takes three rings for her to realise where the sound is coming from. She fumbles at her bedside table for her smartphone, which is vibrating as well as ringing, its white cover glowing with fluorescent light. The time shows 6.03.

'Hello?' Her voice is uncharacteristically bleary.

'Mrs Hammond?' The voice at the other end is male and official.

'Yes?' She is awake now, adrenalin sending sleep packing. An unexpected call this early in the morning is never a good thing. She swings her legs out of the bed and sits up, her bottom perched on the edge of the mattress, poised for action.

'It's Sergeant Steve Tyler here, the custody officer from Southampton central police station. I'm ringing to inform you that your car, your Audi, registration plate AK61 2BU, has been stolen and badly damaged — 'written off', is how we'd put it.

'I also need to inform you that your son Jake was driving it at the time.'

'Jake?' She is standing up now. 'What? Is he all

right? He's not dead is he?' Her voice rises in near-hysteria. Her bowels loosen, liquefied by panic.

'No, he's not dead, madam. He's absolutely fine and, miraculously, no one was injured. But he is in custody here at the station.'

'In custody?'

'In the cells, madam. Don't worry. He's had his rights read to him and seen the duty solicitor. He'll be interviewed later this morning.'

'Interviewed?' His lack of emotion means it takes a while for her to understand what he is saying. She is mortified by the extent to which she asks questions but it all seems so incomprehensible, they are automatic.

'He'll be questioned about several road traffic offences and about the theft of the vehicle.'

'The theft?'

'Section 12 of the Theft Act 1968: taking without owner's consent. A TWOC.'

'Pardon?' He is speaking a different language.

'Sorry. That's the acronym.' He gives a chuckle, and she imagines him: a plump, little man, oozing self-importance. 'What you might call joyriding.'

'But it was my car. He didn't steal it.'

'We need to see if you could make a statement, Mrs Hammond.'

'A statement?'

'You are the victim of this crime, Mrs Hammond, and we need you to make a statement to see if you could press charges.'

The unpleasant truth of what he is asking dawns on her. 'You want me to make a statement against my child so that you can press charges against him?'

'It would be helpful. Unless you gave permission?'

She pauses. It is on the tip of her tongue to swear but she stops herself, aware that she is talking to a police officer. She forces herself to become emollient. 'Well, of course, he can drive it whenever he likes.'

'He hasn't taken his test yet, has he?'

'No.'

'So if you have given him permission, you're permitting him to drive without insurance and without a licence — themselves offences that place you in more trouble than him for taking it. I'd think carefully, madam, before you say that.'

Frustration surges at this official little man who is now playing games.

'I didn't give him permission, no, of course I didn't, Sergeant. But I'm not going to make a statement against him.'

'Well, just think about it. There's no need for you to come in to see him but we'd need to see you to consider bail, if that's appropriate. We've tried your home — but you're not in Winchester, is that right?'

'I'm in Buckinghamshire, taking part in a baking competition.' The explanation — and her presence there — seems suddenly ludicrous. 'I'm leaving right now. I'm on my way.'

'There's no need to rush, Mrs Hammond. Please make sure you drive safely. He's probably asleep in the cells.'

'I doubt it.' The retort is bitter.

There is an uneasy silence.

'I'll come straight in.'

She kills the call, aware he is speaking — telling her that officers will come to her house — but little caring for her abruptness or the foolishness of speaking like this to the police. She has past experience of them, and it wasn't pleasant, or in any way beneficial.

All that matters is that she gets to Jake — and quickly. She throws underwear into her leather holdall and pulls the doors of her wardrobe open, wresting free the shift dress she had planned to wear today. Fear propels her into activity. It suddenly occurs to her that the need to see Jake is stronger than the desire to gather up her things.

She pulls on Pilates bottoms, her cashmere hoodie and ballet pumps. Then rips them off. She needs to look formidable even if her world is crumbling. On go the dress and a blazer. She will add high-heeled ankle boots when she finishes driving. She upends her hair and ties it into a high ponytail; thrusts rings on her fingers. Her hands shaking, she grabs make-up bag, jewellery pouch, iPod and handbag — leaving the rest of the room in disarray.

It has taken her less than five minutes from ending the phone call to reaching her Porsche. During this time, she has tried to call Oliver, pressing callback when he fails to answer home, his mobile, or the pied-à-terre. He is supposed to be in Winchester so where the hell is he and why isn't he answering?

As she reverses across the gravel, tyres

screeching, her phone rings. It's Oliver.

She brakes sharply, spraying gravel; kills the engine. 'It's about Jake. He's been arrested for taking the Audi and crashing it. No one else is injured — neither's he. But he'll need a better solicitor than the duty one. Could you arrange that? I'm on my way.'

She speaks in the way he understands: hard and factual, devoid of emotion.

There is a pause.

'I know. I've been trying to get hold of you.'

'You know?'

'He rang me.'

'He rang *you*?'

Her world shifts perceptibly.

'He's allowed one call.'

'Why did he ring you?'

She is struck by the injustice of it all.

'I suspect because you're the victim so the custody officer wouldn't permit contact.' He sighs in exasperation. 'Come on, Karen, this isn't about which parent he calls. This is about getting him out of this shit.'

She is surprised by the uncharacteristic display of emotion. Her husband is too controlled ever to swear.

'Oliver?'

'He's looking at going to court, Karen. Did you know he was chased by traffic cops before he smashed into a parked car? That he was involved in what they call a 'pursuit' and that he failed to stop? They'll have it all on camera. And that's quite apart from the fact he was driving on a provisional licence with no insurance. He'll be going to court — and he's looking at a possible custodial.'

'Oh my God. What the fuck has he done? Why has he done this?'

His voice is cold. 'This isn't the time for recriminations, or self-loathing. This is about trying to help him.'

'No, no, of course not.' She seeks to recover herself. 'Where are you?'

'London.'

She waits for him to gulp an admission of guilt.

'Livy was staying at Molly's; Jake said he would be at home revising and so there seemed — and clearly this was the wrong decision — no need for me to come back and check. I stayed on in town to get more work done.'

She lets her fury pervade the silence. Only fifty miles from home but he might as well be in a different continent.

She is suddenly exhausted by their virtual separation; by her loneliness. How did this happen? For a moment, she wants to be absolved of responsibility: to be held, secure in his arms, feeling the rise and fall of his chest.

Instead, she issues an order: 'Please sort out a lawyer. I'm going straight to the station. I'll see you at home.'

★   ★   ★

Later, it occurs to her that two members of her family could be charged with speeding offences as she circumnavigates London, her Porsche

339

Cayenne eating up the lights of the M25.

She is acutely aware of how fast she is driving as she zips along the outer lane, occasionally undercutting slower cars that have the temerity to cruise at eighty. At one point, a black Porsche Boxster flirts with her, tagging her in a game of car kiss chase, the blond boy racer grinning inanely.

She pulls into the middle lane; kills her speed; lets him roar off in a display of exhaust and thwarted testosterone. Ahead of her, the traffic is building up, the Porsches and Mercs that owned the road before six now jostling with the Audi saloons and VW Golfs; the pimped-up 4×4s; the people-carrying taxis on their second airport trip of the day.

Round and round they go. The orbital studded with cars. Embracing the capital, like lights encircling a Christmas tree.

Pulling off on to the M3 southbound, the traffic becomes marginally quieter and she zooms up the outer lane, leaving a chain of lorries rumbling behind. The car cleaves through the South Downs, where rabbits bound on the verge and a fox, destined to be roadkill, narrowly escapes. She surges on, the speedometer at 90 mph now. Winchester sleeps and Southampton, when she finally reaches it, is only stirring: the suburbs closed up for the night, the streets empty bar a few early morning runners and disorientated clubbers. The world is carrying on as normal despite Jake being held in a police cell. It is obscene.

She parks in the centre of the city, and crosses

over to the police station: 7.37 a.m. on a beautiful late April Sunday. Around her, lovers are sleeping off the previous night's drinking, curled around each other in bed. Her seventeen-year-old, meanwhile, is having a harsh — perhaps overdue — dose of reality. She imagines him, stripped of his belt and shoes, denied his wallet and iPhone, experiencing a night in a cell deep in the bowels of the police station. His beautiful face will be crumpled, bravado giving way to tears. I didn't cry, she thinks. Not even when he gripped my head.

It is the smell that brings it home to her. The smell peculiar to institutions: a cloying odour of disinfectant and fear. It is a stench that takes her back to the toilets of her comprehensive, where petty extortion and small-time drug dealing were carried out in the small stalls, girls cowering against the metal toilet roll holders or slumped on the urine-stained black seats as their tormenters practised stealthy intimidation. And it takes her back to a memory she has tried to block from her mind for three decades: of herself, as a seventeen-year-old, held at Southend nick. I didn't cry then. I just dealt with it later, in my usual way.

'Can I help you?'

The duty sergeant is surprised to see such a sophisticated woman enter the station so early in the morning. She is dressed as if for a night out: short dress, blazer, high-heeled ankle boots, and yet she seems focused: not noticeably drunk or disorientated.

'Jake Hammond.' She lowers her voice though

341

there is no one around, certainly not the drunks she feared and remembered. 'I believe you are holding him. He's my son.'

'Mrs Hammond? We spoke on the phone. Sergeant Tyler.'

He looks surprised as he equates the woman in front of him with the near-hysterical, increasingly abrasive person he spoke to.

'You made it here pretty quickly. But I told you not to come.'

'I'm sorry. I just wanted to see him as quickly as possible.'

'I'm afraid you can't do that, at the moment. You're the victim, you see, so it's not permitted until after we've interviewed you. And he's seventeen. He doesn't need you as his mother here.'

'Of course he needs me as his mother. He needs me now more than at any other time.'

'Sorry — I should have said he doesn't need an appropriate adult. He doesn't need a parent, or a guardian figure, in with him. We treat him as an adult in that respect.'

'But he's not an adult.'

'In the eyes of the law, he is in that respect.'

Tears well, infuriatingly. 'He is not an adult. He's my little boy.'

* ★ ★

Later, she is more stoic when the road traffic officer, a callow young sergeant only recently out of the Police Staff College tries to extract a statement.

342

It helps that she is on her own ground: in her capacious sitting room, with its polished oak parquet which the officer's comedy black boots risk marking, and its sumptuous cream sofa on which he has lowered his tall frame.

It also helps that Oliver is at her side. To all observers, they are a united couple, anxious for their child's welfare but aware of the seriousness of his behaviour: the fact he has committed a crime.

'I think we can just put it down to youthful high spirits.' Oliver had sought to downplay the situation with a smoothness Karen associated with his professional life but rarely glimpsed.

'With respect, sir. I think it's a little more serious than that,' Sergeant Knapton had begged to differ. 'He was driving at 96 mph on the ring road and was in a pursuit situation.'

'I think what my husband means, Sergeant,' Karen had interposed with a smile at both men, as she had refilled the officer's coffee cup, 'is that Jake isn't a 'bad boy'. He's never been in trouble with the police before and, as his headmaster will tell you, he's an exemplary pupil.

'I think what we both feel is that this was an ill-judged prank that went badly wrong. You can be assured we will be letting him know precisely what we think of his behaviour. But as for pressing charges: I don't think we're going to achieve anything by doing that, other than giving him a criminal record — and risking alienating him.'

'My wife's quite right,' Oliver had added, with a smile at her. 'Thank you, darling.

'I think what we all need to consider, officer,' he went on, 'is that Jake is a high flyer. He's applying to Durham and if we blight his copybook in this way, we will, quite literally, ruin him. So, we won't be pressing charges, officer, and, though we recognise the severity of the driving offences, as our son, we will be supporting him.'

He had given the smile of a rich man used to getting his own way.

'Now about bail . . . '

'That's down to the discretion of the custody officer, sir. Not my job. But if you seem to be suggesting you would support him and wouldn't aid him to abscond, and if it appears he's unlikely to be a risk to himself . . . '

'Jake? A suicide risk? The idea's preposterous.'

' . . . I can't see why it wouldn't be granted.'

'Thank you, Sergeant.' It is Karen. 'So, can he come home now?'

'He needs to be interviewed, first, madam.'

'Oh, of course.' She had forgotten that. 'Well, when he can, I'd like to come and collect him.'

33

Be sure to make time to bake specifically for your children, concocting fairy sandwiches and butterfly cakes just for them. A birthday cake for a special child is a memory they will cherish. Everyone wants to feel loved and to feel unique. And children feel this particularly strongly.

It is a crestfallen Jake who greets her. The arrogance he has worn like a shield over recent months has been discarded revealing him to be more boy than man: soft-featured, vulnerable, scared.

Barefoot and beltless, he seems diminished, his six foot two-inch frame bent over.

'All right, Mum?' His greeting is hesitant. The ironic 'Ma' is missing. He bows his head, shame at his behaviour and at the incipient tears engulfing him.

She goes to put her arms round him.

'Whatcha doing?' He looks, briefly, mortified then surrenders.

'All right, my darling. It's all all right.'

His long, lanky frame in her arms, she realises she has not held him like this for at least four years — since he was twelve or thirteen. Latterly, if he has touched her it has been momentary, a clutch given ironically when fooling around with his friends, or a brief squeeze, his body held away from her, bestowed under sufferance.

He draws away, aware he is being appraised by the inspector who has made quite clear his contempt for him.

'That's not to say Dad and I aren't bloody furious.' She says this partly for the officer's benefit and partly for her son's. She doesn't want them to think he is a rich kid whose misdemeanours will be paid for by Mummy and Daddy — however true this is. Hours later, she will curse him when she becomes embroiled with the insurance firm and finds herself explaining that her car was taken and written off but that the police are not treating it as theft of a vehicle. The threat of the insurance claim not being met hangs heavy and, in the privacy of her shower, she rails against his privilege. But, for now, there are no recriminations. She feels nothing but relief.

She goes through the necessary paperwork with Jake and the custody officer. Can she vouchsafe for him not absconding? It doesn't appear that he is liable to harm himself or to intimidate her, and he has shown that all-important remorse, and so he is bailed until the juvenile court hearing in two weeks.

Jake signs for his belongings, handed over in a labelled plastic bag. His wallet and iPhone; socks, belt and house keys, pitiful in the plastic. The car keys are signed for by Karen, the weighty key fob thrust deep in her handbag, out of sight, out of harm's way.

'You know that your car's not roadworthy now, madam.'

'I am aware of that, yes.'

'You'll need to contact the garage.'

They go through the practicalities; mind-numbing, exhausting, necessary, while, by her side, Jake is eaten up with shame.

By the time they reach the car, across the street from the police station, Jake is crying properly: silent sobs that rack his body, and which, in a rush of irritation, she imagines are put on for effect.

She is silent, unlocking the Porsche, opening the passenger door for him, getting in on her side. It is only when both doors are closed, and she is assured of privacy, that she can trust herself to talk to him.

'So?' Her tone is cold. Anger submerges relief — not just at him writing off the car but at him putting her through all this.

He blurts out a sob. His eyes are red-rimmed and puffy now, his top lip doused in snot and tears.

'Oh, for God's sake, blow your nose.' She hands him a neat tissue from a packet, then another. He sniffs gratefully, tries a watery smile. It is as if, she thinks, looking at him more dispassionately, he is a five-year-old again.

'Why did you do it, Jake? How could you be so stupid, so irresponsible? You could have got yourself killed — or killed someone else. Christ, you could be facing charges of death by dangerous driving.'

He gives another sob but when he looks at her, there is anger and incomprehension in his eyes to match hers.

'Why do you think I did it?'

'I've no bloody idea. Because it seemed like fun? You weren't drunk. Were you high? My God . . . '

'No, nothing like that. Honest. The police did a blood test.'

'Well, why then? To get at me?'

'Yes.' He is crying properly now.

'Yes?' She is dumbfounded. 'Yes?' Her voice escalates.

'Do you really not know?'

'No.' Though of course she knows and her fear is now a certainty.

His voice comes out in a rush. 'Because of Jamie.'

'What about Jamie?' She feels winded.

'He boasted about it . . . '

She wants to retch. The response is physiological not merely psychological. She opens the car door, leans out; waits, breathing in the crisp early morning air until she has calmed herself, averted a catastrophe. *You're fooling no one, Ma. You're fooling no one.*

The move buys her time. She turns back to Jake, whose sobs have become quieter, a gentle riff filling the silence.

'He boasted about it?'

'On Friday night. I bumped into him in town. At the Wetherspoons. Don't think he said it to everyone . . . least I hope not. But to me and Sam. 'Your mum's hot,' that sort of thing . . .

'I told him to lay off and he just said, 'Well, she don't mind. She puts it about.''

He winces; glances at her to gauge her reaction. She looks pale, and angry.

'I tried to deck him, but he just laughed. He laughed at me. And he said, 'I'm talking from experience, Mummy's boy.''

The confession comes out in the rush of a sob. For a moment, a blub fills the Porsche. He wipes a bubble of snot away with his sleeve.

'I tried to deck him again — and got kicked out. Later he sent a text saying: 'Sorry, mate. Only joking.' But he wasn't, Mum. I know he wasn't.'

'Of course, he was.' The lie is automatic.

'Don't fucking patronise me. I'm not stupid.'

His eyes, huge and hazel, fill with tears and resentment. 'I know, Mum. I know . . . '

You're fooling no one, Ma. You're fooling no one. Can't she try, just one last time?

But there's more. 'You were always flirting at the pool with him.'

She sighs, relieved. 'Oh, flirtation . . . You know what I'm like; that's just harmless . . . '

'And there was that time I came home early on a free period . . . He was cycling out of our drive and he ignored me. I couldn't work out why he was here and didn't want to see me . . .

'When I came in, you seemed a bit flustered. You'd been baking — custard tarts, I think, my favourite — and a couple had been eaten. I remember being surprised that you'd tasted them, let alone had two, and you said he'd dropped by with some information about Livy's swimming and you'd given him a couple. To be honest, I was jealous — I couldn't work out why you'd chosen to give the gym lifeguard a coffee, spend time with him. I was jealous you were giving him fucking custard tarts baked for me . . .

'Then you went upstairs for a shower and I realised the real reason you wanted him and how fucking stupid, how fucking juvenile I'd been.'

She is silent. There seems nothing to say. He appears to have conclusive proof. In other circumstances, she would lie but she knows she will not convince Jake. She watches Southampton wake up through her windscreen; dog walkers and joggers returning with the Sunday papers, early churchgoers, dressed smartly for 9 a.m. services, walking briskly across the street. Outside the solid cocoon of her 4×4, life continues. Inside, life has been turned upside down and now appears to be suspended. Yet the digital clock marks another minute.

It is she who breaks the limbo. 'You're not stupid. You're very astute.'

She watches him take in the confession. 'I'm very, very sorry.'

She is not the type to go in for self-flagellation; to prostrate herself in front of others. If there is to be self-recrimination — as she knows there will be — it will be done alone, in the privacy of her bathroom with the taps running.

Nevertheless, her apology feels inadequate: four words that cannot convey the depth of her penitence.

She repeats it, as if repetition will make things better. 'I'm so, so sorry, Jake.'

★ ★ ★

For the rest of the day, she is numb. She listens as Oliver contacts an old college friend — a criminal QC specialising in getting celebrities lenient sentences for driving offences — and secures his agreement to represent Jake at his juvenile court hearing. She expresses relief as her husband tells her that Jake is likely to get a £300–£400 fine for driving without insurance and eighteen months' disqualification before he can take his test. She cooks carefully, lovingly, dutifully: roasting a chicken, making buttery mashed potato, green beans and wine-rich gravy for a son who has refused to eat all day but who, by early evening, is quietly ravenous. She watches as Oliver — having expressed his fulsome disappointment in his son but still ignorant of his wife's role — drives back to London. She checks on Jake, hunkered under the duvet, monosyllabic and exhausted, but safe, under her roof; in bed by 9 p.m.

It is only once she is sure he and Livy are asleep that she retreats to her sanctuary: her bathroom, minimalist and spa-like; as sterile as that of a boutique hotel; little evidence of her complex personality here. She wraps herself in a waffled bathrobe, scrutinising her stomach and thighs as she does so, checking her hip bones jut out at a definite angle so that her thumbs can rest between them and her flesh. Then she takes in her face: hard, lined, cloaked in exhaustion. She slumps to the floor, warmed by the under-floor heating but still shaking — chilled by distress and fear.

The retching does not seem to be enough,

tonight, or it does not satisfy. She has been incapable of eating and finds herself vomiting pale saffron liquid: her stomach juices. Distressed, she seeks oblivion in a bath, the water just about bearable; a degree or two from scalding. She lowers herself gingerly, then relents and turns the cold tap, submerging herself so that the water roars in her ears, a momentary distraction. Her hair unfurls like seaweed, swirls around her: no pre-Raphaelite Ophelia but a tense, reddening Medusa.

When she emerges — gasping for air — the tears come. Hot, angry sobs of guilt, of shame, and of self-pity. Despite her frantic scrubbing, she cannot rid herself of the smell of the police station: the stench of bleach and institutional hot dinners; anxiety and despair.

She plunges under the water again, frantic to cleanse every orifice. She tries to scrub at her nostrils, but ends up spluttering. She emerges then sinks back, her shoulders covered, her hands clutching them in a parody of a lover's embrace.

The image that stays at the front of her mind as she lies there, cocooned in the water, is not of Jake, his voice breaking as he detailed Jamie's taunting; nor of Oliver, his manner cold and efficient as he managed to pull the necessary strings. It is not even of Jamie and herself, stretched across her marital bed one bitter December afternoon — perhaps the day when Jake spotted them — her body still resonating like a bowed viola after a particularly satisfying bout of lovemaking.

352

It is of a figure she has sought to block from her mind for thirty years. The custody officer at Southend police station. A man of medium height but broad-shouldered. Strong and compact: someone who you would not want to take on in a fight. His eyes were dark and knowing. They had sized her up the moment she'd been dragged, handcuffed, into the station. But it is his belt buckle that she most clearly remembers: matt, brass, heavy; a belt that could cause damage, and which pressed into his flesh, delineating his stomach and groin.

'I can see a way to dropping the charges,' he had leered. 'A quick blow job and no one's the wiser.'

'You've got to be fuckin' joking,' she had spat with the bravado that she wore as standard at seventeen.

'Suit yourself. It's your first time in here, isn't it? For shoplifting? The beak are coming down hard on that at the moment. Clever girl like you doesn't want to blot her copybook. Get yourself a record. But if you make my night more interesting, we could wipe the slate clean . . . '

He had unzipped his fly, pulled out his penis, already priapic, thick and winking. With a meaty paw he had gripped the back of her head.

Thirty years on, it is the smell of it she remembers; sour with dried urine, white sediment unfurling underneath the foreskin. That, and the taste.

She hurls herself at the toilet bowl, and retches once again.

34

There will be moments in your life when the very last thing you feel like doing is baking. But do not leave it too long. On the rare occasions I have felt disinclined to bake, I soon miss it and find I am like a ewe separated from her lamb.

'She's not doing it.'

'What do you mean she's not doing it?'

'Karen — she's dropped out of the competition. The Search for the New Mrs Eaden.' Vicki has wasted no time in phoning Claire to pass on the news.

'What do you mean, she's dropped out?'

'Just that. She phoned Jenny to say she was giving her a clear run and wasn't taking part any more. Jenny rang me.'

Despite her excitement, Vicki cannot quite get rid of her irritation that Karen didn't see her as the major competition. OK, so Jenny is the likely winner but it would have been courteous if Karen hadn't been quite so explicit about thinking this and if she had contacted them all.

'But, did she say why?' Claire still seems to be struggling with the concept that anyone would want to bow out of the contest. 'I mean, she was so good. She won at puddings, didn't she, and her YouTube hits are the highest. No offence, but I thought it would be her or Jenny who'd win.'

'Her son's in trouble with the police for

stealing her car and writing it off.' Vicki still can't believe it, and stating the bald facts only makes them more incomprehensible.

There is a pause while Claire digests this. When she speaks, she too is incredulous.

'Karen's son's a joyrider? Oh. My. God.'

'I know. Well . . . it was her car, not anyone else's.'

'That doesn't make it much better.' Claire gives a low whistle. 'She must have been really pissed off.'

'I don't think so.' Vicki is surprised by this turn of events. 'Jenny said she was being hugely supportive. He has a court hearing in a fortnight and Karen wants to be able to focus entirely on him — hence dropping out.'

'That's lovely of her . . . and totally understandable.'

'Yes, but maybe a bit surprising? I don't know about you, but I didn't think she seemed the least maternal. She never talked about her kids, did she? Not like me and you going on about them all the time. Just goes to show, doesn't it? We made all these assumptions but we didn't really know her at all.'

Kathleen

Twenty-three weeks, twenty-four. She reads that her baby is the size of a bag of sugar. She visualises it, then sends Mrs Jennings to bring one from the kitchen. She weighs the paper bag of Tate and Lyle in her hand. One pound feels heavy. Solid. Tangible. A decent, substantial weight.

The baby's foot flutters. Oh my darling, she thinks. Stay in there. Stay in there and remain safe. She reaches to check her inner thighs again. No tackiness; no blood seeping from her. She looks at her Rolex. Ten o'clock: two hours since she last checked. She needs to stop this recent tic; this obsessive checking. She promises herself not to look again before midday.

What to do? Think about something positive, she reminds herself. The cherry blossom in full bloom just below her window; the late April sunshine, bursting in on her. 'This bed thy centre is,' she murmurs, quoting Donne. 'These walls thy sphere.'

Think about *The Art of Baking*. And here she smiles. Completed — and with a publication date for early September, a month after her due date. Time enough to get herself back on to her feet and help with its promotion, she had reassured George. And, yes, of course she wants

356

to do that. After months spent lying alone, as stiff as a board, she wants to sing of the joys of baking and its place at the heart of one's family. She thinks she can manage to play at being Mrs Eaden again.

She stretches out like a cat and points her toes in a parody of exercise, luxuriating in a moment's satisfaction. One project is finished. And, if she can do that then perhaps — please, perhaps — the second — growing her baby — can be achieved.

She crosses her fingers automatically. The guilt of the past two years — the fear that she killed her three earlier babies by virtue of having a weak cervix, and the self-loathing that has come with this — is beginning to ease slightly. I can do this, she prays, as she resists checking her thighs. The baby kicks. We can do this, she corrects herself, stroking her belly and giving it a gentle pat of reassurance. Now just stay in there a little longer. Just stay in there, warm and tight.

The most recent *Home Magazine* is by her bed, containing not just her column but a pattern for newborn bootees. She looks at it but will not knit them — nor order baby clothes from Peter Jones. But when George buys a cot — chosen to match the Ercol furniture she loves and she knows he cannot stand — she thanks him and refuses to listen to the inner voice that continues to mutter that, by doing so, she risks tempting fate.

A celebratory tea

The Duchess of Bedford conceived of the idea of afternoon tea in the 1840s, and, one hundred and twenty years on, it may seem somewhat outmoded. We have no real need of afternoon tea; not in these days when we can just grab a biscuit to nibble alongside our mug of instant coffee. And we may feel we have no time for it with our increasingly busy lives.

But many delightful traditions, though not the least bit necessary, are highly pleasurable. Afternoon tea is one such. Served between 4 and 5 p.m., an occasional afternoon tea will not only restore and revive but cherish and comfort. It will spoil and delight, nurture and sustain.

For form's sake, you will need to make at least some pretence of offering something savoury. Thinly sliced sandwiches will suffice if filled with smoked salmon and cream cheese, finely cut ham and mustard, thin slices of cucumber and butter, or poached salmon and dill mayonnaise.

The savoury element dispatched with, we can focus on the more joyful elements: the scones, the biscuits and the exquisite little cakes. Prettiness is important and so I use a triple-layered cake plate and pile up lemon, raspberry and chocolate macaroons; mini fruit tartlets; and the tiniest of chocolate éclairs or mini Paris-Brests.

For those unsatisfied by such fripperies, you may wish to serve something more substantial such as a ginger cake or almond-encrusted Dundee cake. For my part, I prefer something unashamedly decadent: the richest of chocolate cakes or a strawberry-and-cream-filled gateau. A substantial piece of whimsy.

To drink, one must serve Darjeeling or Earl Grey — and one must use a teapot. This is about the ritual of teatime. Serve with a small jug of milk or slices of lemon and remember: it is not milk in first. Or abandon such anxieties and, for an intimate afternoon tea of sheer decadence, serve with a glass of chilled champagne.

Kathleen Eaden: *The Art of Baking* (1966)

35

Nowhere is the alchemy of baking more evident than when making choux pastry. For this raw, salty dough puffs up into the most ethereal of cases, ready to hold an unctuous treat.

Vicki is in a state: a full-on, frenetic panic in which her kitchen is sprayed with flour, every surface is cluttered, and she cannot think straight.

The competition final is a day away and nothing is going right: her choux pastry is thick and heavy, her mini sponge sandwiches, coloured with raspberry and cocoa, are too lurid. Her millefeuille, inelegantly, irregularly shaped, lack the necessary finesse.

She has worked until two in the morning and then been up since six, when Greg slipped from the house suggesting she have a lie-in. She is running on adrenalin, sugar and caffeine. Too much of all three. And she feels sick.

It is as if she has to finish her school reports, oversee the key stage one nativity, and prepare for an Ofsted inspection all in the same evening. She is never going to manage it.

'Mum-meeeeeeee . . . '

It is Alfie, calling from the garden, with his habitual plea for attention.

'Can you come and play football?'

'Not now, lovely, I'm busy . . . '

'But you *promised* . . . '

'I didn't promise anything, Alfie, no. I said I might play later after I've finished.'

The distinction is lost on her three-year-old who stomps back up the garden, his head down, his shoulders hunched, in an almost comic display of fury.

Vicki feels a momentary twinge of guilt at being pedantic and dismissive. But she hasn't the time to worry about it. She decides to try her choux pastry again and begins to assemble the ingredients: plain flour tipped on to a sheet of greaseproof paper, water, butter and salt placed in a medium-sized saucepan; three free-range eggs, beaten lightly. She heats the butter and water mixture, tipping in the flour as it comes to the boil and removing the pan from the heat. Then, with a wooden spoon, she begins to beat furiously. 'Come on,' she mutters under her breath, as what appears to be a culinary disaster coalesces, beginning to form a smooth, heavy dough. 'Yes, yes, that's better.'

A sporadic thud begins to sound in the kitchen. Vicki is so preoccupied, she doesn't initially register it and then takes a few moments to realise what it is. Alfie, who had been kicking his mini football ineffectively around the back of the garden, is now ramming it against the back of the house and the frame of the open French windows.

'Alf-ieeee . . . '

The ball hurtles into the kitchen, thudding against the units and skittering around her feet.

He laughs hysterically: great gulps of laughter.

Then he sees her anger.

'Alfie Marchant. I am furious!'

She abandons her dough and chases after him, whipping up the garden, fired by fury.

He turns, half fearful, half hopeful it is a game, then sees the look on her face and begins crying. Still running, he stumbles on a tuft of grass, picks himself up, then tries to hide himself in his wigwam, flattening his small body and wriggling backwards as if he can worm his way out of sight.

She reaches in and hauls him out.

'Ow. You're hurting me.' He tries to pull his arms free where she is holding them. She grips harder, her fingers leaving angry red marks in the crook of his elbows.

'I'll hurt you more if you don't behave.' Where had that threat come from — and that choice of a language? The answer is automatic: she hears her mother uttering it. She kneels down, pulling him with her and turns him over, as if to slap the back of his legs.

'Muuuuuuu-meee.'

As she raises her hand, it is as if she were observing herself. Where is calm, kind Miss Taylor, as she was known at St Matthew's? The whole situation seems so ludicrous, so unlike her, that she stops instantly.

She doesn't know what to do with her hand, and finds herself drawing Alfie up into her arms and clinging to him.

'Little Alf, I'm so sorry,' she whispers, confounding him with this sudden change in behaviour. They sit, her hugging him fiercely, stroking his hair and whispering reassurances; him mute, unable to read her mood swings. She is mortified. Why is she behaving like this? It is the closest she has ever got to smacking him.

She carries him back to the house, though he is too heavy for this now and, in normal circumstances, would be running. He holds on to her, dimly aware that this infantilisation is for her benefit.

As she staggers up the garden, she keeps up a steady stream of endearments but her kindness is tempered. She cannot resist the odd admonishment.

'Mummy's sorry she was so angry, but you know you mustn't kick your football inside . . . '

Alfie whimpers softly.

'Oh, but my boy, I am so very sorry.'

When they reach the kitchen she sees that she was interrupted before her choux pastry was properly formed and that her dough is lumpy. She needs to whisk in the eggs but she should have done so immediately.

'I'm going to have to start again now!' The cry, irrational and childish, escapes before she can stop herself.

Alfie, incapable of reading his erratic mother, pulls away.

'Oh, uuuurrrrrgh.' She bends down to hold him and tries to breathe more deeply. It isn't his fault. He's only three. She is overreacting. Her heart races. Calm down, she tells herself. Try to breathe deeply.

She glances at the clock. Ten past ten. Anxiety shoots through her as she contemplates just how much she has to achieve. What can she do with Alfie? She hates herself for fobbing him off on Ali or her mother; feels both guilty and inadequate for being unable to prepare for this competition while looking after him properly. Kathleen Eaden would have managed it, she thinks with a burst of resentment: her daughter Laura spent hours in the kitchen helping her mother bake. But Alfie can't help with these more complicated recipes. Or perhaps it's her fault: the outstanding teacher lacks necessary patience. Either way, she needs some help today.

'Let's just let you watch some CBeebies and I'll contact Granny and see if she'll look after you.' She reaches for this option.

'Not Granny, no.' Alfie looks anguished. 'Want to stay with you, Mummy.'

'Well, I'm sorry, but I'm not able to give you enough attention today, so I think you'll find it a bit boring. You like going to Granny's, don't you?'

She doesn't give him time to answer.

'Of course you do. I'll give her a call now. I'm sure she'll love it.'

Beaming broadly, she leaves him in front of some animated vegetable puppets singing about the joys of compost, and dials her mother's number. Please say yes, she wills her as the number rings out. Please say yes. Don't make me feel terrible about this but, please, just help me.

'Vicki?'

'Mum. Are you OK? Good. Look, I'm ringing for a massive favour. You know the final's tomorrow — yes, yes, of the Search for the New

Mrs Eaden — well, I desperately need to do lots of practice; yes, yes, I do; I know I do; I'm not being perfectionist, or not just being a perfectionist. I'm finding it impossible with Alfie here. So . . . you know what I'm going to ask, don't you? Please, Mum, could you take him? Please, I need some help here.'

There is a pause, so lengthy Vicki wonders if her mother is listening.

'Mum?'

'I'm just thinking, Victoria.' Her tone is tetchy. 'Is there no one else available? What about his nursery?'

'I tried but there aren't any spare spaces today. They're fully booked . . . No, they can't 'just squeeze him in', they need to maintain their staff/child ratios.'

'And Ali?'

'Well, Sam's at nursery today so I can't ask her to look after my child if she's free.'

'Couldn't you?'

'No, I couldn't . . . and I've asked her for too many favours recently.'

'I'm sure she'd help you out, just this once.'

'No, she wouldn't, Mum. And I can't ask her. But, even if I could, I don't think she'd do it for me.'

There is another pause.

'Mum?'

'Victoria . . . I'm thinking.'

Vicki waits, watching the second hand of the kitchen clock revolve a full seven seconds before her mother answers.

'You do realise I had things arranged. I'm

supposed to be doing a shift in Oxfam this afternoon, and I've got my book club this evening. You'd collect him by then, though, wouldn't you?' A note of panic enters her voice.

Vicki squirms with embarrassment.

'It's just I've got to be in Buckinghamshire overnight, in case there are any hiccups. Greg was going to get back here for eight. But is there any chance you could hold on to him overnight? It would just mean I could spend as long as possible practising. You were going to look after him tomorrow, anyway.'

'Yes, I was, wasn't I?'

The reminder seems to weigh against Vicki as Frances contemplates the extent of her generosity.

'I know I'm mucking up your plans, Mum, and I wouldn't ask unless I was absolutely desperate. But this is the final. It's a really big deal, and, to be honest, I'm panicking a bit about it.'

She decides to go full out and opt for flattery.

'I just need to be totally focused and prepared. Isn't that what you always taught me? Well, I ignored you, didn't I, in the run-up to my A-levels. But now I see you were right. Think of this as my A-level equivalent: my chance to shine.'

Silence.

Frances gives an irritated cough. 'I'm not sure that's a good comparison.'

'Not academically, no, of course not.' Vicki realises her mother disapproves of the analogy but refuses to backtrack completely. 'But inasmuch as it's an assessment of my skills then it is comparable, yes.'

There is another pause. I can do no more, thinks Vicki. I have virtually begged her. How else can I persuade her? She thinks of the nuclear option — the issue that can never be discussed — but knows she cannot raise it. And, even if she could, she knows from experience her mother is resistant to a full-on guilt trip.

'All right.' Frances's tone is dry. 'But this will have to be a one-off. I told you when Alfie was born that I wasn't to be relied on for lots of childcare.'

'No, of course not. Well, there's no competition after tomorrow so of course it will be the last time.'

'And you'll bring him to me?'

Vicki looks at the clock. Ten fifteen. Her day is being eaten away but she has no choice.

'Yes, yes, of course I will.'

'OK, then.' Her mother is brisk. 'That's fine.'

Vicki feels wrong-footed and forces herself to smile down the phone. 'Thank you, Mum, thank you so much. You're a star!'

There is a sniff.

'Yes,' says Frances. 'I rather think I am.'

⋆　⋆　⋆

Two and a half hours later, and Vicki is back in her kitchen having hared up the M40 to Oxford. She had spurned the offer of a coffee and given Alfie the most peremptory of cuddles, kissing him fiercely and whispering another apology in his ear.

'Don't leave me, Mummy. Alfie play with Mummy,' he is sobbing as she flees from her mother's small terrace, smiling reassurance. She finds it hard not to fixate on the look on his face.

As she drives back, she comforts herself with the advice of his key worker at nursery: that he is just crying for her benefit. Is that really true, she wonders or a white lie told to appease the consciences of mothers escaping from children's centres as they take advantage of their government-funded fifteen hours of childcare a week?

She texts her mother at a set of traffic lights: 'Is Alfie OK now' but doesn't receive an answer. What should she read into this? That her mother will not respond because she has omitted the obligatory please and thank you, and the grammatically required question mark? Or that her mother has lost her phone again? Ambiguity festers. That is the problem with texts.

The kitchen is in chaos but, in the quiet, she works more calmly, writing a list of the six recipes she wants to get through and ticking them off systematically. Her phone chimes with a text and she checks it to see if it is from Frances. Instead, it is from Jenny.

'How are you doing? Feeling really nervous and can't believe the final's tomorrow! Are you still practising? Xxx'

She sends an effusive one back, surprised not that the older woman is nervous but that she is being so open about this. That's a bad strategy for a competitor, surely? But then the contestants have never been aggressively competitive. A gentle courtesy has coloured their dealings with one another, growing into a genuine friendship. Vicki will miss this solidarity: the feeling of working alongside others who appreciate the joy of creating something delicious and do not see it as sheer indulgence.

The oven timer pings and she switches off her phone to shut down distractions, and inspects a fresh batch of pastry for her millefeuille.

* * *

In Oxford, Frances too is seeking to rid herself of distractions — or, more specifically, a single, albeit noisy, distraction in the form of a three-year-old boy. It is mid-afternoon and she feels she has performed her grandmotherly duty for long enough. She has made boiled egg and soldiers, read him a story and tried to interest him in jigsaws — though the ones she has picked up from Oxfam are too advanced for her small grandson and frustrate him. It seems he cannot manage a one-hundred-piece jigsaw, after all.

Abandoning him in a rush, Vicki had failed to bring the usual boxes of Lego or Playmobil, or his football. 'Can you just get him to do some drawing? He loves that,' she had shouted over her shoulder at her mother as she had virtually run out of Frances's house and back to the sanctuary of her car.

Frances had tried to oblige but refuses to be

enthusiastic about seemingly indiscriminate scribbles and the profligate waste of paper.

'Alfie, please, this is terribly wasteful,' she had chastised him as he had produced a flurry of scrawled masterpieces, scattering sheets of her best printing paper across the table like an unfavourable hand of cards.

'Alfie needs more, Nana.'

'No. No you don't, Alfie, and it's not Nana, that's your other grandmother. It's Frances, remember.' She had given a shudder.

He had looked at her with his almond eyes, fringed with obscenely long lashes, and smiled at her.

'OK, Nana.'

Now she is at a loss as to what to do. He does have Dog, his bedraggled and distinctly smelly teddy bear whom he insists on clutching. But Frances's attempts to engage her only grandchild over his favourite soft toy have fallen flat.

'And what's teddy's name?'

'Dog.'

'Really? He's not a dog; he's a bear, isn't he.'

Alfie had shaken his head emphatically.

'Not bear. Dog.'

'I'm not going to talk to you if you're not going to be sensible.'

He had smiled beatifically then pulled his eyes and mouth aside in imitation of a clown. Jiggling up and down he had laughed nonsensically. 'Okey-dokey, okey-dokey, okey-dokey.'

She had left the room in exasperation.

The trouble, she thinks as she switches on the kettle for a cup of camomile tea, is that she seems to have forgotten how to play with small children. A frisson of anxiety runs through her as she tries to remember how she kept Vicki entertained. Perhaps she didn't need to: she was such a good girl, until her late teens. The thought that Vicki might have liked a little more attention niggles. I didn't play with her as she does with Alfie, she thinks with sudden clarity, and I could have done so. I should have done so.

The kitchen fills with steam and the memory of the Battenburg surfaces. Vicki's face with its look of apprehension — or was it fear? With a sudden flick, she throws her tea bag in a mug and returns next door. Alfie is talking to Dog but breaks off when she enters, as if he doesn't want her to hear.

She bends down, her smile becoming less tentative as an idea forms. 'I know what we should do,' she says. 'We should search for insects in the garden!'

His face breaks into a beam, and he jostles her as she wrestles with the key to the back door.

'Come on, Nana.'

' . . . Of course, Alfie.' She bites her lip.

Being outside in the sunshine makes everything better. He reminds her of a lamb as he careers around the small patch of lawn, running aimlessly, enjoying his freedom. She sits herself down with her tea and a newspaper, provides him with a bucket and small spade, and suggests he start looking for worms.

For a few precious minutes they coexist happily. All that is required of Frances is that she looks into his bucket every so often and feigns enthusiasm; all that is required of Alfie is that he does not trample on the flower beds but stays on the small handkerchief of lawn. Behind her newspaper she watches: intrigued by the care with which he speaks to the worms, curling in the bottom of his bucket, concerned at the amount of grass he keeps showering them with. 'Here you are, wormies, lots of food.'

But then he reaches for one of her purple-headed fritillaries.

'Alfie!' She cannot stop herself.

'Sorry, Nana.' His bottom lip protrudes; his voice is tremulous.

'And I told you: it's Frances; not 'Nana'.'

'Yes, Nana.'

The mistake is automatic and he recognises it immediately. His huge eyes threaten to fill with tears.

'Hello, Frances — having fun?'

It is Julia, Frances's earth mother of a neighbour, who has popped her head over the fence between their gardens. Relaxed, good-natured and distinctly alternative, Julia is the sort of woman Frances would normally shy away from, and yet she cannot help but like her.

Her enquiry, for instance, could rankle, but Frances knows it is not meant maliciously. Indeed, in Julia's world, where four children run riot, a grandmother left alone with a grandchild could not fail to be enjoying herself.

'Does Alfie want to come and play with my lot? They've just got back from school and the big girls would love to play with another little one . . . '

375

Alfie turns to Frances, his eyes gleaming. 'Please, Nana.'

'Oh, well, I really don't want to put you out, Julia . . . '

'It's not putting me out at all. I'll just be getting on with cooking dinner. They'll only be in the garden so you'll be able to hear him. I expect they'll just be bouncing on the trampoline.'

As if on cue, squeals emanate from her side of the fence as her daughters, Saffron and Maisie, scramble on to a trampoline and compete to bounce the highest.

'There they are now. Can you hear them, Alfie? Would you like a go?'

'Oh, well, if you don't mind. I am rather exhausted . . . '

'Then it's sorted. Are you going to lift this little man over or does he want to crawl through the hole in the fence?'

'Oh . . . well, I suppose it makes sense for him to wriggle through it.'

'Come on then, Alfie.'

Julia disappears only to call from the bottom of the garden. Delighted, Alfie runs from his grandmother into a less constrained, more fun-loving world.

Frances sits back with her paper, overwhelmed with tiredness, and allows herself a little doze.

36

At moments of stress, baking can prove most therapeutic, the baker easing her anxieties as she kneads her dough or makes her butter cream. There will be times when it is not practical to bake, but remember: you can always return to it.

The cry, when it rends the air, shortly after four o'clock, barely sounds human. In fact, Frances first thinks of the squeal of a piglet, so ear-piercing is it, and so high-pitched.

On and on it goes, destroying the calm of the afternoon; disturbing the neighbours. Then come the cries of children, frantic, hysterical — 'Mum, Mum, something's wrong with him' — and the heavy footsteps of an overweight woman lumbering up the garden, shouting reassurances.

'It's OK, I'm coming. It's OK, it's OK . . . '

It dawns on Frances, wrenched from her sleep, that the horrific sound comes from next door where she sent Alfie. She rises from her garden chair, inadvertently knocking it over and runs to peer over the fence.

Alfie is prostrate on the trampoline, and the terrible noise seems to be coming from him. Julia is bent over him, her vast bottom blocking him from view.

'Julia? What's wrong, what's happening?'

The younger woman is curt, all lackadaisical good nature gone. 'He's broken his arm, Frances.'

377

She moves aside and gestures at the three-year-old who is writhing in agony, his arm bent like a banana. His screams go on and on.

Frances is in denial. 'He can't have. You were looking after him.'

Incomprehension turns to blame.

Julia turns to face her, her normally florid face drained of colour.

She spits the words out. 'We need to get him to hospital. Just look at him.'

Frances obliges though the sight makes her feel sick. Alfie, his forearm snapped so that it protrudes at an unnatural angle, is white, his eyes dark smudges in the pallor. He looks so very small and vulnerable.

'Mummeee, Mummeee,' he screeches, then gulps great noisy sobs. 'Want Muuuummmmmmeeee.'

'I know, darling, I know,' she seeks to reassure him, constrained by the fence and the trampoline net. She adds a lie, conflating her sense of impotence. 'And Mummy's coming.'

* * *

The landline rings three times before it dawns upon Vicki that someone really wants to get in touch with her and perhaps she should answer. It is a quarter past five. The optimum time for someone in Delhi to claim she has been mis-sold a mortgage. The time she is usually making tea for Alfie and anyone who is close to them knows it is pointless to ring.

She has far more important things to do. She has ticked off four of her six recipes and is about

378

to embark on choux pastry — hoping to perfect the technique she abandoned earlier when she lost her temper with Alfie. Re-reading *The Art of Baking*, she had noticed that Mrs Eaden was particularly partial to a choux bun or mini éclair, and so she is convinced one or other will feature in tomorrow's final.

Which is it going to be? she asks the photo. Kathleen Eaden smiles back, poised and enigmatic as ever. Well, that's a fat lot of use, thinks Vicki, but she smiles, even-tempered. As ever, preparation has calmed her; boosted her confidence once again. You are going to help me, aren't you, she tells the photo: and it is less of a request, more of a conviction. I've done all the hard work. Now I am going to channel your inner calm and bake like you: creatively and effortlessly. Perfectly.

The phone rings again. Bloody hell. It can't be her mother because she'd ring her mobile. A horrible thought occurs to her. She switched it off after texting Jenny. She runs to the phone and picks it up just before it clicks on to the answer machine.

Frances is nervous.

'Vicki? Darling?'

'Mum . . . What is it?'

Her bowels do a flip as the words every parent dreads filter down the mouthpiece.

'There's nothing to worry about — but Alfie's in hospital. He's broken his arm and they need to operate.'

*   *   *

It takes nearly two hours to drive from south-west London to north Oxford during the Friday night rush hour yet it feels much longer, the traffic crawling out of London, belching exhaust and aggressive rhythm and bass. Vicki is fraught by the time she hurtles into the reception of the Radcliffe's Accident and Emergency, having tried to park in a disabled bay — and been upbraided for it.

'But it's my baby . . . my son, he's in hospital.' And she had burst into tears on an unimpressed parking attendant.

'Yes — so's everyone's,' he had said.

A&E is experiencing a relative quiet before the storm of an early summer's Friday night: a mere fifteen patients are clustered in the waiting area, the backs of their thighs sticking to the plastic chairs, their faces reddening in the artificial heat. An overweight man in his mid-fifties clutches his heart, his eyes bulging in panic; a handful of students — the casualties of Friday afternoon sporting disasters — slump, bloodied and muddied. One has a bandage seeped in blood wrapped around his head; another stares at a swollen ankle; a third — whisked behind curtains — is fitting on a trolley, his neck held in a brace.

To Vicki, white-faced and frantic, the atmosphere is surreal — then nightmarish. Boredom coexists with panic; menace with mundanity.

She manages to get out her son's name then races to the paediatric ward where she knows Greg and Frances should be with Alfie. The corridors, decked with cheerful art, seem endless: a labyrinth keeping her from her baby.

Alfie's bed is empty but Frances is beside it, browsing through a copy of the *London Review of Books*.

'Muuumm.' Vicki's voice emerges as a wail. 'Where is he? Where's Alfie?'

Frances gets up, and goes as if to hug her.

'Where is he?' She bats her mother's arms away like a furious child. 'What have they done with him?'

'They haven't done anything with him.' Her mother's voice, firm and more than a touch exasperated, forces Vicki to pull herself together. 'He's just in the anaesthetics room being given the anaesthetic. Greg's with him. Then they're going to take him into theatre, Greg will come back, and they'll bleep us when he's in recovery.'

'What? They can't take him without me seeing him, without me giving him a cuddle!' Vicki is stunned at the surgeon's audacity and confounded by her mother's mastery of hospital jargon.

'They had a slot in theatre and Greg was here. He said you knew this might happen and you'd understand?'

'Yes, yes. He said that on the phone but I didn't think they'd do it. I thought they'd wait for me.'

'They wanted to do what was best for Alfie. I managed to get the paediatric orthopaedic consultant to do it, not the registrar. I know his wife from the Bodleian, volunteering, so I pushed for him to do it before he left for the weekend.'

381

'Oh.' She is stunned by the extent of her mother's influence. Then chastened. That's me told. Frances has managed to achieve far more for Alfie than she has in her directionless panicking.

'I need to see him.' She berates herself for standing there and turns and runs from the ward, through the maze of curtained beds holding sick children, along the corridor with its outdated animal frieze.

'Are you OK, dear?' It is a middle-aged sister. Buxom, implacable, authoritative in her navy uniform.

'Alfie Marchant. My son. He's having his anaesthetic. I need to get to him.' She cannot suppress her mounting frustration.

The nurse shakes her head slowly, as if Vicki has a learning disability or is mad. 'He'll have had his anaesthetic by now and be in theatre. You won't be allowed in. Any minute now your husband' — she raises her voice as if querying whether they are together; Vicki nods frenetically, urging her to speak more quickly — 'will be on his way back and you can wait to be bleeped.'

The nurse smiles, offering condescension and caffeine. 'Why don't you come back to the ward and wait until you can see Alfie in the recovery room. Would you like a nice cup of tea? No? Are you sure?

'Oh, look. There's Alfie's grandmother — your mother? You can sit and have a nice chat.'

* * *

382

'So why did you do it, Mum?' Vicki, bereft of her child, assailed by guilt, is looking for someone to blame. Her voice is tight with anger.

'Why did you let him play on a trampoline with older children when you know that's how fractures happen? And why weren't you there to look after him?'

'I was only in the next-door garden. I'd hardly neglected him!' Frances begins to excuse herself then spots the look of venom on her daughter's face and appears to think better of it. She takes her time; smooths an invisible wrinkle from her skirt.

'I wasn't aware that you didn't want him to go on a trampoline with older children and I assumed — and perhaps I was wrong — that he was being properly supervised. Alfie was desperate to play with other children and so I thought I was being kind.'

Vicki, imagining a dig at Alfie's lack of a sibling as a playmate, is stunned. 'Kind? In what way is it kind to fob him off on your neighbour's children — children he doesn't know?'

Frances bridles. 'I understand that you're upset but I really don't think it's fair to accuse me of 'fobbing him off'. That's a bit like the pot calling the kettle black, Vicki.'

'I was asking for your support, Mum, for your help. It was one day. I know no one else thinks it's important but this competition means so much to me. And tomorrow's the final. I thought you of all people would understand that I wanted to do well.'

'Oh, Vicki.' Frances softens. 'Of course you'll

do well. Why wouldn't you?'

Her daughter gives a bark of incredulity. 'Well, why would I? There's absolutely no guarantee I will and on what basis can you say that? You know nothing about my ability in this sphere, you've shown no interest. Your confidence is groundless.'

She pauses, appalled by her mother's assumed authority, then starts up again.

'I've never really achieved enough, have I? Never done as well as you wanted. Never 'fulfilled my potential'. But this is something I thought I was really good at. And I thought you might recognise that — and support me in it. I thought, for once, you might understand me.'

She waits, wanting a reaction. None is forthcoming.

'Of course, it's all immaterial now,' she goes on, aware as she does so that she is venting all her anger. 'I'll have to drop out. So your childcare was in vain.'

'Why will you have to drop out?'

Vicki stares at her in horror.

'Because the final's tomorrow and my child is in hospital,' she spells it out. 'He's undergoing surgery. How on earth could I leave him? And, if I did, what sort of mother would that make me?'

Frances is silent, her fingers still smoothing the fabric of her skirt, ironing out the non-existent wrinkle. When she looks up, her face is calm, her gaze clear.

'A perfectly normal one,' she says. 'One who is trying to manage a family and some kind of potential career. One who's just been unfortunate in experiencing bad timing.'

Vicki snorts, loudly and derisively. 'You can say that again.'

'Well, that's what it is, isn't it? Alfie isn't in a life-threatening situation. Yes, he'll be uncomfortable tomorrow but he'll have Greg and me here. If you leave him for a day, he won't suffer because of it. If it's important to you to do this final — and I'm sorry I didn't appreciate its full significance to you — then of course you must do it. Perhaps you need to stop beating yourself up and accept that it's OK — that it's acceptable — to put yourself first, for a change?'

'Well, that's the difference between you and me, isn't it?' Vicki hisses, suddenly realising she should lower her voice though the ward is, briefly, empty. 'You're happy to put yourself first; I always feel I should put my child first, even when I'm not doing so. As far as I'm concerned, that's the point of being a mother — though you've never seen it that way.'

She watches, appalled at the strength of her anger, as two spots form on her mother's cheeks. What have I done? she thinks. Then, simultaneously: well, perhaps I should be completely honest. Go for the nuclear option. Let her see my pain.

'I didn't put my baby first once before, Mum, did I? I got rid of it because it was inconvenient. Because, at eighteen, you advised me to have an abortion: told me I should think about my education; that I was too young to have a baby.

'Each month I don't get pregnant, I think I'm

385

being punished for that decision. Punished for my selfishness. And each month it reminds me that, with Alfie, I must never, ever put him last in any way.'

Frances takes her time to answer, as if unsure how to soothe a fourteen-year-old pain she must have hoped had eased to a sad recollection.

'Is that what this is all about — this desire to be a perfect mother? Oh, Vicki.' She moves to put her arm around her but Vicki shrugs it away.

'You were so young. Eighteen but a very young eighteen-year-old. Yes, I wanted what I thought was best for you — but you had so much potential and you were so terrified at the thought of motherhood. I remember you saying: 'A baby's just going to get in the way.''

'I don't think that now — now I can't have another one,' Vicki blurts out.

'I know,' Frances tries to reassure her. 'But your . . . infertility' — she hesitates over the word — 'has absolutely nothing to do with having an abortion. You know that, don't you? You don't need to heap on all this blame.'

Vicki shakes her head. 'It doesn't feel like that. It feels like I have a second chance — a chance to make everything perfect for Alfie.'

'You don't need to be perfect, you need to be *happy*.' Frances reaches for her hands but Vicki snatches them away. 'You ask what the point of being a mother is, and surely it's to be a good and happy role model? One who's fulfilled and not resentful in any way?'

Vicki remains silent and begins to bite at a cuticle; eyes down; refusing to look at Frances.

Her mother pauses, as if aware of the need to tread cautiously.

'I know I'm hardly the best person to lecture you on being a good mother but I've only ever wanted what's best for you. And, if you don't mind me saying, motherhood doesn't seem to leave you entirely satisfied, my darling.'

Vicki draws herself up, self-righteousness flowing through her veins; anger surging through her. And then she begins to cry. Hot tears streak down her cheeks: tears of sorrow, guilt and frustration. For she cannot think of an appropriate reply.

★ ★ ★

Her baby boy is groggy when Vicki and Greg are led into the recovery room. His peaches and cream complexion is now milk white with dark smudges under his eyes. Vicki touches his small, gowned body in its alien hospital garb. His limbs feel slight through the softened cotton, fragile compared to the bulky white cast encasing his right arm.

'Little man,' she coos. A sob catches in her throat and she leans against Greg. 'My poor little man.'

It is not until around midnight that he stirs himself and she sees a little of her true Alfie. By this time, she is ensconced in a camp bed in his room, twisting under the regulation sheet and blanket, her hips too wide for its narrow confines. Greg is propped in the blue plastic armchair beside the bed, his tie and top button loosened, his body slackened in sleep. She feels a rush of tenderness towards them. Father and son look disarmingly similar.

'Mummy.'

In an instant, she is at his side, stumbling to the bed in her rumpled top, socks and M&S knickers.

'Little Alf.'

He opens his eyes wide, scared by the unfamiliar surroundings.

'My arm hurts.'

She feels as if her heart will break.

'I know, darling, I know, darling. Mummy'll make it better.'

She calls for a nurse; smooths his forehead; plants a kiss.

Later, after the nurse has dispensed more diamorphine, and Alfie, and Greg, have fallen back into a deeper slumber, she switches her phone on surreptitiously.

She had phoned Jenny earlier, in the lull when Alfie was sleeping, her mother had returned home, and Greg was on a hunt for coffee and sandwiches.

Her words had tumbled out in a flood, a jumbled explanation as to why she was pulling out of the final that had cascaded over guilt, self-pity and distress.

Jenny had surprised her with her response. 'Well, couldn't you still take part?'

'Jenny!' She had been appalled. 'You sound just like my mother! Of course I couldn't. What kind of mother would that make me?'

Her friend had paused and when she spoke,

her voice was more than usually gentle. 'Don't be too hard on yourself, Vicki. You sound like a perfectly normal mother to me.

'I sacrificed everything I wanted to do for years and look where that got me: home alone — my children having fled the nest, and my husband . . . well . . . rather distant. You were the one who told me it was a waste of time feeling guilty, don't you remember? Would it be so terrible if you did what you wanted?'

Vicki had been silenced; unable to give an articulate response but aware she needed to do so.

'Well — Karen gave up the competition for *her* son.'

'But you're not Karen. She did that because she felt, for some reason, she had to make amends.'

'Well, Kathleen Eaden would never have left a child.' Vicki had reached for irrational sentiment. 'She wouldn't have been like me: indecisive and selfish. She would have known what to do: she would have withdrawn from the competition with dignity.'

There had been a long pause at the end of the phone.

'You don't know that.' Jenny's voice had sounded unusually tight.

'Of course I do. She was completely selfless. She gave up her career and went and lived in Cornwall to give her daughter the most wonderful childhood. You read that article, remember? She always put her family first, Laura Eaden said.'

389

'Yes, but . . . there may have been quite specific reasons for doing that. Look, I'm not saying she wasn't selfless but her retreating, and giving up her writing, may have been more complex than we thought. We've taken it for granted that she just wanted to immerse herself as a full-time mum — but perhaps it was all a bit more complicated.'

There had been a pause while Vicki took this in. 'What do you mean?'

Jenny had paused. 'It's nothing important. Not in the grand scheme of things. But we make assumptions about people all the time and perhaps we did about her. We assumed her life was perfect and that she found motherhood easy but all that stuff about closing the door on a sleeping baby was written before she had a child. I'm not saying she didn't want one — she clearly did — but, to an extent, it was idealised. Perhaps the reality was more difficult. Perhaps it wasn't quite as perfect. Look, it's not something I can explain properly now. Try to make the competition and you'll see.'

Now, in the gloaming, as Vicki runs through the conversation and tries to tease out what Jenny meant by it, her phone reveals a fresh text message. Glancing at Greg, who has slept through its ping, she presses it. A fluorescent glow lights up her screen.

'Dear Vicki, I spent thirty years putting others' needs first. Please don't make my mistake. Besides, I need you as my competition! Hope Alfie has a good sleep and I see you tomorrow. With love, Jen. Xxx'

Kathleen

She wakes to a cramp and an insistent trickle: a ribbon of blood running down her inner thigh.

James Caruthers calls an ambulance at once 'just to be cautious'. But by the time they have arrived at St Stephen's hospital, on the Fulham Road, twenty minutes later, all caution has been thrown to the wind.

The reception area seems to be filled with people: nurses; doctors in what look like pyjamas; Caruthers himself, shirt sleeves rolled to the elbows, a look of intense focus on his face. They move briskly; placing her in a wheelchair, walking en masse through double doors; speaking of 'theatre'; 'paediatricians'; 'resus team in situ'. Words that, as the pain ebbs and flows, she struggles to comprehend.

She is placed on a bed, in a private room, now — and to her horror immediately wets the starched linen. A gush of liquid, pink with blood, soaks the bed.

'Her waters have broken,' a nurse announces to the medical staff. She tries to catch Caruthers' eye to gain some explanation but he is busying himself on the phone, speaking with soft determination. The room whirls with quiet activity.

The tightening intensifies. She watches her

stomach as the skin, taut as a drum, stretches then relaxes. It feels alien; as though this part of her body has a life of its own. She tries to speak — to ask what is happening — but finds she is voiceless; silenced by a fresh crest of pain.

'The contractions are getting closer. Every two minutes,' the nurse, plump and autocratic, says, and Kathleen finally manages an outburst of irrational fury.

'Contractions? They're not contractions!' The idea is ludicrous. 'This baby can't come out yet.'

A surge of pain silences her. The nurse turns aside, her lips pursed. No one looks her in the eye.

It is George who utters the truth she refuses to hear and no one else will tell her. 'My darling, there's nothing they can do to stop it.'

37

If food be love, then baking, surely, is the most nurturing food of all. And, just as you may bake to nurture a love affair, so you may bake to nurture a child. To build them up and make them strong.

She sleeps, of course, badly. Tossing and turning on the narrow camp bed, straining at Alfie's every snuffle, marvelling at how Greg manages to remain so sound asleep.

Her boy sleeps well, though; the sleep of a child exhausted by a long and stressful day and then given an anaesthetic and a hefty dose of diamorphine. He wakes as light filters through the thin curtains at around 6 a.m.

'Mummy, Daddy.' He gives his parents his glorious smile.

'Feeling better, little soldier?' It is Greg, stroking his hair from his brow, smiling down at him. Vicki feels an irrational stab of irritation that he is the first to speak.

Alfie nods. 'I'm hungry.'

They laugh, and Vicki's possessiveness dissipates as Alfie holds out his uncast hand, and Greg puts his arm around her.

'That's got to be a good sign, hasn't it?' She smiles.

'I'd say so. Definitely.' Her husband gives her a squeeze.

The perennial NHS solution of tea, toast and

marmite is dispensed. More painkillers will come later.

'The surgeon will do his ward round at about eight forty-five but I should think this little fellow will be able to go home.' The paediatric sister smiles.

'What — he won't have to stay in for observation?' Greg is surprised.

'Well, if there are no complications you don't need to be here. We'll need the bed for someone else.'

Vicki does a rapid calculation. If Alfie is discharged this morning, will he need her at home? Could she make the Mrs Eaden final? She is supposed to be in the competition kitchen by ten but is confident they could delay the start if she said she was coming.

'Well, if you're sure? That's fantastic, then, isn't it, little Alf? You can have a nice gentle day with Mummy snuggled up on the sofa.' Greg smiles from his son to his wife.

His smile fades. 'What's up, Vicks? You look worried. I'm sure they wouldn't discharge him unless they thought he was ready. But we'll get a second opinion when the consultant comes round.'

'It's not that. I just ... if he's being discharged, I could get to the final of the competition.' She twists her hands as she talks, aware that she is pleading.

Bewilderment crosses Greg's face. 'Really? Is that really what you want to do?'

'Yes. You don't mind, do you?'

He shakes his head in bemusement. 'No, of

394

course not. And of course you must go. Absolutely. But are you sure that Alfie will be OK?'

'He'll be fine,' she hears herself echoing her mother. 'It's for one day. He'll miss me but he'll have you. He won't suffer. I'm sorry, Greg, but I need to do this.'

* * *

Leaving little Alf had been a wrench. No, that was an understatement. She had felt as if she were deserting him.

Greg and her mother had been left to pack together his things; to settle him into his car seat; to drive home to London after the consultant had pronounced him well enough to leave hospital. And she had raced out, without a small hand to clasp, without the requisite bags crammed with childish clobber. She should have felt giddy with excitement. Instead, she felt like the world's biggest bitch.

It didn't help that the only other time Alfie had been in hospital was when he was born — and, then, they had been so very much together. Leaving hospital, she had not been able to take her eyes off him. This red, squished bundle with its surprise shock of dark hair cosseted in a snow suit and strapped into a portable car seat. This little person who had been hidden tight inside her just the day before and who, now, was very definitely a separate individual. And whom she was now being entrusted to take home.

She had felt overwhelmed with love — and terror. She remembered looking up at Greg and seeing the same look of shock and awe as he stared at the car seat cradle.

'Can't quite believe we're allowed to take him away,' he had ventured.

'I know,' she had admitted, incredulous. 'What do we do with him?'

Now, there is no infant with unsmiling eyes to stare at her intently. No little boy, his eyes now smiling, to tug her along, small feet scuffling. She walks faster, boots clattering along the hospital floor, heart lifting as she reaches the concourse, with its newsagents and cafeteria, its smell of fried breakfasts, coffee and disinfectant.

She sees the sign for the exit and rushes to escape the cloying warmth. A couple of patients, clad in pyjamas and dressing gowns, and attached to their drips, stand just outside the entrance drawing on their first cigarettes of the day and she breathes in the nicotine fug. The promise of sweet air dissolves into a smoker's cough.

Minutes later, she swings out of the hospital, and heads for the ring road and the M40. A quick call to Cora, and Eaden and Son are reassured that their fourth contestant is on her way. As she eases her car through a local high street, her guilt at leaving Alfie is tempered with apprehension. She grips the steering wheel and tells herself to focus on the competition. To concentrate on the passion that has driven her for the past three months, since she received the call inviting her to Eaden's headquarters for an audition that dismal February day.

Merging on to the M40, she tries to focus on the last remaining stage of the contest. The theme is a celebratory tea and Harriet has warned them that the bar will be raised for the final. Her head throbs. Even the thought is exhausting.

She suspects they will be asked to create exquisite mouthfuls of sponge and pastry: éclairs, painted with melted chocolate and oozing crème patissière; barquettes glossy with summer fruits; millefeuille, sandwiched with raspberries; bubble-gum pink fondant fancies. The lightest of scones and a cake slick with ganache or teetering under increasingly decadent layers.

She wonders, not for the first time, what prompted Kathleen Eaden to become so interested in, no, so fixated on, baking. The photos show a svelte figure so she clearly didn't gorge on the food. Indeed, she was brought up during the war and rationing so gluttony wasn't an option. Perhaps, like Vicki, she was simply a perfectionist.

Oh, but you make it all look so easy, she tells her. It doesn't look as if you need to practise or to try to be perfect. 'Simply take, whisk, place, ice . . . ' you write, as if it were as natural as 'simply breathe'. When you make bread and butter pudding, you delight your husband. When you bake bread, your children are in raptures, yet again.

Something about that last thought is wrong. It takes a while for her to register what it is. She checks her mirror, indicates, and overtakes a particularly cumbersome lorry that belches black smoke as she glides away.

'*When you bake bread, your children are in raptures.*' But Jenny said you didn't have children when you wrote that. What else did you say about children? '*Close the oven door as gently as on a sleeping baby; biscuits your little ones will love to shape; a milk pudding your children will devour; a birthday cake for a special child . . .* '

What was it Jenny said? That we made assumptions about why you gave up your career. That your life may not have been perfect. And that you may have found aspects of motherhood difficult. Well, what were they?

What caused you to give up your career? Were you hiding something? And why wasn't your life as perfect as we — no, as I — assumed it to be?

She puts her foot down, barely conscious of the flow of cars as she ploughs down the middle lane. Questions crowd her head, pressing out the drone of the traffic, and an alternative reality emerges with a single twist like the shifted prisms of a child's kaleidoscope: not Kathleen Eaden, willingly jettisoning her career for motherhood; Kathleen Eaden, compelled, for some reason, to give up her career.

She moves into sixth gear and speeds into the outside lane, the speedometer soaring to eighty-five as she drives with a new urgency. What did Jenny mean? The sense that she has somehow done Kathleen a disservice grows intense.

Perhaps, she thinks, we have got it all wrong and there should never have been a search for a new Mrs Eaden. Perhaps we should have been looking for the real Kathleen Eaden.

Kathleen

The pain is excruciating now and there is no way she can halt what is happening. Her body seems to have been taken over: reduced to an animal that cries involuntarily and tries to writhe on the floor.

Thank God George can't see me like this, she thinks, as she is forced back on to the bed. Another wave picks her up and she squawks in panic; then another, more turbulent. She begins to shake like a marionette performing a grotesque, uncontrollable dance.

What is happening to me? she wants to scream as a nurse places a nozzle over her mouth and tells her to breathe deeply. And what's that woman doing? How dare she touch me? She feels light-headed then woozily nauseous as the entonox does its work.

'Good girl, good girl,' the nurse tells her and she wants to bat her and her patronising platitudes away. Good girl? How ludicrous. She is a bad mother — or not even that. A bad would-be mother; someone so inept at mother-hood — so inept at the basic function of being a woman — that she can't even keep her baby in her womb.

'Good girl,' the nurse still seems to be saying, as if she hasn't a clue what is happening. 'There,

there. There's a good girl.'

Nausea swells through her, carrying her up on a fresh crest of pain. She spews forth a flame of vomit then begins to shake manically.

'I want this to be over,' she begins to wail. Then: 'She has to stay inside me. She HAS to stay inside me.' Someone is shouting and it seems to be her.

'There, there,' says a nurse, silencing her with the nozzle. 'You're doing so well now. It won't be long before it's over.'

Another wave of nausea. Someone is telling her to push and she wants to scream at them to stop being so stupid; to stop saying that.

Why is everyone telling her how to behave, all of a sudden? Why does everyone always do that? Stay in bed; rest; relax; do what's best for baby. Don't write; don't bake — but do be Mrs Eaden. Smile; pose; nod: nod, smile, pose.

She can't do it any more — or this. But first she needs to explain: this baby needs to stay inside her for six weeks longer. It really has to, though it seems to have a will of its own.

She groans then feels a slither as a hot, warm weight slides through her legs, caught by Caruthers and whisked away immediately. The pain has stopped but an awful silence fills the room.

The men in pyjamas are huddled around what must be the resuscitation trolley. The silence stretches out indefinitely. Her arms ache to hold her child.

I have failed, she thinks, as stars crowd her sight and she risks slipping out of consciousness.

401

She fights against the dizziness. She needs to hold on. That woman is saying something important to her.

By her side, the nurse, looking at the resus trolley where the baby remains silent, mutters her judgement.

'She's looking very blue.'

38

Gingerbread men make the simplest of treats. Children love them the best but, if you have none, you may still indulge yourself. Fashion hearts, or large families.

Bradley Hall, 9.45 a.m., and all involved in the Search for the New Mrs Eaden are waiting for Vicki's Freelander to surge up the drive. The tension is palpable. Harriet and Dan are hovering in the lobby; Cora is checking her phone needlessly and repeatedly, desperate for the final to run to schedule; Claire, perched on a chintz sofa, is rifling through her texts. She re-reads those from Jay — '162,000 hits altogether!' — then double-checks a love letter from Chloe, her passion etched in painstakingly neat joined-up writing. 'You're the bestist mum and the bestist baker in the werld!!!' The pink pencil has pushed into the paper, as if to emphasise her certainty.

It is a glorious day. The former stately home is doing its best to look merely eccentric not architecturally grotesque and the weather is conspiring to help. Early morning sunshine bathes its golden stone, softening its ornate arcading. Lilies of the valley fringe it in white and green. The lush lawn sparkles. The marquee has been erected and, later, the contestants will shiver like guests dressed in summer regalia for a spring wedding.

Jenny stands in the bay window, looking less like the matronly cook she may have appeared to be at the start of the process and more like the lady of the manor. There is a serenity about her in contrast to the agitation that whirls around her. Head up, eyes peering down to the end of the drive, she is poised and still. She seems to have shed some weight but, more than that, she has shed some of her inhibition. She is a picture of self-possession.

As Vicki's car sweeps over the gravel, however, she moves into action, gliding to the door to take her friend in her arms.

Vicki is all of a fluster. 'I'm so late, so late . . . Thank you for waiting for me . . . Has it held you up massively? Can I just go to the loo and grab a drink before we start? Where's Harriet? Are they angry? Oh, Jen, I feel so guilty for leaving poor little Alf . . . '

'Calm down.' Jenny smiles, and envelops her in softness. Her body is more compact than Vicki had imagined: she does not sink into a duvet of flesh but is cushioned in comfort. She feels Jenny's surprisingly strong arms around her, breathes in her clean, neutral smell. This must be what it feels like to be held by your mother, she thinks. What it would feel like if Mum just let herself hold me. Utterly secure.

Her friend releases her.

'Poor you — poor Alfie. How is he?'

'OK. Well, he will be.' Vicki smiles, relief obscuring exhaustion. 'I can't bear to think about him though, to be honest, or I'll just leave immediately. I've got to try to focus — just to get through today.'

'Well, that's good news.' It is Harriet, who has bustled up. 'Great that your little one's feeling better and fantastic that you're here. See you in the kitchen in twenty minutes?' And, imperious, she rushes off.

'So this is it then.' Jenny smiles again. 'Ready?'

'Not really, no.' Vicki is apologetic. She draws Jenny aside as Cora, Claire and Mike begin to move to the kitchen. 'I keep obsessing about Alfie and what you said last night about Kathleen. That we'd all made assumptions. That her life wasn't perfect. What did you mean by that?'

'Oh, it's not important.' Jenny, gathering her cardigan and handbag, avoids looking her in the eye. 'Not in the grand scheme of things.'

'You said that last night, but it is to me . . . '

Jenny stops collecting her things, and looks at her. 'I can see that. Are you sure you want to discuss this now, just before the competition?'

'I wouldn't ask if I didn't!' Vicki's frustration comes out louder than she intended. 'I'm sorry . . . ' She is quick to apologise. 'I just can't stop thinking about her. I feel as if we've somehow done her a disservice.'

The look Jenny gives her — cool, quizzical — is disarming. Slowly, she puts down her handbag and rifles through it. She finds what she's looking for: a sheaf of blue-grey Basildon Bond, inscribed in cobalt-blue ink, neatly folded.

She hands it to Vicki.

'What's this?'

'A letter: I found it in one of Kathleen's cookery books. I'm not sure she ever sent it, but just read it.'

'A private letter? I'm not sure I should do that. How did you get hold of it?'

'I borrowed it.' Jenny blushes. 'I thought you needed to read it. Look, I'm going to take it back once you've done so. Please, take it: it just makes sense.'

As if sleep-walking, Vicki takes the letter from her, carefully unfolds it, and begins to read.

> *Little Haven,*
> *Trecothan,*
> *15th June 1972*

My dearest Charlie,

Wonderful to see you yesterday. To have you down here to help celebrate Lily's sixth birthday. It may seem ridiculously formal my writing but I wanted to stress how grateful we are for you making the effort — and for treating her just like any other child.

She loved the kite. What an inspired choice! We tested it out this morning, at low tide, on the flat sands of Constantine. We took down the wheelchair equipped for sand — the one with the massive wheels you hate carrying — and attached the line handles firmly, in case it should blow away. Then she held the lines and, with George pushing behind, they raced the length of the beach as if pulled by this glorious kite that swooped and soared in the sunshine. I wish you could have heard her peals of laughter.

She sounded so infectiously happy. Squealing with excitement and for fear that her fantastic new toy would blow away.

Needless to say, it didn't. George had tied it on too tight for that — can you imagine the tantrum if he hadn't? — and we must have spent a good hour and a half flying it. I thought George was going to have a heart attack, he was so out of breath from the exercise, so I took over. And I am so glad I did.

It was the closest I've ever come to taking her hand and just running with her — and your kite enhanced that sense of freedom, sprinting ahead of us, up in the blue, like some unencumbered sprite.

Later, we tried another first; and I am so proud of this. I got her to make gingerbread men — a whole family. And she made them herself. Well, she needed help with tipping the ingredients into the bowl but she managed to bind the dough and to roll it and to press down the cutters to make shapes. She may not have been standing on a chair next to me but who cares? We were baking together properly, just as I'd always imagined I would with my daughter. At one point she asked: 'Am I doing this right, Mummy?' I tell you, I almost cried.

Oh Charlie, when I think back six years, this all seemed an impossibility. Do you remember what she was like when she was born? More bird than baby. Skin translucent; veins bright beneath it. Not an ounce of unnecessary, crucial flesh.

It seemed so cruel to have a child like this after my other three losses (I still can't use Caruthers' phrase: habitual abortion). Not the plump, healthy baby I dreamed of but a sickly scrap of a child born at thirty-four weeks. By rights, she shouldn't have survived and, at times, in those first torturous weeks, it seemed incredible and, yes I admit it, unkind — to us, but most of all to her — that she did.

I cannot believe I have just written that but the truth — and you are the only person I can admit this to — is that, for quite a time, I grieved for the child she wasn't and never would be, Charlie. But she persisted with us. And, as it became clear she would survive, my faltering love for her grew more and more intense. She was our little fighter. Perfect except for the cerebral palsy; untroubled except for the odd fit.

Talking of which, I know you are still concerned at our remaining down here, far from the teaching hospitals, but you are worrying unnecessarily. There is the hospital at Treliske and we continue to make six-monthly visits to the neurologist in Harley Street. Living in such a remote place allows her a freer life; one in which no one can ever point a finger and whisper about it being a tragedy; or make any reference to my loss of career. I couldn't exist anonymously in London with a handicapped daughter, or run with her free as a kite through Hyde Park or

Kensington Gardens. Can you imagine it? Someone would always notice, a look of pity on their face.

I've just realised that sounds as if I am ashamed of her. You know I am not. But I cannot bear the attention. I always hated it when I had to do all those wretched openings and now, well, it would seem even more intrusive. It's bad enough that Mrs Eaden — and her naive assumptions about how she can please her perfect family, no, create the perfect family, through baking — still haunts me. I don't need anyone else to flag up my very public identity. Here, I can just be Kitty, Lily's mother. I can focus on my daughter and do everything in my powers to make her life, however long it is, happy.

Enough justification for our hermit-like existence. Every time I breathe in the Atlantic I know we are doing the best for her; and every time we go down to the beach together. Do let me know when we can next entice you down.

You are a stronger wheelchair sprinter than George, and Lily wants to take the kite to Watergate Bay next. The sands there are three miles long so you had better get in training!

With very much love,
Kitty
xxx

The script is so familiar: firm, expansive, looping and the voice as clear and vibrant as

409

ever. But the reality conveyed in the letter is all wrong.

'I don't understand.' Vicki is bewildered. 'Who's this Kitty?'

'Kitty was Kathleen. This was a letter from her to her brother.'

'Kathleen? Kathleen Eaden?'

Jenny nods.

'Then who's Lily? Kathleen's daughter is called Laura and she's only a couple of years older than me. Thirty-five, I think. I remember from that interview. She wouldn't have been six in 1972.'

'Kathleen must have had another child. A child born very early who she wanted to protect from the public eye. It would explain why they sold the business and moved to such a remote part of Cornwall — or remote then, certainly — and why she didn't write anything further. She did always put her family first, as Laura said, and, with such a sick child — a child who had fits and suffered from cerebral palsy — perhaps it seemed the obvious, the only choice.'

The space around Vicki shifts slightly. She feels disorientated as if she has just spun very fast on a roundabout with Alfie.

'She doesn't like being Mrs Eaden . . . She doesn't even think baking necessarily pleases a family.' Every certainty shatters into splinters.

'No. I imagine that, faced with a very premature child, being Mrs Eaden felt a bit — I don't know — silly? No, disingenuous. A child with cerebral palsy — and the experience of multiple miscarriages — doesn't fit in with the

410

serene, controlled, seemingly perfect world she describes.'

'But baking could help? Baking brought her such happiness.' Vicki clings to one certainty.

'And it evidently did.' Jenny seeks to reassure her. 'She made gingerbread men with Lily, didn't she? And you can see that that still brought her joy.

'But her life wasn't perfect, was it? At least, nowhere near as perfect as her book and her photos suggest. And, while perfection might be possible in baking, in life, well, it's impossible.

'The perfect wife, the perfect child, the perfect mother? None of us can be these. They're mere fancies. For you, for me, for Kathleen.'

39

When making crème patissière, whisk the mixture constantly once the hot milk has been added. The custard must boil but not scorch the base of the pan. This is one of those moments when you must pay attention to detail. A moment's distraction and your custard is ruined.

It takes Frances only three rings to pick up her phone, not her customary ten.

Vicki, gripping her mobile, is startled. She had expected a few seconds to compose herself but, suddenly, she has to speak.

'Mum?'

'Victoria?' Her mother's voice is guarded, as if wary of another onslaught from her angry, needy daughter. 'Aren't you at the competition? Shouldn't it start soon?'

'Yes. In five minutes. But I needed to speak to you first. I needed to apologise.' The confession comes out in a rush of relief.

'Go on.' Her mother's voice is low but the tone is calm rather than critical.

'I should be doing this face to face . . . but I needed to tell you, quickly, so that neither of us brooded on this all day. I wanted to say sorry. For blaming you for the abortion. For implying that you forced me to do it. That I only did it because you suggested it.'

There is a long pause. Say something, Vicki

wills her, but then realises her mother is still waiting. And, yes. There is more to say.

'I suppose it suited me to put all the responsibility on you,' Vicki continues. 'I've always felt quietly guilty but managed to justify it before I had a child. Then, since having Alf, it's seemed much more of a momentous thing. I suppose I wanted to share — or to offload — the blame. But I've been unfair. I know I couldn't have coped with having a baby then. I was far too much of a child myself. And I do remember you saying that if I really wanted to go ahead and have it, then you would support me.'

There is a long pause, during which Vicki lets out her breath in a rush.

When her mother answers, she is hesitant but measured.

'You do know that it was your decision to go ahead with it, don't you?'

'Yes, Mum. That's what I'm trying to say. Yes, I do. And I'm sorry.'

'I've only ever wanted what was best for you, my darling. Yes, academically but, far more importantly, emotionally. And I'm very sorry if it hasn't always — hasn't often — felt that way.'

There is another pause.

'I know I've never seemed that motherly. Not particularly maternal. I suppose, if I'm honest, having a baby didn't come that easily to me. I expect these days they'd diagnose it as post-natal depression.' She gives a sniff, as if suspicious of the diagnosis — or irritated at having to admit to such feelings. 'Then, I just thought I wasn't a natural mother, whatever that means.

'There was no lengthy maternity leave in those days. I went back to teach when you were six weeks old, and when I did, I managed to cope better. I was happier. And you seemed calmer. You never seemed to cry with your childminder half as much as you did with me.

'But I did love you, Vicki. I know I must have seemed strict: tough on you over your homework, concerned that you fulfil your potential. Perhaps not very playful. Well, not in the least playful. But I loved you — and I wish I could have shown it in a convincing way.

'I suppose what I'm saying is: I tried my best. And, without wishing to sound trite, that's all any of us can do. It's what you do for Alfie. Please don't agonise about not being a good enough mother, and do what I failed to do: just enjoy him.'

There is an even lengthier pause while Vicki tries to articulate a suitable response. But she finds her throat is thick and she cannot speak properly. A sound comes out, halfway between a gulp and a cry.

'Vicki? Are you all right? You'd better get to your competition. You don't want to be late.'

'Yes, yes, of course.' She manages to pull herself together. 'Thank you — for the pep talk. I suppose I ought to be going so, bye, then.'

Their heart-to-heart seems to have finished, and yet Vicki senses — or perhaps she just hopes — it isn't quite over; that there is more her mother has to say.

'Thank you for calling and, Vicki?'

'Yes?' She grips the phone.

414

'You will remember, won't you: I do love you, darling.'

* * *

'So — here we are.' Harriet, rocking on the balls of her feet at the front of the room, has abandoned any pretence at not being excited. Relief that she has four bakers, even if Karen, the one she had tipped to win, is missing, has made her comparatively skittish.

'A celebratory tea. The fitting finale to a fantastic competition. An over-the-top culinary blow-out — but one that aspires to refinement, not excess.

'Today we want you to create the sort of exquisite afternoon tea that Kathleen Eaden wrote about: a decadent display of choice morsels designed to indulge, to treat. Nothing must be mediocre. There are to be no leaden cupcakes, no wedges of cold bread and butter pudding, no stolid pastries. We want dainty sandwiches from thinly sliced, freshly made bread; French tartlets; millefeuille; a choux pastry, and scones and cream for the most English of guests.'

'Today's test will be one of timing as much as anything else,' Dan adds. 'We are giving you four and a half hours in total. How you divide it up is a matter for your judgement and expertise.

'None of these recipes by themselves is arduous, but getting them all accomplished in under five hours — and ensuring that each baked good is in pristine condition — will be a massive challenge. You have five bakes to

415

complete and you will have to work out a rigorous timetable to ensure each stage is completed in that time.'

There is a pause. Claire looks sick; Mike shell-shocked. Vicki looks relieved, and exhausted. Jenny smiles: composed, serene.

'So, if we can start?' Harriet looks at them all and smiles. 'Let the final stage of the Search for the New Mrs Eaden begin.'

Four heads bow in concentration, each jotting down timings with a pencil as assiduously as if it were some complicated maths formula. Jenny finishes her timetable first, working with a speed in keeping with her usual efficient pace.

She'll start with the bread first, then, while the dough's proving, move on to the crème patissière for the mini tartlets and millefeuille. The various pastries come next; then the baking and constructing. She needs to pull off a delicate conjuring act, creating the freshest, most exquisite products without risking a manic rush at the end.

Assessing her timetable, she wonders if this neat rigidity — each time neatly annotated against a baked product and a culinary process — is a flaw in her baking, and her personality. Perhaps she has been too rigid: not daring to be as imaginative as Kathleen Eaden; and not daring — before now — to step outside the familiar role she has colluded in fulfilling throughout her adult life.

But she knows that this order has saved her. Things fall apart; the centre cannot hold. But sauces need to be stirred, ingredients measured, precision demanded. The structure of the competition — and the demand that she excel — has forced her to focus; to concentrate on the here and now and not allow herself to be ambushed by a skittering imagination. All thoughts of a writhing Gabby Arkwright are reined in when she over-whisks a bowl of egg whites or snaps a chocolate curl.

Of course, she knows she will have to face the reality of a marriage that is disintegrating as inevitably as a cooling soufflé after this competition. The phoney war has continued, but Nigel, his interest piqued by a more animated wife, has shown signs of wanting peace talks. She is not so sure.

The old Jenny, the compliant wife and mother whose world was her Suffolk kitchen, has been subsumed by a revised version: one who has glimpsed an intriguing world outside her walled kitchen garden and thinks she might venture out there. Thinks she is capable of doing so.

This new, improved Jenny — or perhaps a revitalised version of the original — will walk out of the room if she is described as fat, though the description is no longer completely accurate. To her surprise, the stress of the last few weeks means she has had to buy clothes two sizes smaller for this final: she is still large but no longer obese.

She will confront her husband about his affair, not feign ignorance in the hope that it will go away. She would like to gain his admiration and respect; she would like to believe that twenty-eight years of a relationship need not be

417

squandered; that marriage counselling — were she to persuade Nigel to enter into this — could provide a balm to soothe the petty grievances and harsher cruelties. But she fears it is too late for that. She does not want to be with someone capable of describing her as fat. She suspects — no, actually, she knows — she will walk away.

The knowledge leaves her numb, and so she sidelines this idea — putting it on the back burner like a pan of gently simmering pasta — as she kneads the dough for her soft, white bread. Nigel will be in Peterborough tomorrow, running the half marathon, but her girls, her glorious girls, will be here this afternoon to support her. Not her much missed Kate, still in Sydney, but Lizzie — who will come up from Bristol, and Emma, her sometimes spiky, but ultimately steadfast middle child. The thought that she has been willing to leave her new boyfriend and hectic student life in the south of France just to cheer on her mum fills her with happiness, like syrup seeping from warm treacle tart. It floods her veins. I have my girls, she thinks. And I have this skill. Perhaps, at the moment, there is nothing else I need.

Behind her, Claire is also focusing on the positives, giving herself a pep talk as she forms the puff pastry for her millefeuille, rubbing butter into flour then pouring water into a well at the centre to form a rough dough. It has been a struggle to believe she is good enough to be here but she has the proof: 162,000 people have watched her make Chelsea buns, a gingerbread house and a chocolate soufflé of all things on the net; 162,000 people think she was all right. Or, if she is honest, more than all right.

She shapes the dough then starts on the crème patissière, infusing milk with vanilla. That vanilla pod cost two pounds, she thinks, as she watches the flecks of black swim through the milk and breathes in the sweetly evocative scent. She would never have used such ingredients before this competition, but would add a drop of essence, strong and synthetic in comparison but a fraction of the price.

Two pounds. She could get two big bags of pasta; half a kilo of mince; or two packets of fish fingers for that. Ten meals for Chloe or a wizened dark stick that smells heavenly and helps create the most exquisite custard but is still, when all's said and done, just a *flavouring*. She is sure none of the others thinks like that. But then none of them, she is pretty certain, has ever worked for £6.08 an hour. And none has ever had to calculate that to spend two pounds on a vanilla pod they need to forgo two loaves of bread; or four pints of milk and a bag of potatoes or packet of cheap biscuits.

She separates her eggs and whisks the yolks with sugar and cornflour, the orange globes becoming thick, pale and creamy. No one else has ever mentioned the money: the £50,000 contract for being involved in the advertising campaign, for 'fronting' the baked product range, and for writing a weekly column; but the figure broods at the back of Claire's mind.

Fifty thousand pounds. The sum ker-chings periodically like the ring of an old-fashioned fruit machine jackpot. A figure that is conceivable: more tangible than the Lottery millions her neighbour dreams of winning. That is — just — attainable. That is life-changing.

The thought winds her. Fifty thousand pounds. Five times her current salary. Enough to put down a deposit on a small flat, if she could increase her salary to fund a mortgage; to be able to put on the heating; to buy Chloe a computer or a DS; to buy her new clothes — not dress her in hand-me-downs. To take her on holiday.

Perhaps — and, here, she fizzes with excitement — Chloe could be like other kids, and go on an aeroplane? She imagines Chloe's reaction were she to tell her this: huge eyes widening; freckles wrinkling; long limbs wrapping themselves around her and squeezing her so tight she has to squeal for breath.

She whisks furiously. She is not going to win if she slides into daydreams. And then she smiles. Not so long ago, she thought she had lost the capacity for them.

As Claire's custard thickens, the smell of caramel and then burnt sugar fills the room as, to her right, a mixture catches.

'Oh, sugar!!!!'

It is Vicki — working at the next station — who looks close to tears. She sweeps the saucepan from the ring and pours its contents into another saucepan, hoping to confound the inevitable and rescue it. The water hits the pan with a mocking hiss, then spews forth steam. The sides have blackened and the bottom bubbles. Lumps of egg and cornflour congeal like

420

sweetened scrambled eggs.

'It's all ruined.' Vicki's voice breaks, and the strain of the past eighteen hours escapes with her cry.

'Hey, calm down . . . You're just tired — and nervous.' Claire seeks to reassure while keeping an eye on her own mixture. The custard bubbles: thick, smooth and unctuous. She removes it from the heat.

'Why not get something else done while your milk infuses.' She darts to Vicki's work bench and glances at her list. 'Here — the choux pastry. You could make that and put it aside. At least then you could tick something off.'

She takes in the worktop, strewn with broken eggs; cluttered and chaotic. Vicki's bread dough is proving but her burnt custard has put her behind.

'All right,' Vicki sniffs and wipes her eyes with the back of her hand. 'Not doing very well at this,' she says.

'You've had a crappy eighteen hours,' Claire tells her. 'Time to put it right.'

'I guess . . . ' Vicki offers a watery smile.

'Come on.' Claire tries a joke. 'Don't make it too easy for the rest of us.'

Her competitor laughs, involuntarily. 'Oh, Claire. You're brilliant. You don't need me to muck up for you to do well.'

'Well, so are you. And you're not going to muck up. Come on. Pretend you're psyching yourself up in front of thirty six-year-olds. What was it you said? That you had to put on a show in front of them? That you couldn't let them see you were nervous?'

'Something like that,' Vicki mumbles.

'Right. Well, you just need to treat Dan and Harriet like those six-year-olds — and do the same.'

Like a chastened child, Vicki does what she is told, measuring the water, butter and salt for the choux pastry; binding the eggs; weighing the flour. She brings the butter and water to a rolling boil then beats in the flour to form a stolid lump of dough. Then, bit by bit, she adds the eggs — the consistency changing from thick scrambled egg to a smooth, camel-coloured paste. She tastes the mixture and recoils: warm butter, salt and egg seep through her mouth but the effect is unpleasant. Too savoury; too raw. And yet, when baked, this will be transformed into the lightest of pastries: a crisp ball of nothingness to be filled with whipped cream or ice cream, that is integral to some of the lightest, most frivolous of desserts.

Placing it to one side, Vicki decides to go back to creating her crème patissière. But the smell wafting from the infused vanilla pod reminds her of the lotion she used to massage a baby Alfie — before he was capable of jumping up from a nappy mat and wriggling free of her caress.

Oh, this is *hopeless*. Despite her best intentions, she is finding it impossible to focus. Her mind clouds with emotions: guilt at leaving Alfie, grief over her abortion and the row with her mother, and sorrow for Kathleen. All this *baking* seems irrelevant: a mere pastime compared to the important stuff of life: making, and tending to, babies. She splits a yolk, and watches as the streak of gold slips into the bowl of white albumen, tainting the fluid as it dances through it; forcing her to start again.

Oh, bloody hell. She reaches for a new bowl and three fresh eggs then takes a minute to try to compose herself. Alfie's face swims into focus: his big hazel eyes, his face, bleached of colour, his cherry-red bottom lip that jutted out as he called after her, as she retreated from the ward, smiling reassurance as she did so: 'Mummmmmeeee . . . '

I never wanted to be the sort of mother who left her children, she thinks savagely. How could I have left him when he needed me? A wave of self-loathing picks her up then immerses her. How could I have left him in his hospital bed?

Kathleen would never have done that, she thinks automatically. She gave up everything for Lily. A second thought shoots through her with cold certainty: but I'm not Kathleen, am I? And who knows what sort of mother she would have been if her experience hadn't been so traumatic, so extreme.

I'm not very good at just being a stay-at-home mummy, her deep, dark voice persists. It's what you wanted, she chides herself, and you're so lucky to have it. I know, she thinks. I know, but I'm not very happy and I'm far from perfect at it.

I need to do something else, she realises as she separates the eggs successfully and the orange yolks flop into the bowl. The truth, which she has long known, finally surfaces: I want to apply for Amy's job. I need to see if I can go back and teach.

40

Baking is a means of cherishing your loved ones. Of developing an enjoyable, desirable skill. Baking can introduce one to new flavours and cultures. It can educate and open up a whole new world.

The four and a half hours are up. Four cake stands are piled high with millefeuille, choux buns and tartlets, bulging with cream and crème patissière. Fat scones — Mike's huge wedges designed for fuelling walks; Vicki's petite morsels — nest in napkin-lined baskets, their tops shiny with egg wash, sprinkled with sugar. Platters of poached salmon sandwiches jostle with home-cured ham and green tomato chutney; jewel-like jam glistens next to golden-crusted clotted cream.

The judges are taking their time deliberating over who should win and the bakers have been told to relax and mingle with their families and supporters. Groups are spilling out of the house, where they watched events via a live feed.

'Mum, you were wonderful!' Emma rushes across the lawn to Jenny and flings her arms around her, closely followed by Lizzie. Vicki watches with envy as the three women form a tight knot then release each other with a laugh. She has never experienced such unrestrained, such unconscious mothering.

Mike is being hugged too; grabbed by two

children, Pippa and Sam it must be, and then by a woman to whom he bears an uncanny resemblance: it must be his sister. And Claire is the centre of attention in her world: engulfed by a middle-aged couple and a young girl.

'Mum, you were *awesome*,' Chloe cries as she dances round them and then performs a cartwheel. Despite her exhaustion, Vicki bursts out laughing.

Mike's daughter, Pippa, is watching Chloe with interest, and breaks away from her father to sidle up to the older girl, clearly awestruck. Claire introduces her parents to Mike, and Vicki sees, for the first time, the look of frank admiration Mike gives Claire. Shyly, the two groups merge into one.

Everyone has these big supportive families here, thinks Vicki, somewhat mournfully, and flicks to a photo sent by Greg while she was baking. Alfie is nestled on the sofa, clutching Dog, his threadbare teddy. 'All well, Mummy. We love you! Good luck!' is the message and Alfie, who seems to be beaming, is giving her the thumbs up.

One small boy and his dad. Well, it might have to be enough. No, she rephrases that: it might be enough. And then, she begins to smile. Walking across the grass, a little tentatively at first then, as she notes her beam, with quiet resolve, comes the person she least expected — but the one she now realises she most hoped for.

'I hope you don't mind my coming?' says Frances.

And Vicki finds that she is smiling through tears.

The deliberations continue and Jenny, enjoying a glass of bubbly with her girls, hardly hears her mobile.

Then Emma's phone goes off: a fierce, insistent ring.

'Is your mother there?' Nigel's voice, irascible and strident, can be heard by all three of them.

'Nigel?' Jenny takes the phone which Emma hands over. Then: 'Oh . . . Oh . . . Oh, Nigel, I *am* sorry.'

'What is it?' Emma and Lizzie whisper their concern, and try to gain eye contact. But Jenny, preoccupied, is still talking.

'No . . . Well, I can see you do want me to hurry back, but I just can't do that. I'm in the middle of the competition . . . And I can't help you after this. I'm sorry, Nigel, but I can't do this any more.

'I quite understand, but perhaps Gabby could help? I'm sure she'll be a more willing nursemaid and she did encourage you to enter. No . . . No, Nigel, I can't . . . and I can't listen to this any longer.'

She takes the phone from her ear and holds it away from her as a torrent of anger spills out, polluting the gentle swell of chatter.

'Goodbye, Nigel.' She puts the phone to her ear and then, with sudden determination, abruptly kills the call.

'What was that about?' Lizzie finally ventures.

'Your father. He's torn his cruciate ligament

training for tomorrow and needs six weeks' bed rest.'

The girls look dumbstruck.

'I told him I couldn't hurry back to help.'

'Well done you!' Emma gives her a huge hug, though Lizzie seems bewildered.

'I think I've done more than that.' In her daughter's arms, she looks suddenly fearful. 'I think I might have just left him.'

Emma's whisper is ferocious. 'Even more well done.'

$$\star \quad \star \quad \star$$

Oblivious to all this, Claire, surrounded by her family and Mike's, is fizzing with excitement. She has just been asked to talk to Eaden's chief executive about developing a West Country bakery range.

She thinks she could just about manage that. How difficult could it be after what she has just done? She takes another sip of champagne then chinks her glass with Angela.

'This is the life, isn't it?' Her mother smiles.

'I could get used to this, Mum. I really could.'

There is, Claire has realised, a whole new world out there to experience: a world of croquet lawns and cookery demonstrations; of champagne tastings; of basking in the admiration of kind men like Mike. A world in which she can dream.

In front of her, Chloe is demonstrating cartwheels to Pippa and patronising the younger girl. She watches her stretch tall and turn three in quick succession. Then she stops, and runs across the lawn, legs and arms whirling.

'Daaaaaaaaad!'

A man, with the slow strut of a peacock, a suntanned face and golden green eyes is sauntering their way.

'What's he doing here?' Angela emits a growl. 'Did you invite him?'

'No . . . at least, I don't think so. Obviously, he knew you and Chloe were coming to the final. Perhaps I was unclear . . . '

She wants him to disappear immediately.

'All right?' Jay smiles at Claire and flings his arms around Chloe. Angela gives a stiff nod of acknowledgement.

'What are you doing here?' Claire is bemused, and suddenly aware of the contrast between Mike and Jay.

'I thought . . . as we were getting on better . . . I could come: help you schmooze.' He tries a smile, then falters. 'Chloe suggested it, but perhaps it's a bad idea?'

A retort is on the tip of her tongue but she bites it down, aware of her daughter's upturned face, already clouded with confusion.

'That's a lovely idea,' she says for Chloe's sake. 'But can we have a quick word, first? Won't be a moment, lovely,' she tries to reassure her daughter, kissing her freckled cheek.

She needs to get Jay away from the marquee and her new friends. This is her new world, not his. He belongs to the sand dunes of her youth not the kitchens and croquet lawns of her future. Seeing him, she wonders if she has

428

finally outgrown him.

She takes him by the arm, leading him away but trying to do so kindly. He jerks his arm free with an angry flourish.

'Don't be like that,' she tries to placate him, as they continue walking across the lawn and up a mound towards a clump of trees that will offer some privacy.

'You're making me look stupid.' He is suddenly sulky. 'I thought it would be a good surprise.'

'Oh Jay, you thought you'd be in on the action.'

'I did not.' He looks hurt.

'Jay . . . This is me, remember? I know what you're up to. I'm flattered you've come all this way for me but I don't think it was just for me, if you're honest. I think you thought you'd come because it would be a laugh.'

There is silence as he seems to judge his next move.

'Well, where's the harm in that? Perhaps you should try it some time.'

His pride is hurt and he is becoming bolshie.

'None. There's no harm in that; except that you can't be in my and Chloe's life just for the fun bits. It doesn't work like that.'

'Oh, spare me the lecture.' He moves as if to leave her but something — perhaps her steeliness; perhaps the fear of looking even more of a fool — stops him. He stands, shifting his feet, waiting for her to have her say.

'Being a parent — and being a partner — is about being there for the shit bits and the boring bits, not just the fun bits: the YouTube clips; the winning competitions, if I manage that; the swanning around in posh houses, drinking champagne.'

'Don't patronise me.'

'I didn't mean to. I'm sorry. I just don't think you realise what Chloe — and I — would really like from you.'

'Don't I? Well, look.' He wrenches up the sleeve of his T-shirt to reveal a fresh tattoo, the word Chloe, written in an italicised font, curling around his bicep. His skin is freshly pink from the pinpricks.

'I did that to show my commitment: to show you how much she — and you — mean to me.'

Claire swallows. It is the most stupid thing he could have done. The grand gesture that was meant to proclaim his maturity has actually done the reverse. She wants to soothe the poor, raw skin, to kiss it better, and to gouge out the tattoo at the same time.

'Being a parent isn't about having your child's name tattooed on your arm,' she says, and she speaks more in sorrow than anger. 'It's about being there to take her to hospital when she has a high temperature; holding her over the loo when she throws up; changing her sheets if she wets the bed; helping her with her reading; picking her up from school. Playing with her. Listening to her worries. Baking. Trying to give her a happy life.'

'Sounds like you've got it all sewn up.' He kicks at the turf with his trainer.

'No, I haven't. Of course I haven't.' She

430

struggles to keep her voice even, her frustration mounting. 'I try but I can't give her everything. Chloe needs you to be there for her too.'

'And what about you?'

She looks at him gently. 'I don't know, Jay. As Chloe's dad, of course I need you, but as a partner? No, I don't think I need you that way.'

There is a pause.

Shit, she thinks. What have I done? He looks so beautiful when he's crestfallen. If he smiles at me in that lazy way of his then I'm done for: I'll sleep with him tonight. Would that be so bad? Wouldn't it be sexy and celebratory; wouldn't it allow me to feel like Karen? But I'm not her and I don't want to be like her. It would feel like a step backwards. As he looks up at her through those long lashes, the arguments flicker through her mind.

'Cla-aire . . . '

A strident voice breaks the tension. Vicki is marching across the grass towards her. 'Sorry to interrupt — but they're going to announce the winner!'

She runs up the slope and gives Claire a hug, beaming at Jay in a way that suggests she is oblivious to having interrupted something.

Saved by Vicki, thinks Claire. By this funny, posh woman that I cannot help liking; by a new friend who told me — what was it? — not to go backwards and repeat old mistakes but to move onwards and upwards in life.

'God, I'm terrified,' Vicki confesses as she links arms with Claire and the two of them start to march down the hill.

'Come on — Jay, isn't it? You're going to miss the excitement!' Vicki stops their march, races back and grabs him by the hand as though he were a three-year-old.

Claire doubts he has ever met anyone so oblivious to his feelings. He looks steam-rollered and manages to extricate his hand gently.

'It's all right, I'll follow you. You go ahead — I'll come on.'

'Come on. Race you,' Vicki challenges her — and, fuelled by champagne and, on Claire's part, a desire to escape turbulent emotions, the two of them run across the grass.

★   ★   ★

The others are waiting when they dash in. Jenny and Mike are standing to the left of the tasting island on which the cake stands are arranged, Mike wearing an air of wry resignation; Jenny outwardly calm though her smile looks a little fixed.

Claire and Vicki push their way through to the front to stand alongside them and to the right of Dan and Harriet. In front of them, the cake stands are slightly depleted. Claire recognises her éclairs and notes that her tartlets have disappeared altogether. She glances at the tier alongside it — Jenny's, she thinks — and tries to assess if more has been sampled. Can she read anything into this?

The general babble diminishes and then stops abruptly with a few giggled 'shushes'. Harriet holds up one hand and silence descends.

This is it, thinks Claire. The whole point of the competition. The announcement of the winner. Any moment, the New Mrs Eaden will be revealed.

'Thank you.' Harriet looks particularly gracious. 'As you know, this is our inaugural baking competition held in honour of Kathleen Eaden, who sadly passed away last December.'

Oh no, we're in for a long speech, thinks Claire.

'We weren't sure if we'd find anyone to match her. But we have! All four bakers would have made Mrs Eaden proud but one in particular had what we were looking for: her intense passion, her compulsion even, to bake.

'This baker combines a quiet accomplishment with moments of culinary genius and has developed throughout the competition into someone who knows, beyond a shadow of a doubt, that she excels when she bakes.'

Not me then, thinks Claire with a rush, but the disappointment is expected and is mingled with joy when she takes in the announcement and the swell of cheers that greets it.

'Our New Mrs Eaden,' says Harriet, 'is Jenny.'

41

There are many reasons to bake: to feed; to create; to impress; to nourish; to define ourselves; and, sometimes, it has to be said, to perfect. But often we bake to fill a hunger that would be better filled by a simple gesture from a dear one. We bake to love and be loved.

Well, the best woman won, thinks Karen as she watches the live YouTube feed on her laptop in the kitchen.

Jenny appears to be crying: fat tears that spill from her eyes and draw a path through the pressed powder on her cheeks. Vicki is also blubbing. Well, that's no surprise. Claire is smiling and her beam, as she hugs Jenny, seems genuine. Mike embraces them all in one group bear hug and then gives Claire a second squeeze.

She turns from the screen and reaches for a Diet Coke: her security blanket; her poison. It could have been me, a tiny voice pipes up inside her. Well, perhaps it could have been but there's no use thinking of that now, she reproves herself somewhat testily. She runs through some positive thinking gleaned from a cognitive behavioural therapy handbook: she chose to leave the competition; there is still that agent interested in a book on low-fat baking; and nothing can take away the 186,000 hits she received for her three films; the knowledge that she was the clear front-runner in the populist stakes.

Oliver walks into the kitchen, and glances at the laptop, then stands beside her, hands dangling ineffectually. He takes off his titanium-rimmed glasses and cleans them with the tail of his shirt then pushes them back on the bridge of his nose with a sigh.

He has been more of a presence this past fortnight since Jake was arrested. Today has felt decidedly odd. He has been around: not in London; not in the gym; not holed up in his study, but here, in her house, in her bed, in her *kitchen*. And though she is not used to it, is not even sure she likes it, she appreciates what he is doing. In his own, non-verbal way, he is trying to make up for lost time.

Of course, her secret eating and purging rituals have had to change, which has been exhausting. The fear of disclosure at first overwhelmed her but the need to purge herself soon surpassed that. She has just had to choose her times.

She still fears he knows, though. As ever, when he notices her, he really notices her, assessing her with those unflinching eyes.

Take now, for instance.

'Do you wish you were doing it?' He gestures at the Macbook.

'Oh, no, not really . . . ' She is unconvincing.

'Of course you do.' He says it as a given. Then, as if he realises he sounds dismissive: 'I do appreciate what you've given up, you know. And so does Jake. He does know what you've done for him.'

'Oh — it's nothing. A baking competition. And not even one on the telly.' The lady doth protest too much, she thinks, as she turns from the screen and reaches for a cold bottle of sparkling water.

'No. It's not nothing.'

She keeps her back turned, unsure of how to respond. The fridge door has a smear on it and she polishes it clean with an antibacterial wipe, still avoiding his eye.

Jake, ambling into the room, clocks the screen and his mother now sipping a fresh glass of watery bubbles.

'All right, Mum?' He throws a long arm around her shoulders and, slightly self-conscious, gives her a bracing squeeze.

'What's that for?' She is surprised.

'Heard what Dad said . . . And I do appreciate it. Your being here for me . . . '

He drops his arm and reddens.

'Did you put him up to this?' she confronts Oliver.

Her husband is exasperated. 'Perhaps you've just brought up a son who's considerate, after all. Perhaps he's trying to thank you for what you do for him.'

'We've got to sort you out next, though, Mum,' Jake mumbles, and she sees that he has flushed bright red now and is looking at the chewed quicks of his fingers.

Her stomach flips. Is he going to betray her now and bring up Jamie? After all she's done for

436

him? She daren't look at Oliver, standing by his side.

Her son scrutinises his fingernails more intently, then directs his gaze at his father.

'We've got to look after her, too, Dad. Got to stop her starving herself — and then vomiting.'

The room spins, tiny stars crowding in in a wave of dizziness.

'You knew about that?' she wants to cry, but to do so would be a confession. She remains silent, rooted to the spot like a terrified child, hoping that somehow Oliver has not heard or understood.

But nothing gets past her clever husband — or, rather, her husband with a memory for these things.

'You're still doing that?' His face is blanched of colour and she sees the reality of all those missed dinners and impromptu trips to the bathroom flicker through his mind. Perhaps the memory of that night in Rome — of her frozen in the moonlit bathroom as he stumbled upon her, incredulous — has resurfaced. And that incident eight months later, when he came across her in Val d'Isère.

'But . . . I thought you'd got over all that years ago?' he says.

He walks towards her, this cerebral, habitually distant man, and stretches out to touch her arm. His hand falls back, limply.

For God's sake, hold me, she wants to scream as she lowers her head, succumbing to tears.

'Just give her a hug, Dad.' Jake understands her better.

And, tentatively, as though he has not done it for a long time and as if he has difficulty remembering how to, Oliver takes her in his arms.

Epilogue

14 June 2011

Kathleen

She works rhythmically and efficiently, the fingers of her right hand now a little gnarled with arthritis but still adept at shaping the dough.

It rolls easily, spread along the worktop like a pat of soft butter. She calculates how many biscuits she can make with this first rolling then presses down the cutters. Ten adults and now for the fun bit: ten little boys and girls.

With a palette knife, she eases the shapes and places them on a greased baking sheet before pressing in currant eyes and buttons. Then it's into a hot oven while she wipes down her worktop and washes up in preparation for her visitors.

A breeze, fresh off the Atlantic, lifts her washing strung out in the garden, and strokes her cheek as it blows through the window. She smiles. Her face, etched in wrinkles, becomes recognisable: no longer exquisite but still charismatic; still high cheekboned.

'The doyenne of baking with the enviable figure.' The description that once drew a smile now seems absurd. How long did she exist? That stylised dolly bird fled pretty swiftly — kitten heels incompatible with pushing a wheelchair and wet Cornish winters.

Mrs Eaden also vanished. Her friends here

know her as Kitty, and Kitty Pollington since George died in 1993. To all intents and purposes, Kathleen Eaden, the culinary construct and millionaire's widow, has long since disappeared.

Well, a good thing too. She has never missed her. She opens the window wide; breathes in the air sweetened with thyme and honeysuckle; drinks in the cry of skylarks, chattering up high. From her window she can see the sea: a navy strip against the muted gold of the sand, the soft pink of the thrift, the lush green of the cliffs. She is seventy-four and it comforts her to think that this will remain long after she dies.

It is low tide. The sand will be ribboned with the bumps of the waves, christened with puddles of salt water, strewn with shells and bladderwrack. Down on the beach, someone is flying a kite and for a moment she half sees a wheelchair streaking behind it and a small girl, dark hair streaming, screaming in delight.

Silly old fool. She is being uncharacteristically sentimental but that's no surprise. Today would have been Lily's forty-sixth birthday and, though she does not want to dwell on this, she cannot help commemorating her.

The gingerbread men are in her honour, as is the massive Victoria sponge, filled with whipped cream and strawberries — the first of the season — which was always her favourite birthday cake. Her mind crowds with an image from her ninth birthday — her very last: Lily dabbing her nose with whipped cream as she licked it from a plump strawberry, eyes bright with transgression.

442

'Lily . . . ' she had started to reprove her and had been silenced by her giggles.

Oh, she must stop this. They will be here soon and they mustn't see her upset. Laura never knew Lily and Kitty has gone to great lengths to keep her sorrow private. To ensure the dead sister shouldn't haunt the living one, who burst into the world so emphatically, two years after her death.

Laura had been a surprise: a glorious, unexpected treat conceived on the cusp of her fortieth birthday when she could not think of another child and could only just cope with her grief. She had had another stitch, and perhaps, this time, Caruthers had sewed her more tightly. Or perhaps she had no expectations. Laura arrived at thirty-nine weeks. Just five after her sister, but, oh, those five made all the difference.

Enough of this. She peers out of the window and can just spy three figures making their way along the clifftop: two small ones scampering in front and a third: taller, laden with bags and walking more slowly. She is tall, Laura, where Lily was small; blonde where she was dark; broad where she was slight. Physically, she is George's child whereas Lily: Lily was hers entirely.

The timer pings. Better get those gingerbread babies out of the oven. It wouldn't do to burn them for Max and Kit. Right on cue, she hears the garden gate slam and four small feet race up the path, sandals thudding on the slate.

'Careful, boys,' says their mother, more in hope than expectation.

'They've worn you out,' Kitty calls from the door, trying to sound normal, as her grandsons whirl around her legs.

'As ever!' Laura rolls her eyes. She drops her bags and takes her mother in her arms, kissing her cheek. 'Hello, Mum. Are you OK? Gosh, I'm exhausted.'

The boys are circling the women now, yapping for attention like clamouring puppies. Their yelps stop when they spot the baking tray.

'What have you been baking?' Max, the five-year-old, asks, as they cluster around it, jostling each other. 'Oh! Gingerbread men.'

'I used to make them for your mummy when she was small. Do you remember?'

Her daughter gives her a squeeze. 'As if I could forget . . . Oh, look: Granny's made whole families . . . Gingerbread men and women and lots of babies: girls and boys.'

The three-year-old, Kit, reaches to touch one.

'Careful, sweetheart. You'll burn yourself.'

Kitty moves his small fingers from the hot tray and blows on them, pretend-nibbling then kissing them.

'Kit watch?'

'All right, my love.' She lifts up his still-toddlerish body as she eases the biscuits on to a wire rack. He is soft enough to eat.

'Which one would you like?'

He pauses, eyes wide as he deliberates.

'Do you want the biggest?' she whispers.

He nods solemnly.

'Here you are then.' She hands him a gingerbread man, flecked with caster sugar:

444

almost too warm, soft and sweet.

He grasps it in his hand and peers at its currant eyes intently.

'What is it?'

'He looks like he's smiling,' he says.

Then, overwhelmed with shyness, he buries into her and nestles his hot face in her neck.

Acknowledgements

This novel would not be in the state it is were it not for my agent, Lizzy Kremer, who guided me with intelligence, compassion and just the right amount of steel.

Special thanks, too, to Kate Parkin, for her delicate editing and passionate championing; to the team at Hodder for creating such a stunning edition; and to Clare Bowron and Harriet Moore at David Higham Associates.

My sister, Laura Tennant, was the only person who read this before submission and provided typically perceptive comments and a massive boost of confidence. My mother, Bobby Hall, offered continual love and support, as did my father, Chris Hall, and step-parents, David Evans and Lynn Sime.

Mary Goodman listened to me talk about it for far too long; persuaded me to submit it after 30,000 words; and turned up on my doorstep when I had a momentary wobble. Thanks, too, to Nikki Wilkinson for the natural photo; to Hazel Rayment, for the IT help; to Colleen Marshman, for the running advice; to Brenda Bishop for the cookbooks; to Sarah Sharrock for telling me to get on with it; and to all my friends who never appeared to doubt I could pull this off.

A number of experts generously gave their time: James Walker, professor of obstetrics at the University of Leeds; Janet Treasure, professor of psychiatry at Guys, Kings and St Thomas' medical school; Ruth Bender-Atik; Mckenzie Cerri; Nina Aufderheide; and Inspector Mark Rogers, of Cambridgeshire police. Thanks, too, to Dan Lepard, whose recipe from *Short and Sweet* inspired the biscuit-making on page 112.

But my most heartfelt thanks go to Ella and Jack, my children, and to Phil, my husband.

This book is dedicated to the three of you, with love.

We do hope that you have enjoyed reading this large print book.

Did you know that all of our titles are available for purchase?

We publish a wide range of high quality large print books including:
Romances, Mysteries, Classics
General Fiction
Non Fiction and Westerns

Special interest titles available in large print are:
The Little Oxford Dictionary
Music Book
Song Book
Hymn Book
Service Book

Also available from us courtesy of Oxford University Press:
Young Readers' Dictionary
(large print edition)
Young Readers' Thesaurus
(large print edition)

For further information or a free brochure, please contact us at:
Ulverscroft Large Print Books Ltd.,
The Green, Bradgate Road, Anstey,
Leicester, LE7 7FU, England.
Tel: (00 44) 0116 236 4325
Fax: (00 44) 0116 234 0205

Other titles published by Ulverscroft:

THE GOOD ITALIAN

Stephen Burke

1935: Enzo Secchi, harbourmaster of Massawa, Eritrea's main port, is a loyal Italian colonial servant. But he is lonely, and when his friend suggests he find an Eritrean housekeeper to cook, clean — and maybe share his bed, Enzo takes the plunge and advertises. He surprises himself by choosing Aatifa, a sharp-tongued woman in her early 30s with a complicated family life. What neither of them counts on is falling in love. But when Italian forces bent on invading neighbouring Ethiopia begin arriving at the port, they bring with them new laws — including one forbidding 'Relationships of a Conjugal Nature' with Eritrean women. While Enzo and Aatifa strive to keep their relationship hidden, the bitter campaign lays bare all the brutality of Italian colonial ambition, and the consequences will change their lives forever . . .

THE HAREM MIDWIFE

Roberta Rich

1579: Hannah Levi, a Venetian exile, has set up a new life for herself as the best midwife in all of Constantinople, tending to the thousand women of the Sultan's lively and infamous harem. One night, when Hannah is unexpectedly summoned to the palace, she's confronted with Leah, a poor Jewish peasant girl who has been abducted and sold into the harem. The Sultan wants her to produce his heir, but the girl just wants to return to her home and the only life she has ever known. Will Hannah risk her life and livelihood to protect her?

BLACK DOG SUMMER

Miranda Sherry

Yesterday, Sally was living in an idyllic South African farmstead with her teenage daughter Gigi. Now Sally is dead — murdered — and Gigi is alone in the world.

But Sally cannot die. She lingers unseen in her daughter's shadow. When Gigi moves in with her aunt's family, Sally comes too. When Gigi's trauma stirs up long-buried secrets, Sally watches helplessly as the family begins to unravel. Then Gigi's young cousin develops an obsession with African black magic, and events take a darker turn. Now Sally must find a way to stop her daughter from making a mistake that will destroy the lives of all who are left behind . . .

AN APPETITE FOR VIOLETS

Martine Bailey

That's how it is for us servants. No one pays you much heed; mostly you're invisible as furniture. Yet you overhear a conversation, or a writiing desk lies open — and you find something, something you should not have found . . . Biddy Leigh, under-cook at the foreboding Mawton Hall, wants to marry her childhood sweetheart and set up her own tavern. But when her elderly master marries the young Lady Carinna, Biddy is unwittingly swept up in a world of scheming, secrets and lies. Forced to accompany her new mistress to Italy, Biddy takes with her an old household book of recipes, *The Cook's Jewel*, in which she records her observations. When she finds herself embroiled in a murderous conspiracy, Biddy realises that the secrets she holds could be the key to her survival — or her downfall . . .

THE RUNAWAY WOMAN

Josephine Cox

Those looking in from the outside think that Lucy Lovejoy's life is like any other, but at the centre of her family there is a big, empty hole where all the love and warmth should be. Over the years her children have watched while their father chipped away at Lucy's self-confidence. Now the children are following their own paths and Lucy has never felt more alone. When tragedy strikes at the heart of her family, it's a wake-up call for her. Everyone has taken a little piece of her, and she isn't sure who she is anymore. So when Lucy faces a betrayal from those she loves most deeply, she knows that it's time to make a choice. Is she brave enough to find herself again?

VIXEN

Rosie Garland

Brauntone, Devon, 1349: Determined to impress his congregation, new priest Father Thomas quells fears of the coming pestilence with promises of protection. For Anne, the priest's arrival is an opportunity that, at sixteen, she feels all too ready for. Convinced a grand fate awaits, she moves in as Thomas's housekeeper, though hopeful of something more. But his home is a place without love or kindness. So when a strange mute Maid is discovered, washed up in the marshes, and taken in, Anne is grateful for the company. Their friendship gives Anne the chance of happiness she thought she'd never know. But soon the plague strikes Brauntone, spreading panic. And as the villagers' fear turns to anger, Thomas must sacrifice everything to restore their faith in him . . .